Public Speaking

Irvah Lester Winter

Contents

PUBLIC SPEAKING

BY

Irvah Lester Winter

IN OFFERING A BOOK TO STUDENTS OF PUBLIC SPEAKING THE AUTHOR WOULD PAY WHAT TRIBUTE IS HERE POSSIBLE TO CHARLES WILLIAM ELIOT WHO FOR MANY YEARS HAS TAUGHT BY EXAMPLE THE POWER AND BEAUTY OF PERFECTED SPEECH

PREFACE

This book is designed to set forth the main principles of effective platform delivery, and to provide a large body of material for student practice. The work laid out may be used to form a separate course of study, or a course of training running parallel with a course in debating or other original speaking. It has been prepared with a view also to that large number who want to speak, or have to speak, but cannot have the advantage of a teacher. Much is therefore said in the way of caution, and untechnical language is used throughout.

The discussion of principles in Part One is intended as a help towards the student's understanding of his task, and also as a common basis of criticism in the relation between teacher and pupil. The preliminary fundamental work of Part Two, Technical Training, deals first with the right formation of tone, the development of voice as such, the securing of a fixed right vocal habit. Following comes the adapting of this improved voice to the varieties of use, or expressional effect, demanded of the public speaker. After this critical detailed drill, the student is to take the platform, and apply his acquired technique to continued discourse, receiving criticism after each entire piece of work.

The question as to what should be the plan and the content of Part Three, Platform Practice, has been determined simply by asking what are the distinctly varied conditions under which men most frequently speak. It is regarded as profitable for the student to practice, at least to some extent, in all the several kinds of speech here chosen. In thus cultivating versatility, he will greatly enlarge his power of expression, and will, at length, discover wherein lies his own special capability.

The principal aim in choosing the selections has been to have them sufficiently alive to be attractive to younger speakers, and not so heavy as to be unsuited to their powers. Some of them have proved effective by use; many others are new. In all cases they are of good quality.

It is hoped that the new features of the book will be found useful. One of these is a group of lighter after-dinner speeches and anecdotes. It has been said that, in present-day speech-making, humor has supplanted former-day eloquence. It plays anyway a considerable part in various kinds of speaking. The young speaker is generally ineffective in the expression of pleasantry, even his own. Practice in the speaking of wholesome humor is good for cultivating quality of voice and ease of manner, and for developing the faculty of giving humorous turn to one's own thought. It is also entertaining to fellow students. Other new features in the book are a practice section for the kind of informal speaking suited to the club or the classroom, and a section given to the occasional poem, the kind of poem that is associated with speech- making.

A considerable space is given to argumentative selections because of the general interest in debating, and because a need has been felt for something suited for special forensic practice among students of law. Some poetic selections are introduced into Part Two in order to give attractive variety to the student's work, and to provide for the advantage of using verse form in some of the vocal training. The few character sketches introduced may serve for cultivating facility in giving entertaining touches to serious discourse. All the selections for platform practice are designed, as seems most fitting, to occupy about five minutes in delivery. Original speeches, wherein the student presents his own thought, may be intermingled with this more technical work in delivery, or may be taken up in a more special way in a subsequent course.

It should, perhaps, be suggested that the plan of procedure here prescribed can be modified to suit the individual teacher or student. The method of advance explained in the Discussion of Principles is believed to be the best, but some who use the book may prefer, for example, to begin with the second group of selections, the familiar, colloquial passages, and proceed from these to those more elevated and sustained. This or any other variation from the plan here proposed can, of course, be adopted. For any plan the variety of material is deemed sufficient, and the method of grouping will be found convenient and practical.

The making of this kind of book would not be possible except for the generous privileges granted by many authors and many publishers of copyrighted works.

For the special courtesies of all whose writings have a place here the editor would make the fullest acknowledgment of indebtedness. The books from which extracts are taken have been mentioned, in every case, in a prominent place with the title of the selection, in order that so far as possible students may be led carefully to read the entire original, and become fully imbued with its meaning and spirit, before undertaking the vocal work on the selected portion. For the purpose of such reading, it would be well to have these books collected on a section of shelves in school libraries for easy and ready reference.

The publishers from whose books selections have been most liberally drawn are, Messrs. Houghton Mifflin Company, Messrs. Lothrop, Lee and Shepard, Messrs. Little, Brown, and Company, of Boston, and Messrs. Harper and Brothers, Messrs. Charles Scribner's Sons, Messrs. G. P. Putnam's Sons, Messrs. G. W. Dillingham Company, Messrs. Doubleday, Page and Company, and Mr. C. P. Farrell, New York. Several of the after-dinner speeches are taken from the excellent fifteen volume collection, "Modern Eloquence," by an arrangement with Geo. L. Shuman and Company, Chicago, publishers. In the first three volumes of this collection will be found many other attractive after-dinner speeches.

I. L. W. CAMBRIDGE,
MASSACHUSETTS.

INTRODUCTION

Happily, it is no longer necessary to argue that public speaking is a worthy subject for regular study in school and college. The teaching of this subject, in one form or another, is now fairly well established. In each of the larger universities, including professional schools and summer schools, the students electing the courses in speaking number well into the hundreds. These courses are now being more generally placed among those counted towards the academic degrees. The demand for trained teachers in the various branches of the work in schools and colleges is far above the present supply. Educators in general look with more favor upon this kind of instruction, recognizing its practical usefulness and its cultural value. The question of the present time, then, is not whether or not the subject shall have a place. Some sort of place it always has had and always will have. Present discussion should rather bear upon the policy and the method of that instruction, the qualifications to be required of teachers, and the consideration for themselves and their work that teachers have a right to expect.

Naturally, public speaking in the form of debating has received favor among educators. It seems to serve the ends of practice in speaking and it gives also good mental discipline. The high regard for debating is not misplaced. We can hardly overestimate the good that debating has done to the subject of speaking in the schools and colleges. The rigid intellectual discipline involved in debating has helped to establish public speaking in the regular curriculum, thus gaining for it, and for teachers in it, greater respect. To bring training in speech into close relation with training in thought, and with the study of expression in English, is most desirable. This, however, does **not** mean that training in speech, as a distinct object in itself, should be allowed to fall into comparative neglect. It is quite possible that, along with the healthy disapproval of false elocution and meaningless declamation, may come an underestimation of the important place of a right kind and a due degree of technical training in voice and general form.

In a recent book on public speaking, the statement is made that it is all well enough, if it so happens, for a speaker to have a pleasing voice, but it is not essential. This, though true in a sense, is misleading, and much teaching of this sort would be unfortunate for young speakers. It would seem quite unnecessary to say that beauty of voice is not in itself a primary object in vocal training for public speaking. The object is to make voices effective. In the effective use of any other instrument, we apply the utmost skill for the perfect adjustment or coordination of all the means of control. We do this for the attainment of power, for the conserving of energy, for the insuring of endurance and ease of operation. This is the end in the training of the voice. It is to avoid friction. It is to prevent nervous strain, muscular distortion, and failing power, and to secure easy response to the will of the speaker. The point not wholly understood or heeded is that, as a rule, the unpleasing voice is an indi-cation of ill adjustment and friction. It denotes a mechanism wearing on itself--it means a voice that will weaken or fail before its time--a voice that needs repair.

Since speech is to express a speaker's thought, training in speech should not be altogether dissociated from training in thinking. It ought to go hand in hand, indeed, with the study of English, from first to last. But training in voice and in the method of speech is a technical matter. It ought not to be left to the haphaz-ard treatment, the intense spurring on, of vocally unskilled coaches for speaking contests. Discussions about the teaching of speaking are often very curious. We are frequently told by what means a few great orators have succeeded, but we are hardly ever informed of the causes from which many other speakers have been embarrassed or have failed. A book or essay is written to prove, from the individual experience of the author, the infallibility of a method. He was able to succeed, the argument runs, only by this or that means; therefore all should do as he did. It seems very plausible and attractive to read, for instance, that to succeed in speaking, it is only necessary to plunge in and be in earnest. But another writer points out that this is quite absurd; that many poor speakers have not lacked in intense earnestness and sincerity; that it isn't feeling or intense spirit alone that insures success, but it is the attainment as well of a vocal method. Yet he goes on to argue that this vocal method, this forming of a public speaking voice and style, cannot be rightly gained from the teachers; it must be acquired through the exercise of each man's own will; if a man finds he is going wrong he must will to go right--as if many men had not persistently but unsuccessfully exercised their will to this very end. It is so easy, and so attractive, to resolve all problems into one idea. President Woodrow Wilson, of Princeton University, once said that he always avoided the man or the book that proclaimed one idea for the correcting of society's ills. These ideas on which books or essays are written are too obviously fallacious to need extended comment; the wonder is that they are often quoted and commended as being beneficial in their teaching. If we want to row or sprint or play golf, we do not simply go in and do our utmost; we apply the best technical skill to the art; we seek to learn how, from the experience of the past, and through the best instructors obtainable. Both common sense and experience show that the use of the human voice in the art of speaking is not the one thing, among all things, that cannot be successfully taught. The results of vocal teaching show, on the contrary, from multitudes of examples, from volumes of testimony, that there are few branches of instruction wherein the specially trained teacher is so much needed, and can be so effective as in the art of speaking.

In an experience extending over many years, an experience dealing with about all the various forms of public speaking and vocal teaching, the present writer has tried many methods, conducted classes on several different plans, learned the needs, observed the efforts, considered the successes and failures, of many men and women of various ages and of many callings. The constant and insistent fact in all this period of experience has been that skillful, technical instruction, as such, is the one kind of instruction that should always be provided where public speaking is taught, and the one that the student should not fail to secure when it is at hand. Other elements in good speech-making may, if necessary, be obtained from other sources. The teacher of speaking should teach speech. He should teach something else also, but he should, as a technician, teach that. The multitude of men and women who, in earlier and later life, come, in vocal trouble, to seek help from the experienced teacher, and the abundance of testimony as to the satisfactory results; the repeated evidences of failure to produce rightly trained voices wholly by so-called inspirational methods; the frequent evidences of pernicious vocal results from the forcing of young voices in the overintense and hasty efforts made in preparing for prize speaking, acting, and debating,--all these may not come to the understanding of the ordinary observer; they may not often, perhaps, come within the experience of the exceptionally gifted individuals who are usually cited as examples of distinguished success; they cannot impress themselves on educators who have little or no relation with this special subject; they naturally come into the knowledge and experience of the specially trained teacher of public speaking, who is brought into intimate relations with the subject and deals with all sorts and conditions of men. Out of this experience comes the strong conviction that the teacher of public speaking should be a vocal technician and a vocal physician, able to teach constructively and to treat correctively, knowing all he can of all that has been taught before, but teaching only as much of what he knows as is necessary to any individual.

For the dignity and worth of the teaching, the teacher of speaking should be trained, and should be a trainer, as has been indirectly said, in some other subject-- in English literature or composition, in debating, history, or what not. He should be one of the academic faculty--concerned with thought, which speech expresses. He should not, for his other subject, be mainly concerned with gymnastics or athletics; he should not, for his own good and the consequent good of his work, be wholly taken up merely with the teaching of technical form in speaking. He should not be merely--if at all--a coach in inter- collegiate contests; nor should his service to an institution be adjudged mainly by the results of such contests. He should be an independent, intellectually grown and growing man, one who--in his exceptionally intimate relations with students--will have a large and right influence on student life. The offer recently held out by a university of a salary and an academic rank equal to its best, to a sufficiently qualified instructor in public speaking, was one of the several signs of a sure movement of to-day in the right direction--the demand for a man of high character and broad culture, specially skilled in the technical subject he was to teach, and the providing of a worthy position.

One fact that needs to be impressed upon governing bodies of school and college is that the cultivation of good speaking cannot but be unsatisfactory when it is continued over only a very brief time. It may only do mischief. A considerable period is necessary, as is the case with other subjects, for reaching the student intelligence, for molding the faculties, for maturing the powers, for adapting method to the individual, and for bringing the personality out through the method, so that method disappears. Senator George F. Hoar once gave very sensible advice in an address to an audience of Harvard students. He did not content himself with dwelling on the inevitable platitude, first have something to say, and then say it; he said he had been, in all his career, at a special disadvantage in public speaking, from the want of early training in the use of his voice; and he urged that students would do well not only to take advantage of such training in college, but to have their teacher, if it were possible, follow them, for a time, into their professional work. This idea was well exemplified in the case of Phillips Brooks--a speaker of spontaneity, simplicity, and splendid power. It is said that, in the period of his pulpit work, in the midst of his absorbing church labors, he made it a duty to go from time to time for a period of work with his teacher of voice, that he might be kept from falling back into wrong ways. It is often said that, if a man has it in him, he will speak well anyway. It is emphatically the man who has it in him, the man of intense temperament, like that of Phillips Brooks, who most needs the balance wheel, the sure reliance, of technique. That this technique should not be too technical; that form should not be too formal; that teaching should not be too good, or do too much, is one of the principles of good teaching. The point insisted on is that a considerable time is needed, as it is in other kinds of teaching, for thoroughly working out a few essential principles; for overcoming a few obstinate faults; for securing matured results by the right process of gradual development.

There is much cause for gratification in the evidences of a growing appreciation, in all quarters, of the place due to spoken English, as a study to be taught continuously side by side with written English. Much progress has also been made toward making youthful platform speaking, as well as youthful writing, more rational in form, more true in spirit, more useful for its purpose. In good time written and spoken English, conjoined with disciplinary training in thought and imagination, will both become firmly established in their proper place as subjects to be thoroughly and systematically taught. Good teaching will become traditional, and good teachers not rare. And among the specialized courses in public speaking an important place should always be given to an exact training in voice and in the whole art of effective delivery.

PART ONE
A DISCUSSION OF PRINCIPLES

TECHNICAL TRAINING

ESTABLISHING THE TONE

The common trouble in using the voice for the more vigorous or intense forms of speaking is a contraction or straining of the throat. This impedes the free flow of voice, causing impaired tone, poor enunciation, and unhealthy physical conditions. Students should, therefore, be constantly warned against the least beginnings of this fault. The earlier indications of it may not be observed, or the nature of the trouble may not be known, by the untrained speaker. But it ought to have, from the first, the attention of a skilled teacher, for the more deep-seated it becomes, the harder is its cure. So very common is the "throaty" tone and so connected is throat pressure with every other vocal imperfection, that the avoiding or the correcting of this one fault demands constant watchfulness in all vigorous vocal work. The way to avoid the faulty control of voice is, of course, to learn at the proper time the general principles of what singers call voice production. These principles are few and, in a sense, are very simple, but they are not easily made perfectly clear in writing, and a perfect application of them, even in the simpler forms of speaking, often requires persistent practice. It will be the aim here to state only what the student is most likely to understand and profit by, and to leave the rest to the personal guidance of a teacher.

The control of the voice, so far as it can be a conscious physical operation, is determined chiefly by the action of the breathing muscles about the waist and the lower part of the chest. The voice may be said to have its foundation in this part of the physical man. This foundation, or center of control, will be rightly established, not by any very positive physical action; not by a decided raising of the chest; not by any such marked expansion or contraction as to bring physical discomfort or rigid muscular conditions. When the breath is taken in, by an easy, natural expansion, much as air is taken into a bellows, there is, to a certain degree, a firming of the breathing muscles; but this muscular tension is felt by the speaker or singer, if felt at all, simply as a comfortable fullness around, and slightly above, the waistline, probably more in front than elsewhere. An eminent teacher of singing tells his pupils to draw the breath into the stomach. That probably suggests the sensation. When the breath has been taken in, it is to be gently withheld,--not given up too freely,--and the tone is formed on the top, so to speak, of this body of breath, chiefly, of course, in the mouth and head. For the stronger and larger voice the breath is not driven out and dissipated, but the tone is intensified and given completer resonance within--within the nasal or head cavities, somewhat within the pharynx and chest. This body of breath, easily held in good control, by the lower breathing muscles, forms what is called the vocal "support." It is a fixed base of control. It is a fundamental condition, and is to be steadily maintained in all the varied operations of the voice.

Since this fundamental control of voice is so important, breathing exercises are often prescribed for regular practice. Such exercises, when directed by a thoroughly proficient instructor, may be vocally effective, and beneficial to health. Unwisely practiced, they may be unfitted to vocal control and of positive physical harm. Moderately taking the breath at frequent intervals, as a preparation or reenforcement for speaking, should become an unconscious habit. Excessive filling of the lungs or pressing downward upon the abdomen should be avoided. In general, the hearing of the voice, and an expressional purpose in making the voice, are the better means of acquiring good breathing. For the purposes of public speaking, at least, it is seldom necessary to do much more, in regard to the breathing, than to instruct a student against going wrong. The speaker should have a settled feeling of sufficiency; he should hold himself well together, physically and morally, avoiding nervous agitation and physical collapse; he should allow the breath freedom rather than put it under unnatural constraint. Perfect breathing can only be known by certain qualities in the voice. When it is best, the process is least observed. The student learns the method of breathing mainly by noting the result, by rightly hearing his voice. He must, after all, practice through the hearing.

The discussion of vocal support has brought us to the second main principle, the government of the throat. The right control of the voice, by placing a certain degree of tension upon the breathing muscles, tends to take away all pressure and constraint from the throat, leaving that passage seemingly open and free, so that the breath body or column; as some conceive it, seems almost unbroken in continued speech, much as it is, or should be, in prolonging tone in singing. The throat is opened in a relaxed rather than a constrained way, so as to give free play for the involuntary action of the delicate vocal muscles connected with the larynx, which determine all the finer variations of voice. Whatever kind of vocal effort is made, the student should constantly guard himself against the least throat stiffening or contraction, against what vocalists call a "throat grip." He is very likely to make some effort with the throat, or vocal muscles, when putting the voice to any unusual test--when prolonging tone, raising or lowering the pitch, giving sharp inflections, or striking hard upon words for emphasis. In these and other vocal efforts the throat muscles should be left free to do their own work in their own way. The throat is to be regarded as a way through; the motive power is below the throat; the place for giving sound or resonance, to voice, for stamping upon words their form and character, is in the mouth, front and back, and especially in the head.

The last of the three main considerations, the concentration of tone where it naturally seems to be formed, is often termed voice "placing," or "placement." The possible objection to this term is that it may suggest a purely artificial or arbitrary treatment or method. Rightly understood, it is the following of nature. Its value is that it emphasizes the constancy of this one of the constant factors in voice. Its result is a certain kind and degree of monotony; without that particular kind of monotony the voice is faulty. When the tone is forced out of its proper place, it is dissipated and more or less lost. A student once told the writer, when complimented on the good placement of his voice, that he learned this in his summer employment as a public crier at the door of a show tent. He said he could not possibly have endured the daily wear upon the voice in any other way. Voices are heard among teamsters, foremen on the street, and auctioneers, that conform to this and other principles perfectly. We may say that in such cases the process of learning is unconscious. In the case of the untaught student it was conscious, and was exactly what he would have been instructed to do by a teacher. The point is that many cannot learn by themselves, and our more unconscious doings are likely to become our bad habits.

Just what this voice placement is can perhaps be observed simply by sounding the letter "m," or giving an ordinary hum, as the mother sings to the child. It is merely finding the natural, instinctive basal form of the voice, and making all the vowels simply as variations of this form. The hum is often practiced, with a soft pure quality, by singers. It is varied by the sound of "ng," as in "rung" or "hung," and the elemental sound of "l." The practice should always be varied, however, by a fuller sounding of the rounder vowels, lest the voice become too much confined or thinned. The speaker, like the singer, must find out how, by a certain adjustment all along the line from the breathing center to the point of issue of the breath at the front of the mouth, he can easily maintain a constant hitting place, to serve as the hammer head; one singing place for carrying the voice steadily through a sustained passage; one place where, as it were, the tone is held in check so it will not break through itself and go to pieces,--a "placing of the voice," which is to be preserved in every sort of change or play of tone, whether in one's own character or an assumed character; a constant focus or a fixed center of resonance, a forming of tone along the roof of the mouth and well forward in the head, the safeguard and, practically, the one most effective idea in the government of voice.

And now it should be hastily stated that this excellent idea, like other good things, may be easily abused. If the tone is pushed forward or crowded into the head or held tight in its place, in the least degree, there is a drawing or a cramping in the throat; there is a "pressing" of the voice. It should be remembered that the constancy of high placement of tone depends upon the certainty of the tone foundation; that, after all, the voice must rest upon itself, and must not sound as if it were up on tip-toe or on stilts; that tone placement is merely a convenient term for naming a natural condition.

As a final word on this part of the discussion, the student should of course be impressed with the idea that though these three features of vocal mechanism have been considered separately, all ideas about voice are ultimately to become one idea.

The voice is to be thought of as belonging to the whole man, and is to become the spontaneous expression of his feelings and will; it should not draw attention to any particular part of the physical man; whatever number of conditions may be considered, the voice is finally to be one condition, a condition of normal freedom.

A lack of freedom is indicated in the voice, as in other kinds of mechanism by some sign of friction--by a harsh tone from a constrained throat; by a nasal or a muffled tone, from some obstruction in the nasal passages of the head, either because of abnormal physical conditions, or because of an unnatural direction of the breath, mainly due probably to speaking with a closed mouth; by a bound-up, heavy, "chesty" tone, resulting from a labored method of breathing.

Voice in its freer state should be pure, clear, round, fairly musical, and fairly deep and rich. Its multitude of expressive qualities had better be cultivated by the true purpose to express, in the simplest way, sentiments appropriated to one's self through an understanding and a comprehensive appreciation of various passages of good literature. As soon as possible all technique is to be forgotten, unless the consciousness is pricked by something going wrong.

Voices in general need, in the larger development, to be rounded. The vowel forms "oo" as in moon, "o" as in roll, and "a" as in saw, greatly help in giving a rounded form to the general speech; for all vowels can be molded somewhat into the form of these rounder ones. The vowels "e" as in meet, "a" as in late, short "e" as in met, short "a" as in sat, are likely to be made very sharp, thin, and harsh. When a passage for practice begins with round vowels, as for example, "Roll on, thou deep and dark blue ocean, roll!" the somewhat rounded form of the lips, and the opened condition of the throat produced in forming the rounder vowels, can be to some extent maintained through the whole of the passage, in forming all the vowels; and this will give, by repeated practice, a gradually rounded and deepened general character to the voice. On the other hand the thinner, sharper vowels may serve to give keenness and point to tones too thick and dull. In applying these suggestions, as well as all other vocal suggestions, moderation and good sense must be exercised, for the sake of the good outward appearance and the good effect of the speaking. The chief vowel forms running from the deepest to the most shallow are: "oo" as in moon, "o" as in roll, "a" as in saw, "a" as in far, "a" as in say, "e" as in see.

Since the making of tones means practically the shaping of vowels, something should here be said about vowel forms. The mouth opening should of course be freely shaped for the best sounding of the vowels. For the vowel "a" as in far, the mouth is rather fully opened; for "a" as in saw, it is opened deep, that is, the mouth passage is somewhat narrowed, so as to allow increased depth. The vowel "o," as in no, has two forms, the clear open "o," and the "o" somewhat covered by a closer form of the lips, Commonly, when the vowel is prolonged, the initial form, that is the open "o," is held, with the closed form, like "oo" in moon, touched briefly as the tone is finished. So with long "i" (y), as in thy, and "ou," as in thou--the first form is like a broad "a" as in far, with short "i" (sit) ending the "i" (y), and "oo" (moon) ending the "ou." This final sound, though sometimes accentuated for humorous effect, is usually not to be made prominent. The sound of "oi," as in voice, has the main form of "aw" as in saw, and the final form in short "i," as in pin. The vowel "u" is sounded like "oo" (moon) in a few words, as in rule, truth. Generally, it sounds about like "ew" in new or mew. In some of the forms the front of the mouth will be open, in some half open, and in some, as in the case of long "e" (meet), nearly closed. Whatever the degree of opening, the jaw should never be allowed to become stiffly set, nor the tongue nor lips to be held tight, in any degree or way. These faults cause a tightening in the throat, and affect the character of the tone. It will generally be advantage to the tone if the lips are trained to be very slightly protruding, in bell shape, and if the corners of the mouth be not allowed to droop, but be made very slightly to curve upward. The tongue takes of course various positions for different vowels. For our purposes, it may be sufficient to say that it will play its part best if it be not stiffened but is left quite free and elastic, perhaps quite relaxed, and if the tip of it be made to play easily down behind the lower teeth.

Since voice has here been discussed in an objective sort of way, it is fitting to emphasize the importance of what is called naturalness, or more correctly, simplicity. Everybody desires this sort of result. It can readily be seen, however, that about everything we do is a second nature; is done, that is to say, in the acquired, acceptable, conventional way. Voice and speech are largely determined by surrounding influences, and what we come to regard as natural may be only an acquired bad habit, which is, in fact, quite unnatural. Voice should certainly be what we call human. Better it should have some human faults than be smoothed out into negative perfection, without the true ring, the spunk of individuality. There is, nevertheless, a best naturalness, or second nature, and a worst. The object of training is to find the best.

In this discussion of voice some of the ideas often applied to the first steps in the cultivation of singing have been presented, as those most effective also for training in speech. Although, on the surface, singing and speaking are quite different, fundamentally they are the same. Almost all persons have, if they will use it, an ear for musical pitch and tone, and the neglect to cultivate, in early life, the musical hearing and the singing tone is a mistake. To prospective public speakers it is something like a misfortune. The best speakers have had voices that sang in their speaking. This applies distinctly to the speaking, for example, of Wendell Phillips, who is commonly called the most colloquial of our public speakers. It has often been commented on in the case of Gladstone, and applies peculiarly to some of our present-day speakers, who would be called, not orators, but impressive talkers. The meaning is, not of course that speaking should sound like singing, or necessarily like oratory, but that to the trained ear the best speaking has fundamentally the singing conditions, and the voice has singing qualities; and the elementary exercises designed for singing are excellent, in their simpler forms and methods, for the speaking voice. In carrying out this idea in voice training, the selections here given for the earliest exercises, are such as naturally call for some slight approach to the singing tone. Some are in the spirit and style of song or hymn; others are in the form of address to distant auditors, wherein the reciter would call to a distance, or "sing out," as we say. This kind of speaking is a way of quickly "bringing out" the voice. Young students especially are very apt in this, getting the idea at once, though needing, as a rule, special cautions and guidance for keeping the proper vocal conditions, so as to prevent "forcing." The passages are simple in spirit and form. They carry on one dominant feeling, needing little variation of voice. The idea is to render them in a way near to the monotone, that the student may learn to control one tone, so to speak, or to speak nearly in one key, before doing the more varied tones of familiar speech or of complex feeling. We might say the passages are to be read in some degree like the chant; but the chant is likely to bring an excess of head resonance and is too mechanical. The true spirit of the selections is to be given, from the first, but reduced to its very simplest form. Difficulties arise, in this first step, in the case of two classes of student: those who lack sentiment or imagination, or at least the faculty of vocally expressing it, and those with an excess of feeling. The former class have to be mentally awakened; for some motive element, aesthetic appreciation or imaginative purpose, should play a part, as has been said, even in technical vocal training. The latter class must be restrained. Excessive emotion either chokes off expression, or runs away with itself. Calmness, evenness, poise, the easy control that comes from a degree of relaxation, without loss of buoyancy,-- these are the conditions for good accomplishment of any kind. This self-mastery the high-strung, ardent spirit must learn, in order to become really strong. This is accomplished, in the case of a nervous temperament, not by tightening up and trying hard, but by relaxing, by letting down. In the use of these passages the voice will be set at first slightly high in pitch, in order to help in keeping a continuous sounding of tone against the roof of the mouth and to a proper degree in the head. This average pitch, or key, or at least the character of the tone, will be maintained without much change, and with special care that the tone be kept up in its place at the ends of lines or sentences, and be kept well fixed on its breath foundation. The simpler inflections indicating the plain meaning, will of course be observed, the tone will be kept easily supported by the frequently recovered breath that is under it. The back of the mouth will seem to be constantly somewhat open. There will be no attempt at special power, but only a free, mellow, flowing tone of moderate strength. In the exercise each voice will be treated, in detail, according to its particular needs, and in each teacher's own way.

At the time of student life, when physical conditions are not matured, the counsel should repeatedly be given, not only that the voice, though used often and regularly, should be used moderately, but also that the voice should be kept youthful--youthful, if it can be, even in age--but especially in youth, whatever the kind of literature used for practice. Also youth should be counseled not to try to make a voice like the voice of some one else, some speaker, or actor, or teacher. It will be much the best if it is just the student's own.

VOCAL FLEXIBILITY

In the earliest exercises here given the tone will be, for the best and most immediate effect, kept running on somewhat in a straight line, so to speak; will have a certain sameness of sound; will be perhaps somewhat monotonous, because kept pretty much in one key, or in one average degree of pitch. It will perhaps be necessary to make the utterance for the time somewhat artificial. The voice is in the artificial stage, as is the work of an oarsman, for example, in learning the parts of the stroke, or that of a golfer in learning the "swing," although in the case of some students, when the vocal conditions are good and the tone is well balanced, very little of the artificial process is necessary. In that case the voice simply needs, in its present general form, to be developed.

The next step in the training is to try a more varied use of the voice, without a loss of what has been acquired as to formation of tone. The student is to make himself able to slide the voice up and down in pitch, by what is called inflection, to raise or lower the pitch by varied intervals, momentarily to enlarge or diminish the tone, in expressive ways; in short, to adapt the improved tone, the more effective method of voice control, to more varied speech. In the early practice for getting tone variation, the student must guard most carefully against "forcing." Additional difficulties arise when we have vocal changes, and moderate effort, in the degree of the change, is best. In running the tone up, one should let the voice take its own way. The tone should not be pushed or held by any slightest effort at the throat. The control should, as has been said, be far below the throat. In running an inflection from low to high, the tone may be allowed, especially in the earlier practice, to thin out at the top. And always when the pitch is high the tone should be smaller, as it is on a musical instrument, though it should have a consistent depth and dignity from its proper degree of connection with the chest. This consistent character in the upper voice is attained by giving the tone a bit of pomp or nobleness of quality. In taking a low pitch there is, among novices, always a tendency to bear down on the tone in order to gain strength or to give weight to utterance. The voice is thus crowded into, or on, the throat. The voice should never be pushed down or pressed back in the low pitch. This practice leads to raggedness of tone, and finally to virtual loss of the lower voice. The voice should fall of itself with only that degree of force which is legitimately given by the breath tension, produced easily, though firmly, by the breathing muscles. Breadth will be given to the tone by some degree of expansion at the back of the mouth, or in the pharynx. As soon as can be, the speech should be brought down to the utmost of simplicity and naturalness, so that the thought of literature can be expressed with reality and truth; can be made to sound exactly as if it came as an unstudied, spontaneous expression of the student's own mind, and yet so it can be heard, so it will be adequate, so it will be pleasing in sound. The improved tone is to become the student's inevitable, everyday voice.

THE FORMATION OF WORDS

The term enunciation means the formation of words, including right vocal shape to the vowels and right form to the consonants. Pronunciation is scholastic, relating to the word accent and the vowel sound. Authority for this is in the dictionary. Enunciation, belonging to elocution, is the act of forming those authorized sounds into finished speech.

There is a common error regarding enunciation. It is usual, if a speaker is not easily understood, to say that he should "articulate" more clearly; that is, make the consonants more pronounced, and young students are thus often urged into wrongly directed effort with the tongue and lips. Sometimes in books, articulation "stunts," in the form of nonsense alliterations, are prescribed, by which all the vowels are likely to be chewed into consonants. The result is usually an overexertion, and a consequent tightening, of the articulating muscles. At first, and for a time, it may appear that this forcing of the articulation brings the desired result of clearer speech, but it will, in the end, be destructive to voice and bring incoherent utterance. Articulation exercises too difficult for the master, should not be given to the novice. All teachers of singing train voices, at first, on the vowel, and it should be known that, without right vowel, or tone, formation, efforts at good articulation are futile. Every technical vocal fault must be referred back to the fundamental condition of right formation of tone, that is, the vowel. Sputtering, hissing, biting, snapping, of consonants is not enunciation. The student should learn how without constraint, to prolong vowels; learn, if you please, the fundamentals of singing, and articulation, the formation of consonants, the jointing of syllables, will become easy. The reason for this is that when the vowel tone is rightly produced, all the vocal muscles are freed; the tongue, lips, and jaw act without constraint.

The principle of rhythm simplifies greatly the problem of enunciation. It is easier, not only to make good tone, but also to speak words, in the reading of verse than of prose. It is much easier to read a rhythmical piece of prose than one lacking in rhythm. All prose, then, should be rendered with as much rhythmical flow as is allowed consistently with its spirit and meaning. Care must be taken of course that no singsong effect occurs; that the exact meaning receives first attention. In case of long, hard words, ease is attained by making a slight pause before the word or before its preposition or article or other closely attached word, and by giving a strong beat to its accented syllable or syllables, with little effort on the subordinate syllables.

The particular weakness among Americans, in the speaking of words, is failure adequately to form the nasal, or head, sounds. The letters "l," "m," "n," are called vowel consonants. They can be given continuous sound, a head resonance. This sounding may be carried to a fault, or affectation; but commonly it is insufficiently done, and it should be among the first objects of cultivation in vocal practice. The humming of these head sounds, with very moderate force, is excellent for developing and clearing this resonance. The "ng" sound, as in rung, may be added.

Improper division of words into syllables is a common fault. The word "constitution," for example, is made "cons-titution," instead of "con- stitution;" "principle" is pronounced "prints-iple." A clean, correct formation should be made by slightly holding, and completing the accented syllable. The little word "also" is often called "als-o" or "als-so" or "alt-so"; chrysanthemum is pronounced "chrysant-themum"; coun-try is called "country," band so forth. In the case of doubled consonants, as in the word "mellow," "commemorate," "bubble," and the like, a momentary holding of the first consonant, so that a bit of separate impulse is given to the second, makes more perfect speaking. There is a slight difference between "mellow" and "mel-ow," "bub-ble" and "bub-le," "com-memorate" and "com-emorate." These finer distinctions, if one cares to make speech accurate and refined, can be observed in words ending in "ence" and "ance" as in "guidance" and "credence"; in words with the ending "al," "el," or "le," as in "general," "principal," "final," "vessel," "rebel," "principle," and "little." If that troublesome word "separate" were from the beginning rightly pronounced, it would probably be less often wrongly spelled. One should hasten to say, however, that over-nicety in enunciation, pedantic exactness, obtrusive "elocutionary" excellence, or any sort of labored or affected effort should be carefully guarded against. The line of distinction between what is perfect and what is slightly strained is a fine one. Very often, for example, one hears such endings as "or" in "creator," "ed" in "dedicated," "ess" in "readiness," "men" in "gentlemen," pronounced with incorrect prominence. These syllables, being very subordinate, should not be made to stand out with undue distinctness, and though the vowels should not be distorted into a wrong form, they should be obscured. In "gentlemen," for example, the "e" is, according to the dictionary, an "obscure" vowel, and the word is pronounced almost as "gentlem'n,"--not "gentlemun," of course, but not "gentlemen." The fault in such forms is more easily avoided by throwing a sharp accent on the accented syllable, letting the other syllables fall easily out. The expression of greeting, "Ladies and gentlemen," should have a strong accent on each first syllable of the two important words, with little prominence given to other syllables or the connecting word; as, "La'dies 'nd gen'tlem'n."

In the same class of errors is that of making an extra syllable in such words as "even," "seven," "heaven," "eleven," and "given," where properly the "e" is elided, leaving "ev'n," "heav'n," and so forth. The mouth should remain closed when the first syllable is pronounced; the "n" is then simply sounded in the head. The same treatment should be given to such words as "chasm" and "enthusiasm." If the mouth is opened after the first part of the word is sounded, we have "chas-um," "enthusias-um." The little words "and," "as," "at" and the like should, of course, when not emphatic, be very lightly touched, with the vowel hardly formed, and the mouth only slightly opened. The word "and" is best sounded, where not emphatic, with light touch, slight opening of the mouth, and hardly any forming of the vowel; almost like "'nd." These words should be connected closely with the word which follows, as if they were a subordinate syllable of that word.

Often we hear such words as "country," "city," and their plurals, pronounced "countree," "citee," and "citees"; "ladies" is called "ladees." The sound should properly be that of short "i" not of long "e." The vowel sound, short "a," as in "cast," "fast," "can't," must be treated as a localism, and yet it is hardly necessary to adhere to any decided extreme because of local associations. Vocally, the very narrow sound of short "a," called "Western," is impossible. It can't be sung; in speech it is usually dry and harsh. As a matter of taste the very broad sound of the short "a," when it is made like "a" in "far," is objectionable because it is extraordinary. There is a form between these extremes, the correct short "a"; this ought to be acceptable anywhere. It is suggestive to observe that localisms are less pronounced among artists than among untrained persons. Trained singers and actors belonging to different countries or sections of country, show few differences among themselves in English pronunciation. Among localisms the letter "r" causes frequent comment. In singing and dramatic speaking, this letter is best formed at the tip of the tongue. In common speech it may be made only by a very slight movement at the back of the tongue. A decided throaty "burr" should always be avoided. In the case of vigorous dramatic utterance, the "r" may be quite decidedly rolled, on the principle that, in such cases, all consonants become a means of effectiveness in expression. In the expression of fine, delicate, or tender sentiment, all consonants should be lightly touched or should be obscured. Enumeration of the many kinds of carelessness of speech would be to little purpose. Scholarly speech requires a knowledge of correct forms, gained from the dictionary, and vocal care and skill in making these forms clear, smooth, and finished in sound.

This discussion has perhaps suggested the extreme of accuracy in speech. But as has already been said, any degree of overnicety, of pedantic elegance, of stilted correctness, is especially irritating to a sensitive ear. Excessive biting off of syllables, flipping of the tongue, showing of the teeth, twisting of the lips, is carrying excellence to a fault. The inactive jaw, tongue, and lips must be made mobile, and in the working away of clumsiness and slovenliness of speech, some degree of stiltedness must perhaps, for a time, be in evidence, but matured practice ought finally to result, not only in accuracy and finish, but in simplicity and ease in speaking.

MAKING THE POINT

When the student has made a fair degree of progress in the more strictly mechanical features of speech, the formation of tone, and the delivery of words, he is ready to give himself up more fully to the effective expression of thought. Of first importance to the speaker, as it is to the writer, is the way to make himself clear as to his meaning. The question has to be put again and again to the young speaker, What is your point? What is the point in the sentence? What is the point in some larger division of the speech? What is the point, or purpose, of the speech as a whole? This point, or the meaning of what is said, should be so put, should be so clear, that no effort is required of a listener for readily apprehending and appreciating it. Discussing now only the question of delivery, we say that the making of a point depends mainly upon what we commonly call emphasis. Extending the meaning of emphasis beyond the limit of mere stress, or weight, of voice, we may define it as special distinctness or impressiveness of effect. In the case of a sentence there is often one place where the meaning is chiefly concentrated; often the emphasis is laid sharply upon two or more points or words in the sentence; sometimes it is put increasingly on immediately succeeding words, called a climax, and sometimes the stress of utterance seems to be almost equally distributed through all the principal words of the sentence.

The particular point of a sentence is determined, not so much by what the sentence says as it stands by itself, as by its relation to what goes before or what follows after. The first thing, then, for the student to do is to become sure of the precise meaning of the sentence, with reference to the general context. Then he must know whether or not he says, for the understanding of others, exactly what is meant. The means of giving special point to a statement is in some way to set apart, or to make prominent, the word or words of special significance. There are several ways in which this is done. Commonly a stress or added weight of voice is put upon the word; generally, too, there is an inflection, a turning of the tone downward or upward; there is frequently a lengthening out of the vowel sound, and a sudden stop after, in some cases before, the word. Any or all these special noticeable vocal effects serve to draw attention to the word and give it expressive significance. These effects are everywhere common in good everyday speech. In the formal art of speaking, they have to be more or less thought out and consciously practiced.

Emphasis is determined by the comparative importance of ideas. An idea is important when, being the first to arise in the mind, it becomes the motive for utterance. We see an object, the idea of high or broad or beautiful arises in the mind; we so form a sentence as to make that idea stand forth; this idea, or the word expressing it, becomes vocally emphatic. In this sentence, "He has done it in a way to impress upon the Filipinos, so far as action and language can do it, his desire, and the desire of our people, ***to do them good***," the idea "to do them good" is the one that arose first in the mind of the speaker and called up the other ideas that served to set this one prominently forth. It is the emphatic idea. It should be carried in the mind of the student speaker from the beginning of the sentence. Again, an idea is important when it arises as closely related to the first, and becomes the chief means of giving utterance concerning the first. This second idea may be something said about the first; it may be compared or contrasted with the first. Being matched against the first, it may become of equal significance with it. "Who is here so ***base*** that would be a ***bondman***?" Here the idea "base" is used to emphasize the quality of "bondman," and becomes equally emphatic with that idea. Other ideas, or other words expressing them, being formed around these principal ones, will be subordinated or more loosely run over, since they simply serve as the setting for the principal ones, or the connecting links, holding them together. Sometimes an idea arising in the mind grows in intensity, asserting itself by stronger and stronger successive words. For example, "He ***mocks*** and ***taunts*** her, he ***disowns, insults*** and ***flouts*** her"; and, "I impeach him in the name of human nature itself, which he has cruelly ***outraged, injured***, and ***oppressed***, in both sexes in every ***age, rank, situation***, and ***condition of life***." The impressiveness in delivering these successive words is increased not because they are in the form of a climax, but they are in the form of a climax because the thought is so insistent as to require new words for its expression. The student will be true and sure in his emphasis only when he takes ideas into his mind in the natural way; that is, he should seize upon the central idea before he gives utterance to any part of a statement. If that idea is constantly carried foremost in the mind, he will then, in due time, give it its true emphasis. So, in the case of a climax, he must realize the spirit and force behind the utterance, and not depend upon any mechanical process of merely increasing the strength of his tones.

Sometimes emphasis must be made to stand so strong as not merely to arrest the movement of thought, and fix the mind of the hearer upon a point, but to turn the attention of the hearer for the moment aside; to draw his mind to the thought of something very remote in time or place or relation, as in the case of making momentary reference to some historic fact or some well-known expression of literature. Allusions and illustrations, then, should be given, not only with color but also with special emphasis. Byron, contemplating the ruins of Rome, calls her "the *Niobe* of nations." The hearer's mind should be arrested, his imagination stirred, at that word. Words used in contrast with one another are given opposing effect by contrasting emphasis: "Not that I loved *Caesar* less, but that I loved *Rome more*." "My *words fly up*; my *thoughts remain below*." When words are used with a double meaning, as in the case of a pun, or with a peculiar implication, or are repeated for some peculiar effect of mere repetition,--when we have, in any form, what is called a play upon words,--a peculiar pointedness is given, wherein the circumflex inflection plays a large part. "Now is it *Rome* indeed and *room* enough, when there is in it but one only man." "I had rather *bear with* you than *bear* you; yet if I did bear you, I should bear no *cross*, for I think you have no *money* in your purse." "But, sir, the *Coalition*! The *Coalition*! Aye, the *murdered Coalition*!"

Although, as has been said, the usual method of making a point is to give striking force to an idea, very often the same effect, or a better effect, is produced by a striking sudden suppression of utterance, by way of decided contrast. When the discourse has been running vigorously and inflections have been repeatedly sharp and strong, the sudden stop, and the stilled utterance of a word, are most effective. Only, the suppressed word must be set apart. There must be the pause before or after, or both before and after. Robert Ingersoll, when speaking with great animation, would often suddenly stop and ask a question in the quietest and most intimate way. This gave point to the question and was impressive.

We have been considering thus far only primary or principal emphasis. Of equal importance is the question of secondary emphasis. The difference in vocal treatment comes in regarding the principal emphasis as absolute or final, as making the word absolved from, cut off from, the rest of the sentence following, and having a final stop or conclusive effect, while the secondary may be regarded as only relatively emphatic, as being related in a subordinate way to the principal, and as maintaining a connection with the rest of the sentence, or as hanging upon the words which follow, or as being a step leading up to the main idea. The vocal indication of this connective principle is the circumflex inflection. The tone will be raised, as in the principal emphasis, but instead of being allowed to fall straight to a finality, it is turned upward at the finish, to hook on, as it were, to the following. The weight of voice will be less marked, the inflection less long, and the pause usually less decided, than in the case of the primary emphasis. "Recall *romance*, recite the names of heroes of legend and *song*, but there is none that is his peer." At the words romance and song there is a secondary emphasis; the voice is not dropped, it is kept suspended with the pause.

A common failing among students is an inability to avoid a frequent absolute emphatic inflection when it is not in place. Many are unable steadily to sustain a sentence till the real point is reached. They fail to keep the voice suspended when they make a pause. It is very important that a student should have a sure method of determining what the principal emphasis is. He should, as has already been said, follow, in rendering the thought of another, the method of the spontaneous expression of his own ideas. He should take into his mind the principal idea or ideas, before he speaks the words leading thereto. He should then, at every pause, keep the thought suspended, incomplete, till he reaches that principal idea; he should then make the absolute stop, with the effect of finality, afterwards running off in a properly related way, such words as serve to complete the form of expression. Take the following sentence: "I never take up a paper full of Congress squabbles, reported as if sunrise depended upon them, without thinking of that idle English nobleman at Florence, who when his brother, just arrived from London, happened to mention the House of Commons, languidly asked, Ah! is that thing still going?" It is rather curious that very rarely will a student keep the thought of such a sentence suspended and connected until he arrives at the real point at the end. He will first say that he never takes up a paper, though of course he really does take up a paper. Then he says he never takes up this kind of paper; and this he does not mean. So he goes on misleading his audience, instead of helping them properly to anticipate the form of statement and so be prepared for the point at the right moment. He should not, as a general rule, let his voice take an absolute drop at the places of secondary emphasis.

In reference to the emphatic point in a larger division of the speech, and to the main or climactic points of the whole speech, the principles for emphasis in the sentence are applied in a larger way. And the way to make the point is, first of all, to think hard on what that point is, what is the end or purpose to be attained. If this does not bring the result--and very often it does not--then the mechanical means of producing emphasis should be studied and consciously applied--the increase, or perhaps the diminution, of force, the lengthening or shortening of tones on the words; a change in the general level of pitch; the use of the emphatic pause; and a lengthening of the emphatic inflection. A more impressive general effect must, in some way, be given to the parts of greater importance.

INDICATING VALUES AND RELATIONS

Perhaps the most commonly criticized fault among beginners in speaking is that of monotony. Monotony that arises from lack of inflection of voice or from lack of pointed-ness or emphasis in a sentence, will presumably be corrected in the earlier exercises. The monotony that is caused by giving to all sentences an equal value, saying all sentences, or a whole speech, in about the same force, rate, and general pitch, is one that may be considered from another point of view. One fault in the delivery of sentences--perhaps the most frequent one--is that of running them all off in about the same modulation. By modulation we mean the wavelike rise and fall of the voice that always occurs in some degree in speech,--sometimes called melody--and the change of key, or general pitch, in passing from one sentence, or part of a speech, to another. Frequently, novices in speaking and in reading, will swing the voice upward in the first part of every sentence, give it perhaps another rise or two as the sentence proceeds, and swing it down, always in precisely the same way, at the end. The effect of this regular rising at the beginning, and this giving of a similar concluding cadence at the end, is to make it appear that each sentence stands quite independent of the others, that each is a detached statement; and when, besides, each sentence is given with about the same force and rate of speed, they all seem to be of about equal importance, all principal or none principal, but as much alike as Rosalind's halfpence. Sentences that have a close sequence as to thought should be so rendered that one seems to flow out from the other, without the regular marked rise at the beginning or the concluding cadence at the end. Sentences, and parts of sentences, which are of less importance than others with which they are associated, should be made less prominent in delivery. Often students are helped by the suggestion that a sentence, or a part of a sentence, or a group of sentences, it may be, be dropped into an undertone, or said as an aside, or rapidly passed over, or in some way put in the background--said, so to speak, parenthetically. Other portions of the speech, or the sentence, the important ones, should, on the same principle, be made to stand out with marked effect.

Notice, in the following quotation, how the first and the last parts arc held together by the pitch or key and the modulation of the voice, and the middle part, the group of examples, is held together in a different key by being set in the background, as being illustrative or probative. "Why, all these Irish bulls are Greek,--every one of them. Take the Irishman carrying around a brick as a specimen of the house he had to sell; take the Irishman who shut his eyes, and looked into the glass to see how he would look when he was dead; take the Irishman that bought a crow, alleging that crows were reported to live two hundred years, and he meant to set out and try it. Well, those are all Greek. A score or more of them, of the parallel character, come from Athens."

The speaker should cultivate a quick sensitiveness as to close unity and slight diversity, as to what is principal and what is subordinate, as to what is in the direct, main line of thought, and what is by the way, casual, or merely a connecting link. This sense of proportion, of close or remote relation, of directness and indirectness, the feeling for perspective, so-called, can be acquired only by continued practice, for sharpening the faculty of apprehension and appreciation. It is usually the last attainment in the student's work, but the neglect of it may result in a confirmed habit of monotony. The term transition is commonly used to denote a passing from one to another of the main divisions of the discourse. The making of this transition, though often neglected, is not difficult. The finishing of one part and the making of a new beginning on the next, usually with some change of standing position, as well as of voice, has an obvious method. The slighter transition, or variation, within a main division, and the avoidance of the slight transition where none should be made, require the keener, quicker insight.

Sentences will have many other kinds of variation in delivery according to the nature and value of the thought. Some will flow on with high successive waves; some will be run almost straight on as in a monotone. Some will be on a higher average tone, or in a higher key; others will be lower. Some will have lengthened vowel sound, and will be more continuous or sustained, so that groups of successive words seem to run on one unbroken tone; others will be abrupt and irregular. Some will be rapid, some slow; some light, others weighty; some affected by long pauses, others by no pause, and some will be done in a dry, matter-of- fact, or precise, or commonplace, or familiar manner, others will be touched with feeling, colored by imagination, glowing with persuasive warmth, elevated, dignified, or profound. A repetition of the selections to be learned, with full expression by voice and action, repetition again, and again, and again, until the sentiment of them becomes a living reality to the speaker, is the only way to acquire the ability to indicate to others the true proportions, the relative values, and the distinctive character, of what is to be said.

EXPRESSING THE FEELING

We are in the habit of distinguishing between what proceeds from mere thinking, what is, as we say, purely intellectual, and what arises more especially from feeling, what we call emotional. We mean, of course, that one or the other element predominates; and the distinction is a convenient one. The subject, the occasion, to a great extent the man, determine whether a speech is in the main dispassionate or impassioned, whether it is plain or ornate in statement, whether it is urgent or aggressive, or calm and rather impassive. It would be beyond our purpose to consider many of the variations and complexities of feeling that enter into vocal expression. We call attention to only a few of the simpler and more common vocal manifestations of feeling, counselling the student who is to deliver a selected speech, to adapt his speaking to the style of that speech. In so doing he will get a varied training, and at length will find his own most effective style.

The speech which is matter-of-fact and commonplace only, has characteristically much short, sharp inflection of voice, with the rapidly varying intervals of pitch that we notice in one's everyday talking. As the utterance takes on force, it is likely to go in a more direct line of average pitch, with stronger inflection on specially emphatic words. As it rises to sentiment, the inflections are less marked, and in the case of a strain of high, nobler feeling, the voice moves on with some approach to the monotone. According as feeling is stronger and firmer, as in the expression of courage, determination, firm resolve, resistance, intense devotion, the voice is kept sustained, with pauses rather abrupt and decisive; if the feeling, though of high sentiment, is tranquil, without aggressiveness, the voice has more of the wavelike rise and fall, and at the pausing places the tone is gradually diminished, rather than abruptly broken off. In the case of quickly impulsive, passionate feeling, the speech is likely to be much varied in pitch, broken by frequent abrupt stops, and decisive inflections. In the case of the expression of tenderness or pathos, there is a lingering tone, with the quality and inflection of plaintiveness, qualified, in public speech, by such dignity and strength as is fitting. In all cases the quality of voice is of course the main thing, and this, not being technical or mechanical, must depend on the speaker's entering into the spirit of the piece and giving color, warmth, and depth to his tones. The spirit of gladness or triumph has usually the higher, brighter, ringing tone; that of gravity, solemnity, awe, the lower, darker, and less varied tone.

In the case of the expression of irony, sarcasm, scorn, contempt, and kindred feelings, the circumflex inflection is the principal feature. This is the curious quirk or double turn in the voice, that is heard when one says, for example, "You're a *fine* fellow," meaning, "You are anything but a fine fellow." In the earlier part of Webster's reply to Hayne are some of the finest examples of irony, grim or caustic humor, sarcasm, and lofty contempt. They need significant turns and plays of voice, but are often spoiled by being treated as high declamation.

In the expression of the various kinds and degrees of feeling there may be a fully expressed force or a suppressed or restrained force. Often the latter is the more natural and effective. This is intense, but not loud, though at times it may break through its restraint. It is most fitting when the hearers are near at hand, as in the case of a jury or judge in court, when the din of loudness would offend.

The climax is a gradually increasing expression of feeling. It may be by a gradual raising of the voice in pitch; it may be by any sort of increasing effectiveness or moving power. It is rather difficult to manage, and may lead to some strained effort. The speaker should keep a steady, controlled movement, without too much haste, but rather a retarded and broadened utterance as the emphatic point is approached; and always the speaker should keep well within his powers, maintaining always some vocal reserve.

The practice of emotional expression gives warmth, mellowness, sympathy and expansiveness to the voice, and must have considerable cultural value.

SHOWING THE PICTURE

A difficult attainment in speaking is that of vividness. The student may see the picture in his own mind's eye, but his mode of expression does not reveal the fact to others. Imagination in writing he may have, with no suggestion of it in the voice. Too often it is erroneously taken for granted that the human voice, because it is human, will at any call, respond to all promptings of the mind. It will no more do so, of course, than the hand or the eye. It must be trained. Often it is a case not merely of vocal response, but of mental awakening as well, and in that case the student must, if he can, learn to see visions and dream dreams.

A way to begin the suiting of speech to imaginative ideas is to imitate; to make the voice sound like the thing to be suggested. Some things are fast, some slow, some heavy, some light, some dark and dismal, some bright and joyous; some things are noisy, some still; some rattle, others roar; the sea is hoarse; the waves wash; the winds blow; the ocean is level, or it dashes high and breaks; happy things sing, and sad things mourn. All life and nature speak just as we speak. How easy it ought to be for us to speak just as nature speaks. And when our abstract notions are put in concrete expression, or presented as a picture, how easy it would seem, by these simple variations of voice, to speak the language of that picture, telling the length, breadth, action, color, values, spirit of it. That it is a task makes it worth while. It affords infinite variety, and endless delight.

One necessary element in so-called word-painting is that of time. When a speaker expresses himself in pictures for the imagination he must give his hearers time to see these pictures, and to sufficiently see and appreciate the parts, or lines of them, and the significance of them. It is a common fault to hasten over the language of imagination as over the commonplace words. The speaker or reader had better be sure to see the image himself before, and indeed after, he speaks it. Others will then be with him. Although among most young speakers the tone of imagination is lacking, yet often young persons who become proficient vocally are fain greatly to overdo it, till the sound that is suited to the sense becomes sound for its own sake, and thereby obscures the sense. Regard for proportion and fitness, in relation to the central idea or purpose, should control the feeling for color in the detail.

EXPRESSION BY ACTION

It should always be borne in mind that gesture means the bearing or the action of the whole man. It does not mean simply movement of the arm and hand. The practice of gesture should be governed by this understanding of the term. A thought, an emotion, something that moves the man from within, will cause a change, it may be slight, or it may be very marked, in eye, face, body. This is gesture. This change or movement may, from the strength of the feeling that prompts it, extend to the arm and hand. But this latter movement, in arm and hand, is only the fuller manifestation of one's thought or feeling--the completion of the gesture, not the gesture itself. Arm movement, when not preceded or supplemented by body movement, or body pose, is obtrusive action; it brings a member of the body into noticeable prominence, attracting the auditor's eye and taking his mind from the speaker's thought. Better have no gesture than gesture of this kind. The student, then, should first learn to appreciate the force of ideas, to see and feel the full significance of what he would say, and indicate by some general movement of body and expression of face, the changing moods of mind. Then the arm and hand may come--in not too conspicuous a way--to the aid of the body. When Wendell Phillips pointed to the portraits in Faneuil Hall and exclaimed: "I thought those pictured lips would have broken into voice to rebuke the recreant American,--the slanderer of the dead," it was not, we may be sure, the uplifted arm alone, but the pose of the man, the something about his whole being, which bespoke the spirit within him, and which was really the gesture. In less positive or striking degrees of action, the body movement will, of course, be very slight, at times almost imperceptible, but the principle always holds, and should be from the first taught. In gesture, the bodily man acts as a unit.

The amount of gesture is, of course, determined by the temperament of the speaker, the nature of the speech, the character of the audience, and the occasion of the address. One speaker will, under certain conditions, gesticulate nearly all the time; another will, under the same conditions, seem seldom to move in any way. The two may be equally effective. A speech that is charged with lively emotion will usually be accompanied by action; a speech expressive of the profound feeling that subdues to gravity, or resignation, would be comparatively without action. The funeral oration by Mark Antony is full of action because it is really intended to excite the will of his audience; in a funeral address simply expressive of sorrow and appreciation, gesture would, as a rule, be out of place. A sharply contested debate may need action that punctuates and enforces; the pleasantry of after-dinner talk may need only the voice. So, one audience, not quick in grasping ideas, may need, both in language and action, much clear, sharp indication of the point by illustration, much stirring up by physical attack, so to speak, while another audience would be displeased by this unnecessary effort to be clear and expressive. Yet again, given a certain speaker and a certain subject and a certain audience, it is obvious that the occasion will determine largely how the speaker will bear himself. The atmosphere of a college commencement will be different from that of a barbecue, and the speaker would, within the limits set by his own personality and his own dignity, adapt himself to the one or the other. The general law of appropriateness and good taste must determine the amount of gesture.

For the purposes of this work there is probably very little, if any, value in a strict classification of gestures. It may, at times, be convenient to speak of one gesture as merely for emphasis, of another as indicating location, of another as giving illustration, of one as more subjective, expressing a thought that reflects back upon the speaker, or is said more in the way of self-communion, of another as objective, concerned only with outer objects or with ideas more apart from the person or the inward feeling of the speaker. But it can easily be shown that one idea, or one dominant feeling, may be expressed by many kinds of action, in fact, so far at least as prescribed movements are concerned, in directly opposite kinds, and gesture is so largely a matter of the individual, and is governed so much by mixed motive and varying circumstance, that the general public speaker will profit little by searching for its philosophic basis, and trying to practice according to any elaborated system. The observing of life, with the exercise of instinct, taste, sense, above all of honest purpose--these, with of course the help of competent criticism, will serve as sufficient practical guides in the cultivation of expressive action.

Some observations, or perhaps general principles, may be offered as helpful. When a speaker is concerned with driving ideas straight home to his audience, as in putting bare fact in a debate, his action will be more direct; it will move in straighter lines and be turned, like his thought, more directly upon his audience. As his statement is more exactly to a point, so his gesture becomes more pointed and definite. When the speaker is not talking to or at his audience, to move them to his will, but is rather voicing the ideas and feelings already possessed by them, and is in a non-aggressive mood, he is likely to use less of the direct and emphasis-giving gesture, and to employ principally the gesture that is merely illustrative of his ideas, more reposeful, less direct, less tense.

To consider more in detail the principle that the man, and not the arm, is the gesture, a man should look what he is to speak. The eye should always have a relation to gesture. The look may be in the direction of the arm movement or in another direction. No practical rule can be given. It can only be said that the eye must play its part. Observing actions in real life, we see that when one person points out an object to another, he looks now at the object, now at the person, as if to guide that person's look. When he hears a sound he may glance in the direction of it, but then look away to listen. Often a suspended action, with a fixed look of the face, will serve to arrest the attention of auditors and fix it upon an idea. One should cultivate first the look, then the supporting or completing action.

As to the movement of the arm and the form of the hand, one should be careful not to become stiff and precise by following exact rules. In general, it may be said that the beginning of the arm movement, being from the body, is in the upper arm; the finish of it is at the tips of the fingers, with the forefinger leading, or bringing the gesture to a point. There is generally a slightly flexible, rythmical movement of the arm and hand. This should not, as a rule, be very marked, and in specially energetic action is hardly observable. In this arm action there is an early preparatory movement, which indicates or suggests, what is coming. Often a moment of suspense in the preparation enhances the effect of the finish, or stroke, of the gesture, which corresponds usually to the vocal emphasis. At the final pointing of the action, the hand is, for a moment or for moments, fixed, as the mind and the man are fixed, for the purpose of holding the attention of the auditor; then follows the recovery, so-called, from the gesture, or it may be, the passing to another gesture. And all the while, let it again be said, slight changes of bodily pose with proper adjustments of the feet, will make the harmonious, unified action. It should be remembered that, as in viewing a house or a picture we should be impressed by the main body and the general effect, rather than by any one feature, so on the same principle, no striking feature of a man's action should attract attention to itself. On the same principle, no part of the hand should be made conspicuous--the thumb or forefinger should not be too much stuck out, nor the other fingers, except in pointing, be very much curved in. Generally, except in precise pointing, there is a graduated curving, not too nice, from the bent little finger to the straighter forefinger. As the gesture is concerned with thought more delicate, the action of the hand is lighter and tends more to the tips of the fingers; as it is more rugged and strong, the hand is held heavier. It is bad to carry the arm very far back, causing a strained look; to stretch the arms too straight out, or to confine the elbow to the side. The elbow is kept somewhat away even in the smallest gesture. While action should have nerve, it should not become nervous, that is, over- tense and rigid. It should be free and controlled, with good poise in the whole man.

Before leaving this subject, in its physical aspect, let us consider somewhat the matter of standing and moving on the platform. Among imperfections as regards position, that kind of imperfection which takes the form of perfectly fixed feet, strictly upright figure, hands at the side, head erect, and eyes straight-of all bad kinds, this kind is the worst. This is often referred to as school declamation, or the speaking of a piece. We have discarded many old ideas of restriction in education. Let us discard the strait-jacket in platform speaking. Nobody else ever speaks as students are often compelled to speak. Let them speak like boys--not like men even-much less like machines. There is of course a good and a bad way of standing and moving, but much is due to youth, to individuality, and to earnest intention, and a student should have free play in a large degree.

In walking, the step should neither be too fast nor too slow, too long nor too short, too much on the heel or too much on the toe. A simple, straightforward way of getting there is all that is wanted. The arms are left to swing easily, but not too much; nor should one arm swing more than the other. The head, it will be noted, may occasionally rise and fall as one goes up or down steps or walks the platform. Before beginning to speak, one should not obviously take a position and prepare. He should easily stop at his place, and, looking at his auditors, begin simply to say something to them. As to the feet, they will, of course, be variously placed or adjusted according to the pose of the body in the varying moods of the speech. In general, the body will rest more on one foot than on the other. In a position of ease, as usually at the beginning of a speech, one foot will bear most of the weight. In this case, this foot will normally be pointed nearly to the front; the other foot will be only very slightly in advance of this and will be turned more outward. The feet will not be close together; nor noticeably far apart. They need not--they had better not--as it is sometimes pictured in books, be so set that a line passing lengthwise through the freer foot will pass through the heel of the other foot. As a man becomes earnest in speaking, his posture will vary, and often he will stand almost equally on his two feet. In changing one's position, it is best to acquire the habit of moving the freer foot, the one lighter on the floor, first, thus avoiding a swaying, or toppling look of the body.

In connection with the subject of standing, naturally comes the question of the arms in the condition of inaction. It is possibly well to train one's self, when learning to speak, to let the arms hang relaxed at the side, but speakers do not often so hold the arms. Usually there is a desk near, and the speaker when at rest drops one hand upon this, or he lets one arm rest at the waist, or he brings the two hands together. Any of these things may be done, if done simply, easily, without nervous tightening, or too frequent shifting. One thing, for practical reasons, should not be allowed, the too common habit of clasping the hands behind the back. It will become a fixed mannerism, and a bad one, for the hands are thus concealed, the shoulders and head may droop forward, and the hands may be so tightened together behind the back as to cause nervous tension in the body and in the voice. The hands should be in place ready for expressive action. The back is not such a place.

Nearly every movement that a man makes in speaking should have some fitting relation to what he is at the moment saying. These movements will then be varied. When certain repeated actions, without this proper relation, are acquired, they are called mannerisms. They have no meaning, and are obtrusive and annoying. Repeated jerking or bobbing of the head, for a supposed emphasis; regularly turning the head from side to side, for addressing all the audience; nervous shaking of the head, as of one greatly in earnest; repeated, meaningless punching or pounding of the air, always in the same way; shifting of one foot regularly backward and forward; rising on the toes with each emphatic word,--although single movements similar to these often have appropriate place, none of these or others should be allowed to become fixed mannerisms, habitually recurring movements, without a purpose. We are sometimes told that certain manneristic ways are often a speaker's strength. Probably this is at least half true. But eccentricities should not be cultivated or indulged. They will come. We should have as few as possible, or they won't count. One thing, however, should here be said. Positive strength, with positive faults, is much better than spiritless inoffensiveness. One should not give all his attention to the avoiding of faults.

In the application of gesture to the expression of ideas, one is helped, as has been said, by constantly heeding the general principle of suiting the form of the gesture to the nature of the thought, or of suiting the action to the word. Inasmuch as gesture so generally takes the form of objects or actions, it is undoubtedly easier to begin with the more concrete in language, or with the discussion of tangible objects, and work from these to the more abstract and remotely imaginary--from the more, to the less, familiar. Let the student indicate the location, or the height, or the width, or the form of an object. His action will probably be appropriate. Let him apply similar, probably less definite, action to certain abstract ideas. Let him pass to ideas more remote and vague, by action largely suggestive, not definite or literal.

The most important, because the most fundamental, principle to be borne in mind is that gesture should be made to enforce, not the superficial, or incidental, ideas appearing in a statement, but the ideas which lie behind the form of expression and are the real basis, or inhere in the fundamental purpose, of the speaker's discourse.

At the close of Senator Thurston's speech on intervention in behalf of Cuba, there is picturesque language for impressing the contention that force is justified in a worthy cause. The speaker cites graphically examples of force at Bunker Hill, Valley Forge, Shiloh, Chattanooga, and Lookout Heights. The student is here very likely to be led astray by the fine opportunity to make gesture. He may vividly see and picture the snows of Valley Forge, marked with bloodstained feet, and the other scenes suggested, but forget about the central idea, the purpose behind all the vivid forms of expression. Graphic, detailed gestures may have the effect of making the pictures in themselves the main object. The action here should be informal, unstudied, and merely remotely suggestive. The speaker should keep to his one central idea, and keep with his audience. Otherwise the speech will be insincere and purposeless, perhaps absurd. The fundamental, not the superficial, should determine the action. Young speakers almost invariably pick out words or phrases, suggesting the possibility of a gesture, and give exact illustration to them, as if the excellence of gesture were in itself an object, when really the thing primarily to be enforced is not these incidental features in the form of expression, but the underlying idea of the whole passage. It is as if the steeple were made out of proportion to the church, or a hat out of proportion to the man. This misconception of what gesture really means is doubtless, in large measure, the cause of making platform recitation often false and offensive. The remedy does not lie in omitting gesture altogether, as some seem to think, but in making gesture simple and true.

Finally, let the student remember that he goes to the platform, not to make a splendid speech and receive praise for a brilliant exhibition of his art, but that he goes there because the platform is a convenient place from which to tell the people something he has to say. Let him think it nothing remarkable that he should be there; let him so bear himself, entering with simplicity, honesty, earnestness, and modesty, into his work, that no one will think much about how his work is done. Spirited oratory, with the commanding presence, the sweeping action, and an overmastering force of utterance, may at times be called forth, but these are given to a man out of his subject and by the occasion; they are not to be assumed by him merely because he is before an audience, or as necessary features of speech-making. Let the student speak, first and always, as a self-respecting, thinking man, earnest and strong, but self-controlled and sensible.

PLATFORM PRACTICE

THE FORMAL ADDRESS

The selections in the several sections for platform practice are to be used for applying, in appropriate combination, the principles heretofore worked out, one by one. The first group provides practice in the more formal style. The occasion of the formal address requires, in large degree, restraint and dignity. The thought is elevated; the mood serious, in some cases subdued, the form of expression exact and firm. The delivery should correspond. The tone should be, in some degree, ennobled; the movement deliberate, and comparatively even and measured; the modulation not marked by striking variations in pitch; the pauses rather regular, and the gesture always sparing, perhaps wholly omitted. The voice should be generally pure and fine; the enunciation should be finished and true. Whatever action there may be should be restrained, well poised, deliberate, with some degree of grace. In general it should be felt that carelessness or looseness or aggressiveness or undue demonstrativeness would be out of harmony with the spirit of the occasion. Good taste must be exercised at every step, and the audience should be addressed, from the outset, as in sympathy with the speaker and ready at once to approve. The spirit and manner of contention is out of place.

In this style of discourse the liability to failure lies in the direction of dullness, monotony, lack of vitality and warmth. This is because the feeling is deep and still; is an undercurrent, strong but unseen. This restrained, repressed feeling is the most difficult fittingly to express. In this kind of speech some marring of just the right effect is difficult to avoid. Simplicity, absolute genuineness, are the essential qualities. The ideas must be conveyed with power and significance, in due degree; but nothing too much is particularly the watchword regarding the outward features of the work.

THE PUBLIC LECTURE

In the public lecture the element of entertainment enters prominently. The audience, at first in a passive state, must be awakened, and taken on with the speaker. Probably it must be instructed, perhaps amused. The speaker must make his own occasion. He has no help from the circumstance of predisposition among his auditors. He must compel, or he must win; he must charm or thrill; or he must do each in turn. Animation, force, beauty, dramatic contrast, vividness, variety, are the qualities that will more or less serve, according to the style of the composition. Aptness in the story or anecdote, facility in graphic illustration, readiness in expressing emotion, happiness in the imitative faculty, for touching off the eccentric in character or incident, are talents that come into play, and in the exercise of these, gesture of course has an important place.

The lecture platform is perhaps the only field, with possibly the exception of what is properly the after-dinner speech, wherein public speaking may be viewed as strictly an art, something to be taken for its own sake, wherein excellence in the doing is principally the end in view. This means, generally, that individual talent, and training in all artistic requirements, count for more than the subject or any "accidents of office," in holding the auditor's interest. An animated and versatile style can be cultivated by striving to make effective the public lecture.

THE INFORMAL DISCUSSION

Informal discussion is the name chosen for the lecture or talk in the club or the classroom. It implies a rather small audience and familiar relations between audience and speaker. While the subject may be weighty, and the language may be necessarily of the literary or scientific sort, the style of speaking should be colloquial. It ought to bring the hearer pretty near to the speaker. If the subject and language are light, the speaking will be sprightly and comparatively swift.

Since the occasion for this kind of speaking is frequent, and the opportunity for it is likely to fall to almost any educated man, proficiency in it might well be made an object in the course of one's educational training. The end aimed at is the ability to talk well. This accomplishment is not so easy as it may seem. It marks, indeed, the stage of maturity in speech-making. Since authoritative opinion from the speaker and interest in the subject on the part of the audience are prime elements in this form of discussion, little cultivation of form is usually given to this kind of speaking. The result is much complaining from auditors about inaudibleness, dullness, monotony, annoying mannerisms, or a too formal, academic tone that keeps the audience remote, a lack of what is called the human quality. A good talker from the desk not only has the reward of appreciation and gratitude, but is able to accomplish results in full proportion to all that he puts into the improvement of his vocal work. An agreeable tone, easy formation of words, clear, well-balanced emphasis, good phrasing, or grouping of words in the sentence, some vigor without continual pounding, easy, unstudied bodily movement without manneristic repetition of certain motions, in short, good form without any obtrusive appearance of form,--these are the qualities desired.

ARGUMENTATIVE SPEECH

In the case of the forensic, we come nearer to the practical in public speaking. The speaker aims, as a rule, to effect a definite purpose, and he concentrates his powers upon this immediate object. Since the speech is for the most part an appeal to the reason, and therefore deals largely with fact and the logical relations of ideas, precision and clearness of statement are the chief qualities to be cultivated. But since the aim is to overcome opposition, and produce conviction, and so to impress and stir as to affect the will to a desired action, the element of force, and the moving quality of persuasion enters in as a reenforcement of the speaker's logic. Generally the speech is very direct, and often it is intense. It has in greater degree than any other form the feature of aggressiveness. Some form of attack is adopted, for the purpose of overthrowing the opposing force. That attack is followed up in a direct line of argument, and is carried out to a finish. In delivery the continuous line of pursuit thus followed often naturally leads to a kind of effective monotone style, wherein the speaker keeps an even force, or strikes blow after blow, or sends shot after shot. The characteristic feature of the forensic style is the climax--climax in brief successions of words, climax in the sentence, climax in giving sections of the speech, climax in the speech as a whole.

Special notice should be taken of the fact that, in earnest argument, sentences have, characteristically, a different run from that in ordinary expository speaking. Whereas in the expository style the sentence flows, as a rule, easily forth, with the voice rising and falling, in an undulatory sort of way, and dropping restfully to a finish, in the heated forensic style, the sentence is given the effect of being sent straight forth, as if to a mark, with the last word made the telling one, and so kept well up in force and pitch. The accumulating force has the effect of sending the last word home, or of making it the one to clinch the statement.

The dangers to be guarded against in debate are wearying monotony, over-hammering--too frequent, too hard, too uniform an emphasis--too much, or too continued heat, too much speed, especially in speaking against time, a loss of poise in the bearing, a halting or jumbling in speech, nervous tenseness in action, an overcontentious or bumptious spirit. Bodily control, restraint, good temper, balance, are the saving qualities. A debater must remember that he need not be always in a heat. Urbanity and graciousness have their place, and the relief afforded by humor is often welcome and effective.

In no form of speaking, except that of dramatic recitation, is the liability to impairment of voice so great as it is in debating. One of the several excellent features of debating is that of the self- forgetfulness that comes with an earnest struggle to win. But perhaps a man cannot safely forget himself until he has learned to know himself. The intensity of debating often leads, in the case of a speaker vocally untrained, to a tightening of the throat in striving for force, to a stiffening of the tongue and lips for making incisive articulation, to a rigidness of the jaw from shutting down on words to give decisive emphasis. Soon the voice has the juice squeezed out of it. The tone becomes harsh and choked; then ragged and weak. The only remedy is to go straight back and begin all over, just as a golfer usually does when he has gone on without instruction. The necessity of going back is often not realized till later in life; then the process is much harder, and perhaps can never be entirely effective. The teacher in the course of his experience meets many, many such cases. The time to learn the right way is at the beginning.

Among the selections here offered for forensic practice, examples in debate serve for the cultivation of the aggressiveness that comes from immediate opposition; examples in the political speech for acquiring the abandon and enthusiasm of the so-called popular style; in the legal plea for practice in suppressed force. In the case of the last of these, it is well that the audience be near to the speaker, as is the case in an address to a judge or jury. The idea is to be forcible without being loud and high; to cultivate a subdued tone that shall, at the same time, be vital and impressive. The importance of a manner of speaking that is not only clear and effective, but also agreeable, easy to listen to, is quite obvious when we consider the task of a judge or a jury, who have to sit for hours and try to carry in their minds the substance of all that has been said, weighing point against point, balancing one body of facts against another. A student can arrange nearly the same conditions as to space, and can, by exercise of imagination, enter into the spirit of a legal conflict.

THE AFTER-DINNER SPEECH

After-dinner speaking is another form that many men may have an opportunity to engage in. It can also be practiced under conditions resembling those of the actual occasion, that is, members of the class can be so seated that the speaking may become intimate in tone, and speeches can be selected that will serve for cultivating that distinctive, sociable quality of voice that, in itself, goes far in contributing to the comfort and delight of the after-dinner audience. The real after-dinner speech deals much in pleasantry. The tone of voice is characteristically unctuous. Old Fezziwig is described by Dickens as calling out "in a comfortable, rich, fat, jovial, oily voice." Something like this is perhaps the ideal after-dinner voice, although there is a dry humor as well as an unctuous, and each speaker will, after all, have his own way of making his hearers comfortable, happy, and attentive. Ease and deliberation are first requisites. Nervous intensity may not so much mar the effect of earnest debate. The social chat is spoiled by it. Humor, as a rule, requires absolute restfulness. Especially should a beginner guard himself against haste in making the point at the finish of a story. It does no harm to keep the hearer waiting a bit, in expectation. The effect may be thus enhanced, while the effect will be entirely lost if the point, and the true touch, are spoiled by uncontrolled haste. The way to gain this ease and control is not by stiffening up to master one's self, but by relaxing, letting go of one's self. Practice in the speech of pleasantry may have great value in giving a man repose, in giving him that saving grace, an appreciation of the humorous, in affording him a means of relief or enlivenment to the serious speech.

THE OCCASIONAL POEM

The occasional poem is so frequently brought forth in connection with speechmaking that some points regarding metrical reading may be quite in place in a speaker's training. Practice in verse reading is of use also because of the frequency of quoted lines from the poets in connection with the prose speech.

To read a poem well one must become in spirit a poet. He must not only think, he must feel. He must exercise imagination. He must, we will say it again, see visions and dream dreams. What was said about vividness in the discussion of expressional effects applies generally to the reading of poetry. One will read much better if he has tried to write-- in verse as well as in prose. He will then know how to put himself in the place of the poet, and will not be so likely to mar the poet's verses by "reading them ill-favoredly." He will know the value of words that have been so far sought, and may not slur over them; he may feel the sound of a line formed to suggest a sound in nature. He will know that a meter has been carefully worked out, and that, in the reading, that meter is of the spirit of the poem; it is not to be disregarded. Likewise he will appreciate the place of rhyme, and may not try so to cover it up as entirely to lose its effect. In humorous verse, especially, rhyme plays an effective part; and in all verse, alliteration, variations in melody, the lighter and the heavier touch, acceleration and retard in movement, the caesura, or pause in the line, and the happy effect of the occasional cadence, are features which one can come to appreciate and respect only with reading one's favorite poems many times, with spirit warm, with faculties alert.

THE MAKING OF THE SPEECH

Although the use of selected speeches is best for effective drill in delivery, yet a student's training for public speaking is of course not complete until he has had experience in applying his acquired skill to the presenting of his own thought. Thinking and speaking should be made one operation. The principles of composition for the public speech belong to a separate work. A few hints only can be given here, and these will be concerned with the informal, offhand speech rather than with the formal address.

The usual directions regarding the choosing of the subject, the collecting of material, and the arranging of it in the most effective order, with exceptions and variations, hold in all forms of the speech. The subject chosen should be one of special interest to the speaker, one on which it is known he can speak with some degree of authority, because of his personal study of it, or because of his having had exceptional personal relations with it. It must also be, because of the nature of it, or because of some special treatment, of particular interest to the audience to be addressed. Either new, out-of-the-way subjects, or new, fresh phases of old subjects are usually interesting. The subject must be limited in its comprehensiveness to suit the time allowed for speaking, and the title of the speech should be so phrased as to indicate exactly what the subject, or the part of a subject, is to be. To this carefully limited and defined subject, the speaker should rigidly adhere.

How to find a subject is generally a topic on which students are advised. Though it is often a necessity to hunt for a suitable special topic on which to speak, the student should know that when he gets outside the classroom, he will find that he will not be invited to speak because he is ready at finding subjects and clever in speech. It is not strange, in view of the many advertisements that reach young men, offering methods of home training, or promising sure success from this or that special method of schooling, that they may come to believe that any one has only to learn to stand up boldly on a platform, and with voice and gesture exercise some mysterious sort of magical control over an audience, and his success as an orator is secure. They will find that their time and money have been wasted, so far as public speaking is concerned, unless, having at the start some native ability, they have secured, in addition, a kind of training that is fundamental. A man is wanted as a speaker primarily because he stands for something; because he has done some noteworthy work. His subjects for discussion arise out of his personal interests, and, to a large extent, his method of treatment will be determined by his relation to these subjects. A young man may well be advised, then, not simply how to choose and how to present a subject, but first to secure a good mental training, and then to find for himself an all-absorbing work to do. The wisdom that comes from a concentrated intellectual activity, and an interest in men's affairs, both directed to some unselfish end, is the essential qualification of the speaker.

In considering the arrangement of a speech, the student will do well to ask himself first, not what is to be the beginning of it, but what is to be the end of it; what is the purpose of it; and what shall be the central idea; what impression, or what principal thought or thoughts, shall be left with the audience. When this is determined, then a way of working out this central idea or of working up to it--in a short speech, by a few points only--must be carefully and thoroughly planned. Extemporaneous speaking is putting spontaneously into words what has previously been well thought out and well arranged. Without this state of preparation, the way of wisdom is silence.

The language of a speech is largely determined by the man's habit of mind, the nature of his subject, and the character of his audience. Students often err in one of two directions, either by being too bookish in language or by allowing the other extreme of looseness, weak colloquialism in words, and formless monotony of sentence, with the endless repetition of the connective "and." Language should be fresh, vital, varied. It should have some dignity. Much reading, writing, and speaking are necessary to secure an adequate vocabulary, and a readiness in putting in firm form a variety of sentences. Concreteness of expression and occasional illustration are more needed in speech than in writing, and the brief anecdote or story is welcome and useful if there is room for it, and if it comes unbidden, by virtue of its fitness and spontaneity, and is not drawn in by the ears for half- hearted service. The inevitable story at the opening of an after-dinner speech might often be spared. Although a good story is in itself enjoyable, yet when a speaker feels that he must make one fit into the speech, whether or no, by applying it to himself or his subject or the occasion, the effect is often very unhappy. A man is best guided in these things simply by being true, by being sincere rather than artful. On this same principle, a student may need some advice with regard to his spirit and manner in giving expression to his own ideas before an audience. He need not, as students often seem to think they must, appear to have full knowledge or final judgment on the largest of subjects. It is more fitting that he should speak as a student, an inquirer, not as an authority. If his statements are guarded and qualified; if he speaks as one only inclined to an opinion when finality of judgment is obviously beyond his reach; if he directly refers, and defers, to opinions that must be better than his can be, his speech will have much more weight, and he will grow in strength of character by always being true to himself. It is a question whether students are not too often inspired to be bold and absolute, for the sake of apparent strength in speaking, rather than modest and judicious and sensible, for the sake of being strong as men.

In the form of delivering one's thought to an audience, it is of the first importance that one should speak and not declaim. There is, of course, a way of talking on the platform that is merely negatively good, a way that is fitting enough in general style, but weak. There should be breadth, and strength, and reach. But this does not mean any necessity of sending forth pointless successive sentences over the heads of an audience. A college president recently said, "Our boys declaim a good deal, though they're not so bad as they used to be. It seems to me," he added, "that the idea is to say something to your audience." That is what a teacher must be continually insisting on, that the student say something to somebody, not chant or declaim into space. And the student should be continually testing himself on this point, whether he is looking into the faces of his hearers and speaking, though on a larger scale, yet in the usual way of communicating ideas.

It is not desirable that men should become overready speakers. Methods of training in extemporaneous discussion that require speaking without thought, on anything or nothing that can be at the moment invented, are likely to be mischievous. Thought suggests expression, and exact thought will find fit form. Sound thinking is the main thing. Practice for mere fluency tends to the habit of superficial thinking, and produces the wearisome, endless talker. In this connection emphasis may be laid upon the point of ending a speech when its purpose is accomplished, and that as soon as can be. Many speeches are spoiled by the last third or quarter of them, when a point well made has lost its effect by being overenforced or obscured by a wordy conclusion. Let the student study for rare thought and economy of speech.

Books on speaking have repeatedly insisted that after all has been said, the public speaker's word will be taken for what he is known to be worth as a man; that his utterances will have effect according as they are given out with soul-felt earnestness. This has already been touched upon here, and it is well that it should be often repeated. It may be well, however, also to consider quite carefully what part is played in men's efforts by the element of skill. Of two equally worthy and equally earnest men, the man of the superior skill, acquired by persistent training in method, will be the stronger man, the man who will be of more service to his fellows. More than this, inasmuch as public men can seldom be perfectly known or judged as to character, and may often, for a time at least, deceive, it is quite possible that the unscrupulous man with great skill will, at some moment of crisis, make the worse appear to be the better cause. Equally skilled men are therefore wanted to contend for the side of right. The man whose service to men depends largely upon his power of speech--in the pulpit, at the bar, or in non-professional capacity--must have, either from gift or from training, the speaker's full equipment, for matching himself against opposing strength.

REVIEW EXERCISES

For convenience of practice, a few pages of brief exercises, exemplifying the foregoing principles, are given at the end of the book. By using each day one example in each group, and changing from time to time, the student will have sufficient variety to serve indefinitely. This vocal practice may be made a healthful and pleasurable daily exercise.

PART TWO
TECHNICAL TRAINING

ESTABLISHING THE TONE

O SCOTIA!
From "The Cotter's Saturday Night"
BY ROBERT BURNS

O Scotia! my dear, my native soil!
For whom my warmest wish to Heaven is sent,
Long may thy hardy sons of rustic toil
Be blest with health, and peace, and sweet content!
And oh! may Heaven their simple lives prevent
From luxury's contagion, weak and vile!
Then, howe'er crowns and coronets be rent,
A virtuous populace may rise the while, And stand a wall of fire around their much-loved isle.
O Thou! who poured the patriotic tide,
That streamed through Wallace's undaunted heart,
Who dared to nobly stem tyrannic pride,
Or nobly die, the second glorious part,
(The patriot's God, peculiarly Thou art,
His friend, inspirer, guardian and reward!)
Oh never, never, Scotia's realm desert;
But still the patriot, and the patriot bard, In bright succession raise, her orna-

ment and guard!

O ROME! MY COUNTRY!

From "Childe Harold's Pilgrimage"

BY LORD BYRON

O Rome! my country! city of the soul!
The orphans of the heart must turn to thee,
Lone mother of dead empires! and control
In their shut breasts, their petty misery.
What are our woes and sufferance?--Come and see
The cypress, hear the owl, and plod your way
O'er steps of broken thrones and temples, Ye!
Whose agonies are evils of a day:-- A world is at our feet as fragile as our clay.
The Niobe of nations! there she stands,
Childless and crownless, in her voiceless woe;
An empty urn within her withered hands,
Whose holy dust was scattered long ago;--
The Scipios' tomb contains no ashes now;
The very sepulchers lie tenantless
Of their heroic dwellers:--dost thou flow,
Old Tiber! through a marble wilderness? Rise, with thy yellow waves, and mantle her distress!

RING OUT, WILD BELLS!

From "In Memoriam"

BY ALFRED LORD TENNYSON

Ring out, wild bells, to the wild sky, The flying cloud, the frosty light; The year is dying in the night; Ring out, wild bells, and let him die.

Ring out the old, ring in the new, Ring, happy bells, across the snow; The year is going, let him go; Ring out the false, ring in the true.

Ring out the grief that saps the mind, For those that here we see no more; Ring out the feud of rich and poor, Ring in redress to all mankind.

Ring out a slowly dying cause, And ancient forms of party strife; Ring in the nobler modes of life, With sweeter manners, purer laws.

Ring out the want, the care, the sin, The faithless coldness of the times; Ring out, ring out my mournful rhymes, But ring the fuller minstrel in.

Ring out false pride in place and blood, The civic slander and the spite; Ring in the love of truth and right, Ring in the common love of good.

ROLL ON, THOU DEEP!

From "Childe Harold's Pilgrimage"

BY LORD BYRON

Roll on, thou deep and dark blue Ocean, roll!

Ten thousand fleets sweep over thee in vain; Man marks the earth with ruin-- his control

Stops with the shore: upon the watery plain, The wrecks are all thy deed, nor doth remain

A shadow of man's ravage, save his own, When for a moment, like a drop of rain,

He sinks into thy depths with bubbling groan,

Without a grave, unknell'd, uncoffin'd, and unknown.

The armaments, which thunderstrike the walls

Of rock-built cities, bidding nations quake, And monarchs tremble in their capitals;

The oak leviathans, whose huge ribs make Their clay creator the vain title take

Of lord of thee, and arbiter of war; These are thy toys, and, as the snowy flake,

They melt into thy yeast of waves, which mar

Alike th' Armada's pride or spoils of Trafalgar.

Thy shores are empires, changed in all save thee:

Assyria, Greece, Rome, Carthage,--what are they? Thy waters wasted them while they were free,

And many a tyrant since; their shores obey The stranger, slave, or savage; their decay

Has dried up realms to deserts: not so thou; Unchangeable, save to thy wild waves play,

Time writes no wrinkle on thine azure brow;

Such as creation's dawn beheld, thou rollest now.

And I have loved thee, Ocean! and my joy

Of youthful sports was on thy breast to be Borne, like thy bubbles, onward: from a boy

I wanton'd with thy breakers--they to me Were a delight; and if the freshening sea

Made them a terror--'twas a pleasing fear.

THOU, TOO, SAIL ON!

From "The Building of the Ship," by permission of, and by special Arrangement with, Houghton Mifflin Company, authorized publishers of this author's works.

BY HENRY W. LONGFELLOW

Sail forth into the sea, O ship! Through wind and wave, right onward steer! The moistened eye, the trembling lip, Are not the signs of doubt or fear.

Sail forth into the sea of life, O gentle, loving, trusting wife, And safe from all adversity Upon the bosom of that sea Thy comings and thy goings be! For gentleness and love and trust Prevail o'er angry wave and gust; And in the wreck of noble lives Something immortal still survives!

Thou, too, sail on, O Ship of State! Sail on, O Union, strong and great! Humanity with all its fears, With all the hopes of future years, Is hanging breathless on thy fate! We know what Master laid thy keel, What Workmen wrought thy ribs of steel, Who made each mast, and sail, and rope, What anvils rang, what hammers beat, In what a forge and what a heat Were shaped the anchors of thy hope! Fear not each sudden sound and shock, 'Tis of the wave and not the rock;

'Tis but the flapping of the sail, And not a rent made by the gale! In spite of rock and tempest's roar, In spite of false lights on the shore, Sail on, nor fear to breast the sea! Our hearts, our hopes, are all with thee, Our hearts, our hopes, our prayers, our tears, Our faith triumphant o'er our fears, Are all with thee,--are all with thee!

O TIBER, FATHER TIBER!

From "Horatius"

BY LORD MACAULAY

"O Tiber, Father Tiber!

To whom the Romans pray, A Roman's life, a Roman's arms,

Take thou in charge this day!" So he spake, and, speaking, sheathed

The good sword by his side, And, with his harness on his back,

Plunged headlong in the tide.

No sound of joy or sorrow

Was heard from either bank, But friends and foes in dumb surprise, With parted lips and straining eyes,

Stood gazing where he sank; And when above the surges

They saw his crest appear, All Rome sent forth a rapturous cry, And even the ranks of Tuscany

Could scarce forbear to cheer.

But fiercely ran the current,

Swollen high by months of rain, And fast his blood was flowing,

And he was sore in pain, And heavy with his armor,

And spent with changing blows; And oft they thought him sinking,

But still again he rose.

And now he feels the bottom;--

Now on dry earth he stands; Now round him throng the Fathers

To press his gory hands. And now, with shouts and clapping,

And noise of weeping loud, He enters through the River Gate,

Borne by the joyous crowd.

MARULLUS TO THE ROMAN CITIZENS

From "Julius Caesar"

BY WILLIAM SHAKESPEARE

Flavius. Why dost thou lead these men about the streets?

Second Citizen. Indeed, sir, we make holiday, to see Caesar, and to rejoice in his triumph.

Marullus. Wherefore rejoice? What conquest brings he home? What tributaries follow him to Rome, To grace in captive bonds his chariot-wheels? You blocks, you stones, you worse than senseless things! O you hard hearts, you cruel men of Rome, Knew you not Pompey? Many a time and oft Have you climb'd up to walls and battlements, To towers and windows, yea, to chimney-tops, Your infants in your arms, and there have sat The live-long day, with patient expectation To see great Pompey pass the streets of Rome; And when you saw his chariot but appear, Have you not made an universal shout, That Tiber trembled underneath her banks, To hear the replication of your sounds, Made in her concave shores? And do you now put on your best attire? And do you now cull out a holiday? And do you now strew flowers in his way That comes in triumph over Pompey's blood? Be gone! Run to your houses, fall upon your knees, Pray to the gods to intermit the plague That needs must light on this ingratitude.

THE RECESSIONAL

From "Collected Verse," with the permission of A. P. Watt and Son, London, and Doubleday, Page and Company, New York, publishers

BY RUDYARD KIPLING

God of our fathers, known of old--

Lord of our far-flung battle-line-- Beneath whose awful hand we hold

Dominion over palm and pine-- Lord God of Hosts, be with us yet, Lest we forget--lest we forget.

The tumult and the shouting dies--

The captains and the kings depart-- Still stands Thine ancient Sacrifice,

An humble and a contrite heart. Lord God of Hosts, be with us yet, Lest we forget--lest we forget.

Far-called our navies melt away--

On dune and headland sinks the fire, Lo, all our pomp of yesterday

Is one with Nineveh and Tyre. Judge of the Nations, spare us yet, Lest we forget--lest we forget.

If, drunk with sight of power, we loose

Wild tongues that have not Thee in awe-- Such boasting as the Gentiles use

Or lesser breeds without the Law-- Lord God of Hosts, be with us yet, Lest we forget--lest we forget.

For heathen heart that puts her trust

In reeking tube and iron shard-- All valiant dust that builds on dust,

And guarding calls not Thee to guard-- For frantic boast and foolish word, Thy Mercy on Thy People, Lord.

THE CRADLE OF LIBERTY

From Webster's Reply to Hayne, in the United States Senate. Little, Brown and Company, Boston, publishers of "The Great Speeches and Orations of Daniel Webster"

BY DANIEL WEBSTER

Mr. President, I shall enter on no encomium upon Massachusetts; she needs none. There she is. Behold her, and judge for yourselves. There is her history; the world knows it by heart. The past, at least, is secure. There is Boston, and Concord, and Lexington, and Bunker Hill; and there they will remain forever. The bones of her sons, fallen in the great struggle for independence, now lie mingled with the soil of every State from New England to Georgia; and there they will lie forever. And, sir, where American liberty raised its first voice, and where its youth was nurtured and sustained, there it still lives in the strength of its manhood and full of its original spirit. If discord and disunion shall wound it; if party strife and blind ambition shall hawk at and tear it; if folly and madness, if uneasiness under salutary and necessary restraint, shall succeed in separating it from that Union by which alone its existence is made sure,--it will stand, in the end, by the side of that cradle in which its infancy was rocked; it will stretch forth its arm with whatever of vigor it may still retain over the friends who gather round it; and it will fall at last, if fall it must, amidst the proudest monuments of its own glory, and on the very spot of its origin.

THE IMPEACHMENT OF WARREN HASTINGS
Delivered in the House of Lords, February 13, 1788
BY EDMUND BURKE

My Lords, I do not mean to go further than just to remind your Lordships of this,--that Mr. Hastings's government was one whole system of oppression, of robbery of individuals, of spoliation of the public, and of suppression of the whole system of the English government, in order to vest in the worst of the natives all the power that could possibly exist in any government; in order to defeat the ends which all governments ought, in common, to have in view. In the name of the Commons of England, I charge all this villainy upon Warren Hastings, in this last moment of my application to you.

Therefore, it is with confidence that, ordered by the Commons of Great Britain, I impeach Warren Hastings of high crimes and misdemeanors.

I impeach him in the name of the Commons of Great Britain in Parliament assembled, whose parliamentary trust he has abused.

I impeach him in the name of the Commons of Great Britain, whose national character he has dishonored.

I impeach him in the name of the people of India, whose laws, rights, and liberties he has subverted.

I impeach him in the name of the people of India, whose property he has destroyed, whose country he has laid waste and desolate.

I impeach him in the name of human nature itself, which he has cruelly outraged, injured, and oppressed, in both sexes. And I impeach him in the name and by the virtue of those eternal laws of justice, which ought equally to pervade every age, condition, rank, and situation, in the world.

BUNKER HILL

From the oration at the laying of the corner stone of the monument, June 17, 1825. Little, Brown and Company, Boston, publishers of "The Great Speeches and Orations of Daniel Webster"

By DANIEL WEBSTER

This uncounted multitude before me and around me proves the feeling which the occasion has excited. These thousands of human faces, glowing with sympathy and joy, and from the impulses of a common gratitude turned reverently to heaven in this spacious temple of the firmament, proclaim that the day, the place, and the purpose of our assembling have made a deep impression on our hearts.

If, indeed, there be anything in local association fit to affect the mind of man, we need not strive to repress the emotions which agitate us here. We are among the sepulchers of our fathers. We are on ground distinguished by their valor, their constancy, and the shedding of their blood. We are here, not to fix an uncertain date in our annals, nor to draw into notice an obscure and unknown spot. If our humble purpose had never been conceived, if we ourselves had never been born, the 17th of June, 1775, would have been a day on which all subsequent history would have poured its light, and the eminence where we stand a point of attraction to the eyes of successive generations. But we are Americans. We live in what may be called the early age of this great continent; and we know that our posterity, through all time, are here to enjoy and suffer the allotments of humanity. We see before us a probable train of great events; we know that our own fortunes have been happily cast, and it is natural, therefore, that we should be moved by the contemplation of occurrences which have guided our destiny before many of us were born, and settled the condition in which we should pass that portion of our existence which God allows to man on earth.

THE GETTYSBURG ADDRESS
In dedication of the National Cemetery at Gettysburg, Pa., Nov. 19, 1863
BY ABRAHAM LINCOLN

Fourscore and seven years ago our fathers brought forth on this continent a new nation, conceived in Liberty, and dedicated to the proposition that all men are created equal.

Now we are engaged in a great civil war, testing whether that nation, or any nation so conceived and so dedicated, can long endure. We are met on a great battlefield of that war. We have come to dedicate a portion of that field, as a final resting-place for those who here gave their lives that that nation might live. It is altogether fitting and proper that we should do this.

But, in a larger sense, we cannot dedicate--we cannot consecrate--we cannot hallow--this ground. The brave men, living and dead, who struggled here, have consecrated it far above our poor power to add or detract. The world will little note nor long remember what we say here, but it can never forget what they did here. It is for us, the living, rather, to be dedicated here to the unfinished work which they who fought here have thus far so nobly advanced. It is rather for us to be here dedicated to the great task remaining before us--that from these honored dead we take increased devotion to that cause for which they gave the last full measure of devotion; that we here highly resolve that these dead shall not have died in vain; that this nation, under God, shall have a new birth of freedom; and that government of the people, by the people, for the people, shall not perish from the earth.

VOCAL FLEXIBILITY

CAESAR, THE FIGHTER

From "The Courtship of Miles Standish," by permission of, and by Special arrangement with, Houghton Mifflin Company, authorized publishers of this author's works

BY HENRY W. LONGFELLOW

"A wonderful man was this Caesar!

You are a writer, and I am a fighter, but here is a fellow Who could both write and fight, and in both was equally skillful!" Straightway answered and spake John Alden, the comely, the youthful: "Yes, he was equally skilled, as you say, with his pen and his weapons. Somewhere have I read, but where I forget, he could dictate Seven letters at once, at the same time writing his memoirs." "Truly," continued the Captain, not heeding or hearing the other, "Truly a wonderful man was Caius Julius Caesar! Better be first, he said, in a little Iberian village, Than be second in Rome, and I think he was right when he said it. Twice was he married before he was twenty, and many times after; Battles five hundred he fought, and a thousand cities he conquered; He, too, fought in Flanders, as he himself has recorded; Finally he was stabbed by his friend, the orator Brutus! Now, do you know what he did on a certain occasion in Flanders, When the rear-guard of his army retreated, the front giving way too, And the immortal Twelfth Legion was crowded so closely together There was no room for their swords? Why, he seized a shield from a soldier, Put himself straight at the head of his troops, and commanded the captains, Calling on each by his name, to order forward the ensigns; Then to widen the ranks, and give more room for their weapons; So he won the day, the battle of something-or-other. That's what I always say; if you wish a thing to be well done, You must do it yourself, you must not leave it to others!"

OFFICIAL DUTY

BY THEODORE ROOSEVELT

I want to talk to you of the attitude that should properly be observed by legislators, by executive officers, toward wealth, and the attitude that should be observed in return by men of means, and especially by corporations, toward the body politic and toward their fellow citizens.

I utterly distrust the man of whom it is continually said: "Oh, he's a good fellow, but, of course, in politics, he plays politics" It is about as bad for a man to profess, and for those that listen to him by their plaudits to insist upon his professing something which they know he cannot live up to, as it is for him to go below what he ought to do, because if he gets into the habit of lying to himself and to his audience as to what he intends to do, it is certain to eat away his moral fiber.

He won't be able then to stand up to what he knows ought to be done. The temptation of the average politician is to promise everything to the reformers and then to do everything for the organization. I think I can say that, whatever I have promised on the stump or off the stump, either expressly or impliedly, to either organization or reformers, I have kept my promise; and I should keep it just as much if the reformers disapproved.

A public man is bound to represent his constituents, but he is no less bound to cease to represent them when, on a great moral question, he feels that they are taking the wrong side. Let him go out of politics rather than stay in at the cost of doing what his own conscience forbids him to do.

LOOK WELL TO YOUR SPEECH

From "Self-Cultivation in English," with the permission of the author, and of Thomas Y. Crowell Company, New York, publishers

BY GEORGE HERBERT PALMER

First, then, "Look well to your speech." It is commonly supposed that when a man seeks literary power he goes to his room and plans an article for the press. But this is to begin literary culture at the wrong end. We speak a hundred times for every once we write. The busiest writer produces little more than a volume a year, not so much as his talk would amount to in a week. Consequently through speech it is usually decided whether a man is to have command of his language or not. If he is slovenly in his ninety-nine cases of talking, he can seldom pull himself up to strength and exactitude in the hundredth case of writing. A person is made in one piece, and the same being runs through a multitude of performances. Whether words are uttered on paper or to the air, the effect on the utterer is the same. Vigor or feebleness results according as energy or slackness has been in command. I know that certain adaptations to a new field are often necessary. A good speaker may find awkwardnesses in himself when he comes to write, a good writer when he speaks. And certainly cases occur where a man exhibits distinct strength in one of the two, speaking or writing, and not in the other. But such cases are rare. As a rule, language once within our control can be employed for oral or for written purposes. And since the opportunities for oral practice enormously outbalance those for written, it is the oral which are chiefly significant in the development of literary power. We rightly say of the accomplished writer that he shows a mastery of his own tongue.

Fortunate it is, then, that self-cultivation in the use of English must chiefly come through speech; because we are always speaking, whatever else we do. In opportunities for acquiring a mastery of language, the poorest and busiest are at no large disadvantage as compared with the leisured rich. It is true the strong impulse which comes from the suggestion and approval of society may in some cases be absent; but this can be compensated by the sturdy purpose of the learner. A recognition of the beauty of well-ordered words, a strong desire, patience under discouragements, and promptness in counting every occasion as of consequence,--these are the simple agencies which sweep one on to power. Watch your speech, then.

HAMLET TO THE PLAYERS
From "Hamlet"
BY WILLIAM SHAKESPEARE

Hamlet. Speak the speech, I pray you, as I pronounced it to you, trippingly on the tongue; but if you mouth it as many of your players do, I had as lief the town-crier spoke my lines. Nor do not saw the air too much with your hand, thus, but use all gently; for in the very torrent, tempest, and, as I may say, the whirlwind of passion, you must acquire and beget a temperance that may give it smoothness. O, it offends me to the soul to hear a robustious periwig-pated fellow tear a passion to tatters, to very rags, to split the ears of the groundlings, who for the most part are capable of nothing but inexplicable dumb- shows and noise. I could have such a fellow whipped for o'erdoing Termagant; it out-herods Herod: pray you, avoid it.

I Player. I warrant your honor.

Hamlet. Be not too tame neither, but let your own discretion be your tutor: suit the action to the word, the word to the action; with this special observance, that you o'erstep not the modesty of nature; for any thing so overdone is from the purpose of playing, whose end, both at the first and now, was and is, to hold, as 'twere, the mirror up to nature; to show virtue her own feature, scorn her own image, and the very age and body of the time his form and pressure. Now this overdone, or come tardy off, though it make the unskillful laugh, cannot but make the judicious grieve; the censure of the which one must in your allowance o'erweigh a whole theater of others. O, there be players that I have seen play, and heard others praise, and that highly, not to speak it profanely, that, neither having the accent of Christians nor the gait of Christian, pagan, nor man, have so strutted and bellowed that I have thought some of nature's journeymen had made men and not made them well, they imitated humanity so abominably.

BELLARIO'S LETTER

From "The Merchant of Venice"

BY WILLIAM SHAKESPEARE

Duke. This letter from Bellario doth commend A young and learned doctor to our court. Where is he?

Nerissa. He attendeth here hard by, To know your answer, whether you'll admit him.

Duke. With all my heart. Some three or four of you Go give him courteous conduct to this place. Meantime the court shall hear Bellario's letter.

Clerk (reads). "Your grace shall understand that at the receipt of your letter I am very sick; but in the instant that your messenger came, in loving visitation was with me a young doctor of Rome; his name is Balthasar. I acquainted him with the cause in controversy between the Jew and Antonio the merchant: we turned o'er many books together: he is furnished with my opinion; which, bettered with his own learning, the greatness whereof I cannot enough commend, comes with him, at my importunity, to fill up your grace's request in my stead. I beseech you, let his lack of years be no impediment to let him lack a reverend estimation; for I never knew so young a body with so old a head. I leave him to your gracious acceptance, whose trial shall better publish his commendation."

CASCA, SPEAKING OF CAESAR

From "Julius Caesar"

BY WILLIAM SHAKESPEARE

Casca. You pull'd me by the cloak; would you speak with me?

Brutus. Ay, Casca; tell us what hath chanc'd to-day, That Caesar looks so sad.

Casca. Why, you were with him, were you not?

Brutus. I should not, then, ask Casca what had chanc'd.

Casca. Why, there was a crown offered him; and being offered him, he put it by with the back of his hand, thus; and then the people fell a-shouting.

Brutus. What was the second noise for?

Casca. Why, for that too.

Cassius. They shouted thrice: what was the last cry for?

Casca. Why, for that too.

Brutus. Was the crown offered him thrice?

Casca. Ay, marry, was't, and he put it by thrice, every time gentler than other; and at every putting-by mine honest neighbors shouted.

Cassius. Who offered him the crown?

Casca. Why, Antony.

Brutus. Tell us the manner of it, gentle Casca.

Casca. I can as well be hanged as tell the manner of it: it was mere foolery; I did not mark it. I saw Mark Antony offer him a crown;--yet 'twas not a crown neither, 'twas one of these coronets;-- and, as I told you, he put it by once: but, for all that, to my thinking, he would fain have had it. Then he offered it to him again; then he put it by again: but, to my thinking, he was very loth to lay his fingers off it. And then he offered it the third time; he put it the third time by: and still as he refused it, the rabblement shouted, and clapped their chopped hands, and threw up their sweaty nightcaps, and uttered such a deal of stinking breath because Caesar refused the crown, that it had almost choked Caesar; for he swooned, and fell down at it: and for mine own part, I durst not laugh, for fear of opening my lips, and receiving the bad air.

SQUANDERING OF THE VOICE

From "Lectures on Oratory" BY HENRY WARD BEECHER

How much squandering there is of the voice! How little there is of the advantage that may come from conversational tones! How seldom does a man dare to acquit himself with pathos and fervor! And the men are themselves mechanical and methodical in the bad way who are most afraid of the artificial training that is given in the schools, and who so often show by the fruit of their labor that the want of oratory is the want of education.

How remarkable is the sweetness of voice in the mother, in the father, in the household! The music of no chorded instruments brought together is, for sweetness, like the music of familiar affection when spoken by brother and sister, or by father and mother.

Conversation itself belongs to oratory. How many men there are who are weighty in argument, who have abundant resources, and who are almost boundless in their power at other times and in other places, but who, when in company among their kind, are exceedingly unapt in their methods. Having none of the secret instruments by which the elements of nature may be touched, having no skill and no power in this direction, they stand as machines before living, sensitive men. A man may be a master before an instrument; only the instrument is dead; and he has the living hand; and out of that dead instrument what wondrous harmony springs forth at his touch! And if you can electrify an audience by the power of a living man on dead things, how much more should that audience be electrified when the chords are living and the man is alive, and he knows how to touch them with divine inspiration!

THE TRAINING OF THE GENTLEMAN

From "Personal Power," by permission of, and by special arrangement with, Houghton Mifflin Company, authorized publishers of this author's works.

BY WILLIAM J. TUCKER

In this talk about the part which the college may take in the training of a gentleman, I have not dwelt, as you have noticed, upon forms or conventionalities. Every gentleman respects form. Respect for form can be taught, or at least inculcated, but not form itself. One comes to be at ease in society by going into society. Manners come by observation. We imitate, we follow the better fashion of society, the better behavior of men. Good breeding consists first in the attention of others in our behalf to certain necessary details, then in our attention to them. We come in time to draw close and nice distinctions. This little thing is right, that is not quite right. So we grow into the formal habits of a gentleman. "Good manners are made up of constant and petty sacrifices," says Emerson. It is well to keep this saying in mind as a qualification of another of his more familiar sayings: "Give me a thought, and my hands and legs and voice and face will all go right. It is only when mind and character slumber that the dress can be seen."

I like to see the well-bred man, to whom the details of social life have become a second nature. I like also to see the play of that first healthy instinct in a true man which scorns a mean act, which will not allow him to take part in the making of a mean custom, which for example, if he be a college fellow, will not suffer him to treat another fellow as a fag. I am entirely sure that that man is a gentleman.

So then it is, in this world of books, of companionship, of sport, of struggle with some of us, of temptation also, and yet more of high incentives, we are all set to the task of coming out, and of helping one another to come out, as gentlemen. Do not miss, I beseech you, the greatness of the task. Do not miss its constancy. It is more than the incidental work of a college to train the efficient, the honorable, the unselfish man. A college-bred man must be able to show at all times and on all occasions the quality of his distinction.

MAKING THE POINT

BRUTUS TO THE ROMAN CITIZENS
From "Julius Caesar"
BY WILLIAM SHAKESPEARE
Be patient till the last.

Romans, countrymen, and lovers! hear me for my cause, and be silent, that you may hear: believe me for mine honor, and have respect to mine honor, that you may believe: censure me in your wisdom, and awake your senses, that you may the better judge. If there be any in this assembly, any dear friend of Caesar's, to him I say, that Brutus' love to Caesar was no less than his. If, then, that friend demand why Brutus rose against Caesar, this is my answer,--Not that I loved Caesar less, but that I loved Rome more. Had you rather Caesar were living, and die all slaves, than that Caesar were dead, to live all free men? As Caesar loved me, I weep for him; as he was fortunate I rejoice at it; as he was valiant, I honor him: but, as he was ambitious, I slew him. There is tears for his love; joy for his fortune; honor for his valor; and death for his ambition. Who is here so base that would be a bondman? If any, speak; for him have I offended. Who is here so rude that would not be a Roman? If any, speak; for him have I offended. Who is here so vile that will not love his country? If any, speak; for him have I offended. I have done no more to Caesar than you shall do to Brutus. The question of his death is enrolled in the Capitol; his glory not extenuated, wherein he was worthy; nor his offenses enforced, for which he suffered death. Here comes his body, mourned by Mark Antony: who, though he had no hand in his death, shall receive the benefit of his dying, a place in the commonwealth; as which of you shall not? With this I depart,-- that, as I slew my best lover for the good of Rome, I have the same dagger for myself, when it shall please my country to need my death.

THE PRECEPTS OF POLONIUS
From "Hamlet"
BY WILLIAM SHAKESPEARE

Yet here, Laertes! aboard, aboard, for shame! The wind sits in the shoulder of your sail, And you are stay'd for. There; my blessing with thee! And these few precepts in thy memory See thou character. Give thy thoughts no tongue, Nor any unproportion'd thought his act. Be thou familiar, but by no means vulgar. Those friends thou hast, and their adoption tried, Grapple them to thy soul with hoops of steel; But do not dull thy palm with entertainment Of each new-hatch'd, unfledg'd comrade. Beware Of entrance to a quarrel, but, being in, Bear't that the opposed may beware of thee. Give every man thy ear, but few thy voice; Take each man's censure, but reserve thy judgment. Costly thy habit as thy purse can buy, But not express'd in fancy; rich, not gaudy; For the apparel oft proclaims the man, And they in France of the best rank and station Are most select and generous, chief in that. Neither a borrower nor a lender be; For loan oft loses both itself and friend, And borrowing dulls the edge of husbandry. This above all: to thine own self be true, And it must follow, as the night the day, Thou canst not then be false to any man. Farewell; my blessing season this in thee!

THE HIGH STANDARD
From the Lord Rector's address, University of Edinburgh, 1882
BY LORD ROSEBERY

Let us win in the competition of international well-being and prosperity. Let us have a finer, better educated, better lodged, and better nourished race than exists elsewhere; better schools, better universities, better tribunals, ay, and better churches. In one phrase, let our standard be higher, not in the jargon of the Education Department, but in the acknowledgment of mankind. The standard of mankind is not so exalted but that a nobler can be imagined and attained. The dream of him who loved Scotland best would lie not so much in the direction of antiquarian revival, as in the hope that his country might be pointed out as one that in spite of rocks, and rigor, and poverty, could yet teach the world by precept and example, could lead the van and point the moral, where greater nations and fairer states had failed. Those who believe the Scots to be so eminently vain a race, will say that already we are in our opinion the tenth legion of civilization. Well, vanity is a centipede with corns on every foot: I will not tread where the ground is most dangerous. But if we are not foremost, we may at any rate become so. Our fathers have declared unto us what was done in their days and in the old time before them: we know that we come of a strenuous stock. Do you remember the words that young Carlyle wrote to his brother nine years after he had left this University as a student, forty-three years before he returned as its Rector?--

"I say, Jack, thou and I must never falter. Work, my boy, work unweariedly. I swear that all the thousand miseries of this hard fight, and ill-health, the most terrific of them all, shall never chain us down. By the river Styx it shall not! Two fellows from a nameless spot in Annandale shall yet show the world the pluck that is in Carlyles."

Let that be your spirit to-day. You are citizens of no mean city, members of no common state, heirs of no supine empire. You will many of you exercise influence over your fellow men: some will study and interpret our laws, and so become a power; others will again be in a position to solace and exalt, as destined to be doctors and clergymen, and so the physical and spiritual comforters of mankind. Make the best of these opportunities. Raise your country, raise your University, raise yourselves.

ON TAXING THE COLONIES
Delivered in the House of Commons, March, 1775
BY EDMUND BURKE

Reflect, sirs, that when you have fixed a quota of taxation for every colony, you have not provided for prompt and punctual payment. You must make new Boston Port Bills, new restraining laws, new acts for dragging men to England for trial. You must send out new fleets, new armies. All is to begin again. From this day forward the empire is never to know an hour's tranquillity. An intestine fire will be kept alive in the bowels of the colonies, which one time or other must consume this whole empire.

Instead of a standing revenue, you will therefore have a perpetual quarrel. Indeed, the noble lord who proposed this project seems himself to be of that opinion. His project was rather designed for breaking the union of the colonies than for establishing a revenue. But whatever his views may be, as I propose the peace and union of the colonies as the very foundation of my plan, it cannot accord with one whose foundation is perpetual discord.

Compare the two. This I offer to give you is plain and simple; the other full of perplexed and intricate mazes. This is mild; that harsh. This is found by experience effectual for its purposes; the other is a new project. This is universal; the other calculated for certain colonies only. This is immediate in its conciliatory operation; the other remote, contingent, full of hazard. Mine is what becomes the dignity of a ruling people--gratuitous, unconditional, and not held out as a matter of bargain and sale. I have done my duty in proposing it to you. I have indeed tried you by a long discourse; but this is the misfortune of those to whose influence nothing will be conceded, and who must win every inch of their ground by argument. You have heard me with goodness. May you decide with wisdom!

JUSTIFYING THE PRESIDENT

From a speech in the Senate, 1900

By JOHN C. SPOONER

Some one asked the other day why the President did not bring about a cessation of hostilities. Upon what basis could he have brought about a cessation of hostilities? Should he have asked Aguinaldo for an armistice? If so, upon what basis should he have requested it? What should he say to him? "Please stop this fighting"? "What for," Aguinaldo would say; "do you propose to retire?" "No." "Do you propose to grant us independence?" "No, not now." "Well, why, then, an armistice?" The President would doubtless be expected to reply: "Some distinguished gentlemen in the United States, members of the United States Senate, and others, have discovered a doubt about our right to be here at all, some question whether we have acquired the Philippines, some question as to whether we have correctly read the Declaration of Independence; and I want an armistice until we can consult and determine finally whether we have acquired the Philippines or not, whether we are violating the Declaration of Independence or not, whether we are trampling upon the Constitution or not." That is practically the proposition.

No, Mr. President, men may say in criticism of the President what they choose. He has been grossly insulted in this chamber, and it appears upon the record. He has gone his way patiently, exercising the utmost forbearance, all his acts characterized by a desire to do precisely what the Congress had placed upon him by its ratification of the treaty and its increase of the army. He has done it in a way to impress upon the Filipinos, so far as language and action could do it, his desire, and the desire of our people, to do them good, to give them the largest possible measure of liberty.

BRITAIN AND AMERICA

From an address in the House of Commons, March, 1865

BY JOHN BRIGHT

Why should we fear a great nation on the American Continent? Some people fear that, should America become a great nation, she will be arrogant and aggressive. But that does not follow. The character of a nation does not depend altogether upon its size, but upon the intelligence, instruction, and morals of its people. You fancy the supremacy of the sea will pass away from you; and the noble lord, who has had much experience, and is supposed to be wiser on the subject than any other man in the House, will say that "Rule Britannia," that noble old song, may become obsolete. Well, inasmuch as the supremacy of the seas means arrogance and the assumption of dictatorial power on the part of this country, the sooner that becomes obsolete the better. I do not believe that it is for the advantage of this country, or of any country in the world, that any one nation should pride itself upon what is termed the supremacy of the sea; and I hope the time is coming--I believe the hour is hastening--when we shall find that law and justice will guide the councils and will direct the policy of the Christian nations of the world. Nature will not be baffled because we are jealous of the United States--the decrees of Providence will not be overthrown by aught we can do.

The population of the United States is now not less than 35,000,000. When the next Parliament of England has lived to the age which this has lived to, that population will be 40,000,000, and you may calculate the increase at the rate of rather more than 1,000,000 of persons per year. Who is to gainsay it? Will constant snarling at a great republic alter this state of things, or swell us up in these islands to 40,000,000 or 50,000,000, or bring them down to our 30,000,000? Honorable members and the country at large should consider these facts, and learn from them that it is the interest of the nations to be at one--and for us to be in perfect courtesy and amity with the great English nation on the other side of the Atlantic.

VALUES AND TRANSITIONS

KING ROBERT OF SICILY

From "King Robert of Sicily," by permission of, and by special arrangement with, Houghton Mifflin Company, authorized publishers of this author's works.

BY HENRY W. LONGFELLOW

Days came and went; and now returned again To Sicily the old Saturnian reign; Under the Angel's governance benign The happy island danced with corn and wine.

Meanwhile King Robert yielded to his fate, Sullen and silent and disconsolate. Dressed in the motley garb that Jesters wear, With look bewildered and a vacant stare, Close shaven above the ears, as monks are shorn, By courtiers mocked, by pages laughed to scorn, His only friend the ape, his only food What others left,--he still was unsubdued. And when the Angel met him on his way, And half in earnest, half in jest, would say, Sternly, though tenderly, that he might feel The velvet scabbard held a sword of steel, "Art thou the King?" the passion of his woe Burst from him in resistless overflow, And, lifting high his forehead, he would fling The haughty answer back, "I am, I am the King!" Almost three years were ended; when there came Ambassadors of great repute and name From Valmond, Emperor of Allemaine, Unto King Robert, saying that Pope Urbane By letter summoned them forthwith to come On Holy Thursday to his city of Rome. And lo! among the menials, in mock state, Upon a piebald steed, with shambling gait, His cloak of fox-tails flapping in the wind, The solemn ape demurely perched behind, King Robert rode, making huge merriment In all the country towns through which they went. The Pope received them with great pomp and blare Of bannered trumpets, on Saint Peter's square, Giving his benediction and embrace Fervent and full of apostolic grace. While with congratulations and with prayers He entertained the Angel unawares,

Robert, the Jester, bursting through the crowd, Into their presence rushed, and cried aloud: "I am the King! Look, and behold in me Robert, your brother, King of Sicily! This man who wears my semblance to your eyes, Is an imposter in a king's disguise. Do you not know me? does no voice within Answer my cry, and say we are akin?" The Pope in silence, but with troubled mien, Gazed at the Angel's countenance serene; The Emperor, laughing, said, "It is strange sport To keep a madman for thy Fool at court!" And the poor, baffled Jester in disgrace Was hustled back among the populace.

LAYING THE ATLANTIC CABLE

An extract from "Masters of the Situation," a lecture

BY JAMES T. FIELDS

When I talk across an ocean of 3000 miles, with my friends on the other side of it, and feel that I may know any hour of the day if all goes well with them, I think with gratitude of the immense energy and perseverance of that one man, Cyrus W. Field, who spent so many years of his life in perfecting a communication second only in importance to the discovery of this country. Think what that enthusiast accomplished by his untiring energy. He made fifty voyages across the Atlantic. Eight years more he encountered the odium of failure, but still kept plowing across the Atlantic, flying from city to city, soliciting capital, holding meetings and forcing down this most colossal discouragement. At last day dawned again, and another cable was paid out--this time from the deck of the "Great Eastern." Twelve hundred miles of it were laid down, and the ship was just lifting her head to a stiff breeze then springing up, when, without a moment's warning, the cable suddenly snapped short off, and plunged into the sea. Nine days and nights they dragged the bottom of the sea for this lost treasure, and though they grappled it three times, they could not bring it to the surface. In five months another cable was shipped on board the "Great Eastern," and this time, by the blessing of heaven, the wires were stretched unharmed from continent to continent. Then came that never- to-be-forgotten search, in four ships, for the lost cable. In the bow of one of these vessels stood Cyrus Field, day and night, in storm and fog, squall and calm, intensely watching the quiver of the grapnel that was dragging two miles down on the bottom of the deep.

At length on the last night of August, a little before midnight, the spirit of this great man was rewarded. I shall here quote his own words, as none others could possibly convey so well the thrilling interest of that hour. He says: "All felt as if life and death hung on the issue. It was only when the cable was brought over the bow and onto the deck that men dared to breathe. Even then they hardly believed their eyes. Some crept toward it to feel of it to be sure it was there. Then we carried it along to the electricians' room, to see if our long- sought treasure was dead or alive. A few minutes of suspense and a flash told of the lightning current again set free. Then the feeling long pent up burst forth. Some turned away their heads and wept. Others broke into cheers, and the cry ran from man to man, and was heard down in the engine rooms, deck below deck, and from the boats on the water, and the other ships, while the rockets lighted up the darkness of the sea. Then, with thankful hearts, we turned our faces again to the West. But soon the wind rose, and for thirty-six hours we were exposed to all the dangers of a storm on the Atlantic. Yet, in the very height and fury of the gale, as I sat in the electricians' room, a flash of light came up from the deep, which, having crossed to Ireland, came back to me in mid-ocean, telling me that those so dear to me, whom I had left on the banks of the Hudson, were well, and following us with their wishes and their prayers. This was like a whisper of God from the sea, bidding me keep heart and hope."

And now, after all those thirteen years of almost superhuman struggle and that one moment of almost superhuman victory, I think we may safely include Cyrus Field among the masters of the situation.

O'CONNELL, THE ORATOR

From "Speeches and Lectures," with the permission of Lothrop, Lee and Shepard, Boston, publishers.

BY WENDELL PHILLIPS

Broadly considered, O'Connell's eloquence has never been equaled in modern times, certainly not in English speech. Do you think I am partial? I will vouch John Randolph of Roanoke, the Virginia slaveholder, who hated an Irishman almost as much as he hated a Yankee, himself an orator of no mean level. Hearing O'Connell, he exclaimed, "This is the man, these are the lips, the most eloquent that speak the English tongue in my day!" I think he was right. I remember the solemnity of Webster, the grace of Everett, the rhetoric of Choate; I know the eloquence that lay hid in the iron logic of Calhoun; I have melted beneath the magnetism of Sergeant S. Prentiss of Mississippi, who wielded a power few men ever had; it has been my fortune to sit at the feet of the great speakers of the English tongue on the other side of the ocean; but I think all of them together never surpassed, and no one of them ever equaled O'Connell.

Nature intended him for our Demosthenes. Never, since the great Greek, has she sent forth one so lavishly gifted for his work as a tribune of the people. In the first place, he had a magnificent presence, impressive in bearing, massive, like that of Jupiter. Webster himself hardly outdid him in the majesty of his proportions. To be sure, he had not Webster's craggy face, and precipice of brow, not his eyes glowing like anthracite coal. Nor had he the lion roar of Mirabeau. But his presence filled the eye. A small O'Connell would hardly have been an O'Connell at all. These physical advantages are half the battle.

I remember Russell Lowell telling us that Mr. Webster came home from Washington at the time the Whig party thought of dissolution, a year or two before his death, and went down to Faneuil Hall to protest; drawing himself up to his loftiest proportion, his brow clothed with thunder, before the listening thousands, he said, "Well, gentlemen, I am a Whig, a Massachusetts Whig, a Faneuil-Hall Whig, a revolutionary Whig, a constitutional Whig. If you break the Whig party, sir, where am I to go?" And says Lowell, "We held our breath, thinking where he *could* go. If he had been five feet three, we should have said, 'Who cares where you go?'" So it was with O'Connell. There was something majestic in his presence before he spoke; and he added to it what Webster had not, what Clay might have lent--infinite grace, that magnetism that melts all hearts into one. I saw him at over sixty-six years of age; every attitude was beauty, every gesture grace. You could only think of a greyhound as you looked at him; it would have been delightful to watch him, if he had not spoken a word. Then he had a voice that covered the gamut. The majesty of his indignation, fitly uttered in tones of superhuman power, made him able to "indict" a nation. Carlyle says, "He is God's own anointed king whose single word melts all wills into his." This describes O'Connell. Emerson says, "There is no true eloquence unless there is a man behind the speech." Daniel O'Connell was listened to because all England and all Ireland knew that there was a man behind the speech.

I heard him once say, "I send my voice across the Atlantic, careering like the thunderstorm against the breeze, to remind the bondman that the dawn of his redemption is already breaking." You seemed to hear the tones come echoing back to

London from the Rocky Mountains. Then, with the slightest possible Irish brogue, he would tell a story, while all Exeter Hall shook with laughter. The next moment, tears in his voice like a Scotch song, five thousand men wept. And all the while no effort. He seemed only breathing.

"As effortless as woodland nooks
Send violets up, and paint them blue."

JUSTIFICATION FOR IMPEACHMENT

Against Warren Hastings, House of Lords, February, 1788

BY EDMUND BURKE

In the name of the Commons of England, I charge all this villainy upon Warren Hastings, in this last moment of my application to you.

My Lords, what is it that we want here to a great act of national justice? Do we want a cause, my Lords? You have the cause of oppressed princes, of undone women of the first rank, of desolated provinces, and of wasted kingdoms.

Do you want a criminal, my Lords? When was there so much iniquity ever laid to the charge of any one? No, my Lords, you must not look to punish any other such delinquent from India. Warren Hastings has not left substance enough in India to nourish such another delinquent.

My Lords, is it a prosecutor you want? You have before you the Commons of Great Britain as prosecutors; and I believe, my Lords, that the sun, in his beneficent progress round the world, does not behold a more glorious sight than that of men, separated from a remote people by the material bounds and barriers of nature, united by the bonds of a social and moral community--all the Commons of England resenting, as their own, the indignities and cruelties that are offered to all the people of India.

Do we want a tribunal? My Lords, no example of antiquity, nothing in the modern world, nothing in the range of human imagination, can supply us with a tribunal like this. My Lords, here we see virtually, in the mind's eye, that sacred majesty of the Crown, under whose authority you sit and whose power you exercise.

We have here all the branches of the royal family, in a situation between majesty and subjection, between the sovereign and the subject-- offering a pledge, in that situation, for the support of the rights of the Crown and the liberties of the people, both of which extremities they touch.

WENDELL PHILLIPS, THE ORATOR

From "The Orations and Addresses of George William Curtis," Vol. III. Copyright, 1894, by Harper and Brothers.

BY GEORGE WILLIAM CURTIS

It was not until Lovejoy fell, while defending his press at Alton, in November, 1837, that an American citizen was killed by a raging mob for declaring, in a free State, the right of innocent men and women to their personal liberty. This tragedy, like the deadly blow at Charles Sumner in the Senate Chamber, twenty years afterward, awed the whole country with a sense of vast and momentous peril. Never since the people of Boston thronged Faneuil Hall on the day after the massacre in State Street, had that ancient hall seen a more solemn and significant assembly. It was the more solemn, the more significant, because the excited multitude was no longer, as in the Revolutionary day, inspired by one unanimous and overwhelming purpose to assert and maintain liberty of speech as the bulwark of all other liberty. It was an unwonted and foreboding scene. An evil spirit was in the air.

When the seemly protest against the monstrous crime had been spoken, and the proper duty of the day was done, a voice was heard,--the voice of the high officer solemnly sworn to prosecute, in the name of Massachusetts, every violation of law, declaring, in Faneuil Hall, sixty years after the battle of Bunker Hill, and amid a howling storm of applause, that an American citizen who was put to death by a mad crowd of his fellow citizens for defending his right of free speech, died as the fool dieth. Boston has seen dark days, but never a moment so dark as that. Seven years before, Webster had said, in the famous words that Massachusetts binds as frontlets between her eyes, "There are Boston and Concord, and Lexington and Bunker Hill, and there they will remain forever." Had they already vanished? Was the spirit of the Revolution quite extinct? In the very Cradle of Liberty did no son survive to awake its slumbering echoes? By the grace of God such a son there was. He had come with the multitude, and he had heard with sympathy and approval the speeches that condemned the wrong; but when the cruel voice justified the murderers of Lovejoy, the heart of the young man burned within him. This speech, he said to himself, must be answered. As the malign strain proceeded, the Boston boy, all on fire, with Concord and Lexington tugging at his heart, unconsciously murmured,

"Such a speech in Faneuil Hall must be answered in Faneuil Hall." "Why not answer it yourself?" whispered a neighbor, who overheard him. "Help me to the platform and I will,"--and pushing and struggling through the dense and threatening crowd, the young man reached the platform, was lifted upon it, and, advancing to speak, was greeted with a roar of hostile cries. But riding the whirlwind undismayed, as for many a year afterward he directed the same wild storm, he stood upon the platform in all the beauty and grace of imperial youth,--the Greeks would have said a god descended,--and in words that touched the mind and heart and conscience of that vast multitude, as with fire from heaven, recalling Boston to herself, he saved his native city and her Cradle of Liberty from the damning disgrace of stoning the first martyr in the great struggle for personal freedom. "Mr. Chairman," he said, "when I heard the gentleman lay down principles which placed the rioters, incendiaries, and murderers of Alton, side by side with Otis and Hancock, and Quincy and Adams, I thought those pictured lips would have broken into voice to rebuke the recreant American--the slanderer of the dead." And even as he spoke the vision was fulfilled. Once more its native music rang through Faneuil Hall. In the orator's own burning words, those pictured lips did break into immortal rebuke. In Wendell Phillips, glowing with holy indignation at the insult to America and to man, John Adams and James Otis, Josiah Quincy and Samuel Adams, though dead, yet spake.

In the annals of American speech there had been no such scene since Patrick Henry's electrical warning to George the Third. It was that greatest of oratorical triumphs when a supreme emotion, a sentiment which is to mold a people anew, lifted the orator to adequate expression. Three such scenes are illustrious in our history: that of the speech of Patrick Henry at Williamsburg, of Wendell Phillips in Faneuil Hall, of Abraham Lincoln in Gettysburg,--three, and there is no fourth.

ON THE DISPOSAL OF PUBLIC LANDS

From reports of the Webster-Hayne debate in the United States Senate, January, 1830

BY ROBERT Y. HAYNE

In 1825 the gentleman told the world that the public lands "ought not to be treated as a treasure." He now tells us that "they must be treated as so much treasure." What the deliberate opinion of the gentleman on this subject may be, belongs not to me to determine; but I do not think he can, with the shadow of justice or propriety, impugn my sentiments, while his own recorded opinions are identical with my own. When the gentleman refers to the conditions of the grants under which the United States have acquired these lands, and insists that, as they are declared to be "for the common benefit of all the States," they can only be treated as so much treasure, I think he has applied a rule of construction too narrow for the case. If, in the deeds of cession, it has been declared that the grants were intended "for the common benefit of all the States," it is clear, from other provisions, that they were not intended merely as so much property; for it is expressly declared that the object of the grants is the erection of new States; and the United States, in accepting this trust, bind themselves to facilitate the foundation of those States, to be admitted into the Union with all the rights and privileges of the original States.

This, sir, was the great end to which all parties looked, and it is by the fulfillment of this high trust that "the common benefit of all the States" is to be best promoted. Sir, let me tell the gentleman that, in the part of the country in which I live, we do not measure political benefits by the money standard. We consider as more valuable than gold, liberty, principle, and justice. But, sir, if we are bound to act on the narrow principles contended for by the gentleman, I am wholly at a loss to conceive how he can reconcile his principles with his own practice. The lands are, it seems, to be treated "as so much treasure," and must be applied to the "common benefit of all the States." Now, if this be so, whence does he derive the right to appropriate them for partial and local objects? How can the gentleman consent to vote away immense bodies of these lands for canals in Indiana and Illinois, to the Louisville and Portland Canal, to Kenyon College in Ohio, to schools for the deaf and dumb, and other objects of a similar description?

THE DECLARATION OF INDEPENDENCE

From "Speeches and Presidential Addresses," Current Literature Publishing Company, New York.

BY ABRAHAM LINCOLN

I am filled with deep emotion at finding myself standing in this place, where were collected together the wisdom, the patriotism, the devotion to principle, from which sprang the institutions under which we live. You have kindly suggested to me that in my hands is the task of restoring peace to our distracted country. I can say in return, sir, that all the political sentiments I entertain have been drawn, so far as I have been able to draw them, from the sentiments which originated in, and were given to the world from, this hall. I have never had a feeling, politically, that did not spring from the sentiments embodied in the Declaration of Independence. I have often pondered over the dangers which were incurred by the men who assembled here and framed and adopted that Declaration. I have pondered over the toils that were endured by the officers and soldiers of the army who achieved that independence. I have often inquired of myself what great principle or idea it was that kept this Confederacy so long together. It was not the mere matter of separation of the colonies from the motherland, but that sentiment in the Declaration of Independence which gave liberty not alone to the people of this country, but hope to all the world, for all future time. It was that which gave promise that in due time the weights would be lifted from the shoulders of all men, and that all should have an equal chance. This is the sentiment embodied in the Declaration of Independence. Now, my friends, can this country be saved on that basis? If it can, I shall consider myself one of the happiest men in the world if I can help to save it. If it cannot be saved upon that principle, it will be truly awful. But if this country cannot be saved without giving up that principle, I was about to say I would rather be assassinated on this spot than surrender it. Now, in my view of the present aspect of affairs, there is no need of bloodshed and war. There is no necessity for it. I am not in favor of such a course; and I may say in advance that there will be no bloodshed unless it is forced upon the government. The government will not use force, unless force is used against it.

My friends, this is wholly an unprepared speech. I did not expect to be called on to say a word when I came here. I supposed I was merely to do something toward raising a flag. I may, therefore, have said something indiscreet. But I have said nothing but what I am willing to live by, and, if it be the pleasure of Almighty God, to die by.

EXPRESSING THE FEELING

NORTHERN GREETING TO SOUTHERN VETERANS
From "Speeches and Addresses," with the permission of the author and of Houghton Mifflin Company, publishers.
BY HENRY CABOT LODGE

I was a boy ten years old when the troops marched away to defend Washington. I saw the troops, month after month, pour through the streets of Boston. I saw Shaw go forth at the head of his black regiment, and Bartlett, shattered in body, but dauntless in soul, ride by to carry what was left of him once more to the battlefields of the Republic. I saw Andrew, standing bareheaded on the steps of the State House, bid the men godspeed. I cannot remember the words he said, but I can never forget the fervid eloquence which brought tears to the eyes and fire to the hearts of all who listened. To my boyish mind one thing alone was clear, that the soldiers, as they marched past, were all, in that supreme hour, heroes and patriots. Other feelings have, in the progress of time, altered much, but amid many changes that simple belief of boyhood has never altered.

And you, brave men who wore the gray, would be the first to hold me or any other son of the North in just contempt if I should say that now it was all over I thought the North was wrong and the result of the war a mistake. To the men who fought the battles of the Confederacy we hold out our hands freely, frankly, and gladly. We have no bitter memories to revive, no reproaches to utter. Differ in politics and in a thousand other ways we must and shall in all good nature, but never let us differ with each other on sectional or state lines, by race or creed.

We welcome you, soldiers of Virginia, as others more eloquent than I have said, to New England. We welcome you to old Massachusetts. We welcome you to Boston and to Faneuil Hall. In your presence here, and at the sound of your voices beneath this historic roof, the years roll back, and we see the figure and hear again the ringing tones of your great orator, Patrick Henry, declaring to the first Continental Congress, "The distinctions between Virginians, Pennsylvanians, New Yorkers, and New Englanders are no more. I am not a Virginian, but an American."

A distinguished Frenchman, as he stood among the graves of Arlington, said: "Only a great people is capable of a great civil war." Let us add with thankful hearts that only a great people is capable of a great reconciliation. Side by side Virginia and Massachusetts led the colonies into the War for Independence. Side by side they founded the government of the United States. Morgan and Greene, Lee and Knox, Moultrie and Prescott, men of the South and men of the North, fought shoulder to shoulder, and wore the same uniform of buff and blue,--the uniform of Washington.

Mere sentiment all this, some may say. But it is sentiment, true sentiment, that has moved the world. Sentiment fought the war, and sentiment has reunited us.

So I say that the sentiment manifested by your presence here, brethren of Virginia, sitting side by side with those who wore the blue, tells us that if war should break again upon the country the sons of Virginia and Massachusetts would, as in the olden days, stand once more shoulder to shoulder, with no distinction in the colors that they wear. It is fraught with tidings of peace on earth, and you may read its meaning in the words on yonder picture, "Liberty and union, now and forever, one and inseparable!"

MATCHES AND OVERMATCHES

From Webster's reply to Hayne in the United States Senate, January, 1830, Little, Brown and Company, Boston, publishers.

BY DANIEL WEBSTER

If, sir, the honorable member, *modestia gratia*, had chosen thus to defer to his friend and to pay him a compliment without intentional disparagement to others, it would have been quite according to the friendly courtesies of debate, and not at all ungrateful to my own feelings. I am not one of those, sir, who esteem any tribute of regard, whether light and occasional or more serious and deliberate, which may be bestowed on others, as so much unjustly withholden from themselves. But the tone and manner of the gentleman's question forbid me thus to interpret it, I am not at liberty to consider it as nothing more than a civility to his friend. It had an air of taunt and disparagement, something of the loftiness of asserted superiority, which does not allow me to pass it over without notice. It was put as a question for me to answer, and so put as if it were difficult for me to answer, whether I deemed the member from Missouri an overmatch for myself in debate here. It seems to me, sir, that this is extraordinary language and an extraordinary tone for the discussions of this body.

Matches and overmatches! Those terms are more applicable elsewhere than here, and fitter for other assemblies than this. Sir, the gentleman seems to forget where and what we are. This is a senate, a senate of equals, of men of individual honor and personal character and of absolute independence. We know no masters, we acknowledge no dictators. This is a hall for mutual consultation and discussion; not an arena for the exhibitions of champions. I offer myself, sir, as a match for no man; I throw the challenge of debate at no man's feet. But then, sir, since the honorable member has put the question in a manner that calls for an answer, I will give him an answer; and tell him that, holding myself to be the humblest of the members here, I yet know nothing in the arm of his friend from Missouri, either alone or when aided by the arm of *his* friend from South Carolina, that need deter even me from espousing whatever opinions I may choose to espouse, from debating whenever I may choose to debate, or from speaking whatever I may see fit to say on the floor of the Senate.

THE COALITION

From the reply to Hayne

"The Great Speeches and Orations of Daniel Webster," Little, Brown and Company, Boston, publishers.

BY DANIEL WEBSTER

Sir, I shall not allow myself, on this occasion, I hope on no occasion, to betray myself into any loss of temper; but if provoked, as I trust I never shall be, into crimination and recrimination, the honorable member may perhaps find that, in that contest, there will be blows to take as well as to give; that others can state comparisons as significant, at least, as his own, and that his impunity may possibly demand of him whatever powers of taunt and sarcasm he may possess. I commend him to a prudent husbandry of his resources.

But, sir, the Coalition! The Coalition! Aye, "the murdered Coalition!" The gentleman asks if I were led or frighted into this debate by the specter of the Coalition. "Was it the ghost of the murdered Coalition," he exclaims, "which haunted the member from Massachusetts; and which, like the ghost of Banquo, would never down?" "The murdered Coalition!" Sir, this charge of a coalition, in reference to the late administration, is not original with the honorable member. It did not spring up in the Senate. Whether as a fact, as an argument, or as an embellishment, it is all borrowed. He adopts it, indeed, from a very low origin, and a still lower present condition. It is one of the thousand calumnies with which the press teemed during an excited political canvass. It was a charge of which there was not only no proof or probability, but which was in itself wholly impossible to be true. No man of common information ever believed a syllable of it. Yet it was of that class of falsehoods which, by continued repetition, through all the organs of detraction and abuse, are capable of misleading those who are already far misled, and of further fanning passion already kindling into flame. Doubtless it served in its day, and in greater or less degree, the end designed by it. Having done that, it has sunk into the general mass of stale and loathed calumnies. It is the very cast-off slough of a polluted and shameless press. Incapable of further mischief, it lies in the sewer, lifeless and despised. It is not now, sir, in the power of the honorable member to give it dignity or decency by attempting to elevate it and to introduce it into the Senate. He cannot change it from what it is, an object of general disgust and scorn. On the contrary, the contact, if he choose to touch it, is more likely to drag him down, down to the place where it lies itself.

IN HIS OWN DEFENSE
BY ROBERT EMMET

I am asked what I have to say why sentence of death should not be pronounced on me, according to law.

I am charged with being an emissary of France. An emissary of France! and for what end? It is alleged that I wish to sell the independence of my country; and for what end? Was this the object of my ambition? And is this the mode by which a tribunal of justice reconciles contradictions? No; I am no emissary; and my ambition was to hold a place among the deliverers of my country, not in power nor in profit, but in the glory of the achievement. Sell my country's independence to France! and for what? Was it for a change of masters? No, but for ambition. O my country! was it personal ambition that could influence me? Had it been the soul of my actions, could I not by my education and fortune, by the rank and consideration of my family, have placed myself amongst the proudest of your oppressors? My country was my idol! To it I sacrificed every selfish, every endearing sentiment; and for it I now offer up my life.

My lords, you are impatient for the sacrifice. Be yet patient! I have but a few more words to say--I am going to my cold and silent grave--my lamp of life is nearly extinguished--my race is run--the grave opens to receive me, and I sink into its bosom. I have but one request to ask at my departure from this world: it is--the charity of its silence. Let no man write my epitaph; for, as no man who knows my motives dares now vindicate them, let not prejudice or ignorance asperse them. Let them and me rest in obscurity and peace, and my tomb remain uninscribed, until other times and other men can do justice to my character. When my country takes her place among the nations of the earth, then, and not till then, let my epitaph be written. I have done.

ON RESISTANCE TO GREAT BRITAIN

From a speech in the Provincial Convention, Virginia, March, 1775

BY PATRICK HENRY

I ask gentlemen, sir, what means this martial array, if its purpose be not to force us to submission? Can gentlemen assign any other possible motive for it? Has Great Britain any enemy in this quarter of the world, to call for all this accumulation of navies and armies? No, sir, she has none. They are meant for us; they can be meant for no other. They are sent over to bind and to rivet upon us those chains which the British ministry have been so long forging. And what have we to oppose them? Shall we try argument? Sir, we have been trying that for the last ten years. Have we anything new to offer upon the subject? Nothing. We have held the subject up in every light of which it is capable; but it has been all in vain. Shall we resort to entreaty and humble supplication? What terms shall we find which have not been already exhausted? Let us not, I beseech you, sir, deceive ourselves longer. Sir, we have done everything that could be done to avert the storm which is now coming on. We have petitioned, we have remonstrated, we have supplicated, we have prostrated ourselves before the throne, and have implored its interposition to arrest the tyrannical hands of the ministry and parliament. Our petitions have been slighted;

our remonstrances have produced additional violence and insult; our supplications have been disregarded; and we have been spurned with contempt from the foot of the throne. In vain, after all these things, may we indulge the fond hope of peace and reconciliation. There is no longer any room for hope. If we wish to be free, if we mean to preserve inviolate these inestimable privileges for which we have been so long contending; if we mean not basely to abandon the noble struggle in which we have been so long engaged, and which we have pledged ourselves never to abandon until the glorious object of our contest shall be obtained, we must fight; I repeat it, sir, we must fight! An appeal to arms, and to the God of Hosts, is all that is left us!

INVECTIVE AGAINST LOUIS BONAPARTE

From a reprint in "A Modern Reader and Speaker," by George Ridde, Duffield and Company, New York, publishers.

BY VICTOR HUGO

I have entered the lists with the actual ruler of Europe, for it is well for the world that I should exhibit the picture. Louis Bonaparte is the intoxication of triumph. He is the incarnation of merry yet savage despotism. He is the mad plenitude of power seeking for limits, but finding them not, neither in men nor facts. Louis Bonaparte holds France; and he who holds France holds the world. He is master of the votes, master of consciences, master of the people; he names his successor, does away with eternity, and places the future in a sealed envelope. Thirty eager newspaper correspondents inform the world that he has frowned, and every electric wire quivers if he raises his little finger. Around him is heard the clanking of the saber and the roll of the drum. He is seated in the shadow of the eagles, begirt by ramparts and bayonets. Free people tremble and conceal their liberty lest he should rob them of it. The great American Republic even hesitates before him, and dares not withdraw her ambassador.

Europe awaits his invasion. He is able to do as he wishes, and he dreams of impossibilities. Well, this master, this triumphant conqueror, this vanquisher, this dictator, this emperor, this all- powerful man, one lonely man, robbed and ruined, dares to rise up and attack.

Yes, I attack Louis Napoleon; I attack him openly, before all the world. I attack him before God and man. I attack him boldly and recklessly for love of the people and for love of France. He is going to be an emperor. Let him be one; but let him remember that, though you may secure an empire, you cannot secure an easy conscience!

This is the man by whom France is governed! Governed, do I say?-- possessed in supreme and sovereign sway! And every day, and every morning, by his decrees, by his messages, by all the incredible drivel which he parades in the "Moniteur," this emigrant, who knows not France, teaches France her lesson! and this ruffian tells France he has saved her! And from whom? From herself! Before him, Providence committed only follies; God was waiting for him to reduce everything to order; at last he has come!

For thirty-six years there had been in France all sorts of pernicious things,--the tribune, a vociferous thing; the press, an obstreperous thing; thought, an insolent thing, and liberty, the most crying abuse of all. But he came, and for the tribune he has substituted the Senate; for the press, the censorship; for thought, imbecility; and for liberty, the saber; and by the saber and the Senate, by imbecility and censorship, France is saved. Saved, bravo! And from whom, I repeat? From herself. For what was this France of ours, if you please? A horde of marauders and thieves, of anarchists, assassins, and demagogues. She had to be manacled, had this mad woman, France; and it is Monsieur Louis Bonaparte who puts the handcuffs on her. Now she is in a dungeon, on a diet of bread and water, punished, humiliated, garotted, safely cared for. Be not disturbed; Monsieur Bonaparte, a policeman stationed at the Elysee, is answerable for her to Europe. He makes it his business to be so; this wretched France is in the straitjacket, and if she stirs--Ah, what is this spectacle before our eyes? Is it a dream? Is it a nightmare? On one side a nation, the first of nations, and on the other, a man, the last of men; and this is what this man does to this nation. What! he tramples her under his feet, he laughs in her face, he mocks and taunts her, he disowns, insults, and flouts her! What! he says, "I alone am worthy of consideration!" What! in this land of France where none would dare to slap the face of his fellow, this man can slap the face of the nation? Oh, the abominable shame of it all! Every time that Monsieur Bonaparte spits, every face must be wiped! And this can last! and you tell me it will last! No! No! by every drop in every vein, no! It shall not last! Ah, if this did last, it would be in very truth because there would no longer be a God in heaven, nor a France on earth!

SHOWING THE PICTURE

MOUNT, THE DOGE OF VENICE!
From the play, "Foscari"
BY MARY RUSSELL MITFORD

Doge. What! didst thou never hear Of the old prediction that was verified When I became the Doge?

Zeno. An old prediction!

Doge. Some seventy years ago--it seems to me As fresh as yesterday--being then a lad No higher than my hand, idle as an heir, And all made up of gay and truant sports, I flew a kite, unmatched in shape or size, Over the river--we were at our house Upon the Brenta then; it soared aloft, Driven by light vigorous breezes from the sea Soared buoyantly, till the diminished toy Grew smaller than the falcon when she stoops To dart upon her prey. I sent for cord, Servant on servant hurrying, till the kite Shrank to the size of a beetle: still I called For cord, and sent to summon father, mother, My little sisters, my old halting nurse,-- I would have had the whole world to survey Me and my wondrous kite. It still soared on, And I stood bending back in ecstasy, My eyes on that small point, clapping my hands, And shouting, and half envying it the flight That made it a companion of the stars, When close beside me a deep voice exclaimed-- Aye, mount! mount! mount!--I started back, and saw A tall and aged woman, one of the wild Peculiar people whom wild Hungary sends Roving through every land. She drew her cloak About her, turned her black eyes up to Heaven, And thus pursued: Aye, like his fortunes, mount, The future Doge of Venice! And before For very wonder any one could speak She disappeared.

Zeno. Strange! Hast thou never seen That woman since?

Doge. I never saw her more.
THE REVENGE

From "Tennyson's Poetical Works," published by Houghton Mifflin Company, Boston.

BY ALFRED LORD TENNYSON

"Shall we fight or shall we fly? Good Sir Richard, tell us now, For to fight is but to die! There'll be little of us left by the time this sun be set." And Sir Richard said again: "We be all good Englishmen. Let us bang these dogs of Seville, the children of the devil, For I never turned my back upon don or devil yet." Sir Richard spoke and he laughed, and we roar'd a hurrah, and so The little *Revenge* ran on sheer into the heart of the foe, With her hundred fighters on deck, and her ninety sick below; For half of their fleet to the right and half to the left were seen. And the little *Revenge* ran on thro' the long sea lane between.

And while now the great *San Philip* hung above us like a cloud Whence the thunderbolt will fall Long and loud, Four galleons drew away From the Spanish fleet that day, And two upon the larboard and two upon the starboard lay, And the battle-thunder broke from them all.

And the sun went down, and the stars came out, far over the summer sea, But never a moment ceased the fight of the one and the fifty-three. Ship after ship, the whole night long, their high-built galleons came, Ship after ship, the whole night long, with her battle-thunder and

flame; Ship after ship, the whole night long, drew back with her dead and her

shame, For some were sunk, and many were shatter'd, and so could fight us

no

more-- God of battles, was ever a battle like this in the world before?

For he said: "Fight on! fight on!" Tho' his vessel was all but a wreck; And it chanced that, when half of the summer night was gone, With a grisly wound to be dressed, he had left the deck, But a bullet struck him that was dressing it suddenly dead, And himself he was wounded again, in the side and the head, And he said: "Fight on! Fight on!"

And the night went down, and the sun smiled out far over the summer

sea, And the Spanish fleet with broken sides lay round us all in a ring; But they dared not touch us again, for they feared that we still could

sting, So they watched what the end would be. And we had not fought them in vain, But in perilous plight were we, Seeing forty of our poor hundred were slain and half of the rest of us maimed for life In the crash of the cannonades and the desperate strife; And the sick men down in the hold were most of them stark and cold, And the pikes were all broken and bent, and the powder was all of it

spent; And the masts and the rigging were lying over the side; But Sir Richard cried in his English pride, "We have fought such a fight for a day and a night As may never be fought again! We have won great glory, my men! And a day less or more At sea or ashore, We die--does it matter when? Sink me the ship, Master Gunner--sink her, split her in twain! Fall into the hands of God, not into the hands of Spain!"

A VISION OF WAR

From a Memorial Day address, with the permission of C. P. Farrell, New York, publisher and owner of the Ingersoll copyrighted books.

BY ROBERT G. INGERSOLL

The past rises before me like a dream. Again we are in the great struggle for national life. We hear the sounds of preparation; the music of boisterous drums; the silver voices of heroic bugles. We see thousands of assemblages, and hear the appeals of orators. We see the pale cheeks of women, and the flushed faces of men; and in those assemblages we see all the dead whose dust we have covered with flowers. We lose sight of them no more. We are with them when they enlist in the great army of freedom. We see them part with those they love. Some are walking for the last time in quiet, woody places with the maidens they adore. We hear the whisperings and the sweet vows of eternal love as they lingeringly part forever. Others are bending over cradles, kissing babes that are asleep. Some are receiving the blessings of old men. Some are parting with mothers who hold them and press them to their hearts again and again and say nothing. Kisses and tears, tears and kisses--divine mingling of agony and joy! And some are talking with wives, and endeavoring with brave words, spoken in the old tones, to drive from their hearts the awful fear. We see them part. We see the wife standing in the door with the babe in her arms--standing in the sunlight, sobbing. At the turn in the road a hand waves--she answers by holding high in her loving arms the child. He is gone, and forever.

We see them all as they march proudly away under the flaunting flags, keeping time to the grand, wild music of war,--marching down the streets of the great cities, through the towns and across the prairies, down to the fields of glory, to do and to die for the eternal right.

A vision of the future rises:--

I see our country filled with happy homes, with firesides of content-- the foremost of all the earth.

I see a world where thrones have crumbled and kings are dust. The aristocracy of idleness has perished from the earth.

I see a world without a slave. Man at last is free. Nature's forces have by science been enslaved. Lightning and light, wind and wave, frost and flame, and all the secret-subtle powers of earth and air are the tireless toilers for the human race.

I see a world at peace, adorned with every form of art, with music's myriad voices thrilled, while lips are rich with words of love and truth; a world in which no exile sighs, no prisoner mourns; a world on which the gibbet's shadow does not fall; a world where labor reaps its full reward, where work and worth go hand in hand, where the poor girl trying to win bread with the needle--the needle that has been called "the asp for the breast of the poor"--is not driven to the desperate choice of crime or death, of suicide or shame.

I see a world without the beggar's outstretched palm, the miser's heartless, stony stare, the piteous wail of want, the livid lips of lies, the cruel eyes of scorn.

I see a race without disease of flesh or brain,--shapely and fair,--the married harmony of form and function,--and, as I look, life lengthens, joy deepens, love canopies the earth; and over all, in the great dome, shines the eternal star of human hope.

SUNSET NEAR JERUSALEM

From an article in the *Century Magazine*, June, 1906, with the Permission of the Century Company and of the author.

BY CORWIN KNAPP LINSON

To our Northern eyes the intense brilliancy of the tropical and semi- tropical sky comes as a revelation. Sometimes at noon it is painfully dazzling; but the evening is a vision of prismatic light holding carnival in the air, wherein Milton's "twilight gray" has no part. Unless the sky is held in the relentless grip of a winter storm, the Orient holds no gray in its evening tones; these are translucent and glowing from the setting of the sun until the stars appear. In Greece we are dreamers in that subtle atmosphere, and in Egypt visionaries under the spell of an ethereal loveliness where the filigree patterning of white dome and minaret and interlacing palm and feathery pepper tree leaves little wonder in the mind that the ornamentation of their architecture is so ravishing in its tracery.

Outside the walls of Jerusalem on the north there is a point on a knoll which commands the venerable city that David took for his own. From here you can watch the variable glow of color spread over the whole breadth of country, from the ground at one's feet to the distant purple hilltops of Bethlehem. The fluid air seems to swim, as if laden with incense. The rocks underfoot are of all tones of lavender in shadow, and of tender, warm gleams in the light, casting vivid violet shadows athwart the mottled orange of the ground.

Down in the little valley just below us a tiny vineyard nestles in the half-light; the gray road trails outside; and beyond rise the walls, serene and stately, catching on their highest towers the last rays of the sun.

The pointed shaft of the German church lifts a gray-green finger tipped with rose into the ambient air. The sable dome of the Holy Sepulcher yields a little to the subtle influence, and shows a softer and more becoming purple.

All the unlovely traits and the squalor of the city are lost, so delicately tender is the mass of buildings painted against the background of distance.

It had been one of those days in March when the clouds of "the latter rains" had been blowing from the west. As the day drew near its close, the heavy mists assembled in great masses of ominous gray and blue, golden-edged against the turquoise sky. With such speed did they move that they seemed suddenly to leap from the horizon, and the vast dome of the heaven became filled with weird, flying monsters racing overhead. The violence of the wind tore the blue into fragments, so that what only a moment since was a colossal weight of cloud threatening to ingulf the universe, was now like a great host marshaled in splendid array, flying banners of crimson, whose ranks were ever changing, until they scattered in disordered flight across the face of the sky.

As the lowering sun neared the horizon, the color grew more and more vivid, until the whole heaven was aflame with a whirlwind of scarlet and gold and crimson, of violet and blue and emerald, flecked with copper and bronze and shreds of smoky clouds in shadow, a tempestuous riot of color so wild and extraordinary as to hold one spellbound.

Had not David beheld a similar sky when he wrote:--

  O Lord my God, thou art very great;

Thou art clothed with honor and majesty.

Who coverest thyself with light as with a garment:

Who stretchest out the heavens like a curtain:

Who layeth the beams of his chambers in the waters:

Who maketh the clouds his chariot:

Who walketh upon the wings of the wind:

Who maketh winds his messengers;

His ministers a flaming fire.

A RETURN IN TRIUMPH

From a speech before the New England Society of New York, December, 1886

BY T. DE WITT TALMAGE

I never so realized what this country was and is as on the day when I first saw some of these gentlemen of the Army and Navy. It was when at the close of the War our armies came back and marched in review before the President's stand at Washington. I do not care whether a man was a Republican or a Democrat, a Northern man or a Southern man, if he had any emotion of nature, he could not look upon it without weeping. God knew that the day was stupendous, and He cleared the heaven of cloud and mist and chill, and sprung the blue sky as the triumphal arch for the returning warriors to pass under. From Arlington Heights the spring foliage shook out its welcome, as the hosts came over the hills, and the sparkling waters of the Potomac tossed their gold to the feet of the battalions as they came to the Long Bridge and in almost interminable line passed over. The Capitol never seemed so majestic as on that morning: snowy white, looking down upon the tides of men that came surging down, billow after billow. Passing in silence, yet I heard in every step the thunder of conflicts through which they had waded, and seemed to see dripping from their smoke-blackened flags the blood of our country's martyrs. For the best part of two days we stood and watched the filing on of what seemed endless battalions, brigade after brigade, division after division, host after host, rank beyond rank; ever moving, ever passing; marching, marching; tramp, tramp, tramp-- thousands after thousands, battery front, arms shouldered, columns solid, shoulder to shoulder, wheel to wheel, charger to charger, nostril to nostril.

Commanders on horses with their manes entwined with roses, and necks enchained with garlands, fractious at the shouts that ran along the line, increasing from the clapping of children clothed in white, standing on the steps of the Capitol, to the tumultuous vociferation of hundreds of thousands of enraptured multitudes, crying "Huzza! Huzza!" Gleaming muskets, thundering parks of artillery, rumbling pontoon wagons, ambulances from whose wheels seemed to sound out the groans of the crushed and the dying that they had carried. These men came from balmy Minnesota, those from Illinois prairies. These were often hummed to sleep by the pines of Oregon, those were New England lumbermen. Those came out of the coal-shafts of Pennsylvania. Side by side in one great cause, consecrated through fire and storm and darkness, brothers in peril, on their way home from Chancellorsville and Kenesaw Mountain and Fredericksburg, in lines that seemed infinite they passed on.

We gazed and wept and wondered, lifting up our heads to see if the end had come, but no! Looking from one end of that long avenue to the other, we saw them yet in solid column, battery front, host beyond host, wheel to wheel, charger to charger, nostril to nostril, coming as it were from under the Capitol. Forward! Forward! Their bayonets, caught in the sun, glimmered and flashed and blazed, till they seemed like one long river of silver, ever and anon changed into a river of fire. No end of the procession, no rest for the eyes. We turned our heads from the scene, unable longer to look. We felt disposed to stop our ears, but still we heard it, marching, marching; tramp, tramp, tramp. But hush,--uncover every head! Here they pass, the remnant of ten men of a full regiment. Silence! Widowhood and orphanage look on and wring their hands. But wheel into line, all ye people! North, South, East, West--all decades, all centuries, all millenniums! Forward, the whole line! Huzza! Huzza!

A RETURN IN DEFEAT

From "The New South," with the permission of Henry W. Grady, Junior

BY HENRY W. GRADY

Dr. Talmage has drawn for you, with a master hand, the picture of your returning armies. He has told you how, in the pomp and circumstance of war, they came back to you, marching with proud and victorious tread, reading their glory in a nation's eyes! Will you bear with me while I tell you of another army that sought its home at the close of the late war? An army that marched home in defeat and not in victory--in pathos and not in splendor, but in glory that equaled yours, and to hearts as loving as ever welcomed heroes home. Let me picture to you the footsore Confederate soldier, as, buttoning up in his faded gray jacket the parole which was to bear testimony to his children of his fidelity and faith, he turned his face southward from Appomattox in April, 1865. Think of him, as ragged, half-starved, heavy-hearted, enfeebled by want and wounds, having fought to exhaustion, he surrenders his gun, wrings the hands of his comrades in silence, and, lifting his tear-stained and pallid face for the last time to the graves that dot the old Virginia hills, pulls his gray cap over his brow and begins the slow and painful journey. What does he find?--let me ask you who went to your homes eager to find, in the welcome you had justly earned, full payment for four years' sacrifice--what does he find when, having followed the battle-stained cross against overwhelming odds, dreading death not half so much as surrender, he reaches the home he left so prosperous and beautiful? He finds his house in ruins, his farm devastated, his slaves free, his stock killed, his barn empty, his trade destroyed, his money worthless; his social system, feudal in its magnificence, swept away; his people without law or legal status; his comrades slain, and the burdens of others heavy on his shoulders. Crushed by defeat, his very traditions gone; without money, credit, employment, material training; and besides all this, confronted with the gravest problem that ever met human intelligence--the establishing of a status for the vast body of his liberated slaves.

What does he do--this hero in gray, with a heart of gold? Does he sit down in sullenness and despair? Not for a day. Surely God, who had stripped him of his prosperity, inspired him in his adversity. As ruin was never before so overwhelming, never was restoration swifter. The soldier stepped from the trenches into the furrow; horses that had charged Federal guns marched before the plow, and the fields that ran red with human blood in April were green with the harvest in June; women reared in luxury cut up their dresses and made breeches for their husbands, and, with a patience and heroism that fit women always as a garment, gave their hands to work. There was little bitterness in all this. Cheerfulness and frankness prevailed. I want to say to General Sherman--who is considered an able man in our parts, though some people think he is kind of careless about fire--that from the ashes he left us in 1864 we have raised a brave and beautiful city; that somehow or other we have caught the sunshine in the bricks and mortar of our homes, and have builded therein not one ignoble prejudice or memory.

But in all this what have we accomplished? What is the sum of our work? We have found that in the general summary the free negro counts more than he did as a slave. We have planted the schoolhouse on the hilltop and made it free to white and black. We have sowed towns and cities in the place of theories, and put business above politics.

Above all, we know that we have achieved in these "piping times of peace" a fuller independence for the South than that which our fathers sought to win in the forum by their eloquence, or compel on the field by their swords.

EXPRESSION BY ACTION

IN OUR FOREFATHERS' DAY
From a speech before the New England Society of New York, December, 1886
BY T. DE WITT TALMAGE

I must not introduce a new habit into these New England dinners, and confine myself to the one theme. For eighty-one years your speakers have been accustomed to make the toast announced the point from which they start, but to which they never return. So I shall not stick to my text, but only be particular to have all I say my own, and not make the mistake of a minister whose sermon was a patchwork from a variety of authors, to whom he gave no credit. There was an intoxicated wag in the audience who had read about everything, and he announced the authors as the minister went on. The clergyman gave an extract without any credit to the author, and the man in the audience cried out: "That's Jeremy Taylor." The speaker went on and gave an extract from another author without credit for it, and the man in the audience said: "That is John Wesley." The minister gave an extract from another without credit for it, and the man in the audience said: "That is George Whitefield." When the minister lost his patience and cried out, "Shut up, you old fool!" the man in the audience replied: "That is your own."

Well, what about this Forefathers' Day? In Brooklyn they say the Landing of the Pilgrims was December the 21st; in New York you say it was December the 22d. You are both right. Not through the specious and artful reasoning you have sometimes indulged in, but by a little historical incident that seems to have escaped your attention. You see, the Forefathers landed in the morning of December the 21st, but about noon that day a pack of hungry wolves swept down the bleak American beach looking for a New England dinner and a band of savages out for a tomahawk picnic hove in sight, and the Pilgrim Fathers thought it best for safety and warmth to go on board the Mayflower and pass the night. And during the night there came up a strong wind blowing off shore that swept the Mayflower from its moorings clear out to sea, and there was a prospect that our Forefathers, having escaped oppression in foreign lands, would yet go down under an oceanic tempest. But the next day they fortunately got control of their ship and steered her in, and the second time the Forefathers stepped ashore.

Brooklyn celebrated the first landing; New York the second landing. So I say Hail! Hail! to both celebrations, for one day, anyhow, could not do justice to such a subject; and I only wish I could have kissed the blarney stone of America, which is Plymouth Rock, so that I might have done justice to this subject. Ah, gentlemen, that Mayflower was the ark that floated the deluge of oppression, and Plymouth Rock was the Ararat on which it landed.

But let me say that these Forefathers were of no more importance than the Foremothers. As I understand it, there were eight of them--that is, four fathers and four mothers--from whom all these illustrious New Englanders descended.

Now I was not born in New England, but though not born in New England, in my boyhood I had a New England schoolmaster, whom I shall never forget. He taught us our A, B, C's. "What is that?" "I don't know, sir." "That's A" (with a slap). "What is that?" "I don't know, sir." (With a slap)--"That is B." I tell you, a boy that learned his letters in that way never forgot them; and if the boy was particularly dull, then this New England schoolmaster would take him over his knee, and then the boy got his information from both directions.

But all these things aside, no one sitting at these tables has higher admiration for the Pilgrim Fathers than I have--the men who believed in two great doctrines, which are the foundation of every religion that is worth anything: namely, the fatherhood of God and the brotherhood of Man--these men of backbone and endowed with that great and magnificent attribute of stick-to-it-iveness.

CASSIUS AGAINST CAESAR

From "Julius Caesar"

BY WILLIAM SHAKESPEARE

I know that virtue to be in you, Brutus, As well as I do know your outward favor. Well, honor is the subject of my story.-- I cannot tell what you and other men Think of this life; but, for my single self, I had as lief not be as live to be In awe of such a thing as I myself. I was born free as Caesar; so were you: We both have fed as well; and we can both Endure the winter's cold as well as he: For once, upon a raw and gusty day, The troubled Tiber chafing with her shores, Caesar said to me, "Dar'st thou, Cassius, now Leap in with me into this angry flood, And swim to yonder point?" Upon the word, Accoutred as I was, I plunged in, And bade him follow: so, indeed, he did. The torrent roar'd, and we did buffet it With lusty sinews, throwing it aside And stemming it with hearts of controversy; But ere we could arrive the point propos'd, Caesar cried, "Help me, Cassius, or I sink!" I, as Aeneas, our great ancestor, Did from the flames of Troy upon his shoulder The old Anchises bear, so from the waves of Tiber Did I the tired Caesar. And this man Is now become a god; and Cassius is A wretched creature, and must bend his body, If Caesar carelessly but nod on him. He had a fever when he was in Spain, And, when the fit was on him, I did mark How he did shake: 'tis true, this god did shake: His coward lips did from their color fly; And that same eye, whose bend doth awe the world, Did lose his luster: I did hear him groan: Ay, and that tongue of his, that bade the Romans Mark him, and write his speeches in their books, Alas, it cried, "Give me some drink, Titinius," As a sick girl. Ye gods, it doth amaze me A man of such a feeble temper should So get the start of the majestic world, And bear the palm alone.

II

Why, man, he doth bestride the narrow world Like a Colossus, and we petty men Walk under his huge legs and peep about To find ourselves dishonourable graves. Men at some time are masters of their fates; The fault, dear Brutus, is not in our stars, But in ourselves, that we are underlings. Brutus and Caesar: what should be in that "Caesar"? Why should that name be sounded more than yours? Write them together, yours is as fair a name; Sound them, it doth become the mouth as well; Weigh them, it is as heavy; conjure with 'em, Brutus will start a spirit as soon as Caesar. Now, in the names of all the gods at once, Upon what meat doth this our Caesar feed, That he is grown so great? Age, thou art shamed! Rome, thou hast lost the breed of noble bloods! When went there by an age, since the great flood, But it was fam'd with more than with one man? When could they say till now, that talked of Rome, That her wide walls encompass'd but one man? Now is it Rome indeed, and room enough, When there is in it but one only man. O, you and I have heard our fathers say, There was a Brutus once that would have brook'd The eternal devil to keep his state in Rome As easily as a king.

THE SPIRIT OF THE SOUTH

From "The New South," with the permission of Henry W. Grady Junior

BY HENRY W. GRADY

The New South is enamored of her new work. Her soul is stirred with the breath of a new life. The light of a grander day is falling fair on her face. She is thrilling with the consciousness of growing power and prosperity. As she stands upright, full-statured and equal among the people of the earth, breathing the keen air and looking out upon the expanding horizon, she understands that her emancipation came because in the inscrutable wisdom of God her honest purpose was crossed and her brave armies were beaten.

This is said in no spirit of time-serving or apology. The South has nothing for which to apologize. She believes that the late struggle between the States was war and not rebellion, revolution and not conspiracy, and that her convictions were as honest as yours. I should be unjust to the dauntless spirit of the South and to my own convictions if I did not make this plain in this presence. The South has nothing to take back. In my native town of Athens is a monument that crowns its central hills--a plain, white shaft. Deep cut into its shining side is a name dear to me above the names of men, that of a brave and simple man who died in brave and simple faith. Not for all the glories of New England--from Plymouth Rock all the way-- would I exchange the heritage he left me in his soldier's death. To the foot of that shaft I shall send my children's children to reverence him who ennobled their name with his heroic blood. But, sir, speaking from the shadow of that memory, which I honor as I do nothing else on earth, I say that the cause in which he suffered and for which he gave his life was adjudged by higher and fuller wisdom than his or mine, and I am glad that the omniscient God held the balance of battle in his Almighty hand, and that human slavery was swept forever from American soil--the American Union saved from the wreck of war.

This message, Mr. President, comes to you from consecrated ground. Every foot of the soil about the city in which I live is sacred as a battle ground of the Republic. Every hill that invests it is hallowed to you by the blood of your brothers, sacred soil to all of us, rich with memories that make us purer and stronger and better, speaking an eloquent witness in its white peace and prosperity to the indissoluble union of American States and the imperishable brotherhood of the American people.

Now what answer has New England to this message? Will she permit the prejudices of war to remain in the hearts of the conquerors, when it has died in the hearts of the conquered? Will she transmit this prejudice to the next generation, that in their hearts, which never felt the generous ardor of conflict, it may perpetuate itself? Will she withhold, save in strained courtesy, the hand which straight from his soldier's heart Grant offered to Lee at Appomattox? Will she make the vision of a restored and happy people, which gathered above the couch of your dying captain, [1] filling his heart with grace, touching his lips with praise and glorifying his path to the grave; will she make this vision on which the last sigh of his expiring soul breathed a benediction, a cheat and a delusion? If she does, the South, never abject in asking for comradeship, must accept with dignity a refusal; but if she does not, if she accepts in frankness and sincerity this message of good will and friendship, then will the prophecy of Webster, delivered in this very society forty years ago amid tremendous applause, be verified in its fullest and final sense, when he said: "Standing hand to hand and clasping hands, we should remain united as we have been for sixty years, citizens of the same country, members of the same government, united, all united now and united forever. There have been difficulties, contentions, and controversies, but I tell you that in my judgment,--

"'Those opposed eyes,
Which like the meteors of a troubled heaven,
All of one nature, of one substance bred,
Did lately meet in th' intestine shock,
Shall now, in mutual well-beseeming ranks,
March all one way.'"

SOMETHING RANKLING HERE

From the reply to Hayne, in the United States Senate, January, 1830. Little, Brown and Company, Boston, Publishers of "The Great Speeches and Orations of Daniel Webster"

BY DANIEL WEBSTER

---

1 General Ulysses S. Grant.

The gentleman, sir, in declining to postpone the debate, told the Senate, with the emphasis of his hand upon his heart, that there was something rankling *here* which he wished to relieve. It would not, Mr. President, be safe for the honorable member to appeal to those around him upon the question whether he did in fact make use of that word. But he may have been unconscious of it. At any rate, it is enough that he disclaims it. But still, with or without the use of that particular word, he had yet something *here*, he said, of which he wished to rid himself by an immediate reply. In this respect, sir, I have a great advantage over the honorable gentleman. There is nothing *here*, sir, which gives me the slightest uneasiness; neither fear, nor anger, nor that which is sometimes more troublesome than either, the consciousness of having been in the wrong. There is nothing, either originating *here*, or now received *here* by the gentleman's shot. Nothing originating here, for I had not the slightest feeling of unkindness towards the honorable member. Some passages, it is true, had occurred since our acquaintance in this body, which I could have wished might have been otherwise; but I had used philosophy and forgotten them. I paid the honorable member the attention of listening with respect to his first speech; and when he sat down, though surprised, and I must even say astonished, at some of his opinions, nothing was farther from my intention than to commence any personal warfare. Through the whole of the few remarks I made in answer, I avoided, studiously and carefully, everything which I thought possible to be construed into disrespect. And, sir, while there is thus nothing originating *here* which I wished at any time or now wish to discharge, I must repeat also, that nothing has been received *here* which *rankles*, or in any way gives me annoyance. I will not accuse the honorable member of violating the rules of civilized war; I will not say that he poisoned his arrows. But whether his shafts were or were not dipped in that which would have caused rankling if they had reached their destination, there was not, as it happened, quite strength enough in the bow to bring them to their mark. If he wishes now to gather up those shafts, he must look for them elsewhere; they will not be found fixed and quivering in the object at which they were aimed.

But the gentleman inquires why *he* was made the object of such a reply. Why was *he* singled out? If an attack has been made on the East, he, he assures us, did not begin it; it was made by the gentleman from Missouri. Sir, I answered the gentleman's speech because I happened to hear it; and because, also, I chose to give an answer to that speech, which, if unanswered, I thought most likely to produce injurious impressions. I did not stop to inquire who was the original drawer of the bill. I found a responsible indorser before me, and it was my purpose to hold him liable, and to bring him to his just responsibility, without delay.

FAITH IN THE PEOPLE

BY JOHN BRIGHT

Our opponents have charged us with being the promoters of a dangerous excitement. They have the effrontery to say that I am the friend of public disorder. I am one of the people. Surely, if there be one thing in a free country more clear than another, it is, that any one of the people may speak openly to the people. If I speak to the people of their rights, and indicate to them the way to secure them,--if I speak of their danger to the monopolists of power,--am I not a wise counsellor, both to the people and to their rulers?

Suppose I stood at the foot of Vesuvius, or Aetna, and, seeing a hamlet or a homestead planted on its slope, I said to the dwellers in that hamlet, or in that homestead, "You see that vapor which ascends from the summit of the mountain. That vapor may become a dense, black smoke, that will obscure the sky. You see the trickling of lava from the crevices in the side of the mountain. That trickling of lava may become a river of fire. You hear that muttering in the bowels of the mountain. That muttering may become a bellowing thunder, the voice of violent convulsion, that may shake half a continent. You know that at your feet is the grave of great cities, for which there is no resurrection, as histories tell us that dynasties and aristocracies have passed away, and their names have been known no more forever."

If I say this to the dwellers upon the slope of the mountain, and if there comes hereafter a catastrophe which makes the world to shudder, am I responsible for that catastrophe? I did not build the mountain, or fill it with explosive materials. I merely warned the men that were in danger. So, now, it is not I that am stimulating men to the violent pursuit of their acknowledged constitutional rights.

The class which has hitherto ruled in this country has failed miserably. It revels in power and wealth, whilst at its feet, a terrible peril for its future, lies the multitude which it has neglected. If a class has failed, let us try the nation.

That is our faith, that is our purpose, that is our cry. Let us try the nation. This it is which has called together these countless numbers of the people to demand a change; and from these gatherings, sublime in their vastness and their resolution, I think I see, as it were, above the hilltops of time, the glimmerings of the dawn of a better and a nobler day for the country and the people that I love so well.

THE FRENCH AGAINST HAYTI

From a lecture, "Toussaint L'Ouverture," with the permission of Lothrop, Lee and Shepard, Boston, publishers

BY WENDELL PHILLIPS

You remember when Bonaparte returned from Elba, and Louis XVIII sent an army against him, Bonaparte descended from his carriage, opened his coat, offering his breast to their muskets, and saying, "Frenchmen, it is the Emperor!" and they ranged themselves behind him, his soldiers shouting, "Vive l'Empereur!" That was in 1815. Twelve years before, Toussaint, finding that four of his regiments had deserted and gone to Leclerc, drew his sword, flung it on the grass, went across the field to them, folded his arms, and said, "Children, can you point a bayonet at me?" The blacks fell on their knees, praying his pardon. It was against such a man that Napoleon sent his army, giving to General Leclerc, the husband of his beautiful sister Pauline, thirty thousand of his best troops, with orders to reintroduce slavery. Among these soldiers came all of Toussaint's old mulatto rivals and foes.

Holland lent sixty ships. England promised by special message to be neutral; and you know neutrality means sneering at freedom, and sending arms to tyrants. England promised neutrality, and the black looked out on the whole civilized world marshaled against him. America, full of slaves, of course was hostile. Only the Yankee sold him poor muskets at a very high price. Mounting his horse, and riding to the eastern end of the island, Samana, he looked out on a sight such as no native had ever seen before. Sixty ships of the line, crowded by the best soldiers of Europe, rounded the point. They were soldiers who had never yet met an equal, whose tread, like Caesar's, had shaken Europe,--soldiers who had scaled the Pyramids, and planted the French banners on the Walls of Rome. He looked a moment, counted the flotilla, let the reins fall on the neck of his horse, and turning to Christophe, exclaimed: "All France is come to Hayti; they can only come to make us slaves; and we are lost!" He then recognized the only mistake of his life,--his confidence in Bonaparte, which had led him to disband his army.

Returning to the hills, he issued the only proclamation which bears his name and breathes vengeance: "My children, France comes to make us slaves. God gave us liberty; France has no right to take it away. Burn the cities, destroy the harvests, tear up the roads with cannon, poison the wells, show the white man the hell he comes to make";--and he was obeyed. When the great William of Orange saw Louis XIV cover Holland with troops, he said, "Break down the dikes, give Holland back to ocean"; and Europe said, "Sublime!" When Alexander saw the armies of France descend upon Russia, he said, "Burn Moscow, starve back the invaders"; and Europe said, "Sublime!" This black saw all Europe marshaled to crush him, and gave to his people the same heroic example of defiance.

THE NECESSITY OF FORCE

From a speech in the United States Senate, March 24, 1898

BY JOHN M. THURSTON

I counseled silence and moderation from this floor when the passion of the nation seemed at white heat over the destruction of the *Maine*; but it seems to me the time for action has now come. No greater reason for it can exist to-morrow than exists to-day. Every hour's delay only adds another chapter to the awful story of misery and death. Only one power can intervene--the United States of America. Ours is the one great nation of the New World, the mother of American republics. She holds a position of trust and responsibility toward the peoples and affairs of the whole Western Hemisphere. It was her glorious example which inspired the patriots of Cuba to raise the flag of liberty in her eternal hills. We cannot refuse to accept this responsibility which the God of the universe has placed upon us as the one great power in the New World. We must act! What shall our action be? Some say, The acknowledgment of the belligerency of the revolutionists. The hour and the opportunity for that have passed away. Others say, Let us by resolution or official proclamation recognize the independence of the Cubans. It is too late for even such recognition to be of great avail. Others say, Annexation to the United States. God forbid! I would oppose annexation with my latest breath. The people of Cuba are not our people; they cannot assimilate with us; and beyond all that, I am utterly and unalterably opposed to any departure from the declared policy of the fathers, which would start this republic for the first time upon a career of conquest and dominion utterly at variance with the avowed purposes and the manifest destiny of popular government.

There is only one action possible, if any is taken; that is, intervention for the independence of the island. We cannot intervene and save Cuba without the exercise of force, and force means war; war means blood. The lowly Nazarene on the shores of Galilee preached the divine doctrine of love, "Peace on earth, good will toward men." Not peace on earth at the expense of liberty and humanity. Not good will toward men who despoil, enslave, degrade, and starve to death their fellow-men. I believe in the doctrine of Christ. I believe in the doctrine of peace; but men must have liberty before there can come abiding peace. When has a battle for humanity and liberty ever been won except by force? What barricade of wrong, injustice, and oppression has ever been carried except by force?

Force compelled the signature of unwilling royalty to the great Magna Charta; force put life into the Declaration of Independence and made effective the Emancipation Proclamation; force waved the flag of revolution over Bunker Hill and marked the snows of Valley Forge with bloodstained feet; force held the broken line of Shiloh, climbed the flame-swept hill at Chattanooga, and stormed the clouds on Lookout Heights; force marched with Sherman to the sea, rode with Sheridan in the Valley of the Shenandoah, and gave Grant victory at Appomattox; force saved the Union, kept the stars in the flag, made "niggers" men. The time for God's force has come again. Let the impassioned lips of American patriots once more take up the song:--

In the beauty of the lilies Christ was born across the sea,
With a glory in His bosom that transfigured you and me.
As He died to make men holy, let us die to make men free,
For God is marching on.

Others may hesitate, others may procrastinate, others may plead for further diplomatic negotiation, which means delay, but for me, I am ready to act now, and for my action, I am ready to answer to my conscience, my country, and my God.

AGAINST WAR WITH MEXICO
From a speech to the United States Senate, February 11, 1847
BY THOMAS CORWIN

The President has said he does not expect to hold Mexican territory by conquest. Why, then, conquer it? Why waste thousands of lives and millions of money fortifying towns and creating governments, if, at the end of the war, you retire from the graves of your soldiers and the desolated country of your foes, only to get money from Mexico for the expense of all your toil and sacrifice? Who ever heard, since Christianity was propagated among men, of a nation taxing its people, enlisting its young men, and marching off two thousand miles to fight a people merely to be paid for it in money? What is this but hunting a market for blood, selling the lives of your young men, marching them in regiments to be slaughtered and paid for like oxen and brute beasts?

Sir, this is, when stripped naked, that atrocious idea first promulgated in the President's message, and now advocated here, of fighting on till we can get our indemnity for the past as well as the present slaughter. We have chastised Mexico, and if it were worth while to do so, we have, I dare say, satisfied the world that we can fight.

Sir, I have read in some account of your Battle of Monterey, of a lovely Mexican girl, who, with the benevolence of an angel in her bosom and the robust courage of a hero in her heart, was busily engaged during the bloody conflict, amid the crash of falling houses, the groans of the dying, and the wild shriek of battle, in carrying water to slake the burning thirst of the wounded of either host. While bending over a wounded American soldier, a cannonball struck her and blew her to atoms! Sir, I do not charge my brave, generous-hearted countrymen who fought that fight with this. No, no! We who send them-- we who know what scenes like this, which might send tears of sorrow "down Pluto's iron cheek," are the invariable, inevitable attendants on war--we are accountable for this. And this--this is the way we are to be made known to Europe. This--this is to be the undying renown of free, republican America! "She has stormed a city--killed many of its inhabitants of both sexes--she has room"! So it will read. Sir, if this were our only history, then may God of His mercy grant that its volume may speedily come to a close.

Why is it, sir, that we, the United States, a people of yesterday compared with the older nations of the world, should be waging war for territory--for "room?" Look at your country, extending from the Alleghany Mountains to the Pacific Ocean, capable itself of sustaining in comfort a larger population than will be in the whole Union for one hundred years to come. Over this vast expanse of territory your population is now so sparse that I believe we provided, at the last session, a regiment of mounted men to guard the mail from the frontier of Missouri to the mouth of the Columbia; and yet you persist in the ridiculous assertion, "I want room." One would imagine, from the frequent reiteration of the complaint, that you had a bursting, teeming population, whose energy was paralyzed, whose enterprise was crushed, for want of space. Why should we be so weak or wicked as to offer this idle apology for ravaging a neighboring Republic? It will impose on no one at home or abroad.

Do we not know, Mr. President, that it is a law never to be repealed that falsehood shall be short-lived? Was it not ordained of old that truth only shall abide for ever? Whatever we may say to-day, or whatever we may write in our books, the stern tribunal of history will review it all, detect falsehood, and bring us to judgment before that posterity which shall bless or curse us, as we may act now, wisely or otherwise. We may hide in the grave (which awaits us all) in vain; we may hope there, like the foolish bird that hides its head in the sand, in the vain belief that its body is not seen; yet even there this preposterous excuse of want of "room" shall be laid bare and the quick- coming future will decide that it was a hypocritical pretense under which we sought to conceal the avarice which prompted us to covet and to seize by force that which was not ours.

THE MURDER OF LOVEJOY

From "Speeches and Lectures," with the permission of Lothrop, Lee and Shepard, Boston, publishers.

BY WENDELL PHILLIPS

Mr. Chairman: We have met for the freest discussion of these resolutions, and the events which gave rise to them. I hope I shall be permitted to express my surprise at the sentiments of the last speaker,--surprise not only at such sentiments from such a man, but at the applause they have received within these walls. A comparison has been drawn between the events of the Revolution and the tragedy at Alton. We have heard it asserted here, in Faneuil Hall, that Great Britain had a right to tax the Colonies, and we have heard the mob at Alton, the drunken murderers of Lovejoy, compared to those patriot fathers who threw the tea overboard! Fellow citizens, is this Faneuil Hall doctrine? The mob at Alton were met to wrest from a citizen his just rights,--met to resist the laws. We have been told that our fathers did the same; and the glorious mantle of Revolutionary precedent has been thrown over the mobs of our day. To make out their title to such defense, the gentleman says that the British Parliament had a *right* to tax these colonies. It is manifest that, without this, his parallel falls to the ground; for Lovejoy had stationed himself within constitutional bulwarks. He was not only defending the freedom of the press, but he was under his own roof, in arms with the sanction of the civil authority. The men who assailed him went against and over the laws. The *mob*, as the gentleman terms it,--mob, forsooth! certainly we sons of the tea-spillers are a marvelously patient generation!--the "orderly mob" which assembled in the Old South to destroy the tea were met to resist, not the laws, but illegal exactions. Shame on the American who calls the tea tax and stamp act *laws!* Our fathers resisted, not the King's prerogative, but the King's usurpation. To find any other account, you must read our Revolutionary history upside down. Our state archives are loaded with arguments of John Adams to prove the taxes laid by the British Parliament unconstitutional,--beyond its power. It was not till this was made out that the men of New England rushed to arms. The arguments of the Council Chamber and the House of Representatives preceded and sanctioned the contest. To draw the conduct of our ancestors into a precedent for mobs, for a right to resist laws we ourselves have enacted, is an insult to their memory. The difference between the excitements of those days and our own, which the gentleman in kindness to the latter has overlooked, is simply this: the man of that day went for the right, as secured by the laws. They were the people rising to sustain the laws and constitution of the Province. The rioters of our day go for their own wills, right or wrong. Sir, when I heard the gentleman lay down principles which place the murderers of Alton side by side with Otis and Hancock, with Quincy and Adams, I thought those pictured lips [pointing to the portraits in the Hall] would have broken into voice to rebuke the recreant American,--the slanderer of the dead. The gentleman said that he should sink into insignificance if he dared to gainsay the principles of these resolutions. Sir, for the sentiments he has uttered, on soil consecrated by the prayers of Puritans and the blood of patriots, the earth should have yawned and swallowed him up.

I am glad, Sir, to see this crowded house. It is good for us to be here. When Liberty is in danger, Faneuil Hall has the right, it is her duty, to strike the keynote for these United States.

DEPICTING CHARACTER

A TALE OF THE PLAINS
From "Hunting the Grizzly," with the permission of G. P. Putnam's Sons, New York and London, publishers.
BY THEODORE ROOSEVELT
One of my valued friends in the mountains, and one of the best hunters with whom I ever traveled, was a man who had a peculiarly light-hearted way of looking at conventional social obligations. Though in some ways a true backwoods Donatello, he was a man of much shrewdness and of great courage and resolution. Moreover, he possessed what only a few men do possess, the capacity to tell the truth. He saw facts as they were, and could tell them as they were, and he never told an untruth unless for very weighty reasons. He was preeminently a philosopher, of a happy, skeptical turn of mind. He had no prejudices.

On one occasion when we were out together we killed a bear, and after skinning it, took a bath in a lake. I noticed he had a scar on the side of his foot, and asked him how he got it, to which he responded, with indifference:--

"Oh, that? Why, a man shoo tin' at me to make me dance, that was all."

I expressed some curiosity in the matter, and he went on:

"Well, the way of it was this: It was when I was keeping a saloon in New Mexico, and there was a man there by the name of Fowler, and there was a reward on him of three thousand dollars--"

"Put on him by the State?"

"No, put on by his wife," said my friend; "and there was this--"

"Hold on," I interrupted; "put on by his wife, did you say?"

"Yes, by his wife. Him and her had been keepin' a faro bank, you see, and they quarreled about it, so she just put a reward on him, and so--"

"Excuse me," I said, "but do you mean to say that this reward was put on publicly?" to which my friend answered with an air of gentlemanly boredom at being interrupted to gratify my thirst for irrelevant detail:--

"Oh, no, not publicly. She just mentioned it to six or eight intimate personal friends."

"Go on," I responded, somewhat overcome by this instance of the primitive simplicity with which New Mexican matrimonial disputes were managed, and he continued:--

"Well, two men come ridin' in to see me to borrow my guns. My guns was Colt's self-cockers. It was a new thing then, and they was the only ones in town. These come to me, and 'Simpson,' says they, 'we want to borrow your guns; we are goin' to kill Fowler.'

"'Hold on for a moment,' said I, 'I am willin' to lend you them guns, but I ain't goin' to know what you'r' goin' to do with them, no, sir; but of course you can have the guns.'" Here my friend's face lightened pleasantly, and he continued:--

"Well, you may easily believe I felt surprised next day when Fowler come ridin' in, and, says he, 'Simpson, here's your guns!' He had shot them two men! 'Well, Fowler,' says I, 'if I had known them men was after you, I'd never have let them have the guns nohow,' says I. That wasn't true, for I did know it, but there was no cause to tell him that."

I murmured my approval of such prudence, and Simpson continued, his eyes gradually brightening with the light of agreeable reminiscence:--

"Well, they up and they took Fowler before the justice of peace. The justice of the peace was a Turk."

"Now, Simpson, what do you mean by that?" I interrupted.

"Well, he come from Turkey," said Simpson, and I again sank back, wondering briefly what particular variety of Mediterranean outcast had drifted down to Mexico to be made a justice of the peace. Simpson laughed and continued: "That Fowler was a funny fellow. The Turk, he committed Fowler, and Fowler, he riz up and knocked him down and tromped all over him and made him let him go!"

"That was an appeal to a higher law," I observed. Simpson assented cheerily, and continued:--

"Well, that Turk, he got nervous for fear Fowler was goin' to kill him, and so he comes to me and offers me twenty-five dollars a day to protect him from Fowler; and I went to Fowler, and 'Fowler,' says I, 'that Turk's offered me twenty-five dollars a day to protect him from you. Now, I ain't goin' to get shot for no twenty-five dollars a day, and if you are goin' to kill the Turk, just say so and go and do it; but if you ain't goin' to kill the Turk, there's no reason why I shouldn't earn that twenty-five dollars a day!' and Fowler, says he, 'I ain't goin' to touch the Turk; you just go right ahead and protect him.'"

So Simpson "protected" the Turk from the imaginary danger of Fowler, for about a week, at twenty-five dollars a day.

Then one evening he happened to go out and meet Fowler, "and," said he, "the moment I saw him I know he felt mean, for he begun to shoot at my feet," which certainly did seem to offer presumptive evidence of meanness. Simpson continued:--

"I didn't have no gun, so I just had to stand there and take it until something distracted his attention, and I went off home to get my gun and kill him, but I wanted to do it perfectly lawful; so I went up to the mayor (he was playin' poker with one of the judges), and says I to him, 'Mr. Mayor,' says I, 'I am goin' to shoot Fowler.' And the mayor he riz out of his chair and he took me by the hand, and says he, 'Mr. Simpson, if you do I will stand by you'; and the judge he says, 'I'll go on your bond.'"

Fortified by this cordial approval of the executive and judicial branches of the government, Mr. Simpson started on his quest. Meanwhile, however, Fowler had cut up another prominent citizen, and they already had him in jail. The friends of law and order, feeling some little distrust as to the permanency of their own zeal for righteousness, thought it best to settle the matter before there was time for cooling, and accordingly, headed by Simpson, the mayor, the judge, the Turk, and other prominent citizens of the town, they broke into the jail and hanged Fowler. The point in the hanging which especially tickled my friend's fancy as he lingered over the reminiscence was one that was rather too ghastly to appeal to our own sense of humor. In the Turk's mind there still rankled the memory of Fowler's very unprofessional conduct while figuring before him as a criminal. Said Simpson, with a merry twinkle of the eye: "Do you know, that Turk, he was a right funny fellow too after all. Just as the boys were going to string up Fowler, says he, 'Boys, stop; one moment, gentlemen,--Mr. Fowler, good-by,' and he blew a kiss to him!"

GUNGA DIN

From "Departmental Ditties," with the permission of A. P. Watt and Son, London, and Doubleday, Page and Company, New York.

BY RUDYARD KIPLING

You may talk o' gin and beer

When you're quartered safe out 'ere, An' you're sent to penny-fights an' Aldershot it;

But when it comes to slaughter

You will do your work on water, An' you'll lick the bloomin' boots of 'im that's got it.

Now in Injia's sunny clime,

Where I used to spend my time A-servin' of 'Er Majesty the Queen,

Of all them blackfaced crew

The finest man I knew Was our regimental bhisti, Gunga Din.

He was "Din! Din! Din! You limping lump o' brick-dust, Gunga Din!

Hi! slippery hitherao!

Water, get it! Panee lao![2]   You squidgy-nosed old idol, Gunga Din."

The uniform 'e wore

Was nothin' much before, An' rather less than 'arf o' that be'ind,

For a piece o' twisty rag

An' a goatskin water-bag Was all the field-equipment 'e could find.

When the sweatin' troop-train lay

In a sidin' through the day, Where the 'eat would make your bloomin' eyebrows crawl,

We shouted "Harry By!"[3]

Till our throats were bricky-dry, Then we wopped 'im 'cause 'e couldn't serve us all.

It was "Din! Din! Din!

You 'eathen, where the mischief 'ave you been?

You put some juldee in it

---

2   Bring water swiftly.
3   O Brother

Or I'll marrow you this minute,[4] If you don't fill up my helmet, Gunga Din!"
  'E would dot an' carry one
Till the longest day was done; An' 'e didn't seem to know the use o' fear.
If we charged or broke or cut,
You could bet your bloomin' nut, 'E'd be waitin' fifty paces right flank rear.
With 'is mussick [5] on 'is back,
'E would skip with our attack, An' watch us till the bugles made "Retire,"
An' for all 'is dirty 'ide
'E was white, clear white, inside When 'e went to tend the wounded under fire!
It was "Din! Din! Din!" With the bullets kickin' dust-spots on the green.
When the cartridges ran out,
You could hear the front-files shout, "Hi! ammunition-mules an' Gunga Din!"
  I sha'n't forgit the night
When I dropped be'ind the fight With a bullet where my belt-plate should 'a' been.
I was chokin' mad with thirst,
An' the man that spied me first Was our good old grinnin', gruntin' Gunga Din.
'E lifted up my 'ead,
An' he plugged me where I bled, An' 'e guv me 'arf-a-pint o' water-green:
It was crawlin' and it stunk,
But of all the drinks I've drunk, I'm gratefullest to one from Gunga Din.
It was "Din! Din! Din!" 'Ere's a beggar with a bullet through 'is spleen;
'E's chawin' up the ground,
An' 'e's kickin' all around: "For Gawd's sake git the water, Gunga Din!"
  'E carried me away
To where a dooli lay, An' a bullet come an' drilled the beggar clean.
'E put me safe inside,
An' just before 'e died: "I 'ope you liked your drink," sez Gunga Din.
So I'll meet 'im later on
At the place where 'e is gone-- Where it's always double drill and no canteen;

4 Hit you
5 Water skin

'E'll be squattin' on the coals, Givin' drink to poor damned souls, An' I'll get a swig in hell from Gunga Din!

Yes, Din! Din! Din! You Lazarushian-leather Gunga Din!

Though I've belted you and flayed you,

By the living Gawd that made you, You're a better man than I am, Gunga Din!

ADDRESS OF SERGEANT BUZFUZ
From "The Pickwick Papers"
BY CHARLES DICKENS

Sergeant Buzfuz rose with all the majesty and dignity which the grave nature of the proceedings demanded, and having whispered to Dodson, and conferred briefly with Fogg, pulled his gown over his shoulders, settled his wig, and addressed the jury.

Sergeant Buzfuz began by saying that never, in the whole course of his professional experience,--never, from the very first moment of his applying himself to the study and practice of the law, had he approached a case with such a heavy sense of the responsibility imposed upon him,--a responsibility he could never have supported, were he not buoyed up and sustained by a conviction, so strong that it amounted to positive certainty, that the cause of truth and justice, or, in other words, the cause of his much-injured and most oppressed client, *must* prevail with the high-minded and intelligent dozen of men whom he now saw in that box before him.

Counsel always begin in this way, because it puts the jury on the best terms with themselves, and makes them think what sharp fellows they must be. A visible effect was produced immediately; several jurymen beginning to take voluminous notes.

"The plaintiff is a widow; yes, gentlemen, a widow. The late Mr. Bardell, after enjoying, for many years, the esteem and confidence of his sovereign, as one of the guardians of his royal revenues, glided almost imperceptibly from the world, to seek elsewhere for that repose and peace which a custom-house can never afford."

This was a pathetic description of the decease of Mr. Bardell, who had been knocked on the head with a quart-pot in a public-house cellar.

"Of this man Pickwick I will say little; the subject presents but few attractions;

and I, gentlemen, am not the man, nor are you, gentlemen, the men, to delight in the contemplation of revolting heartlessness and of systematic villainy."

Here Mr. Pickwick, who had been writhing in silence, gave a violent start, as if some vague idea of assaulting Sergeant Buzfuz, in the august presence of justice and law, suggested itself to his mind.

"I say systematic villainy, gentlemen," said Sergeant Buzfuz, looking through Mr. Pickwick, and talking *at* him, "and when I say systematic villainy, let me tell the defendant, Pickwick,--if he be in court, as I am informed he is,--that it would have been more decent in him, more becoming, in better judgment, and in better taste, if he had stopped away.

"I shall show you, gentlemen, that for two years Pickwick continued to reside without interruption or intermission at Mrs. Bardell's house. I shall show you that, on many occasions, he gave halfpence, and on some occasions even sixpences, to her little boy; and I shall prove to you, by a witness whose testimony it will be impossible for my learned friend to weaken or controvert, that on one occasion he patted the boy on the head, and, after inquiring whether he had won any *alley tors* or *commoneys* lately (both of which I understand to be a particular species of marbles much prized by the youth of this town), made use of this remarkable expression: 'How should you like to have another father?' I shall prove to you, gentlemen, on the testimony of three of his own friends,--most unwilling witnesses, gentlemen,--most unwilling witnesses,--that on that morning he was discovered by them holding the plaintiff in his arms, and soothing her agitation by his caresses and endearments.

"And now, gentlemen, but one word more. Two letters have passed between these parties,--letters which are admitted to be in the handwriting of the defendant. Let me read the first:--'Garraway's, twelve o'clock. Dear Mrs. B.--Chops and Tomato sauce. Yours, Pickwick.' Gentlemen, what does this mean? Chops! Gracious heavens! and Tomato sauce! Gentlemen, is the happiness of a sensitive and confiding female to be trifled away by such shallow artifices as these? The next has no date whatever, which is in itself suspicious. 'Dear Mrs. B., I shall not be at home till to-morrow. Slow coach.' And then follows this very remarkable expression. 'Don't trouble yourself about the warming-pan.' Why, gentlemen, who *does* trouble himself about a warming-pan? Why is Mrs. Bardell so earnestly entreated not to agitate herself about this warming-pan, unless it is, as I assert it to be, a mere cover for hidden fire,--a mere substitute for some endearing word or promise, agreeably to a preconcerted system of correspondence, artfully contrived by Pickwick with a view to his contemplated desertion, and which I am not in a condition to explain?

"Enough of this. My client's hopes and prospects are ruined. But Pickwick, gentlemen,--Pickwick, the ruthless destroyer of this domestic oasis in the desert of Goswell Street,--Pickwick, who has choked up the well, and thrown ashes on the sward,--Pickwick, who comes before you to-day with his heartless Tomato sauce and warming-pans,--Pickwick still rears his head with unblushing effrontery, and gazes without a sigh on the ruin he has made. Damages, gentlemen, heavy damages, are the only punishment with which you can visit him, the only recompense you can award to my client. And for those damages she now appeals to an enlightened, a high-minded, a right-feeling, a conscientious, a dispassionate, a sympathizing, a contemplative jury of her civilized countrymen."

A NATURAL PHILOSOPHER

BY MACCABE

Ladies and Gentlemen: I see so many foine-lookin' people sittin' before me that if you'll excuse me I'll be after takin' a seat meself. You don't know me, I'm thinking, as some of yees 'ud be noddin' to me afore this. I'm a walkin' pedestrian, a travelin' philosopher. Terry O'Mulligan's me name. I'm from Dublin, where many philosophers before me was raised and bred. Oh, philosophy is a foine study! I don't know anything about it, but it's a foine study! Before I kirn over I attended an important meetin' of philosophers in Dublin, and the discussin' and talkin' you'd hear there about the world 'ud warm the very heart of Socrates or Aristotle himself. Well, there was a great many *imminent* and learned *min* there at the meetin', and I was there too, and while we was in the very thickest of a heated argument, one comes to me and says he, "Do you know what we're talkin' about?" "I do," says I, "but I don't understand yees." "Could ye explain the sun's motion around the earth?" says he. "I could," says I, "but I'd not know could you understand or not." "Well," says he, "we'll see," says he. Sure'n I didn't know anything, how to get out of it then, so I piled in, "for," says I to myself, "never let on to any one that you don't know anything, but make them believe that you do know all about it." So says I to him, takin' up me shillalah this way (holding a very crooked stick perpendicular), "We'll take that for the straight line of the earth's equator"--how's that for gehography? (to the audience). Ah, that was straight till the other day I bent it in an argument. "Wery good," says he. "Well," says I, "now the sun rises in the east" (placing the disengaged hand at the eastern end of the stick). Well, he couldn't deny that. "And when he gets up he

Darts his rosy beams
Through the mornin' gleams."

Do you moind the poetry there? (to the audience with a smile). "And he keeps on risin' and risin' till he reaches his meriden." "What's that?" says he. "His dinner-toime," says I; "sure'n that's my Latin for dinner-toime, and when he gets his dinner

He sinks to rest
Behind the glorious hills of the west."

Oh, begorra, there's more poetry! I fail it creepin' out all over me. "There," says I, well satisfied with myself, "will that do for ye?" "You haven't got done with him yet," says he. "Done with him," says I, kinder mad like; "what more do you want me to do with him? Didn't I bring him from the east to the west? What more do you want?" "Oh," says he, "you'll have to bring him back again to the east to rise next mornin'." By Saint Patrick! and wasn't I near betrayin' me ignorance, Sure'n I thought there was a large family of suns, and they rise one after the other. But I gathered meself quick, and, says I to him, "Well," says I, "I'm surprised you axed me that simple question. I thought any man 'ud know," says I, "when the sun sinks to rest in the west--when the sun--" says I. "You said that before," says he. "Well, I want to press it stronger upon you," says I. "When the sun sinks to rest in the east--no--west, why he--why he waits till it grows dark, and then he goes ***back in the noight toime***!"

RESPONSE TO A TOAST
From "A Charity Dinner"
BY LITCHFIELD MOSELEY

"Milors and Gentlemans!" commences the Frenchman, elevating his eyebrows and shrugging his shoulders. "Milors and Gentlemans--You excellent chairman, M. le Baron de Mount-Stuart, he have say to me, 'Make de toast.' Den I say to him dat I have no toast to make; but he nudge my elbow ver soft, and say dat dere is von toast dat nobody but von Frenchman can make proper; and, derefore, wid your kind permission, I vill make de toast. 'De brevete is de sole of de feet,' as you great philosophere, Dr. Johnson, do say, in dat amusing little vork of his, de Pronouncing Dictionnaire; and, derefore, I vill not say ver moch to de point. Ven I vas a boy, about so moch tall, and used for to promenade de streets of Marseilles et of Rouen, vid no feet to put onto my shoe, I nevare to have expose dat dis day vould to have arrive. I vas to begin de vorld as von garcon--or, vat you call in dis countrie, von vaitaire in a cafe--vere I vork ver hard, vid no habillemens at all to put onto myself, and ver little food to eat, excep' von old blue blouse vat vas give to me by de proprietaire, just for to keep myself fit to be showed at; but, tank goodness, tings dey have change ver moch for me since dat time, and I have rose myself, seulement par mon industrie et perseverance. Ah! mes amis! ven I hear to myself de flowing speech, de oration magnifique of you Lor' Maire, Monsieur Gobbledown, I feel dat it is von great privilege for von etrange to sit at de same table, and to eat de same food, as dat grand, dat majestique man, who are de terreur of de voleurs and de brigands of de metropolis; and who is also, I for to suppose, a halterman and de chef of you common scoundrel. Milors and gentlemans, I feel dat I can perspire to no greatare honneur dan to be von common scoundrelman myself; but, helas! dat plaisir are not for me, as I are not freeman of your great cite, not von liveryman servant of von of you compagnies joint-stock. But I must not forget de toast. Milors and Gentlemans! De immortal Shakispeare he have write, 'De ting of beauty are de joy for nevermore.' It is de ladies who are de toast. Vat is more entrancing dan de charmante smile, de soft voice, der vinking eye of de beautiful lady! It is de ladies who do sweeten de cares of life. It is de ladies who are de guiding stars of our existence. It is de ladies who do cheer but not inebriate, and, derefore, vid all homage to de dear sex, de toast dat I have to propose is, "De Ladies! God bless dem all!"

PARTRIDGE AT THE PLAY

From "Tom Jones"

BY HENRY FIELDING

In the first row of the first gallery did Mr. Jones, Mrs. Miller, her youngest daughter, and Partridge, take their places. Partridge immediately declared it was the finest place he had ever been in. When the first music was played, he said, "It was a wonder how so many fiddlers could play at one time, without putting one another out." While the fellow was lighting the upper candles, he cried out to Mrs. Miller, "Look, look, madam, the very picture of the man in the end of the common-prayer book before the gunpowder-treason service." Nor could he help observing, with a sigh, when all the candles were lighted, "That here were candles enough burnt in one night, to keep an honest poor family for a whole twelvemonth."

As soon as the play, which was Hamlet, Prince of Denmark, began, Partridge was all attention, nor did he break silence till the entrance of the ghost; upon which he asked Jones, "What man that was in the strange dress; something," said he, "like what I have seen in a picture. Sure it is not armor, is it?" Jones answered, "That is the ghost." To which Partridge replied with a smile, "Persuade me to that, sir, if you can. ... No, no, sir, ghosts don't appear in such dresses as that, neither." In this mistake, which caused much laughter in the neighborhood of Partridge, he was suffered to continue, till the scene between the ghost and Hamlet, when Partridge gave that credit to Mr. Garrick, which he had denied to Jones, and fell into so violent a trembling, that his knees knocked against each other. Jones asked him what was the matter, and whether he was afraid of the warrior upon the stage? "O la! sir," said he, "I perceive now it is what you told me. ... Nay, you may call me coward if you will; but if that little man there upon the stage is not frightened, I never saw any man frightened in my life. Ay, ay: go along with you: Ay, to be sure! Who's fool then? Will you? Lud have mercy upon such foolhardiness!--Whatever happens, it is good enough for you.--Follow you? I'd follow the devil as soon. Nay, perhaps it is the devil--for they say he can put on what likeness he pleases.--Oh! here he is again.--No farther! No, you have gone far enough already; farther than I'd have gone for all the king's dominions." Jones offered to speak, but Partridge cried, "Hush, hush! dear sir, don't you hear him?" And during the whole speech of the ghost, he sat with his eyes fixed partly on the ghost and partly on Hamlet, and with his mouth open; the same passions which succeeded each other in Hamlet, succeeding likewise in him.

During the second act, Partridge made very few remarks. He greatly admired the fineness of the dresses; nor could he help observing upon the king's countenance. "Well," said he, "how people may be deceived by faces! *Nulla fides fronti* is, I find, a true saying. Who would think, by looking into the king's face, that he had ever committed a murder?" He then inquired after the ghost; but Jones, who intended he should be surprised, gave him no other satisfaction than "that he might possibly see him again soon, and in a flash of fire."

Partridge sat in a fearful expectation of this; and now, when the ghost made his next appearance, Partridge cried out, "There, sir, now; what say you now? is he frightened now or no? As much frightened as you think me, and, to be sure, nobody can help some fears. I would not be in so bad a condition as what's his name, squire Hamlet, is there, for all the world. Bless me! what's become of the spirit! As I am a living soul, I thought I saw him sink into the earth." "Indeed, you saw right," answered Jones, "Well, well," cries Partridge, "I know it is only a play: and besides, if there was any thing in all this, Madam Miller would not laugh so; for as to you, sir, you would not be afraid, I believe, if the devil was here in person.--There, there--Aye, no wonder you are in such a passion; shake the vile wicked wretch to pieces. If she was my own mother, I would serve her so. To be sure all duty to a mother is forfeited by such wicked doings.--Aye, go about your business, I hate the sight of you."

Little more worth remembering occurred during the play, at the end of which Jones asked him which of the players he had liked best? To this he answered, with some appearance of indignation at the question, "The king, without doubt." "Indeed, Mr. Partridge," says Mrs. Miller, "you are not of the same opinion with the town; for they are all agreed, that Hamlet is acted by the best player who ever was on the stage." "He the best player!" cries Partridge, with a contemptuous sneer, "why, I could act as well as he myself. I am sure, if I had seen a ghost, I should have looked in the very same manner, and done just as ne did. And then, to be sure, in that scene, as you called it, between him and his mother, where you told me he acted so fine, why, Lord help me, any man, that is, any good man, that had such a mother, would have done exactly the same. I know you are only joking with me; but indeed, madam, though I was never at a play in London, yet I have seen acting before in the country; and the king for my money; he speaks all his words distinctly, half as loud again as the other.--Anybody may see he is an actor."

A MAN'S A MAN FOR A' THAT
BY ROBERT BURNS

Is there for honest poverty
That hings his head, an' a' that? The coward slave, we pass him by--
We dare be poor for a' that. For a' that, an' a' that,
Our toils obscure, an' a' that, The rank is but the guinea's stamp,
The man's the gowd[6] for a' that!

What tho' on hamely[7] fare we dine,
Wear hoddin[8] gray, an' a' that; Gie fools their silks, and knaves their wine--
A man's a man, for a' that. For a' that, an' a' that,
Their tinsel show, an' a' that, The honest man, though e'er sae poor,
Is king o' men for a' that!

Ye see yon birkie[9], ca'd a lord,
Wha struts, an' stares, an' a' that; Tho' hundreds worship at his word,
He's but a coof[10] for a' that; For a' that, an' a' that,
His riband, star, an' a' that; The man of independent mind,
He looks an' laughs at a' that.

A prince can mak a belted knight,
A marquis, duke, an' a' that; But an honest man's aboon[11] his might--
Gude faith, he maunna fa'[12] that! For a' that, an' a' that,
Their dignities, an' a' that, The pith o' sense, an' pride o' worth,
Are higher ranks than a' that.

---

6   gold
7   homely, plain
8   homespun
9   fellow
10   fool (pronounce like German *o* or oe)
11   above
12   must not claim (to make the honest man)

Then let us pray that come it may,
As come it will for a' that, That sense an' worth, o'er a' the earth,
Shall bear the gree,[13] an' a' that. For a' that, an' a' that,
It's comin' yet, for a' that-- That man to man, the warld o'er,
Shall brothers be for a' that.

ARTEMUS WARD'S LECTURE
From "Complete Works of Artemus Ward" with the permission of the G. W. Dillingham Company, New York, publishers.
BY CHARLES FARRAR BROWN (ARTEMUS WARD)
I don't expect to do great things here--but I have thought that if I could make money enough to buy me a passage to New Zealand I should feel that I had not lived in vain. I don't want to live in vain. I'd rather live in Texas--or here.

If you should be dissatisfied with anything here to-night--I will admit you all free in New Zealand--if you will come to me there for the orders. Any respectable cannibal will tell you where I live. This shows that I have a forgiving spirit.

I really don't care for money. I only travel round to see the world and to exhibit my clothes. These clothes I have on have been a great success in America.

How often do large fortunes ruin young men! I should like to be ruined, but I can get on very well as I am.

I am not an Artist. I don't paint myself--though perhaps if I were a middle-aged single lady I should--yet I have a passion for pictures.--I have had a great many pictures--photographs--taken of myself. Some of them are very pretty--rather sweet to look at for a short time--and as I said before, I like them. I've always loved pictures. I could draw on wood at a very tender age. When a mere child I once drew a small cartload of raw turnips over a wooden bridge.--The people of the village noticed me. I drew their attention. They said I had a future before me. Up to that time I had an idea it was behind me.

Time passed on. It always does, by the way. You may possibly have noticed that Time passes on.--It is a kind of way Time has.

I became a man. I haven't distinguished myself at all as an artist--but I have always been more or less mixed up with art. I have an uncle who takes photographs-

13 prize

-and I have a servant who--takes anything he can get his hands on.

When I was in Rome--Rome in New York State, I mean--a distinguished sculpist wanted to sculp me. But I said "No." I saw through the designing man. My model once in his hands--he would have flooded the market with my busts--and I couldn't stand it to see everybody going round with a bust of me. Everybody would want one of course--and wherever I should go I should meet the educated classes with my bust, taking it home to their families. This would be more than my modesty could stand--and I should have to return home--where my creditors are.

I like art. I admire dramatic art--although I failed as an actor.

It was in my schoolboy days that I failed as an actor.--The play was "The Ruins of Pompeii."--I played the ruins. It was not a very successful performance--but it was better than the "Burning Mountain." He was not good. He was a bad Vesuvius.

The remembrance often makes me ask--"Where are the boys of my youth?" I assure you this is not a conundrum. Some are amongst you here--some in America--some are in jail.

Hence arises a most touching question--"Where are the girls of my youth?" Some are married--some would like to be.

Oh, my Maria! Alas! she married another. They frequently do. I hope she is happy--because I am.--Some people are not happy. I have noticed that.

A gentleman friend of mine came to me one day with tears in his eyes. I said, "Why these weeps?" He said he had a mortgage on his farm--and wanted to borrow $200. I lent him the money--and he went away. Some time afterward he returned with more tears. He said he must leave me forever. I ventured to remind him of the $200 he borrowed. He was much cut up. I thought I would not be hard upon him--so told him I would throw off $100. He brightened--shook my hand--and said,--"Old friend-- I won't allow you to outdo me in liberality--I'll throw off the other hundred."

I like Music.--I can't sing. As a singist I am not a success. I am saddest when I sing. So are those who hear me. They are sadder even than I am.

I met a man in Oregon who hadn't any teeth--not a tooth in his head-- yet that man could play on the bass drum better than any man I ever met. He kept a hotel. They have queer hotels in Oregon. I remember one where they gave me a bag of oats for a pillow--I had nightmares of course. In the morning the landlord said,-- "How do you feel--old hoss-- hay?"--I told him I felt my oats.

As a manager I was always rather more successful than as an actor.

Some years ago I engaged a celebrated Living American Skeleton for a tour through Australia. He was the thinnest man I ever saw. He was a splendid skeleton. He didn't weigh anything scarcely--and I said to myself--the people of Australia will flock to see this tremendous cu- riosity. It is a long voyage--as you know--from New York to Melbourne-- and to my utter surprise the skeleton had no sooner got out to sea than he commenced eating in the most horrible manner. He had never been on the ocean before--and he said it agreed with him--I thought so!--I never saw a man eat so much in my life. Beef, mutton, pork--he swallowed them all like a shark--and between meals he was often discovered behind barrels eating hard-boiled eggs. The result was that, when we reached Melbourne, this infamous skel-eton weighed sixty-four pounds more than I did!

I thought I was ruined--but I wasn't. I took him on to California-- another very long sea voyage--and when I got him to San Francisco I exhibited him as a fat man.

This story hasn't anything to do with my entertainment, I know--but one of the principal features of my entertainment is that it contains so many things that don't have anything to do with it.

JIM BLUDSO, OF THE PRAIRIE BELLE

By permission of, and by special arrangement with, Houghton Mifflin Company, authorized publishers of this author's work.

BY JOHN HAY

Wall, no! I can't tell whar he lives, Because he don't live, you see; Leastways, he's got out of the habit Of livin' like you and me. Whar have you been for the last three year That you haven't heard folks tell How Jimmy Bludso passed in his checks The night of the "Prairie Belle"?

He weren't no saint,--them engineers Is all pretty much alike,-- One wife in Natchez-under-the-Hill And another one here, in Pike; A keerless man in his talk was Jim, And an awkward hand in a row, But he never flunked, and he never lied,-- I reckon he never knowed how.

And this was all the religion he had,-- To treat his engine well; Never be passed on the river; To mind the pilot's bell; And if ever the "Prairie Belle" took fire,-- A thousand times he swore, He'd hold her nozzle agin the bank Till the last soul got ashore.

All boats has their day on the Mississip, And her day come at last,-- The "Movastar" was a better boat, But the "Belle" she *wouldn't* be passed. And so she come tearin' along that night-- The oldest craft on the line-- With a nigger squat on her safety valve, And her furnace crammed, rosin and pine.

The fire bust out as she cleared the bar, And burnt a hole in the night, And quick as a flash she turned, and made For that willer-bank on the right. There was runnin' and cursing but Jim yelled out, Over all the infernal roar, "I'll hold her nozzle agin the bank Till the last galoot's ashore."

Through the hot, black breath of the burnin' boat Jim Bludso's voice was heard, And they all had trust in his cussedness, And knowed he would keep his word. And, sure's you're born, they all got off Afore the smokestacks fell,-- And Bludso's ghost went up alone In the smoke of the "Prairie Belle."

He weren't no saint,--but at jedgment I'd run my chance with Jim, 'Longside of some pious gentlemen That wouldn't shake hands with him. He seen his duty, a dead-sure thing,-- And he went for it thar and then; And Christ ain't agoing to be too hard On a man that died for men.

THE TRIAL OF ABNER BARROW

From "The Boy Orator of Zepata City" in "The Exiles and Other Stories." Copyrighted, 1894, Harper and Brothers. Reprinted with permission.

BY RICHARD HARDING DAVIS

Abe Barrow had been closely associated with the early history of Zepata; he had killed in his day several of the Zepata citizens. His fight with Thompson had been a fair fight--as those said who remembered it--and Thompson was a man they could well spare; but the case against Barrow had been prepared by the new and youthful district attorney, and the people were satisfied and grateful.

Harry Harvey, "The Boy Orator of Zepata City," as he was called, turned slowly on his heels, and swept the court room carelessly with a glance of his clever black eyes. The moment was his.

"This man," he said, and as he spoke even the wind in the corridors hushed for the moment, "is no part or parcel of Zepata city of to-day. He comes to us a relic of the past--a past that was full of hardships and glorious efforts in the face of daily disappointments, embitterments and rebuffs. But the part *this* man played in that past lives only in the court records of that day. This man, Abe Barrow, enjoys, and has enjoyed, a reputation as a 'bad man,' a desperate and brutal ruffian. Free him today, and you set a premium on such reputations; acquit him of this crime, and you encourage others to like evil. Let him go, and he will walk the streets with a swagger, and boast that you were afraid to touch him--afraid, gentlemen--and children and women will point after him as the man who has sent nine others into eternity, and who yet walks the streets a free man. And he will become, in the eyes of the young and the weak, a hero and a god.

"For the last ten years, your honor, this man, Abner Barrow, has been serving a term of imprisonment in the state penitentiary; I ask you to send him back there again for the remainder of his life. Abe Barrow is out of date. This Rip Van Winkle of the past returns to find a city where he left a prairie town; a bank where he spun his roulette-wheel; this magnificent courthouse instead of a vigilance committee! He is there, in the prisoner's pen, a convicted murderer and an unconvicted assassin, the last of his race,--the bullies and bad men of the border,--a thing to be forgotten and put away forever from the sight of men. And I ask you, gentlemen, to put him away where he will not hear the voice of man nor children's laughter, nor see a woman's smile. Bury him with the bitter past, with the lawlessness that has gone--that has gone, thank God--and which must not return."

The district attorney sat down suddenly, and was conscious of nothing until the foreman pronounced the prisoner at the bar guilty of murder in the second degree.

Judge Truax leaned across his desk and said, simply, that it lay in his power to sentence the prisoner to not less than two years' confinement in the state penitentiary, or for the remainder of his life.

"Before I deliver sentence on you, Abner Barrow," he said with an old man's kind severity, "is there anything you have to say on your own behalf?"

Barrow's face was white with the prison tan, and pinched and hollow-eyed and worn. When he spoke his voice had the huskiness which comes from non-use, and cracked and broke like a child's.

"I don't know, Judge," he said, "that I have anything to say in my own behalf. I guess what the gentleman said about me is all there is to say. I *am* a back number, I *am* out of date; I *was* a loafer and a blackguard. He told you I had no part or parcel in this city, or in this world; that I belonged to the past; that I ought to be dead. Now that's not so. I have just one thing that belongs to this city, and to this world--and to me; one thing that I couldn't take to jail with me, and I'll have to leave behind me when I go back to it. I mean my wife. You, sir, remember her, sir, when I married her twelve years ago. She gave up everything a woman ought to have, to come to me. She thought she was going to be happy with me; that's why she come, I guess. Maybe she was happy for about two weeks. After that first two weeks her life, sir, was a hell, and I made it a hell. Respectable women wouldn't speak to her because she was my wife--and she had no children. That was her life. She lived alone over the dance-hall, and sometimes when I was drunk--I beat her.

"At the end of two years I killed Welsh, and they sent me to the pen for ten years, and she was free. She could have gone back to her folks and got a divorce if she'd wanted to, and never seen me again. It was an escape most women'd gone down on their knees and thanked their Maker for.

"But what did this woman do--my wife, the woman I misused and beat and dragged down in the mud with me? She was too mighty proud to go back to her people, or to the friends who shook her when she was in trouble; and she sold out the place, and bought a ranch with the money, and worked it by herself, worked it day and night, until in ten years she had made herself an old woman, as you see she is to-day.

"And for what? To get *me* free again; to bring *me* things to eat in jail, and picture papers, and tobacco--when she was living on bacon and potatoes, and drinking alkali water--working to pay for a lawyer to fight for *me*--to pay for the *best* lawyer.

"And what I want to ask of you, sir, is to let me have two years out of jail to show her how I feel about it. It's all I've thought of when I was in jail, to be able to see her sitting in her own kitchen with her hands folded, and me working and sweating in the fields for her, working till every bone ached, trying to make it up to her.

"And I can't, I can't! It's too late! It's too late! Don't send me back for life! Give me a few years to work for her--to show her what I feel here, what I never felt for her before. Look at her, gentlemen, look how worn she is, and poorly, and look at her hands, and you men must feel how I feel--I don't ask you for myself. I don't want to go free on my own account. My God! Judge, don't bury me alive, as that man asked you to. Give me this last chance. Let me prove that what I'm saying is true."

Judge Truax looked at the papers on his desk for some seconds, and raised his head, coughing as he did so.

"It lies--it lies at the discretion of this Court to sentence the prisoner to a term of imprisonment of two years, or for an indefinite period, or for life. Owing to--on account of certain circumstances which were--have arisen--this sentence is suspended. This Court stands adjourned."

PART THREE
PLATFORM PRACTICE

THE SPEECH OF FORMAL OCCASION

THE BENEFITS OF A COLLEGE EDUCATION
From an address by the President to the students of Harvard University, at the announcement of Academic Distinctions, 1909
BY ABBOTT LAWRENCE LOWELL

This meeting is held not merely to honor the men who have won prizes, attained high rank, or achieved distinction in studies. In a larger sense it is a tribute paid by the University to the ideals of scholarship. It is a public confession of faith in the aims for which the University was established. We may, therefore, not inappropriately consider here the nature and significance of scholarship.

Without attempting an exhaustive catalogue of the benefits of education, we may note three distinct objects of college study. The first is the development of the mental powers with a view to their use in any subsequent career. In its broadest sense this may be called training for citizenship, for we must remember that good citizenship does not consist exclusively in rendering public service in political and philanthropic matters. It includes also conducting an industrial or professional career so as not to leave the public welfare out of sight.

Popular government is exacting. It implies that in some form every man shall voluntarily consecrate a part of his time and force to the state, and the better the citizen, the greater the effort he will make. On the function of colleges in fitting men for citizenship and for active work, much emphasis has been laid of late. Yet it is not the only aim of college studies. Another object is cultivation of the mind, refinement of taste, a development of the qualities that distinguish the civilized man from the barbarian. Nor does the value of these things lie in personal satisfaction alone. There is a culture that is selfish and exclusive, that is self-centered and conceited. The intellectual snob is quite as repellant as any other. But this is true of the moral distortion of all good qualities. The culture that narrows the sympathies, instead of enlarging them, has surely missed the object that should give its chief worth and dignity. The culture that reveals beauty in all its forms, that refines the sensibilities, and expands the mental horizon, that, without a sense of superiority, desires to share these things with others, and makes the lives of all men better worth living, is like the glow of fire in a cold room. It is a form of social service of a high order.

A third benefit of college education is the contact it affords with the work of creative imagination. The highest type of scholar is the creative scholar, just as the highest type of citizen is the statesman. The greatest figures in history, as almost every one will admit, are the thinkers and the rulers of men. People will always differ in the relative value they ascribe to these two supreme forms of human power. But if one may indulge in apocalyptic visions, I should prefer in another world to be worthy of the friendship of Aristotle rather than of Alexander, of Shakespeare or Newton than of Napoleon or Frederick the Great.

When I spoke of the benefit of college life in training for citizenship, and in imparting culture, I was obviously dealing with things which lie within the reach of every student; but in speaking of creative scholarship you may think that I am appealing only to the few men who have the rare gift of creative genius. But happily the progress of the world is not in the exclusive custody of the occasional men of genius. Great originality is, indeed, rare; but on a smaller scale it is not uncommon, and the same principles apply to the production of all creative work. The great scholar and the lesser intellectual lights differ in brilliancy, but the same process must be followed to bring them to their highest splendor. Nor is it the genius alone, or even the man of talent, who can enjoy and aid productive thought. It is not given to all men to possess creative scholarship themselves; but most men by following its footsteps can learn to respect it and feel its charm; and for any man who passes through college without doing so, college education has been in one of its most vital elements a failure. If he has not recognized the glowing imagination, the lofty ideals, the patience and the modesty, that characterize the true scholar, his time here has been spent, not perhaps without profit, but without inspiration.

All productive work is largely dependent upon appreciation by the community. The great painters of Italy would have been sterile had not the citizens of Florence been eager to carry Cimabue's masterpiece in triumph through the streets. Kant would never have written among a people who despised philosophy; and the discoveries of our own day would have been impossible in an unscientific age. Every man who has learned to respect creative scholarship can enter into its spirit, and by respecting it he helps to foster it.

WHAT THE COLLEGE GIVES

From "Girls and Education," a commencement address, Bryn Mawr College, 1911, by permission of, and by special arrangement with, Houghton Mifflin Company, authorized publishers of this author's works.

BY LE BARON RUSSELL BRIGGS

One of the best gifts that a college can bestow is the power of taking a new point of view through putting ourselves into another's place. To many students this comes hard, but come it must, as they hope to be saved.

To the American world the name of Charles Eliot Norton stands for all that is fastidious, even for what is over-fastidious; but Charles Eliot Norton's collection of verse and prose called "The Heart of Oak Books" shows a catholicity which few of his critics could approach, a refined literary hospitality not less noteworthy than the refined human hospitality of his Christmas Eve at Shady Hill. As an old man this interpreter of Dante saw and hailed with delight the genius of Mr. Kipling. If you leave college without catholicity of taste, something is wrong either with the college or with you.

As in literature, so in life. The greatest teachers--even Christ himself--have taught nothing greater than the power of seeing with the eyes of another soul. "Browning," said a woman who loves poetry, "seems to me not so much man as God." For Browning, beyond all men in the past century, beyond nearly all men of all time, could throw himself into the person of another.

"God be thanked, the meanest of his creatures
Boasts two soul-sides, one to face the world with,

One to show a woman when he loves her,"

said this same great poet, writing to his wife. But Browning has as many soul-sides as humanity. Hence it has been truly called a new life, like conversion, or marriage, or the mystery of a great sorrow,--a change and a bracing change in our outlook on the whole world, to discover Browning. The college should be our Browning, revealing the motive power of every life, the poetry of good and bad. It is only the "little folk of little soul" who come out of college as the initiated members of an exclusive set. Justify yourself and your college years by your catholic democracy.

It is the duty of the college not to train only, but to inspire; to inspire not to learning only, but to a disciplined appreciation of the best in literature, in art, and in life, to a catholic taste, to a universal sympathy. It is the duty of the student to take the inspiration, to be not disobedient to the heavenly vision, but to justify four years of delight, by scholarship at once accurate and sympathetic, by a finer culture, by a leadership without self-seeking or pride, by a whole-souled democracy. How simple and how old it all is! Yet it is not so simple that any one man or woman has done it to perfection; nor so old that any one part of it fails to offer fresh problems and fresh stimulus to the most ambitious of you all.

Nothing is harder than to take freely and eagerly the best that is offered us, and never turn away to the pursuit of false gods. Now the best that is offered in college is the inspiration to learn, and having learned, to do:--

> "Friends of the great, the high, the perilous years,
> Upon the brink of mighty things we stand--
> Of golden harvests and of silver tears,
> And griefs and pleasures that like grains of sand
> Gleam in the hourglass, yield their place and die."
> So said the college poet.

"Art without an ideal," said a great woman, "is neither nature nor art. The question involves the whole difference between Phidias and Mme. Tussaud." Let us never forget that the chief business of college teachers and college taught is the giving and receiving of ideals, and that the ideal is a burning and a shining light, not now only, or now and a year or two more, but for all time. What else is the patriot's love of country, the philosopher's love of truth, the poet's love of beauty, the teacher's love of learning, the good man's love of an honest life, than keeping the ideal, not merely to look at, but to see by? In its light, and only in its light, the greatest things are done. Thus the ideal is not merely the most beautiful thing in the world; it is the source of all high efficiency. In every change, in every joy or sorrow that the coming years may bring, do you who graduate to-day remember that nothing is so practical as a noble ideal steadily and bravely pursued, and that now, as of old, it is the wise men who see and follow the guiding star.

MEMORIAL DAY ADDRESS

From "After-Dinner and Other Speeches," with the permission of the author.

BY JOHN D. LONG

In memory of the dead, in honor of the living, for inspiration to our children, we gather to-day to deck the graves of our patriots with flowers, to pledge commonwealth and town and citizen to fresh recognition of the surviving soldier, and to picture yet again the romance, the reality, the glory, the sacrifice of his service. As if it were but yesterday, you recall him. He had but turned twenty. The exquisite tint of youthful health was in his cheek. His pure heart shone from frank, outspeaking eyes. His fair hair clustered from beneath his cap. He had pulled a stout oar in the college race, or walked the most graceful athlete on the village green. He had just entered on the vocation of his life. The doorway of his home at this season of the year was brilliant in the dewy morn with the clambering vine and fragrant flower, as in and out he went, the beloved of mother and sisters, and the ideal of a New England youth:--

> "In face and shoulders like a god he was;
> For o'er him had the goddess breathed the charm
> Of youthful locks, the ruddy glow of youth,
> A generous gladness in his eyes: such grace
> As carver's hand to ivory gives, or when
> Silver or Parian stone in yellow gold
> Is set."

And when the drum beat, when the first martyr's blood sprinkled the stones of Baltimore, he took his place in the ranks and went forward. You remember his ingenuous and glowing letters to his mother, written as if his pen were dipped in his very heart. How novel seemed to him the routine of service, the life of camp and march! How eager the wish to meet the enemy and strike his first blow for the good cause! What pride at the promotion that came and put its chevron on his arm or its strap upon his shoulder!

They took him prisoner. He wasted in Libby and grew gaunt and haggard with the horror of his sufferings and with pity for the greater horror of the sufferings of his comrades who fainted and died at his side. He tunneled the earth and escaped. Hungry and weak, in terror of recapture, he followed by night the pathway of the railroad. He slept in thickets and sank in swamps. He saw the glitter of horsemen who pursued him. He knew the bloodhound was on his track. He reached the line; and, with his hand grasping at freedom, they caught and took him back to his captivity. He was exchanged at last; and you remember, when he came home on a short furlough, how manly and war-worn he had grown. But he soon returned to the ranks and to the welcome of his comrades. They recall him now alike with tears and pride. In the rifle pits around Petersburg you heard his steady voice and firm command. Some one who saw him then fancied that he seemed that day like one who forefelt the end. But there was no flinching as he charged. He had just turned to give a cheer when the fatal ball struck him. There was a convulsion of the upward hand. His eyes, pleading and loyal, turned their last glance to the flag. His lips parted. He fell dead, and at nightfall lay with his face to the stars. Home they brought him, fairer than Adonis over whom the goddess of beauty wept. They buried him in the village churchyard under the green turf. Year by year his comrades and his kin, nearer than comrades, scatter his grave with flowers. Do you ask who he was? He was in every regiment and every company. He went out from every Massachusetts village. He sleeps in every Massachusetts burying ground. Recall romance, recite the names of heroes of legend and song, but there is none that is his peer.

WILLIAM MCKINLEY

From an address in the United States Senate

BY JOHN HAY

For the third time the Congress of the United States are assembled to commemorate the life and the death of a President slain by the hand of an assassin. The attention of the future historian will be attracted to the features which reappear with startling sameness in all three of these awful crimes: the uselessness, the utter lack of consequence of the act; the obscurity, the insignificance of the criminal; the blamelessness--so far as in our sphere of existence the best of men may be held blameless--of the victim. Not one of our murdered Presidents had an enemy in the world; they were all of such preeminent purity of life that no pretext could be given for the attack of passional crime; they were all men of democratic instincts, who could never have offended the most jealous advocates of equality; they were of kindly and generous nature, to whom wrong or injustice was impossible; of moderate fortune, whose slender means nobody could envy. They were men of austere virtue, of tender heart, of eminent abilities, which they had devoted with single minds to the good of the Republic. If ever men walked before God and man without blame, it was these three rulers of our people. The only temptation to attack their lives offered was their gentle radiance--to eyes hating the light that was offense enough.

The obvious elements which enter into the fame of a public man are few and by no means recondite. The man who fills a great station in a period of change, who leads his country successfully through a time of crisis; who, by his power of persuading and controlling others, has been able to command the best thought of his age, so as to leave his country in a moral or material condition in advance of where he found it,--such a man's position in history is secure. If, in addition to this, his written or spoken words possess the subtle qualities which carry them far and lodge them in men's hearts; and, more than all, if his utterances and actions, while informed with a lofty morality, are yet tinged with the glow of human sympathy,-- the fame of such a man will shine like a beacon through the mists of ages--an object of reverence, of imitation, and of love. It should be to us an occasion of solemn pride that in the three great crises of our history such a man was not denied us. The moral value to a nation of a renown such as Washington's and Lincoln's and McKinley's is beyond all computation. No loftier ideal can be held up to the emulation of ingenuous youth. With such examples we cannot be wholly ignoble. Grateful as we may be for what they did, let us be still more grateful for what they were. While our daily being, our public policies, still feel the influence of their work, let us pray that in our spirits their lives may be voluble, calling us upward and onward.

There is not one of us but feels prouder of his native land because the august figure of Washington presided over its beginnings; no one but vows it a tenderer love because Lincoln poured out his blood for it; no one but must feel his devotion for his country renewed and kindled when he remembers how McKinley loved, revered, and served it, showed in his life how a citizen should live, and in his last hour taught us how a gentleman could die.

ROBERT E. LEE

From an address at the unveiling of a statue of General Lee, at Washington and Lee University, 1883

BY JOHN W. DANIEL

Mounted in the field and at the head of his troops, a glimpse of Lee was an inspiration. His figure was as distinctive as that of Napoleon. The black slouch hat, the cavalry boots, the dark cape, the plain gray coat without an ornament but the three stars on the collar, the calm, victorious face, the splendid, manly figure on the gray war horse,--he looked every inch the true knight--the grand, invincible champion of a great principle.

The men who wrested victory from his little band stood wonder-stricken and abashed when they saw how few were those who dared oppose them, and generous admiration burst into spontaneous tribute to the splendid leader who bore defeat with the quiet resignation of a hero. The men who fought under him never revered or loved him more than on the day he sheathed his sword. Had he but said the word, they would have died for honor. It was because he said the word that they resolved to live for duty.

Plato congratulated himself, first, that he was born a man; second, that he had the happiness of being a Greek; and third, that he was a contemporary of Sophocles. And in this audience to-day, and here and there the wide world over, is many an one who wore the gray, who rejoices that he was born a man to do a man's part for his suffering country; that he had the glory of being a Confederate; and who feels a justly proud and glowing consciousness in his bosom when he says unto himself: "I was a follower of Robert E. Lee. I was a soldier in the army of Northern Virginia."

As president of Washington and Lee University, General Lee exhibited qualities not less worthy and heroic than those displayed on the broad and open theater of conflict when the eyes of nations watched his every action. In the quiet walks of academic life, far removed from "war or battle's sound," came into view the towering grandeur, the massive splendor, and the loving-kindness of his character. There he revealed in manifold gracious hospitalities, tender charities, and patient, worthy counsels, how deep and pure and inexhaustible were the fountains of his virtues. And loving hearts delight to recall, as loving lips will ever delight to tell, the thousand little things he did which sent forth lines of light to irradiate the gloom of the conquered land and to lift up the hopes and cheer the works of his people.

Come we then to-day in loyal love to sanctify our memories, to purify our hopes, to make strong all good intent by communion with the spirit of him who, being dead, yet speaketh. Let us crown his tomb with the oak, the emblem of his strength, and with the laurel, the emblem of his glory. And as we seem to gaze once more on him we loved and hailed as Chief, the tranquil face is clothed with heaven's light, and the mute lips seem eloquent with the message that in life he spoke, "There is a true glory and a true honor; the glory of duty done, the honor of the integrity of principle."

FAREWELL ADDRESS TO THE UNITED STATES SENATE
BY HENRY CLAY

From 1806, the period of my entrance upon this noble theater, with short intervals, to the present time, I have been engaged in the public councils, at home or abroad. Of the services rendered during that long and arduous period of my life it does not become me to speak; history, if she deign to notice me, and posterity, if the recollection of my humble actions shall be transmitted to posterity, are the best, the truest, and the most impartial judges.

I have not escaped the fate of other public men, nor failed to incur censure and detraction of the bitterest, most unrelenting, and most malignant character. But I have not meanwhile been unsustained. Everywhere throughout the extent of this great continent I have had cordial, warmhearted, faithful, and devoted friends, who have known me, loved me, and appreciated my motives.

In the course of a long and arduous public service, especially during the last eleven years in which I have held a seat in the Senate, from the same ardor and enthusiasm of character, I have no doubt, in the heat of debate, and in an honest endeavor to maintain my opinions against adverse opinions alike honestly entertained, as to the best course to be adopted for the public welfare, I may have often inadvertently and unintentionally, in moments of excited debate, made use of language that has been offensive, and susceptible of injurious interpretation towards my brother Senators. If there be any here who retain wounded feelings of injury or dissatisfaction produced on such occasions, I beg to assure them that I now offer the most ample apology for any departure on my part from the established rules of parliamentary decorum and courtesy. On the other hand, I assure Senators, one and all, without exception and without reserve, that I retire from this chamber without carrying with me a single feeling of resentment or dissatisfaction toward the Senate or any one of its members.

In retiring, as I am about to do, forever, from the Senate, suffer me to express my heartfelt wishes that all the great and patriotic objects of the wise framers of our Constitution may be fulfilled; that the high destiny designed for it may be fully answered; and that its deliberations, now and hereafter, may eventuate in securing the prosperity of our beloved country, in maintaining its rights and honor abroad, and upholding its interests at home. I retire, I know, at a period of infinite distress and embarrassment. I wish I could take my leave of you under more favorable auspices; but, without meaning at this time to say whether on any or on whom reproaches for the sad condition of the country should fall, I appeal to the Senate and to the world to bear testimony to my earnest and continued exertions to avert it, and to the truth that no blame can justly attach to me.

May the most precious blessings of heaven rest upon the whole Senate and each member of it, and may the labors of every one redound to the benefit of the nation and the advancement of his own fame and renown. And when you shall retire to the bosom of your constituents, may you receive that most cheering and gratifying of all human rewards--their cordial greeting of "Well done, good and faithful servant."

And now, Mr. President, and Senators, I bid you all a long, a lasting, and a friendly farewell.

THE DEATH OF GARFIELD
From an address before both houses of Congress, February, 1882
BY JAMES G. BLAINE

Surely, if happiness can ever come from the honors or triumphs of this world, on that quiet July morning James A. Garfield may well have been a happy man. No foreboding of evil haunted him, no slightest premonition of danger clouded his sky. His terrible fate was upon him in an instant. One moment he stood erect, strong, confident in the years stretching peacefully out before him. The next he lay wounded, bleeding, helpless, doomed to weary weeks of torture, to silence and the grave.

Great in life, he was surpassingly great in death. For no cause, in the very frenzy of wantonness and wickedness, by the red hand of Murder he was thrust from the full tide of this world's interest, from its hopes, its aspirations, its victories, into the visible presence of death. And he did not quail. Not alone for the one short moment in which, stunned and dazed, he could give up life, hardly aware of its relinquishment, but through days of deadly languor, through weeks of agony that was not less agony because silently borne, with clear sight and calm courage he looked into his open grave. What blight and ruin met his anguished eyes whose lips may tell--what brilliant broken plans, what baffled high ambitions, what sundering of strong, warm, manhood's friendships, what bitter rending of sweet household ties! Behind him a proud, expectant nation; a great host of sustaining friends; a cherished and happy mother wearing the full, rich honors of her early toil and tears; the wife of his youth, whose whole life lay in his; the little boys not yet emerged from childhood's day of frolic; the fair young daughter; the sturdy sons just springing into closest companionship, claiming every day, and every day rewarding, a father's love and care; and in his heart the eager, rejoicing power to meet all demand. Before him desolation and great darkness! And his soul was not shaken. His countrymen were thrilled with instant, profound, and universal sympathy. Masterful in his mortal weakness, he became the center of a nation's love, enshrined in the prayers of a world. But all the love and all the sympathy could not share with him his suffering. He trod the winepress alone. With unfaltering front he faced death. With unfailing tenderness he took leave of life. Above the demoniac hiss of the assassin's bullet he heard the voice of God. With simple resignation he bowed to the divine decree.

As the end drew near, his early craving for the sea returned. The stately mansion of power had been to him the wearisome hospital of pain, and he begged to be taken from its prison walls, from its oppressive, stifling air, from its homelessness and its hopelessness. Gently, silently, the love of a great people bore the pale sufferer to the longed-for healing of the sea, to live or to die, as God should will, within sight of its heaving billows, within sound of its manifold voices. With wan, fevered face tenderly lifted to the cooling breeze he looked out wistfully upon the ocean's changing wonders--on its far sails whitening in the morning light; on its restless waves rolling shoreward to break and die beneath the noonday sun; on the red clouds of evening arching low to the horizon; on the serene and shining pathway of the stars. Let us think that his dying eyes read a mystic meaning which only the rapt and parting soul may know. Let us believe that in the silence of the receding world he heard the great waves breaking on a farther shore, and felt already upon his wasted brow the breath of the eternal morning.

THE SECOND INAUGURAL ADDRESS

Delivered from the steps of the Capitol at Washington, 1865.

BY ABRAHAM LINCOLN

FELLOW COUNTRYMEN,--At this second appearing to take the oath of the Presidential office there is less occasion for an extended address than there was at first. Then a statement, somewhat in detail, of a course to be pursued seemed very fitting and proper. Now, at the expiration of four years, during which public declarations have been constantly called forth on every point and phase of the great contest which still absorbs the attention and engrosses the energies of the nation, little that is new could be presented.

The progress of our arms, upon which all else chiefly depends, is as well known to the public as to myself, and it is, I trust, reasonably satisfactory and encouraging to all. With high hope for the future, no prediction in regard to it is ventured.

On the occasion corresponding to this four years ago, all thoughts were anxiously directed to an impending civil war. All dreaded it, all sought to avoid it. While the inaugural address was being delivered from this place, devoted altogether to saving the Union without war, insurgent agents were in the city seeking to destroy it with war-- seeking to dissolve the Union and divide the effects by negotiation. Both parties deprecated war, but one of them would make war rather than let the nation survive, and the other would accept war rather than let it perish, and the war came.

One eighth of the whole population were colored slaves, not distributed generally over the Union, but localized in the Southern part of it. These slaves constituted a peculiar and powerful interest. All knew that this interest was somehow the cause of the war. To strengthen, perpetuate, and extend this interest was the object for which the insurgents would rend the Union by war, while the Government claimed no right to do more than to restrict the territorial enlargement of it.

Neither party expected for the war the magnitude or the duration which it has already attained. Neither anticipated that the cause of the conflict might cease when, or even before, the conflict itself should cease. Each looked for an easier triumph, and a result less fundamental and astounding. Both read the same Bible, and pray to the same God, and each invokes His aid against the other. It may seem strange that any men should dare to ask a just God's assistance in wringing their bread from the sweat of other men's faces; but let us judge not, that we be not judged. The prayer of both could not be answered. That of neither has been answered fully. The Almighty has His own purposes. Woe unto the world because of offenses, for it must needs be that offenses come, but woe to that man by whom the offense cometh. If we shall suppose that American slavery is one of those offenses which, in the providence of God, must needs come, but which having continued through His appointed time, He now wills to remove, and that He gives to both North and South this terrible war as the woe due to those by whom the offense came, shall we discern there any departure from those divine attributes which the believers in a living God always ascribe to Him? Fondly do we hope, fervently do we pray, that this mighty scourge of war may speedily pass away. Yet if God wills that it continue until all the wealth piled by the bondsman's two hundred and fifty years of unrequited toil shall be sunk, and until every drop of blood drawn with the lash shall be repaid by another drawn with the sword, as was said three thousand years ago, so still it must be said, that the judgments of the Lord are true and righteous altogether.

With malice toward none, with charity for all, with firmness in the right as God gives us to see the right, let us finish the work we are in, to bind up the nation's wounds, to care for him who shall have borne the battle, and for his widow and his orphans, to do all which may achieve and cherish a just and a lasting peace among ourselves and with all nations.

THE DEATH OF PRINCE ALBERT
From an address in the House of Commons, February, 1862
BY BENJAMIN DISRAELI

No person can be insensible to the fact that the House meets to-night under circumstances very much changed from those which have attended our assembling for many years. Of late years--indeed, for more than twenty years past--whatever may have been our personal rivalries, and whatever our party strife, there was at least one sentiment in which we all coincided, and that was a sentiment of admiring gratitude to that Throne whose wisdom and whose goodness had so often softened the acerbities of our free public life, and had at all times so majestically represented the matured intelligence of an enlightened people.

Sir, all that is changed. He is gone who was "the comfort and support" of that Throne. It has been said that there is nothing which England so much appreciates as the fulfillment of duty. The Prince whom we have lost not only was eminent for the fulfillment of duty, but it was the fulfillment of the highest duty under the most difficult circumstances. Prince Albert was the Consort of his Sovereign--he was the father of one who might be his Sovereign--he was the Prime Councillor of a realm, the political constitution of which did not even recognize his political existence.

Sir, it is sometimes deplored by those who admired and loved him that he was thwarted occasionally in his undertakings, and that he was not duly appreciated. But these are not circumstances for regret, but for congratulation. They prove the leading and original mind which has so long and so advantageously labored for this country. Had he not encountered these obstacles, had he not been subject to this occasional distrust and misconception, it would only have shown that he was a man of ordinary mold and temper. Those who improve must change, those who change must necessarily disturb and alarm men's prejudices. What he had to encounter was only a demonstration that he was a man superior to his age, and therefore admirably adapted for the work of progress. There is one other point, and one only, on which I will presume for a moment to dwell, and it is not for the sake of you, Sir, or those who now hear me, or of the generation to which we belong, but it is that those who come after us may not misunderstand the nature of this illustrious man. Prince Albert was not a mere patron; he was not one of those who by their gold or by their smiles reward excellence or stimulate exertion. His contributions to the cause of State were far more powerful and far more precious. He gave to it his thought, his time, his toil; he gave to it his life. On both sides and in all parts of the House I see many gentlemen who occasionally have acted with the Prince at those council boards where they conferred and consulted upon the great undertakings with which he was connected. I ask them, without fear of a denial, whether he was not the leading spirit, whether his was not the mind which foresaw the difficulty, his not the resources that supplied the remedy; whether his was not the courage which sustained them under apparently overpowering difficulties; whether every one who worked with him did not feel that he was the real originator of those plans of improvement which they assisted in carrying into effect?

But what avail these words? This House to-night has been asked to condole with the Crown upon this great calamity. No easy office. To condole, in general, is the office of those who, without the pale of sorrow, still feel for the sorrowing. But in this instance the country is as heart-stricken as its Queen. Yet in the mutual sensibility of a Sovereign and a people there is something ennobling--something which elevates the spirit beyond the level of mere earthly sorrow. The counties, the cities, the corporations of the realm--those illustrious associations of learning and science and art and skill, of which he was the brightest ornament and the inspiring spirit, have bowed before the Throne. It does not become the Parliament of the country to be silent. The expression of our feelings may be late, but even in that lateness may be observed some propriety. To-night the two Houses sanction the expression of the public sorrow, and ratify, as it were, the record of a nation's woe.

AN APPRECIATION OF MR. GLADSTONE

From an address in the House of Commons

BY ARTHUR J. BALFOUR

I feel myself unequal even to dealing with what is, perhaps, more strictly germane to this address--I mean, Mr. Gladstone as a politician, as a Minister, as a leader of public thought, as an eminent servant of the Queen; and if I venture to say anything, it is rather of Mr. Gladstone, the greatest member of the greatest deliberative assembly, which, so far, the world has seen.

Sir, I think it is the language of sober and unexaggerated truth to say that there is no gift which would enable a man to move, to influence, to adorn an assembly like this that Mr. Gladstone did not possess in a supereminent degree. Debaters as ready there may have been, orators as finished. It may have been given to others to sway as skillfully this assembly, or to appeal with as much directness and force to the simpler instincts of the great masses in the country; but, sir, it has been given to no man to combine all these great gifts as they were combined in the person of Mr. Gladstone. From the conversational discussion appropriate to our work in committees, to the most sustained eloquence befitting some great argument, and some great historic occasion, every weapon of Parliamentary warfare was wielded by him with the success and ease of a perfect, absolute, and complete mastery. I would not venture myself to pronounce an opinion as to whether he was most excellent in the exposition of a somewhat complicated budget of finance or legislation, or whether he showed it most in the heat of extemporary debate. At least this we may say, that from the humbler arts of ridicule or invective to the subtlest dialectic, the most persuasive eloquence, the most cogent appeals to everything that was highest and best in the audience that he was addressing, every instrument which could find place in the armory of a member of this House, he had at his command without premeditation, without forethought, at the moment and in the form which appeared best suited to carry out his purpose.

It may, perhaps, be asked whether I have nothing to say about Mr. Gladstone's place in history, about the judgment we ought to pass upon the great part which he has played in the history of his country and the history of the world during the many years in which he held a foremost place in this assembly. These questions are legitimate questions. But they are not to be discussed by me to-day. Nor, indeed, do I think that the final answer can be given to them--the final judgment pronounced--in the course of this generation. But one service he did--in my opinion incalculable--which is altogether apart from the judgment which we may be disposed to pass on the particular opinions, the particular views, or the particular lines of policy which Mr. Gladstone may from time to time have adopted. Sir, he added a dignity and he added a weight to the deliberations of this House by his genius which I think it is impossible adequately to express.

It is not enough, in my opinion, to keep up simply a level, though it be a high level, of probity and of patriotism. The mere virtue of civic honesty is not sufficient to preserve this assembly from the fate which has overcome so many other assemblies, the products of democratic forces. More than this is required, more than this was given to us by Mr. Gladstone. Those who seek to raise in the public estimation the level of our proceedings will be the most ready to admit the infinite value of those services, and realize how much the public prosperity is involved in the maintenance of the work of public life. Sir, that is a view which, it seems to me, places the services of Mr. Gladstone to this assembly, which he loved so well, and of which he was so great a member, in as clear a light and on as firm a basis as it is possible to place them.

WILLIAM E. GLADSTONE
From an address in the House of Lords, May, 1898
BY LORD ROSEBERY

My Lords, this is, as has been pointed out, an unique occasion. Mr. Gladstone always expressed a hope that there might be an interval left to him between the end of his political and of his natural life. That period was given to him, for it is more than four years since he quitted the sphere of politics. Those four years have been with him a special preparation for his death, but have they not also been a preparation for his death with the nation at large? Had he died in the plenitude of his power as Prime Minister, would it have been possible for a vigorous and convinced Opposition to allow to pass to him, without a word of dissent, the honors which are now universally conceded? Hushed for the moment are the voices of criticism; hushed are the controversies in which he took part; hushed for the moment is the very sound of party conflict. I venture to think that this is a notable fact in our history. It was not so with the elder Pitt. It was not so with the younger Pitt. It was not so with the elder Pitt--in spite of his tragic end, of his unrivaled services, and of his enfeebled old age. It was not so with the younger Pitt--in spite of his long control of the country and his absolute and absorbed devotion to the State. I think that we should remember this as creditable not merely to the man, but to the nation.

My Lords, there is one deeply melancholy feature of Mr. Gladstone's death--by far the most melancholy--to which I think none of my noble friends have referred. I think that all our thoughts must be turned, now that Mr. Gladstone is gone, to that solitary and pathetic figure who, for sixty years, shared all the sorrows and all the joys of Mr. Gladstone's life; who received his every confidence and every aspiration; who shared his triumphs with and cheered him under his defeats; who, by her tender vigilance, I firmly believe, sustained and prolonged his years. I think that the occasion ought not to pass without letting Mrs. Gladstone know that she is in all our thoughts to- day. And yet, my Lords--putting that one figure aside--to me, at any rate, this is not an occasion for absolute and entire and unreserved lamentation. Were it, indeed, possible so to protract the inexorable limits of human life that we might have hoped that future years, and even future generations, might see Mr. Gladstone's face and hear his matchless voice, and receive the lessons of his unrivaled experience-- we might, perhaps, grieve to-day as those who have no hope. But that is not the case. He had long exceeded the span of mortal life; and his latter months had been months of unspeakable pain and distress. He is now in that rest for which he sought and prayed, and which was to give him relief from an existence which had become a burden to him. Surely this should not be an occasion entirely for grief; when a life prolonged to such a limit, so full of honor, so crowned with glory, had come to its termination. The nation lives that produced him. The nation that produced him may yet produce others like him; and, in the meantime, it is rich in his memory, rich in his life, and rich, above all, in his animating and inspiring example. Nor do I think that we should regard this heritage as limited to our own country or to our own race. It seems to me that, if we may judge from the papers of to-day, that it is shared by, that it is the possession of, all civilized mankind, and that generations still to come, through many long years, will look for encouragement in labor, for fortitude in adversity, for the example of a sublime Christianity, with constant hope and constant encouragement, to the pure, the splendid, the dauntless figure of William Ewart Gladstone.

THE SOLDIER'S CREED

From a centennial address at the United States Military Academy at West Point, with the author's permission.

BY HORACE PORTER

As we stand here to-day a hundred years of history pass in review before us. The present permanent Academy was founded in 1802. The class that year contained two cadets. During the ten years following the average number was twenty. We might say of the cadets of those days what Curran said of the books in his library--"not numerous, but select."

And now a word to the Corps of Cadets, the departure of whose graduating class marks the close of the first century of the Academy's life. The boy is father to the man. The present is the mold in which the future is cast. The dominant characteristics of the cadet are seen in the future general. You have learned here how to command, and a still more useful lesson, how to obey. You have been taught obedience to the civil, as well as to the military, code, for in this land the military is always subordinate to the civil law. Not the least valuable part of your education is your service in the cadet ranks, performing the duties of a private soldier. That alone can acquaint you with the feelings and the capabilities of the soldiers you will command. It teaches you just how long a man can carry a musket in one position without overfatigue, just how hard it is to keep awake on sentry duty after an exhausting day's march. You will never forget this part of your training. When Marshal Lannes's grenadiers had been repulsed in an assault upon the walls of a fortified city, and hesitated to renew the attack, Lannes seized a scaling ladder and, rushing forward, cried: "Before I was a marshal I was a grenadier, and I have not forgotten my training." Inspired by his example, the grenadiers carried the walls and captured everything before them.

Courage is the soldier's cardinal virtue. You will seldom go amiss in following General Grant's instructions to his commanders, "When in doubt move to the front."

A generous country has with fostering care equipped you for your career. It is entitled to your undivided allegiance. In closing, let me mention, by way of illustration, a most touching and instructive scene which I once witnessed at the annual meeting in the great hall of the Sorbonne in Paris for the purpose of awarding medals of honor to those who had performed acts of conspicuous bravery in saving human life at sea. A bright-eyed boy of scarcely fourteen summers was called to the platform. The story was recounted of how one winter's night when a fierce tempest was raging on the rude Normandy coast, he saw signals of distress at sea and started with his father, the captain of a small vessel, and the mate to attempt a rescue. By dint of almost superhuman effort the crew of a sinking ship was safely taken aboard. A wave then washed the father from the deck. The boy plunged into the seething waves to save him, but the attempt was in vain, and the father perished. The lad struggled back to the vessel to find that the mate had also been washed overboard. Then lashing himself fast, he took the wheel and guided the boat, with its precious cargo of human souls, through the howling storm safely into port. The minister of public instruction, after paying a touching tribute to the boy's courage in a voice broken with emotion, pinned the medal on his breast, placed in his hands a diploma of honor, and then, seizing the brave lad in his arms, imprinted a kiss on each cheek. For a moment the boy seemed dazed, not knowing which way to turn, as he stood there with the tears streaming down his bronzed cheeks while every one in that vast hall wept in sympathy. Suddenly his eyes turned toward his old peasant mother, she to whom he owed his birth and his training, as she sat at the back of the platform with bended form and wearing her widow's cap. He rushed to her, took the medal from his breast, and, casting it and his diploma into her lap, threw himself on his knees at her feet.

Men of West Point, in the honorable career which you have chosen, whatever laurels you may win, always be ready to lay them at the feet of your country to which you owe your birth and your education.

COMPETITION IN COLLEGE

From an address at Columbia University, June, 1909

BY ABBOTT LAWRENCE LOWELL

We have seen that the sifting out of young men capable of scholarship is receiving to-day less attention than it deserves; and that this applies not only to recruiting future leaders of thought, but also to prevailing upon every young man to develop the intellectual powers he may possess. We have seen also that, while the graduate school can train scholars, it cannot create love of scholarship. That work must be done in undergraduate days. We have found reasons to believe that during the whole period of training, mental and physical, which reaches its culmination in college, competition is not only a proper but an essential factor; and we have observed the results that have been achieved at Oxford and Cambridge by its use. In this country, on the other hand, several causes, foremost among them the elective system, have almost banished competition in scholarship from our colleges; while the inadequate character of our tests, and the corporate nature of self-interest in these latter times, raise serious difficulties in making it effective.

Nevertheless, I have faith that these obstacles can be overcome, and that we can raise intellectual achievement in college to its rightful place in public estimation. We are told that it is idle to expect young men to do strenuous work before they feel the impending pressure of earning a livelihood; that they naturally love ease and self- indulgence, and can be aroused from lethargy only by discipline, or by contact with the hard facts of a struggle with the world. If I believed that, I would not be president of a college for a moment. It is not true. A normal young man longs for nothing so much as to devote himself to a cause that calls forth his enthusiasm, and the greater the sacrifice involved, the more eagerly will he grasp it. If we were at war and our students were told that two regiments were seeking recruits, one of which would be stationed at Fortress Monroe, well- housed and fed, living in luxury, without risk of death or wounds, while the other would go to the front, be starved and harassed by fatiguing marches under a broiling sun, amid pestilence, with men falling from its ranks killed or suffering mutilation, not a single man would volunteer for the first regiment, but the second would be quickly filled. Who is it that makes football a dangerous and painful sport? Is it the faculty or the players themselves?

A young man wants to test himself on every side, in strength, in quickness, in skill, in courage, in endurance; and he will go through much to prove his merit. He wants to test himself, provided he has faith that the test is true, and that the quality tried is one that makes for manliness; otherwise he will have none of it. Now we have not convinced him that high scholarship is a manly thing worthy of his devotion, or that our examinations are faithful tests of intellectual power; and in so far as we have failed in this we have come short of what we ought to do. Universities stand for the eternal worth of thought, for the preeminence of the prophet and the seer; but instead of being thrilled by the eager search for truth, our classes too often sit listless on the bench. It is not because the lecturer is dull, but because the pupils do not prize the end enough to relish the drudgery required for skill in any great pursuit, or indeed in any sport. To make them see the greatness of that end, how fully it deserves the price that must be paid for it, how richly it rewards the man who may compete for it, we must learn--and herein lies the secret--we must learn the precious art of touching their imagination.

A MASTER OF THE SITUATION

From a lecture, entitled "Masters of the Situation"

BY JAMES T. FIELDS

There was once a noble ship full of eager passengers, freighted with a rich cargo, steaming at full speed from England to America. Two thirds of a prosperous voyage thus far were over, as in our mess we were beginning to talk of home. Fore and aft the songs of good cheer and hearty merriment rose from deck to cabin.

"As if the beauteous ship enjoyed the beauty of the sea,
She lifteth up her stately head, and saileth joyfully,
A lovely path before her lies, a lovely path behind;
She sails amid the loveliness like a thing of heart and mind."

Suddenly, a dense fog came, shrouding the horizon, but as this was a common occurrence in the latitude we were sailing, it was hardly mentioned in our talk that afternoon. There are always croakers on board ship, if the weather changes however slightly, but the ***Britannia*** was free, that voyage, of such unwelcome passengers. A happier company never sailed upon an autumn sea! The storytellers are busy with their yarns to audiences of delighted listeners in sheltered places; the ladies are lying about on couches, and shawls, reading or singing; children in merry companies are taking hands and racing up and down the decks,--when a quick cry from the lookout, a rush of officers and men, and we are grinding on a ledge of rocks off Cape Race! One of those strong currents, always mysterious, and sometimes impossible to foresee, had set us into shore out of our course, and the ship was blindly beating on a dreary coast of sharp and craggy rocks.

I heard the order given, "Every one on deck!" and knew what that meant-- the masts were in danger of falling. Looking over the side, we saw bits of the keel, great pieces of plank, floating out into the deep water. A hundred pallid faces were huddled together near the stern of the ship where we were told to go and wait. I remember somebody said that a little child, the playfellow of passengers and crew, could not be found, and that some of us started to find him; and that when we returned him to his mother she spake never a word, but seemed dumb with terror at the prospect of separation and shipwreck, and that other specter so ghastly when encountered at sea.

Suddenly we heard a voice up in the fog in the direction of the wheelhouse, ringing like a clarion above the roar of the waves, and the clashing sounds on shipboard, and it had in it an assuring, not a fearful tone. As the orders came distinctly and deliberately through the captain's trumpet, to "ship the cargo," to "back her," to "keep her steady," we felt somehow that the commander up there in the thick mist on the wheelhouse knew what he was about, and that through his skill and courage, by the blessing of heaven, we should all be rescued. The man who saved us so far as human aid ever saves drowning mortals, was one fully competent to command a ship; and when, after weary days of anxious suspense, the vessel leaking badly, and the fires in danger of being put out, we arrived safely in Halifax, old Mr. Cunard, agent of the line, on hearing from the mail officer that the steamer had struck on the rocks and had been saved only by the captain's presence of mind and courage, simply replied, "Just what might have been expected in such a disaster; Captain Harrison is always master of the situation." Now, no man ever became master of the situation by accident or indolence. I believe with Shelley, that the Almighty has given men and women arms long enough to reach the stars if they will only put them out! It was an admirable saying of the Duke of Wellington, "that no general ever blundered into a great victory." St. Hilaire said, "I ignore the existence of a blind chance, accident, and haphazard results." "He happened to succeed," is a foolish, unmeaning phrase. No man happens to succeed.

WIT AND HUMOR

Reprinted from "American Wit and Humor," copyrighted in "Modern Eloquence," Geo. L. Shuman and Company, Chicago, publishers.

BY MINOT J. SAVAGE

Wit may take many forms, but it resides essentially in the thought or the imagination. In its highest forms it does not deal in things but with ideas. It is the shock of pleased surprise which results from the perception of unexpected likeness between things that differ or of an unexpected difference between things that are alike. Or it is where utterly incongruous things are apparently combined in the expression of one idea. Wit may be bitter or kindly or entirely neutral so far as the feelings are concerned. When extremes of feeling, one way or the other, are concerned, then it takes on other names which will be considered by themselves.

But not to stop any longer with definition, it is almost pure wit when some one said of an endless talker that he had "occasional brilliant flashes of silence." So of the saying of Mr. Henry Clapp. You know it is said of Shakespeare, "He is not for a day, but for all time." Speaking of the bore who calls when you are busy and never goes, Mr. Clapp said, "He is not for a time, but for all day." And what could be more deliciously perfect than the following: Senator Beck of Kentucky was an everlasting talker. One day a friend remarked to Senator Hoar, "I should think Beck would wear his brain all out talking so much." Whereupon Mr. Hoar replied, "Oh, that doesn't affect him any: he rests his mind when he is talking." This has, indeed, a touch of sarcasm; but it is as near the pure gold of wit as you often get. Or, take this. There being two houses both of which are insisted on as the real birthplace of the great philosopher and statesman, Mark Twain gravely informs us that "Franklin was twins, having been born simultaneously in two different houses in Boston."

One of the finest specimens of clear-cut wit is the saying of the Hon. Carroll D. Wright. Referring to the common saying, he once keenly remarked: "I know it is said that figures won't lie, but, unfortunately, liars will figure."

In contradistinction from wit, humor deals with incidents, characters, situations. True humor is altogether kindly; for, while it points out and pictures the weaknesses and foibles of humanity, it feels no contempt and leaves no sting. It has its root in sympathy and blossoms out in toleration.

It would take too long at this point in my lecture to quote complete specimens of humor; for that would mean spreading out before you detailed scenes or full descriptions. But fortunately it is not necessary. Cervantes, Shakespeare, Charles Lamb, Dickens, and a host of others will readily occur to you. But what could be better of its kind than this? General Joe Johnston was one day riding leisurely behind his army on the march. Food had been scarce and rations limited. He spied a straggler in the brush beside the road. He called out sharply, "What are you doing here?" Being caught out of the ranks was a serious offense, but the soldier was equal to the emergency. So to the General's question he replied, "Pickin' 'simmons." The persimmon, as you know, has the quality of puckering the mouth, as a certain kind of wild cherry used to mine when I was a boy. "What are you picking 'simmons for?" sharply rejoined the General. Then came the humorous reply that disarmed all of the officer's anger and appealed to his sympathy, while it hinted all "the boys" were suffering for the cause. "Well, the fact of it is, General, I'm trying to shrink up my stomach to the size of my rations, so I won't starve to death."

A MESSAGE TO GARCIA

From an article in The Philistine, with the permission of the author

BY ELBERT HUBBARD

When war broke out between Spain and the United States, it was very necessary to communicate quickly with the leader of the Insurgents. Garcia was somewhere in the mountain fastnesses of Cuba--no one knew where. No mail or telegraph message could reach him. The President must secure his cooperation, and quickly.

What to do!

Some one said to the President, "There's a fellow by the name of Rowan will find Garcia for you if anybody can." Rowan was sent for and given a letter to be delivered to Garcia. How "the fellow by the name of Rowan" took the letter, sealed it up in an oilskin pouch, strapped it over his heart, in four days landed by night off the coast of Cuba from an open boat, disappeared into the jungle, and in three weeks came out on the other side of the island, having traversed a hostile country on foot, and delivered his letter to Garcia, are things I have no special desire now to tell in detail.

The point I wish to make is this: McKinley gave Rowan a letter to be delivered to Garcia; Rowan took the letter and did not ask, "Where is he at?" By the Eternal! there is a man whose form should be cast in deathless bronze and the statue placed in every college of the land. It is not book learning young men need, nor instruction about this and that, but a stiffening of the vertebrae which will cause them to be loyal to a trust, to act promptly, concentrate their energies; do the thing--"Carry a message to Garcia!"

General Garcia is dead now, but there are other Garcias. No man who has endeavored to carry out an enterprise where many hands were needed, but has been well-nigh appalled at times by the imbecility of the average man--the inability or unwillingness to concentrate on a thing and do it. Slipshod assistance, foolish inattention, dowdy indifference, and half-hearted work seem the rule; and no man succeeds, unless by hook or crook, or threat, he forces or bribes other men to assist him; or mayhap, God in His goodness performs a miracle, and sends him an angel of light for an assistant.

And this incapacity for independent action, this moral stupidity, this infirmity of the will, this unwillingness to catch hold and lift, are the things that put pure socialism so far into the future. If men will not act for themselves, what will they do when the benefit of the effort is for all?

My heart goes out to the man who does his work when the "boss" is away as well as when he is at home. And the man, who, when given a letter for Garcia, quietly takes the missive, without asking any idiotic questions, and with no lurking intention of chucking it into the nearest sewer, or of doing aught else but deliver it, never gets "laid off," nor has to go on a strike for higher wages. Civilization is one long anxious search for just such individuals. Anything such a man asks shall be granted; his kind is so rare that no employer can afford to let him go. He is wanted in every city, town, and village--in every office, shop, store, and factory. The world cries out for such; he is needed, and needed badly-the man who can carry a message to Garcia.

SHAKESPEARE'S "MARK ANTONY"

ANONYMOUS

A Roman, an orator, and a triumvir, a conqueror when all Rome seemed armed against him only to have his glory "false played" by a woman "unto an enemy's triumph,"--such is Shakespeare's story of Mark Antony. Passion alternates with passion, purpose with purpose, good with evil, and strength with weakness, until his whole nature seems changed, and we find the same and yet another man.

In "Julius Caesar" Antony is seen at his best. He is the one triumphant figure of the play. Caesar falls. Brutus and Cassius are in turn victorious and defeated, but Antony is everywhere a conqueror. Antony weeping over Caesar's body, Antony offering his breast to the daggers which have killed his master, is as plainly the sovereign power of the moment as when over Caesar's corpse he forces by his magnetic oratory the prejudiced populace to call down curses on the heads of the conspirators.

Caesar's spirit still lives in Antony,--a spirit that dares face the conspirators with swords still red with Caesar's blood and bid them,

Whilst their purple hands do reek and smoke,

fulfill their pleasure,--a spirit that over the dead body of Caesar takes the hand of each and yet exclaims:--

"Had I as many eyes as thou hast wounds,
Weeping as fast as they stream forth thy blood,
It would become me better than to close
In terms of friendship with thine enemies."

Permission is granted Antony to speak a farewell word over the body of Caesar in the crowded market place. Before the populace, hostile and prejudiced, Antony stands as the friend of Caesar. Slowly, surely, making his approach step by step, with consummate tact he steals away their hearts and paves the way for his own victory. The honorable men gradually turn to villains of the blackest dye. Caesar's mantle, which but a moment before had called forth bitter curses, now brings tears to every Roman's eye. The populace fast yields to his eloquence. He conquers every vestige of distrust as he says:--

"I am no orator, as Brutus is;
But, as you know me all, a plain, blunt man,
That love my friend; and that they know full well
That gave me public leave to speak of him."

And now the matchless orator throws off his disguise. With resistless vehemence he pours forth a flood of eloquence which bears the fickle mob like straws before its tide:--

"I tell you that which you yourselves do know;
Show you sweet Caesar's wounds, poor, poor dumb mouths,
And bid them speak for me; but were I Brutus,
And Brutus Antony, there were an Antony
Would ruffle up your spirits, and put a tongue
In every wound of Caesar, that would move
The stones of Rome to rise and mutiny."

The effect is magical. The rage of the populace is quickened to a white heat; and, baffled, beaten by a plain, blunt man, the terror-stricken conspirators ride like madness through the gates of Rome.

ANDR. AND HALE

From "Orations and After-Dinner Speeches," the Cassell Publishing Company, New York, publishers.

BY CHAUNCEY M. DEPEW

Andre's story is the one overmastering romance of the Revolution. American and English literature is full of eloquence and poetry in tribute to his memory and sympathy for his fate. After the lapse of a hundred years, there is no abatement of absorbing interest. What had this young man done to merit immortality? The mission whose tragic issue lifted him out of the oblivion of other minor British officers, in its inception was free from peril or daring, and its objects and purposes were utterly infamous.

Had he succeeded by the desecration of the honorable uses of passes and flags of truce, his name would have been held in everlasting execration. In his failure the infant Republic escaped the dagger with which he was feeling for its heart, and the crime was drowned in tears for his untimely end. His youth and beauty, the brightness of his life, the calm courage in the gloom of his death, his early love and disappointment, surrounded him with a halo of poetry and pity which have secured for him what he most sought and could never have won in battles and sieges,--a fame and recognition which have outlived that of all the generals under whom he served.

Are kings only grateful, and do not republics forget? Is fame a travesty, and the judgment of mankind a farce? America had a parallel case in Captain Nathan Hale. Of the same age as Andre, he, after graduation at Yale College with high honors, enlisted in the patriot cause at the beginning of the contest, and secured the love and confidence of all about him. When none else would go upon a most important and perilous mission, he volunteered, and was captured by the British.

While Andre received every kindness, courtesy, and attention, and was fed from Washington's table, Hale was thrust into a noisome dungeon in the sugar-house. While Andre was tried by a board of officers and had ample time and every facility for defense, Hale was summarily ordered to execution the next morning. While Andre's last wishes and bequests were sacredly followed, the infamous Cunningham tore from Hale his cherished Bible and destroyed before his eyes his last letter to his mother and sister, and asked him what he had to say. "All I have to say," was his reply, "is, I regret I have but one life to lose for my country."

The dying declarations of Andre and Hale express the animating spirit of their several armies, and teach why, with all her power, England could not conquer America. "I call upon you to witness that I die like a brave man," said Andre, and he spoke from British and Hessian surroundings, seeking only glory and pay. "I regret I have but one life to lose for my country," said Hale; and, with him and his comrades, self was forgotten in that absorbing, passionate patriotism which pledges fortune, honor, and life to the sacred cause.

THE BATTLE OF LEXINGTON

BY THEODORE PARKER

One raw morning in spring--it will be eighty years the nineteenth day of this month--Hancock and Adams, the Moses and Aaron of that Great Deliverance, were both at Lexington; they also had "obstructed an officer" with brave words. British soldiers, a thousand strong, came to seize them and carry them over sea for trial, and so nip the bud of Freedom auspiciously opening in that early spring. The town militia came together before daylight, "for training." A great, tall man, with a large head and a high, wide brow, their captain,--one who had "seen service,"--marshaled them into line, numbering but seventy, and bade "every man load his piece with powder and ball." "I will order the first man shot that runs away," said he, when some faltered. "Don't fire unless fired upon, but if they want to have a war, let it begin here."

Gentlemen, you know what followed; those farmers and mechanics "fired the shot heard round the world." A little monument covers the bones of such as before had pledged their fortune and their sacred honor to the Freedom of America, and that day gave it also their lives. I was born in that little town, and bred up amid the memories of that day. When a boy, my mother lifted me up, on Sunday, in her religious, patriotic arms, and held me while I read the first monumental line I ever saw-- "Sacred to Liberty and the Rights of Mankind."

Since then I have studied the memorial marbles of Greece and Rome, in many an ancient town; nay, on Egyptian obelisks, have read what was written before the Eternal roused up Moses to lead Israel out of Egypt, but no chiseled stone has ever stirred me to such emotion as these rustic names of men who fell "In the Sacred Cause of God and their Country."

Gentlemen, the Spirit of Liberty, the Love of Justice, was early fanned into a flame in my boyish heart. The monument covers the bones of my own kinsfolk; it was their blood which reddened the long, green grass at Lexington. It was my own name which stands chiseled on that stone; the tall Captain who marshaled his fellow farmers and mechanics into stern array, and spoke such brave and dangerous words as opened the war of American Independence,--the last to leave the field,-- was my father's father. I learned to read out of his Bible, and with a musket he that day captured from the foe, I learned also another religious lesson, that "Rebellion to Tyrants is Obedience to God." I keep them both "Sacred to Liberty and the Rights of Mankind," to use them both "In the Sacred Cause of God and my Country."

THE HOMES OF THE PEOPLE

Reprinted with the permission of Henry W. Grady, Jr.

BY HENRY W. GRADY

I went to Washington the other day, and I stood on the Capitol Hill; my heart beat quick as I looked at the towering marble of my country's Capitol, and the mist gathered in my eyes as I thought of its tremendous significance, and the armies and the treasury, and the judges and the President, and the Congress and the courts, and all that was gathered there. And I felt that the sun in all its course could not look down on a better sight than that majestic home of a republic that had taught the world its best lessons of liberty. And I felt that if honor and wisdom and justice abided therein, the world would at last owe that great house in which the ark of the covenant of my country is lodged, its final uplifting and its regeneration.

Two days afterward, I went to visit a friend in the country, a modest man, with a quiet country home. It was just a simple, unpretentious house, set about with big trees, encircled in meadow and field rich with the promise of harvest.

Inside was quiet, cleanliness, thrift, and comfort. Outside, there stood my friend, the master, a simple, upright man, with no mortgage on his roof, no lien on his growing crops, master of his own land and master of himself. There was his old father, an aged, trembling man, but happy in the heart and home of his son.

They started to their home, and as they reached the door the old mother came with the sunset falling fair on her face, and lighting up her deep, patient eyes, while her lips, trembling with the rich music of her heart, bade her husband and son welcome to their home. Beyond was the housewife, busy with her household cares, clean of heart and conscience, the buckler and helpmeet of her husband. Down the lane came the children, trooping home after the cows, seeking as truant birds do the quiet of their home nest.

And I saw the night come down on that house, falling gently as the wings of the unseen dove. And the old man--while a startled bird called from the forest, and the trees were shrill with the cricket's cry, and the stars were swarming in the sky--got the family around him, and, taking the old Bible from the table, called them to their knees, the little baby hiding in the folds of its mother's dress, while he closed the record of that simple day by calling down God's benediction on that family and on that home. And while I gazed, the vision of that marble Capitol faded. Forgotten were its treasures and its majesty, and I said, "Oh, surely here in the homes of the people are lodged at last the strength and the responsibility of this government, the hope and the promise of this republic."

GENERAL ULYSSES S. GRANT
BY CANON G. W. FARRAR

When Abraham Lincoln sat, book in hand, day after day, under the tree, moving round it as the shadow crossed, absorbed in mastering his task; when James Garfield rang the bell at Hiram Institute on the very stroke of the hour and swept the schoolroom as faithfully as he mastered his Greek lesson; when Ulysses Grant, sent with his team to meet some men who came to load his cart with logs, and, finding no men, loaded the cart with his own boy's strength, they showed in the conscientious performance of duty the qualities which were to raise them to become kings of men. When John Adams was told that his son, John Quincy Adams, had been elected President of the United States, he said, "He has always been laborious, child and man, from infancy."

But the youth was not destined to die in the deep valley of obscurity and toil, in which it is the lot--and perhaps the happy lot--of most of us to spend our little lives. The hour came; the man was needed. In 1861 there broke out that most terrible war of modern days. Grant received a commission as Colonel of Volunteers, and in four years the struggling toiler had been raised to the chief command of a vaster army than has ever been handled by any mortal man. Who could have imagined that four years would make that enormous difference? But it is often so. The great men needed for some tremendous crisis have stepped often, as it were, out of a door in the wall which no man had noticed; and, unannounced, unheralded, without prestige, have made their way silently and single-handed to the front. And there was no luck in it. It was a work of inflexible faithfulness, of indomitable resolution, of sleepless energy, and iron purpose and tenacity. In the campaigns at Fort Donelson; in the desperate battle at Shiloh; in the siege of Corinth; in battle after battle, in seige after seige; whatever Grant had to do, he did it with his might. Other generals might fail--he would not fail. He showed what a man could do whose will was strong. He undertook, as General Sherman said of him, what no one else would have ventured and his very soldiers began to reflect something of his indomitable determination.

His sayings revealed the man. "I have nothing to do with opinions," he said at the outset," and shall only deal with armed rebellion." "In riding over the field," he said at Shiloh, "I saw that either side was ready to give way, if the other showed a bold front. I took the opportunity, and ordered an advance along the whole line." "No terms," he wrote to General Buckner at Fort Donelson (and it is pleasant to know that General Buckner stood as a warm friend beside his dying bed); "no terms other than unconditional surrender can be accepted." "My headquarters," he wrote from Vicksburg, "will be on the field." With a military genius which embraced the vastest plans while attending to the smallest details, he defeated, one after another, every great general of the Confederates except Stonewall Jackson. The Southerners felt that he held them as in the grasp of a vise; that this man could neither be arrested nor avoided. For all this he has been severely blamed. He ought not to be blamed. He has been called a butcher, which is grossly unjust. He loved peace; he hated bloodshed; his heart was generous and kind. His orders were to save lives, to save treasure, but at all costs to save his country--and he did save his country.

After the surrender at Appomattox Court House, the war was over. He had put his hand to the plow and had looked not back. He had made blow after blow, each following where the last had struck; he had wielded like a hammer the gigantic forces at his disposal, and had smitten opposition into the dust. It was a mighty work, and he had done it well. Surely history has shown that for the future destinies of a mighty nation it was a necessary and blessed work!

AMERICAN COURAGE

From the copyrighted print in "A Modern Reader and Speaker," by George Riddle, with the permission of Duffield and Company, New York, publishers.

BY SHERMAN HOAR

I fear we undervalue the devotion to country which comes from a contemplation of what has been done and suffered in her name. I feel that we teach those who are to make or mar the future of this nation too much of what has been done elsewhere, and too little of what has been done here. Courage is the characteristic of no one land or time. The world's history is full of it and the lessons it teaches. American courage, however, is of this nation; it is ours, and if the finest national spirit is worth the creating; if patriotism is still a quality to be engendered in our youth; if love of country is still to be a strong power for good, those acts of devotion and of heroic personal sacrifice with which our history is filled, are worthy of earnest study, of continued contemplation, and of perpetual consideration.

"Let him who will, sing deeds done well across the sea,
Here, lovely Land, men bravely live and die for Thee."

The particular example I desire to speak about is of that splendid quality of courage which dares everything not for self or country, but for an enemy. It is of that kind which is called into existence not by dreams of glory, or by love of land, but by the highest human desire; the desire to mitigate suffering in those who are against us.

In the afternoon of the day after the battle of Fredericksburg, General Kershaw of the Confederate army was sitting in his quarters when suddenly a young South Carolinian named Kirkland entered, and, after the usual salutations, said: "General, I can't stand this." The general, thinking the statement a little abrupt, asked what it was he could not stand, and Kirkland replied: "Those poor fellows out yonder have been crying for water all day, and I have come to you to ask if I may go and give them some." The "poor fellows" were Union soldiers who lay wounded between the Union and Confederate lines. To go to them, Kirkland must go beyond the protection of the breastworks and expose himself to a fire from the Union sharpshooters, who, so far during that day, had made the raising above the Confederate works of so much as a head an act of extreme danger. General Kershaw at first refused to allow Kirkland to go on his errand, but at last, as the lad persisted in his request, declined to forbid him, leaving the responsibility for action with the boy himself. Kirkland, in perfect delight, rushed from the general's quarters to the front, where he gathered all the canteens he could carry, filled them with water, and going over the breastworks, started to give relief to his wounded enemies. No sooner was he in the open field than our sharpshooters, supposing he was going to plunder their comrades, began to fire at him. For some minutes he went about doing good under circumstances of most imminent personal danger. Soon, however, those to whom he was taking the water recognized the character of his undertaking. All over the field men sat up and called to him, and those too hurt to raise themselves, held up their hands and beckoned to him. Soon our sharpshooters, who luckily had not hit him, saw that he was indeed an Angel of Mercy, and stopped their fire, and two armies looked with admiration at the young man's pluck and loving- kindness. With a beautiful tenderness, Kirkland went about his work, giving of the water to all, and here and there placing a knapsack pillow under some poor wounded fellow's head, or putting in a more comfortable position some shattered leg or arm. Then he went back to his own lines and the fighting went on. Tell me of a more exalted example of personal courage and self-denial than that of that Confederate soldier, or one which more clearly deserves the name of Christian fortitude. In that terrible War of the Rebellion, Kirkland gave up his life for a mistaken cause in the battle of Chickamauga, but I cannot help thanking God that, in our reunited country, we are joint heirs with the men from the South in the glory and inspiration that come from such heroic deeds as his.

THE MINUTEMEN OF THE REVOLUTION

Reprinted, with permission, from "The Orations and Addresses of George William Curtis," Vol. III. Copyright, 1894, by Harper and Brothers.

BY GEORGE WILLIAM CURTIS

The Minuteman of the Revolution! And who was he? He was the old, the middle-aged, and the young. He was the husband and the father, who left his plow in the furrow and his hammer on the bench, and marched to die or be free. He was the son and lover, the plain, shy youth of the singing school and the village choir, whose heart beat to arms for his country, and who felt, though he could not say with the old English cavalier:--

"I could not love thee, dear, so much,

Loved I not honor more."

He was the man who was willing to pour out his life's blood for a principle. Intrenched in his own honesty, the king's gold could not buy him; enthroned in the love of his fellow citizens, the king's writ could not take him; and when, on the morning of Lexington, the king's troops marched to seize him, his sublime faith saw, beyond the clouds of the moment, the rising sun of the America we behold, and, careless of himself, mindful only of his country, he exultingly exclaimed, "Oh, what a glorious morning!" And then, amid the flashing hills, the ringing woods, the flaming roads, he smote with terror the haughty British column, and sent it shrinking, bleeding, wavering, and reeling through the streets of the village, panic-stricken and broken.

Him we gratefully recall to-day; him we commit in his immortal youth to the reverence of our children. And here amid these peaceful fields,-- here in the heart of Middlesex County, of Lexington and Concord and Bunker Hill, stand fast, Son of Liberty, as the minuteman stood at the old North Bridge. But should we or our descendants, false to justice or humanity, betray in any way their cause, spring into life as a hundred years ago, take one more step, descend, and lead us, as God led you in saving America, to save the hopes of man.

No hostile fleet for many a year has vexed the waters of our coast; nor is any army but our own likely to tread our soil. Not such are our enemies to-day. They do not come, proudly stepping to the drumbeat, their bayonets flashing in the morning sun. But wherever party spirit shall strain the ancient guarantees of freedom; or bigotry and ignorance shall lay their fatal hands on education; or the arrogance of caste shall strike at equal rights; or corruption shall poison the very springs of national life,--there, Minuteman of Liberty, are your Lexington Green and Concord Bridge. And as you love your country and your kind, and would have your children rise up and call you blessed, spare not the enemy. Over the hills, out of the earth, down from the clouds, pour in resistless might. Fire from every rock and tree, from door and window, from hearthstone and chamber. Hang upon his flank from morn to sunset, and so, through a land blazing with indignation, hurl the hordes of ignorance and corruption and injustice back--back in utter defeat and ruin.

PAUL REVERE'S RIDE

Reprinted with permission from "The Orations and Addresses of George William Curtis," Vol. III. Copyright 1894, by Harper and Brothers.

BY GEORGE WILLIAM CURTIS

On Tuesday, April 18, 1775, Gage, the royal governor, who had decided to send a force to Concord to destroy the stores, picketed the roads from Boston into Middlesex, to prevent any report of the intended march from spreading into the country. But the very air was electric. In the tension of the popular mind, every sound and sight was significant. In the afternoon, one of the governor's grooms strolled into a stable where John Ballard was cleaning a horse. John Ballard was a son of liberty; and when the groom idly remarked in nervous English "about what would occur to-morrow," John's heart leaped and his hand shook, and, asking the groom to finish cleaning the horse, he ran to a friend, who carried the news straight to Paul Revere.

Gage thought that his secret had been kept, but Lord Percy, who had heard the people say on the Common that the troops would miss their aim, undeceived him. Gage instantly ordered that no one should leave the town. But Dr. Warren was before him, and, as the troops crossed the river, Paul Revere was rowing over the river farther down to Charlestown, having agreed with his friend, Robert Newman, to show lanterns from the belfry of the Old North Church,--

"One, if by land, and two, if by sea,"

as a signal of the march of the British. It was a brilliant April night. The winter had been unusually mild and the spring very forward. The hills were already green; the early grain waved in the fields, and the air was sweet with blossoming orchards. Under the cloudless moon the soldiers silently marched, and Paul Revere swiftly rode, galloping through Medford and West Cambridge, rousing every house as he went, spurring for Lexington and Hancock and Adams, and evading the British patrols, who had been sent out to stop the news.

Stop the news! Already the village church bells were beginning to ring the alarm, as the pulpits beneath them had been ringing for many a year. In the awakening houses lights flashed from window to window. Drums beat faintly far away and on every side. Signal guns flashed and echoed. The watchdogs barked; the cocks crew.

Stop the news! Stop the sunrise! The murmuring night trembled with the summons so earnestly expected, so dreaded, so desired. And as, long ago, the voice rang out at midnight along the Syrian shore, wailing that great Pan was dead, but in the same moment the choiring angels whispered, "Glory to God in the highest, for Christ is born," so, if the stern alarm of that April night seemed to many a wistful and loyal heart to portend the passing glory of British dominion and the tragical chance of war, it whispered to them with prophetic inspiration, "Good will to men; America is born!"

There is a tradition that long before the troops reached Lexington an unknown horseman thundered at the door of Captain Joseph Robbins in Acton, waking every man and woman and babe in the cradle, shouting that the regulars were marching to Concord and that the rendezvous was the old North Bridge. Captain Robbins' son, a boy of ten years, heard the summons in the garret where he lay, and in a few minutes was on his father's old mare, a young Paul Revere, galloping along the road to rouse Captain Isaac Davis, who commanded the minutemen of Acton. The company assembled at his shop, formed, and marched a little way, when he halted them and returned for a moment to his house. He said to his wife, "Take good care of the children," kissed her, turned to his men, gave the order to march, and saw his home no more. Such was the history of that night in how many homes!

The hearts of those men and women of Middlesex might break, but they could not waver. They had counted the cost. They knew what and whom they served; and, as the midnight summons came, they started up and answered, "Here am I!"

THE ARTS OF THE ANCIENTS

From "Speeches and Lectures," with the permission of Lothrop, Lee and Shepard, Boston, publishers.

BY WENDELL PHILLIPS

We have a pitying estimate, a tender compassion, for the narrowness, ignorance, and darkness of the bygone ages. We seem to ourselves not only to monopolize, but to have begun, the era of light. In other words, we are all running over with a fourth-day-of-July spirit of self-content. I am often reminded of the German whom the English poet Coleridge met at Frankfort. He always took off his hat with profound respect when he ventured to speak of himself. It seems to me, the American people might be painted in the chronic attitude of taking off its hat to itself.

Considering their employment of the mechanical forces, and their movement of large masses from the earth, we know that the Egyptians had the five, seven, or three mechanical powers; but we cannot account for the multiplication and increase necessary to perform the wonders they accomplished.

There is a book telling how Domenico Fontana of the sixteenth century set up the Egyptian obelisk at Rome on end, in the Papacy of Sixtus V. Wonderful! Yet the Egyptians quarried that stone, and carried it a hundred and fifty miles, and the Romans brought it seven hundred and fifty miles, and never said a word about it.

Take canals. The Suez canal absorbs half its receipts in cleaning out the sand which fills it continually, and it is not yet known whether it is a pecuniary success. The ancients built a canal at right angles to ours; because they knew it would not fill up if built in that direction, and they knew such a one as ours would. There were magnificent canals in the land of the Jews, with perfectly arranged gates and sluices. We have only just begun to understand ventilation properly for our houses; yet late experiments at the Pyramids in Egypt show that those Egyptian tombs were ventilated in the most perfect and scientific manner.

Again, cement is modern, for the ancients dressed and joined their stones so closely, that, in buildings thousands of years old the thin blade of a penknife cannot be forced between them. The railroad dates back to Egypt. Arago has claimed that they had a knowledge of steam. A painting has been discovered of a ship full of machinery, and a could only be accounted for by supposing the motive power to have been steam. Bramah acknowledges that he took the idea of his celebrated lock from an ancient Egyptian pattern. De Tocqueville says that there was no social question that was not discussed to rags in Egypt.

"Well," say you, "Franklin invented the lightning rod." I have no doubt he did; but years before his invention, and before muskets were invented, the old soldiers on guard on the towers used Franklin's invention to keep guard with; and if a spark passed between them and the spearhead, they ran and bore the warning of the state and condition of affairs. After that you will admit that Benjamin Franklin was not the only one that knew of the presence of electricity, and the advantages derived from its use. Solomon's Temple you will find was situated on an exposed point of the hill: the temple was so lofty that it was often in peril, and was guarded by a system exactly like that of Benjamin Franklin.

Well, I may tell you a little of ancient manufactures. The Duchess of Burgundy took a necklace from the neck of a mummy, and wore it to a ball given at the Tuileries; and everybody said they thought it was the newest thing there. A Hindoo princess came into court; and her father, seeing her, said, "Go home, you are not decently covered,--go home;" and she said, "Father, I have seven suits on;" but the suits were of muslin so thin that the king could see through them, A Roman poet says, "the girl was in the poetic dress of the country." I fancy the French would be rather astonished at this. Four hundred and fifty years ago the first spinning machine was introduced into Europe. I have evidence to show that it made its first appearance two thousand years before.

Why have I groped among these ashes? I have told you these facts to show you that we have not invented everything--that we do not monopolize the encyclopedia. The past had knowledge. But it was the knowledge of the classes, not of the masses. "The beauty that was Greece and the grandeur that was Rome" were exclusive, the possession of the few. The science of Egypt was amazing; but it meant privilege-- the privilege of the king and the priest. It separated royalty and priesthood from the people, and was the engine of oppression. When Cambyses came down from Persia and thundered across Egypt, treading out royalty and priesthood, he trampled out at the same time civilization itself.

The distinctive glory of the nineteenth century is that it distributes knowledge; that it recognizes the divine will, which is that every man has a right to know whatever may be serviceable to himself or to his fellows; that it makes the church, the schoolhouse, and the town hall, its symbols, and humanity its care. This democratic spirit will animate our arts with immortality, if God means that they shall last.

A MAN WITHOUT A COUNTRY

An extract from "A Man Without a Country"

BY EDWARD EVERETT HALE

Philip Nolan was as fine a young officer as there was in the "Legion of the West," as the Western division of our army was then called. When Aaron Burr made his first dashing expedition down to New Orleans in 1805, at Fort Massac, or somewhere above on the river, he met, as the devil would have it, this gay, dashing, bright young fellow; at some dinner party, I think. Burr marked him, talked to him, walked with him, took him a day or two's voyage in his flatboat, and, in short, fascinated him. For the next year, barrack life was very tame to poor Nolan. He occasionally availed himself of the permission the great man had given him to write to him. Long, high-worded, stilted letters the poor boy wrote and rewrote and copied. But never a line did he have in reply from the gay deceiver. The other boys in the garrison sneered at him, because he sacrificed in this unrequited affection for a politician the time which they devoted to Monongahela, hazard, and high-low-jack. But one day Nolan had his revenge. This time Burr came down the river, not as an attorney seeking a place for his office, but as a disguised conquerer. He had defeated I know not how many district attorneys; he had dined at I know not how many public dinners; he had been heralded in I don't know how many "Weekly Arguses," and it was rumored that he had an army behind him and an empire before him. It was a great day--his arrival--to poor Nolan. Burr had not been at the fort an hour before he sent for him. That evening he asked Nolan to take him out in his skiff, to show him a canebrake or a cottonwood tree, as he said--really to seduce him; and by the time the sail was over, Nolan was enlisted body and soul. From that time, though he did not yet know it, he lived as A MAN WITHOUT A COUNTRY.

What Burr meant to do I know no more than you. It is none of our business just now. Only, when the grand catastrophe came, and Jefferson and the House of Virginia of that day undertook to break on the wheel all the possible Clarences of the then House of York, by the great treason trial at Richmond, some of the lesser fry in that distant Mississippi Valley, which was farther from us than Puget's Sound is to-day, introduced the like novelty on their provincial stage; and, to while away the monotony of the summer at Fort Adams, got up, for "spectacles," a string of court-martials on the officers there. One and another of the colonels and majors were tried, and, to fill out the list, little Nolan, against whom, Heaven knows, there was evidence enough--that he was sick of the service, had been willing to be false to it, and would have obeyed any order to march any-whither with any one who would follow him had the order been signed, "By command of His Exc. A. Burr." The courts dragged on. The big flies escaped--rightly for all I know. Nolan was proved guilty enough, as I say; yet you and I would never have heard of him, but that, when the president of the court asked him at the close whether he wished to say anything to show that he had always been faithful to the United States, he cried out, in a fit of frenzy:--"Damn the United States! I wish I may never hear of the United States again!"

I suppose he did not know how the words shocked old Colonel Morgan, who was holding the court. He, on his part, had grown up in the West of those days, in the midst of "Spanish plot," "Orleans plot," and all the rest. He had spent half his youth with an older brother, hunting horses in Texas; and, in a word, to him "United States" was scarcely a reality. Yet he had been fed by "United States" for all the years since he had been in the army. He had sworn on his faith as a Christian to be true to "United States." It was "United States" which gave him the uniform he wore, and the sword by his side. I do not excuse Nolan; I only explain to the reader why he damned his country, and wished he might never hear her name again.

He never did hear her name but once again. From that moment, September 23, 1807, till the day he died, May 11, 1863, he never heard her name again. For that half century and more he was a man without a country.

Old Morgan, as I said, was terribly shocked. He called the court into his private room, and returned in fifteen minutes, with a face like a sheet, to say:--

"Prisoner, hear the sentence of the court! The court decides, subject to the approval of the president, that you never hear the name of the United States again."

Nolan laughed. But nobody else laughed. Old Morgan was too solemn, and the whole room was hushed dead as night for a minute. Even Nolan lost his swagger in a moment. Then Morgan added:--

"Mr. Marshal, take the prisoner to Orleans in an armed boat, and deliver him to the naval commander there."

The marshal gave his orders and the prisoner was taken out of court.

"Mr. Marshal," continued old Morgan, "see that no one mentions the United States to the prisoner. Mr. Marshal, make my respects to Lieutenant Mitchell at Orleans, and request him to order that no one shall mention the United States to the prisoner while he is on board ship. You will receive your written orders from the officer on duty here this evening. The court is adjourned without day."

The plan then adopted was substantially the same which was necessarily followed ever after. The Secretary of the Navy was requested to put Nolan on board a government vessel bound on a long cruise, and to direct that he should be only so far confined there as to make it certain that he never saw or heard of the country. One afternoon a lot of the men sat on the deck smoking and reading aloud. Well, so it happened that in his turn Nolan took the book and read to the others; and he read very well. Nobody in the circle knew a line of the poem, only it was all magic and Border chivalry, and was ten thousand years ago. Poor Nolan read steadily through the fifth canto without a thought of what was coming:--

"Breathes there the man with soul so dead,
Who never to himself hath said,"--

It seems impossible to us that anybody ever heard this for the first time; but all these fellows did then, and poor Nolan himself went on, still unconsciously or mechanically:--

"This is my own, my native land!"

Then they all saw something was to pay; but he expected to get through, I suppose, turned a little pale, but plunged on:--

"Whose heart hath ne'er within him burned
As home his footsteps he hath turned
From wandering on a foreign strand?--
If such there breathe, go, mark him well,"--

By this time the men were all beside themselves, wishing there was any way to make him turn over two pages; but he had not quite presence of mind for that; he gagged a little, colored crimson, and staggered on:--

"For him no minstrel raptures swell;
High though his titles, proud his name,
Boundless his wealth as wish can claim,
Despite these titles, power, and pelf,
The wretch, concentred all in self,"--

and here the poor fellow choked, could not go on, but started up, swung the book into the sea, vanished into his stateroom, and we did not see him for two months again. He never entered in with the young men exactly as a companion again; but generally he had the nervous, tired look of a heart-wounded man.

And when Nolan died, there was found in his Bible a slip of paper at the place where he had marked the text:--

"They desire a country, even a heavenly; wherefore God is not ashamed to be called their God; for He hath prepared for them a city."

On this slip of paper he had written:--

"Bury me in the sea; it has been my home, and I love it. But will not some one set up a stone for my memory at Fort Adams or at Orleans, that my disgrace may not be more than I ought to bear? Say on it:--

"In Memory of

"PHILIP NOLAN,

"Lieutenant in the Army of the United States.

"He loved his country as no other man has loved her; but no man deserved less at her hands."

THE EXECUTION OF RODRIGUEZ

From "Cuba in War Time," with the author's permission

BY RICHARD HARDING DAVIS

Adolfo Rodriguez was the only son of a Cuban farmer. When the revolution broke out, young Rodriguez joined the insurgents, leaving his father and mother and two sisters at the farm. He was taken by the Spanish, was tried by a military court for bearing arms against the government, and sentenced to be shot by a fusillade some morning before sunrise. His execution took place a half mile distant from the city, on the great plain that stretches from the forts out to the hills, beyond which Rodriguez had lived for nineteen years.

There had been a full moon the night preceding the execution, and when the squad of soldiers marched out from town, it was still shining brightly through the mists. It lighted a plain two miles in extent broken by ridges and gullies and covered with thick, high grass and with bunches of cactus and palmetto.

The execution was quickly finished with rough, and, but for one frightful blunder, with merciful swiftness. The crowd fell back when it came to the square of soldiery, and the condemned man, the priests, and the firing squad of six young volunteers passed in and the lines closed behind them.

Rodriguez bent and kissed the cross which the priest held up before him. He then walked to where the officer directed him to stand, and turned his back to the square and faced the hills and the road across them which led to his father's farm. As the officer gave the first command he straightened himself as far as the cords would allow, and held up his head and fixed his eyes immovably on the morning light which had just begun to show above the hills.

The officer had given the order, the men had raised their pieces, and the condemned man had heard the clicks of the triggers as they were pulled back, and he had not moved. And then happened one of the most cruelly refined, though unintentional, acts of torture that one can very well imagine. As the officer slowly raised his sword, preparatory to giving the signal, one of the mounted officers rode up to him and pointed out silently--the firing squad were so placed that when they fired they would shoot several of the soldiers stationed on the extreme end of the square.

Their captain motioned his men to lower their pieces, and then walked across the grass and laid his hand on the shoulder of the waiting prisoner. It is not pleasant to think what that shock must have been. The man had steeled himself to receive a volley of bullets in the back. He believed that in the next instant he would be in another world; he had heard the command given, had heard the click of the Mausers as the locks caught--and then, at that supreme moment, a human hand had been laid upon his shoulder and a voice spoke in his ear.

You would expect that any man who had been snatched back to life in such a fashion would start and tremble at the reprieve, or would break down altogether, but this boy turned his head steadily, and followed with his eyes the direction of the officer's sword, then nodded his head gravely, and with his shoulders squared, took up a new position, straightened his back again, and once more held himself erect. As an exhibition of self-control this should surely rank above feats of heroism performed in battle, where there are thousands of comrades to give inspiration. This man was alone, in sight of the hills he knew, with only enemies about him, with no source to draw on for strength but that which lay within himself.

The officer of the firing squad, mortified by his blunder, hastily whipped up his sword, the men once more leveled their rifles, the sword rose, dropped, and the men fired. At the report the Cuban's head snapped back almost between his shoulders, but his body fell slowly, as though some one had pushed him gently forward from behind and he had stumbled. He sank on his side in the wet grass without a struggle or sound, and did not move again.

At that moment the sun, which had shown some promise of its coming in the glow above the hills, shot up suddenly from behind them in all the splendor of the tropics, a fierce, red disk of heat, and filled the air with warmth and light.

THE INFORMAL DISCUSSION

THE FLOOD OF BOOKS
From "Essays in Application," with the permission of Charles Scribner's Sons, New York, publishers.
BY HENRY VAN DYKE

There is the highest authority for believing that a man's life, even though he be an author, consists not in the abundance of things that he possesses. Rather is its real value to be sought in the quality of the ideas and feelings that possess him, and in the effort to embody them in his work.

The work is the great thing. The delight of clear and steady thought, of free and vivid imagination, of pure and strong emotion; the fascination of searching for the right words, which sometimes come in shoals like herring, so that the net can hardly contain them, and at other times are more shy and fugacious than the wary trout which refuse to be lured from their hiding places; the pleasure of putting the fit phrase in the proper place, of making a conception stand out plain and firm with no more and no less than is needed for its expression, of doing justice to an imaginary character so that it shall have its own life and significance in the world of fiction, of working a plot or an argument clean through to its inevitable close: these inward and unpurchasable joys are the best wages of the men and women who write.

What more will they get? Well, unless history forgets to repeat itself, their additional wages, their personal dividends under the profit- sharing system, so to speak, will be various. Some will probably get more than they deserve, others less.

The next best thing to the joy of work is the winning of gentle readers and friends who find some good in your book, and are grateful for it, and think kindly of you for writing it.

The next best thing to that is the recognition, on the part of people who know, that your work is well done, and of fine quality. That is called fame, or glory, and the writer who professes to care nothing for it is probably deceiving himself, or else his liver is out of order. Real reputation, even of a modest kind and of a brief duration, is a good thing; an author ought to be able to be happy without it, but happier with it.

EFFECTIVENESS IN SPEAKING

From the Introduction to "The World's Famous Orations," with the permission of Funk and Wagnalls Company, New York and London, publishers.

BY WILLIAM JENNINGS BRYAN

While it is absolutely necessary for the orator to master his subject and to speak with earnestness, his speech can be made more effective by the addition of clearness, brevity and apt illustrations.

Clearness of statement is of very great importance. It is not sufficient to say that there are certain self-evident truths; it is more accurate to say that all truth is self-evident. Because truth is self-evident, the best service that one can render a truth is to state it so clearly that it can be comprehended, needs no argument in its support. In debate, therefore, one's first effort should be to state his own side so clearly and concisely as to make the principles involved easily understood. His second object should be so to divest his opponent's argument of useless verbiage as to make it stand forth clearly; for as truth is self-evident, so error bears upon its face its own condemnation. Error needs only to be exposed to be overthrown.

Brevity of statement also contributes to the force of a speaker. It is possible so to enfold a truth in long-drawn-out sentences as practically to conceal it. The epigram is powerful because it is full of meat and short enough to be remembered. To know when to stop is almost as important as to know where to begin and how to proceed. The ability to condense great thoughts into small words and brief sentences is an attribute of genius. Often one lays down a book with the feeling that the author has "said nothing with elaboration," while in perusing another book one finds a whole sermon in a single sentence, or an unanswerable argument couched in a well-turned phrase.

The interrogatory is frequently employed by the orator, and when wisely used is irresistible. What dynamic power for instance, there is in that question propounded by Christ, "What shall it profit a man if he gain the whole world and lose his own soul?" Volumes could not have presented so effectively the truth that he sought to impress upon his hearers.

The illustration has no unimportant place in the equipment of the orator. We understand a thing more easily when we know that it is like something which we have already seen. Illustrations may be drawn from two sources--nature and literature--and of the two, those from nature have the greater weight. All learning is valuable; all history is useful. By knowing what has been we can better judge the future; by knowing how men have acted heretofore we can understand how they will act again in similar circumstances. But people know nature better than they know books, and the illustrations drawn from everyday life are the most effective.

If the orator can seize upon something within the sight or hearing of his audience,--something that comes to his notice at the moment and as if not thought of before,--it will add to the effectiveness of the illustration. For instance, Paul's speech to the Athenians derived a large part of its strength from the fact that he called attention to an altar near by, erected "to the Unknown God," and then proceeded to declare unto them the God whom they ignorantly worshiped.

Abraham Lincoln used scripture quotations very frequently and very powerfully. Probably no Bible quotation, or, for that matter, no quotation from any book ever has had more influence upon a people than the famous quotation made by Lincoln in his Springfield speech of 1858,--"A house divided against itself cannot stand." It is said that he had searched for some time for a phrase which would present in the strongest possible way the proposition he intended to advance--namely, that the nation could not endure half slave and half free.

It is a compliment to a public speaker that the audience should discuss what he says rather than his manner of saying it; more complimentary that they should remember his arguments, than that they should praise his rhetoric. The orator should seek to conceal himself behind his subject. If he presents himself in every speech he is sure to become monotonous, if not offensive. If, however, he focuses attention upon his subject, he can find an infinite number of themes and, therefore, give variety to his speech.

BOOKS, LITERATURE, AND THE PEOPLE

From "Essays in Application," with the permission of Charles Scribner's Sons, New York, publishers.

BY HENRY VAN DYKE

Every one knows what books are. But what is literature? It is the ark on the flood. It is the light on the candlestick. It is the flower among the leaves; the consummation of the plant's vitality, the crown of its beauty, and the treasure house of its seeds. It is hard to define, easy to describe.

Literature is made up of those writings which translate the inner meanings of nature and life, in language of distinction and charm, touched with the personality of the author, into artistic forms of permanent interest. The best literature, then, is that which has the deepest significance, the most lucid style, the most vivid individuality, and the most enduring form.

On the last point contemporary judgment is but guess-work, but on the three other points it should not be impossible to form, nor improper to express, a definite opinion.

Literature has its permanent marks. It is a connected growth, and its life history is unbroken. Masterpieces have never been produced by men who have had no masters. Reverence for good work is the foundation of literary character. The refusal to praise bad work, or to imitate it, is an author's personal chastity.

Good work is the most honorable and lasting thing in the world. Four elements enter into good work in literature:--An original impulse--not necessarily a new idea, but a new sense of the value of an idea. A first-hand study of the subject and the material. A patient, joyful, unsparing labor for the perfection of form. A human aim--to cheer, console, purify, or ennoble the life of the people. Without this aim literature has never sent an arrow close to the mark. It is only by good work that men of letters can justify their right to a place in the world. The father of Thomas Carlyle was a stonemason, whose walls stood true and needed no rebuilding. Carlyle's prayer was, "Let me write my books as he built his houses."

EDUCATION FOR BUSINESS

From an address before the New York Chamber of Commerce, 1890

BY CHARLES WILLIAM ELIOT

Before we can talk together to advantage about the value of education in business, we ought to come to a common understanding about the sort of education we mean and the sort of business.

We must not think of the liberal education of to-day as dealing with a dead past--with dead languages, buried peoples, exploded philosophies; on the contrary, everything which universities now teach is quick with life and capable of application to modern uses. They teach indeed the languages and literature of Judea, Greece, and Rome; but it is because those literatures are instinct with eternal life. They teach mathematics, but it is mathematics mostly created within the lifetime of the older men here present. In teaching English, French, and German, they are teaching the modern vehicles of all learning--just what Latin was in medieval times. As to history, political science, and natural science, the subjects, and all the methods by which they are taught, may properly be said to be new within a century. Liberal education is not to be justly regarded as something dry, withered, and effete; it is as full of sap as the cedars of Lebanon.

And what sort of business do we mean? Surely the larger sorts of legitimate and honorable business; that business which is of advantage both to buyer and seller, and to producer, distributor, and consumer alike, whether individuals or nations, which makes common some useful thing which has been rare, or makes accessible to the masses good things which have been within reach only of the few--I wish I could say simply which make dear things cheap; but recent political connotations of the word cheap forbid. We mean that great art of production and exchange which through the centuries has increased human comfort, cherished peace, fostered the fine arts, developed the pregnant principle of associated action, and promoted both public security and public liberty.

With this understanding of what we mean by education on the one hand and business on the other, let us see if there can be any doubt as to the nature of the relations between them. The business man in large affairs requires keen observation, a quick mental grasp of new subjects, and a wide range of knowledge. Whence come these powers and attainments--either to the educated or to the uneducated--save through practice and study? But education is only early systematic practice and study under guidance. The object of all good education is to develop just these powers--accuracy in observation, quickness and certainty in seizing upon the main points of new subjects, and discrimination in separating the trivial from the important in great masses of facts. This is what liberal education does for the physician, the lawyer, the minister, and the scientist. This is what it can do also for the man of business; to give a mental power is one of the main ends of the higher education.

Is not active business a field in which mental power finds full play? Again, education imparts knowledge, and who has greater need to know economics, history, and natural science than the man of large business?

Further, liberal education develops a sense of right, duty, and honor; and more and more, in the modern world, large business rests on rectitude and honor, as well as on good judgment. Education does this through the contemplation and study of the moral ideals of our race; not in drowsiness or dreaminess or in mere vague enjoyment of poetic and religious abstractions, but in the resolute purpose to apply spiritual ideals to actual life. The true university fosters ideals, but always to urge that they be put into practice in the real world. When the universities hold up before their youth the great Semitic ideals which were embodied in the Decalogue, they mean that those ideals should be applied in politics. When they teach their young men that Asiatic ideal of unknown antiquity, the Golden Rule, they mean that their disciples shall apply it to business; when they inculcate that comprehensive maxim of Christian ethics, "Ye are all members of one another," they mean that this moral principle is applicable to all human relations, whether between individuals, families, states, or nations.

THE BEGINNINGS OF AMERICAN ORATORY

From the author's lectures on oratory, with his permission

BY THOMAS WENTWORTH HIGGINSON

It is a singular fact that the three leaders of the revolution, in the Massachusetts colony, John Adams, Sam Adams, and Oxenbridge Thatcher, were all trained originally to be clergymen, and all afterwards determined to be lawyers, and get their legal training in addition. John Adams did it; Oxenbridge Thatcher did it. Sam Adams's parents held so hard to the doctrine that the law was a disreputable profession that they never allowed him to enter it. He went into business, but before he got through, mixed himself up with legal questions more than the two others put together. And what is more, and what has only lately been brought out distinctly, there existed in the southern colonies represented by Virginia very much the same feeling, only coming from a different source. It was not a question of church membership or of ecclesiastical training--the southern colonies never troubled themselves very much about those things--but turned upon a wholly different thing. The southern colonies were based on land ownership; the aim was to build up a type of society like the English type, an aristocratic system of landowners as in England. And these miscellaneous men who, without owning large estates or large numbers of slaves, came forward to try cases in court, were regarded with the same sort of suspicion which the same class had to meet in Massachusetts.

Patrick Henry, the greatest of Virginians for the purpose for which Providence had marked him out, was always regarded by Jefferson in very much the same light in which Sam Adams was by his uncles, who were afraid he wanted to be a lawyer. Henry was regarded as a man from the people, an irregularly trained man. Jefferson, you will find, criticizes his pronunciation severely. He talked about "yearth" instead of "earth." He said that a man's "nateral" parts needed to be improved by "eddication." Jefferson had traveled in Europe and talked with cultivated men in other countries. He did not do that sort of thing, and he, not being a man of the most generous or candid nature, always tries to make us think that Patrick Henry was a nobody who had very little practice. And it was not until the admirable life of him written for the "American Statesmen" series by my predecessor in this lectureship, Moses Coit Tyler, whose loss we so greatly mourn, that it was clearly made out that, on the contrary, he had an immense legal practice and was wonderfully successful in a great variety of cases.

So, both North and South, there was this antagonism to this new class coming forward; and yet that new class stepped forward and took the leadership of the American Revolution. Not that the clergy were false to their duty. They did their duty well. There is a book by J. Wingate Thornton, called "The Clergy of the American Revolution," which contains an admirable and powerful series of sermons by those very clergymen whom I have criticized for their limitations. They did their part admirably, and yet one sees as time goes on that the lawyers are taking matters into their own hands.

But the change was not always a benefit to the style of oratory. It was a period of somewhat formal style; it was not a period when the English language was reaching to its highest sources. You will be surprised to find, for instance, in the books and addresses of that period how little Shakespeare is quoted, how much oftener much inferior poets. In Edmund Burke's orations he quotes Shakespeare very little; and Edmund Burke's orations are interesting especially for this, that they are not probably the original addresses which he gave, are literature rather than oratory, and are now generally supposed to have been written out afterwards.

Like Burke most of the orators of that period have a certain formal style. When all is said and done, the clergy got a certain pithiness from that terrific habit they had of going back every little while and pinning down their thought with a text. One English clergyman of the period compared his text to a horse block on which he ascended when he wished to mount his horse, and then he rode his horse as long as he wished and might or might not come back to that horse block again. Therefore we see in the oratory of that time a certain formality.

Moreover, in the absence of the modern reporter, we really do not know exactly what was said in the greatest speeches of that day. The modern reporter, whose aim is to report everything that is said, and who generally succeeds in putting in a great many fine things which haven't occurred to the orators--the modern reporter was not known, and we have but very few descriptions even of the great orations.

DANIEL WEBSTER, THE MAN

From the author's lectures on oratory, with his permission

BY THOMAS WENTWORTH HIGGINSON

It happened to me, when I was in college, to be once on some business at an office on State Street in Boston, then as now the central business street of the place, in a second-story office where there were a number of young men writing busily at their desks. Presently one of the youths, passing by accident across the room, stopped suddenly and said,--

"There is Daniel Webster!"

In an instant every desk in that room was vacated, every pane in every window was filled with a face looking out, and I, hastening up behind them, found it difficult to get a view of the street so densely had they crowded round it. And once looking out, I saw all up and down the street, in every window I could see, just the same mass of eager faces behind the windows. Those faces were all concentrated on a certain figure, a farmer-like, sunburned man who stood, roughly clothed, with his hands behind him, speaking to no one, looking nowhere in particular; waiting, so far as I could see, for nothing, with broad shoulders and heavy muscles, and the head of a hero above. Such a brow, such massive formation, such magnificent black eyes, such straight black eyebrows I had never seen before.

That man, it appeared, was Daniel Webster! I saw people go along the street sidling along past him, looking up at him as if he were the Statue of Liberty Enlightening the World in New York harbor. Nobody knew what he wanted, it never was explained; he may have been merely waiting for some companion to go fishing. But there he was, there he stands in my memory. I don't know what happened afterwards, or how these young men ever got back to their desks--if they ever did.

For me, however, that figure was revealed by one brief duplicate impression, which came in a few months afterwards when I happened to be out in Brookline, a suburb of Boston, where people used to drive then, as they drive now, on summer afternoons for afternoon tea--only, afternoon tea not having been invented, they drove out to their neighbors' houses for fruit or a cup of chocolate.

You have heard Boston perhaps called the "Hub of the universe." A lady, not a Bostonian, once said that if Boston were the hub of the universe, Brookline ought to be called the "Sub-hub." In the "sub-hub" I was sitting in the house of a kinsman who had a beautiful garden; who was the discoverer, in fact, of the Boston nectarine, which all the world came to his house to taste. I heard voices in the drawing-room and went in there. And there I saw again before me the figure of that day on State street, but it was the figure of a man with a beamingly good- natured face, seated in a solid chair brought purposely to accommodate his weight, sitting there with the simple culinary provision of a cup of chocolate in his hand.

It so happened that the great man, the godlike Daniel, as the people used to call him, had expressed the very mortal wish for a little more sugar in his chocolate; and I, if you please, was the fortunate youth who, passing near him, was selected as the Ganymede to bring to him the refreshment desired. I have felt ever since that I, at least, was privileged to put one drop of sweetness into the life of that great man, a life very varied and sometimes needing refreshment. And I have since been given by my classmates to understand--I find they recall it to this day--that upon walking through the college yard for a week or two after that opportunity, I carried my head so much higher than usual as to awaken an amount of derision which undoubtedly, if it had been at West Point, would have led to a boxing match.

That was Daniel Webster, one of the two great lawyers of Boston--I might almost say, of the American bar at that time.

THE ENDURING VALUE OF SPEECH

From the author's lectures on oratory, with his permission

BY THOMAS WENTWORTH HIGGINSON

The Englishman, as far as I have observed, as a rule gets up with reluctance, and begins with difficulty. Just as you are beginning to feel seriously anxious for him, you gradually discover that he is on the verge of saying some uncommonly good thing. Before you are fully prepared for it he says that good thing, and then to your infinite amazement he sits down!

The American begins with an ease which relieves you of all anxiety. The anxiety begins when he talks a while without making any special point. He makes his point at last, as good perhaps as the Englishman's, possibly better. But then when he has made it, you find that he goes on feeling for some other good point, and he feels and feels so long, that perhaps he sits down at last without having made it.

My ideal of a perfect speech in public would be that it should be conducted by a syndicate or trust, as it were, of the two nations, and that the guaranty should be that an American should be provided to begin every speech and an Englishman provided to end it.

Then, when we go a little farther and consider the act of speech itself, and its relation to the word, we sometimes meet with a doubt that we see expressed occasionally in the daily papers provided for us with twenty pages per diem and thirty-two on Sunday, whether we will need much longer anything but what is called sometimes by clergymen "the printed word"--whether the whole form of communication through oral speech will not diminish or fade away.

It seems to me a truly groundless fear--like wondering whether there will ever be a race with only one arm or one leg, or a race of people who live only by the eye or by the ear. The difference between the written word and the spoken word is the difference between solitude and companionship, between meditation and something so near action that it is at least halfway to action and creates action. It is perfectly supposable to imagine a whole race of authors of whom not one should ever exchange a word with a human being while his greatest work is being produced.

The greatest work of American literature, artistically speaking, Hawthorne's "Scarlet Letter," was thus produced. His wife records that during the year that he was writing it, he shut himself up in his study every day. She asked no questions; he volunteered no information. She only knew that something was going on by the knot in his forehead which he carried all that year. At the end of the year he came from his study and read over to her the whole book; a work of genius was added to the world. It was the fruit of solitude.

And sometimes solitude, I regret as an author to say, extends to the perusal of the book, for I have known at least one volume of poems of which not a copy was ever sold; and I know another of which only one copy was sold through my betraying the secret of the author and mentioning the book to a classmate, who bought that one copy.

Therefore, in a general way, we may say that literature speaks in a manner the voice of solitude. As soon as the spoken word comes in, you have companionship. There can be no speech without at least one person present, if it is only the janitor of the church. Dean Swift in reading the Church of England service to his man-servant only, adapted the service as follows: "Dearly beloved Roger, the Scripture moveth thee and me in sundry places," etc.; but in that very economy of speech he realized the presence of an audience. It takes a speaker and an audience together to make a speech--I can say to you what I could not first have said to myself. "The sea of upturned faces," as Daniel Webster said, borrowing the phrase, however, from Scott's "Rob Roy"-- "the sea of upturned faces makes half the speech." And therefore we may assume that there will always be this form of communication. It has, both for the speaker and for the audience, this one vast advantage.

TO COLLEGE GIRLS

From "Girls and Education," by permission of, and by special arrangement with, Houghton Mifflin Company, authorized publishers of this author's works.

BY LE BARON RUSSELL BRIGGS

I doubt whether any one has told more effectively what a college may do for a girl's mind than Dr. Thomas Fuller. In his "Church History of Britain" he gives a short chapter to "The Conveniency of She-Colleges." (I once quoted this chapter at Smith College, and was accused of making it up.) "Nunneries also," he observes, "were good She-Schools, wherein the girls and maids of the neighborhood were taught to read and work; and sometimes a little Latin was taught them therein. Yea, give me leave to say, if such feminine foundations had still continued, haply the weaker sex might be heightened to a higher perfection than hitherto hath been attained. That sharpness of their wits, and suddenness of their conceits, which their enemies must allow unto them, might by education be improved into a judicious solidity."

The feminine mind, with its quick intuitions and unsteady logic, may keep the intuitions and gain a firmness which makes it more than transiently stimulating. The emotional mind has its charm, especially if its emotions are favorable to ourselves.

In some things it may be well that emotion is greater than logic; but emotion *in logic* is sad to contend with, sad even to contemplate--and such is too often the reasoning of the untrained woman. Do not for a moment suppose that I believe such reasoning peculiar to women; but from the best men it has been in great measure trained out.

In a right-minded, sound-hearted girl, college training tends toward control of the nervous system; and control of the nervous system-- making it servant and not master--is almost the supreme need of women. Without such control they become helpless; with it they know scarcely a limit to their efficiency. The world does not yet understand that for the finest and highest work it looks and must look to the naturally sensitive, whether women or men. I remember expressing to the late Professor Greenough regret that a certain young teacher was nervous. His answer has been a comfort to me ever since. "I wouldn't give ten cents for any one who isn't." The nervous man or woman is bound to suffer; but the nervous man or woman may rise to heights that the naturally calm can never reach and can seldom see. To whom do you go for counsel? To the calm, no doubt; but never to the phlegmatic-never to the calm who are calm because they know no better (like the man in Ruskin "to whom the primrose is very accurately the primrose because he does not love it"). You go to the calm who have fought for their calmness, who have known what it is to quiver in every nerve, but have put through whatever they have taken in hand.

There are numberless sweet and patient women who never studied beyond the curriculum of the district school, women who help every one near them by their own unselfish loveliness; but the intelligently patient, the women who can put themselves into the places of all sorts of people, who can sympathize not merely with great and manifest griefs, but with every delicate jarring of the human soul-- hardest of all, with the ambitions of the dull--these women, who must command a respect intellectual as well as moral, reach their highest efficiency through experience based on college training.

College life, designed as it is to strengthen a girl's intellect and character, should teach her to understand better, and not worse, herself as distinguished from other beings of her own sex or the opposite, should fortify her individuality, her power of resisting, and her determination to resist, the contagion of the unwomanly. Exaggerated study may lessen womanly charm; but there is nothing loud or masculine about it. Nor should we judge mental training or anything else by scattered cases of its abuse. The only characteristics of women that the sensible college girl has lost are feminine frivolity, and that kind of headless inaccuracy in thought and speech which once withheld from the sex--or from a large part of it--the intellectual respect of educated men.

At college, if you have lived rightly, you have found enough learning to make you humble, enough friendship to make your hearts large and warm, enough culture to teach you the refinement of simplicity, enough wisdom to keep you sweet in poverty and temperate in wealth. Here you have learned to see great and small in their true relation, to look at both sides of a question, to respect the point of view of every honest man or woman, and to recognize the point of view that differs most widely from your own. Here you have found the democracy that excludes neither poor nor rich, and the quick sympathy that listens to all and helps by the very listening. Here too, it may be at the end of a long struggle, you have seen--if only in transient glimpses--that after doubt comes reverence, after anxiety peace, after faintness courage, and that out of weakness we are made strong. Suffer these glimpses to become an abiding vision, and you have the supreme joy of life.

THE ART OF ACTING

From an address to the students of Harvard University, 1885. Published in "The Drama; Addresses by Henry Irving," William Heinemann, London, publisher, 1893

BY HENRY IRVING

What is the art of acting? I speak of it in its highest sense, as the art to which Roscius, Betterton, and Garrick owed their fame. It is the art of embodying the poet's creations, of giving them flesh and blood, of making the figures which appeal to your mind's eye in the printed drama live before you on the stage. "To fathom the depths of character, to trace its latent motives, to feel its finest quiverings of emotion, to comprehend the thoughts that are hidden under words, and thus possess one's self of the actual mind of the individual man"--such was Macready's defini-tion of the player's art; and to this we may add the testimony of Talma. He describes tragic acting as "the union of grandeur without pomp and nature without trivial-ity." It demands, he says, the endowment of high sensibility and intelligence.

You will readily understand from this that to the actor the well-worn maxim that art is long and life is short has a constant significance. The older we grow the more acutely alive we are to the difficulties of our craft. I cannot give you a better illustration of this fact than a story which is told of Macready. A friend of mine, once a dear friend of his, was with him when he played Hamlet for the last time. The curtain had fallen, and the great actor was sadly thinking that the part he loved so much would never be his again. And as he took off his velvet mantle and laid it aside, he muttered almost unconsciously the words of Horatio, "Good-night, sweet Prince" then turning to his friend, "Ah," said he, "I am just beginning to realise the sweetness, the tenderness, the gentleness of this dear Hamlet!" Believe me, the true artist never lingers fondly upon what he has done. He is ever thinking of what re-mains undone: ever striving toward an ideal it may never be his fortune to attain.

It is often supposed that great actors trust to the inspiration of the moment. Nothing can be more erroneous. There will, of course, be such moments, when an actor at a white heat illumines some passage with a flash of imagination (and this mental condition, by the way, is impossible to the student sitting in his armchair); but the great actor's surprises are generally well weighed, studied, and balanced. We know that Edmund Kean constantly practiced before a mirror effects which startled his audience by their apparent spontaneity. It is the accumulation of such effects which enables an actor, after many years, to present many great characters with remarkable completeness.

I do not want to overstate the case, or to appeal to anything that is not within common experience, so I can confidently ask you whether a scene in a great play has not been at some time vividly impressed on your minds by the delivery of a single line, or even of one forcible word. Has not this made the passage far more real and human to you than all the thought you have devoted to it? An accomplished critic has said that Shakespeare himself might have been surprised had he heard the "Fool, fool, fool!" of Edmund Kean. And though all actors are not Keans, they have in varying degree this power of making a dramatic character step out of the page, and come nearer to our hearts and our understandings.

After all, the best and most convincing exposition of the whole art of acting is given by Shakespeare himself: "To hold, as 'twere, the mirror up to nature, to show virtue her own feature, scorn her own image, and the very age and body of the time his form and pressure." Thus the poet recognized the actor's art as a most potent ally in the representation of human life. He believed that to hold the mirror up to nature was one of the worthiest functions in the sphere of labor, and actors are content to point to his definition of their work as the charter of their privileges.

ADDRESS TO THE FRESHMAN CLASS AT HARVARD UNIVERSITY
From "The Harvard Graduates Magazine"
BY CHARLES WILLIAM ELIOT

Just in the last few years we have had a striking illustration of strong reaction against prevailing educational policies. There has come upon us right here on these grounds and among Harvard's constituents, and widespread over the country as well, a distrust of freedom for students, of freedom for citizens, of freedom for backward races of men. This is one of the striking phenomena of our day, a distrust of freedom.

Now, there is no moment in life when there comes a greater sudden access of freedom than this moment in which you find yourselves. When young men come to an American college, I care not at all which college--to any American college from the parents' home or from school, they experience a tremendous access of freedom. Is it an injury? Is it a danger? Are you afraid of it? Has society a right to be afraid of it? What is freedom for? What does it do for us? Does it hurt us or help us? Do we grow in it, or do we shrink in it? That is quite an important question in the management of Harvard University. It is the important question in modern government. It is pretty clear that when young men or old men are free, they make mistakes, and they go wrong; having freedom to do right or wrong, they often do right and they often do wrong. When you came hither, you found yourselves in possession of a new freedom. You can overeat yourselves, for example; you can overdrink; you can take no care for sleep; you can take no exercise or too much; you can do little work or too much; you can indulge in harmful amusements: in short, you have a great new freedom here. Is it a good thing for you or a bad thing? Clearly you can go astray, for the road is not fenced. You can make mistakes; you can fall into sin. Have you learned to control yourselves? Have you got the will-power in you to regulate your own conduct? Can you be your own taskmaster? You have been in the habit of looking to parents, perhaps, or to teachers, or to the heads of your boarding schools or your day schools for control in all these matters. Have you got it in yourselves to control yourselves? That is the prime question which comes up with regard to every one of you when you come to the University. Have you the sense and the resolution to regulate your own conduct?

It is pretty clear that in other spheres freedom is dangerous. How is it with free political institutions? Do they always yield the best government? Look at the American cities and compare them with the cities of Europe. Clearly, free institutions do not necessarily produce the best government. Are then free institutions wrong or inexpedient? What is freedom for? Why has God made men free, as he has not made the plants and the animals? Is freedom dangerous? Yes! but it is necessary to the growth of human character, and that is what we are all in the world for, and that is what you and your like are in college for. That is what the world was made for, for the occupation of men who in freedom through trial win character. It is choice which makes the dignity of human nature. It is habitual choosing after examination, consideration, reflection, and advice, which makes the man of power. It is through the internal motive power of the will that men imagine, invent, and thrust thoughts out into the obscure beyond, into the future. The will is the prime motive power; and you can only train your wills, in freedom. That is what freedom is for, in school and college, in society, industries, and governments. Fine human character is the ultimate object, and freedom is the indispensable condition of its development.

Now, there are some clear objects for choice here in college, for real choice, for discreet choice. I will mention only two. In the first place, choose those studies--there is a great range of them here--which will, through your interest in them, develop your working power. You know it is only through work that you can achieve anything, either in college or in the world. Choose those studies on which you can work intensely with pleasure, with real satisfaction and happiness. That is the true guide to a wise choice. Choose that intellectual pursuit which will develop within you the power to do enthusiastic work, an internal motive power, not an external compulsion. Then choose an ennobling companionship. You will find out in five minutes that this man stirs you to good, that man to evil. Shun the latter; cling to the former. Choose companionship rightly, choose your whole surroundings so that they shall lift you up and not drag you down. Make these two choices wisely, and be faithful in labor, and you will succeed in college and in after life.

WITH TENNYSON AT FARRINGFORD

From "Alfred Lord Tennyson, A Memoir by His Son," with the permission of The Macmillan Company, New York and London, publishers.

Before leaving for Aldworth we spent some delightful sunny days in the Farringford gardens. In the afternoons my father sat in his summerhouse and talked to us and his friends.

This spring he had enjoyed seeing the unusually splendid blossom of apple and pear tree, of white lilacs, and of purple aubretia that bordered the walks.

At intervals he strolled to the bottom of the kitchen garden to look at the roses, or at the giant fig tree ("like a breaking wave," as he said) bursting into leaf; or he marked the "branching grace" of the stately line of elms, between the boles of which, from his summerhouse, he caught a glimpse of far meadows beyond. He said that he did not believe in Emerson's pretty lines:--

"Only to children children sing,
Only to youth the Spring is Spring."

"For age does feel the joy of spring, though age can only crawl over the bridge while youth skips the brook." His talk was grave and gay together. In the middle of anecdotes he would stop short and say something of what he felt to be the sadness and mystery of life.

What impressed all his friends was his choice of language, the felicity of his turns of expression, his imagery, the terseness of his unadorned English, and his simple directness of manner, which none will ever be able to reproduce, however many notes they may have taken. His dignity and repose of manner, his low musical voice, and the power of his magnetic dark eye kept the attention riveted. His argument was clear and logical and never wandered from the point except by way of illustration, and his illustrations were the most various I have ever heard, and were taken from nature and science, from high and low life, from the rich and from the poor, and his analysis of character was always subtle and powerful.

While he talked of the mysteries of the universe, his face, full of the strong lines of thought, was lighted up; and his words glowed as it were with inspiration.

When conversing with my brother and myself or our college friends, he was, I used to think, almost at his best, for he would quote us the fine passages from ancient or modern literature and show us why they are fine, or he would tell us about the great facts and discoveries in astronomy, geology, botany, chemistry, and the great problems in philosophy, helping us toward a higher conception of the laws which govern the world and of "the law behind the law." He was so sympathetic that the enthusiasm of youth seemed to kindle his own. He spoke out of the fullness of his heart, and explained more eloquently than ever where his own difficulties lay, and what he, as an old man, thought was the true mainspring of human life and action; and

> "How much of act at human hands
> The sense of human will demands
> By which we dare to live or die."

The truth is that real genius, unless made shallow by prejudice, is seldom frozen by age, and that, until absolute physical decay sets in, the powers of the mind may become stronger and stronger.

On one of these June mornings, Miss L--, who was a stranger to us, but whose brother we had known for some time, called upon us. My father took her over the bridge to the summerhouse looking on the Down. After a little while he said: "Miss L--, my son says I am to read to you," and added, "I will read whatever you like." He read some of "Maud," "The Spinster's Sweet-Arts," and some "Enoch Arden."

His voice, as Miss L-- noticed, was melodious and full of change, and quite unimpaired by age. There was a peculiar freshness and passion in his reading of "Maud," giving the impression that he had just written the poem, and that the emotion which created it was fresh in him. This had an extraordinary influence on the listener, who felt that the reader had been ***present*** at the scenes he described, and that he still felt their bliss or agony.

He thoroughly enjoyed reading his "The Spinster's Sweet-Arts," and when he was reading "Enoch Arden" he told Miss L-- to listen to the sound of the sea in the line,

> "The league-long roller thundering on the reef,"

and to mark Miriam Lane's chatter in

"He ceased; and Miriam Lane
Made such a voluble answer promising all."
NOTES ON SPEECH-MAKING

From "Notes on Speech-Making," with the permission of Longmans, Green and Company, New York and London, publishers.

BY BRANDER MATTHEWS

We are told that the five-minute speeches with which Judge Hoar year after year delighted the Harvard chapter of the Phi Beta Kappa contained but one original idea, clearly stated, and but one fresh story, well told. This is indeed a model to be admired of all men; yet how few of us will take the trouble of copying it!

The speaker who rambles and ambles along, saying nothing, and his fellow, the speaker who links jest to jest, saying little more, are both of them unabashed in the presence of an audience. They are devoid of all shyness. They are well aware that they have "the gift of the gab"; they rejoice in its possession; they lie in wait for occasions to display it. They have helped to give foreigners the impression that every American is an oratorical revolver, ready with a few remarks whenever any chairman may choose to pull the trigger. And yet there are Americans not a few to whom the making of an after-dinner speech is a most painful ordeal. When the public dinner was given to Charles Dickens in New York, on his first visit to America, Washington Irving was obviously the predestined presiding officer. Curtis tells us that Irving went about muttering: "I shall certainly break down; I know I shall break down." When the dinner was eaten, and Irving arose to propose the health of Dickens, he began pleasantly and smoothly in two or three sentences; then hesitated, stammered, smiled, and stopped; tried in vain to begin again; then gracefully gave it up, announced the toast, "Charles Dickens, the guest of the nation," and sank into his chair amid immense applause, whispering to his neighbor, "There! I told you I should break down, and I've done it."

When Thackeray came, later, Irving "consented to preside at a dinner, if speeches were absolutely forbidden; the condition was faithfully observed" (so Curtis records), "but it was the most extraordinary instance of American self-command on record." Thackeray himself had no fondness for after-dinner speaking, nor any great skill in the art. He used to complain humorously that he never could remember all the good things he had thought of in the cab; and in "Philip" he went so far as to express a hope that "a day will soon arrive (but I own, mind you, that I do not carve well) when we shall have the speeches done by a skilled waiter at a side table, as we now have the carving."

Hawthorne was as uncomfortable on his feet as were Thackeray and Irving; but his resolute will steeled him for the trial. When he dined with the Mayor of Liverpool, he was called upon for the toast of the United States. "Being at bay, and with no alternative, I got upon my legs and made a response," he wrote in his notebook, appending this comment: "Anybody may make an after-dinner speech who will be content to talk onward without saying anything. My speech was not more than two or three inches long; ... but, being once started, I felt no embarassment, and went through it as coolly as if I were going to be hanged."

He also notes that his little speech was quite successful, "considering that I did not know a soul there, except the Mayor himself, and that I am wholly unpracticed in all sorts of oratory, and that I had nothing to say." To each of these three considerations of Hawthorne's it would be instructive to add a comment, for he spoke under a triple disadvantage. A speech cannot really be successful when the speaker has nothing to say. It is rarely successful unless he knows the tastes and the temper of those he is addressing. It can be successful only casually unless he has had some practice in the simpler sort of oratory.

HUNTING THE GRIZZLY

From "Hunting the Grizzly" with the permission of G. P. Putnam's Sons, New York and London, publishers.

BY THEODORE ROOSEVELT

For half a mile I walked quickly and silently over the pine needles, across a succession of slight ridges separated by narrow, shallow valleys. The forest here was composed of lodge-pole pines, which on the ridges grew close together, with tall slender trunks, while in the valleys the growth was more open. Though the sun was behind the mountains, there was yet plenty of light by which to shoot, but it faded rapidly.

At last, as I was thinking of turning toward camp, I stole up to the crest of one of the ridges, and looked over into the valley some sixty yards off. Immediately I caught the loom of some large, dark object; and another glance showed me a big grizzly walking slowly off with his head down. He was quartering to me, and I fired into his flank, the bullet, as I afterward found, ranging forward and piercing one lung. At the shot he uttered a loud, moaning grunt and plunged forward at a heavy gallop, while I raced obliquely down the hill to cut him off. After going a few hundred feet, he reached a laurel thicket, some thirty yards broad, and two or three times as long, which he did not leave. I ran up to the edge and there halted, not liking to venture into the mass of twisted, close-growing stems and glossy foliage. Moreover, as I halted, I heard him utter a peculiar, savage kind of whine from the heart of the brush. Accordingly, I began to skirt the edge, standing on tiptoe and gazing earnestly to see if I could not catch a glimpse of his hide. When I was at the narrowest part of the thicket, he suddenly left it directly opposite, and then wheeled and stood broadside to me on the hillside, a little above. He turned his head stiffly toward me; scarlet strings of froth hung from his lips; his eyes burned like embers in the gloom.

I held true, aiming at the shoulder, and my bullet shattered the point or lower end of his heart, taking out a big nick. Instantly the great bear turned with a harsh roar of fury and challenge, blowing the bloody foam from his mouth, so that I saw the gleam of his white fangs; and then he charged straight at me, crashing and bounding through the laurel bushes, so that it was hard to aim. I waited till he came to a fallen tree, raking him as he topped it with a ball, which entered his chest and went through the cavity of his body, but he neither swerved nor flinched, and at the moment I did not know that I had struck him. He came steadily on, and in another second was almost upon me. I fired for his forehead, but my bullet went low, entering his open mouth, smashing his lower jaw and going into the neck. I leaped to one side almost as I pulled the trigger; and through the hanging smoke the first thing I saw was his paw as he made a vicious side blow at me. The rush of his charge carried him past. As he struck he lurched forward, leaving a pool of bright blood where his muzzle hit the ground; but he recovered himself and made two or three jumps onward, while I hurriedly jammed a couple of cartridges into the magazine, my rifle holding only four, all of which I had fired. Then he tried to pull up, but as he did so his muscles seemed suddenly to give way, his head dropped, and he rolled over and over like a shot rabbit. Each of my first three bullets had inflicted a mortal wound.

It was already twilight, and I merely opened the carcass, and then trotted back to camp. Next morning I returned and with much labor took off the skin. The fur was very fine, the animal being in excellent trim, and unusually bright colored. Unfortunately, in packing it out I lost the skull, and had to supply its place with one of plaster. The beauty of the trophy, and the memory of the circumstances under which I produced it, make me value it perhaps more highly than any other in my house.

ARGUMENT AND PERSUASION

DEBATES AND CAMPAIGN SPEECHES

ON RETAINING THE PHILIPPINE ISLANDS
SPEECH OF GEORGE F. HOAR

A famous orator once imagined the nations of the world uniting to erect a column to Jurisprudence in some stately capital. Each country was to bring the name of its great jurist to be inscribed on the side of the column, with a sentence stating what he and his country through him had done toward establishing the reign of law and justice for the benefit of mankind.

I have sometimes fancied that we might erect here in the capital of the country a column to American Liberty which alone might rival in height the beautiful and simple shaft which we have erected to the fame of the Father of the Country. I can fancy each generation bringing its inscription, which should recite its own contribution to the great structure of which the column should be but the symbol.

The generation of the Puritan and the Pilgrim and the Huguenot claims the place of honor at the base. "I brought the torch of freedom across the sea. I cleared the forest. I subdued the savage and the wild beast. I laid in Christian liberty and law the foundations of empire."

The next generation says: "What my fathers founded I builded. I left the seashore to penetrate the wilderness. I planted schools and colleges and churches."

Then comes the generation of the great colonial day: "I stood by the side of England on many a hard-fought field. I helped humble the power of France."

Then comes the generation of the revolutionary time: "I encountered the power of England. I declared and won the independence of my country. I placed that declaration on the eternal principles of justice and righteousness which all mankind have read, and on which all mankind will one day stand. I affirmed the dignity of human nature and the right of the people to govern themselves."

The next generation says: "I encountered England again. I vindicated the right of an American ship to sail the seas the wide world over without molestation. I made the American sailor as safe at the ends of the earth as my fathers had made the American farmer safe in his home."

Then comes the next generation: "I did the mighty deeds which in your younger years you saw and which your fathers told. I saved the Union. I freed the slave. I made of every slave a freeman, and of every freeman a citizen, and of every citizen a voter."

Then comes another who did the great work in peace, in which so many of you had an honorable share: "I kept the faith. I paid the debt. I brought in conciliation and peace instead of war. I built up our vast domestic commerce. I made my country the richest, freest, strongest, happiest people on the face of the earth."

And now what have we to say? What have we to say? Are we to have a place in that honorable company? Must we engrave on that column: "We repealed the Declaration of Independence. We changed the Munroe Doctrine from a doctrine of eternal righteousness and justice, resting on the consent of the governed, to a doctrine of brutal selfishness, looking only to our own advantage. We crushed the only republic in Asia. We made war on the only Christian people in the East. We converted a war of glory into a war of shame. We vulgarized the American flag. We introduced perfidy into the practice of war. We inflicted torture on unarmed men to extort confession. We put children to death. We established reconcentrado camps. We devastated provinces. We baffled the aspirations of a people for liberty"?

No, Mr. President. Never! Never! Other and better counsels will yet prevail. The hours are long in the life of a great people. The irrevocable step is not yet taken.

Let us at least have this to say: "We, too, have kept the faith of the fathers. We took Cuba by the hand. We delivered her from her age-long bondage. We welcomed her to the family of nations. We set mankind an example never beheld before of moderation in victory. We led hesitating and halting Europe to the deliverance of their beleaguered ambassadors in China. We marched through a hostile country--a country cruel and barbarous--without anger or revenge. We returned benefit for injury, and pity for cruelty. We made the name of America beloved in the East as in the West. We kept faith with the Philippine people. We kept faith with our own history. We kept our national honor unsullied. The flag which we received without a rent we handed down without a stain."

SPEECH OF WILLIAM MCKINLEY

I do not know why in the year 1899 this Republic has unexpectedly had placed before it mighty problems which it must face and meet. They have come and are here, and they could not be kept away. We have fought a war with Spain.

The Philippines, like Cuba and Porto Rico, were intrusted to our hands by the war, and to that great trust, under the Providence of God and in the name of human progress and civilization, we are committed. It is a trust we have not sought; it is a trust from which we will not flinch. The American people will hold up the hands of their servants at home to whom they commit its execution, while Dewey and Otis and the brave men whom they command will have the support of the country in upholding our flag where it now floats, the symbol and assurance of liberty and justice.

There is universal agreement that the Philippines shall not be turned back to Spain. No true American consents to that. Even if unwilling to accept them ourselves, it would have been a weak evasion of manly duty to require Spain to transfer them to some other power or powers, and thus shirk our own responsibility. Even if we had had, as we did not have, the power to compel such a transfer, it could not have been made without the most serious international complications. Such a course could not be thought of. And yet had we refused to accept the cession of them, we should have had no power over them even for their own good.

We could not discharge the responsibilities upon us until these islands became ours, either by conquest or treaty. There was but one alternative, and that was either Spain or the United States in the Philippines. The other suggestions--first, that they should be tossed into the arena of contention for the strife of nations; or, second, be left to the anarchy and chaos of no protectorate at all--were too shameful to be considered.

The treaty gave them to the United States. Could we have required less and done our duty? Could we, after freeing the Filipinos from the domination of Spain, have left them without government and without power to protect life or property or to perform the international obligations essential to an independent state? Could we have left them in a state of anarchy and justified ourselves in our own consciences or before the tribunal of mankind? Could we have done that in the sight of God or man?

No imperial designs lurk in the American mind. They are alien to American sentiment, thought, and purpose. Our priceless principles undergo no change under a tropical sun. They go with the flag. They are wrought in every one of its sacred folds, and are indistinguishable as its shining stars.

"Why read ye not the changeless truth,

The free can conquer but to save?"

If we can benefit these remote peoples, who will object? If in the years of the future they are established in government under law and liberty, who will regret our perils and sacrifices? Who will not rejoice in our heroism and humanity? Always perils, and always after them safety; always darkness and clouds, but always shining through them the light and the sunshine; always cost and sacrifice, but always after them the fruition of liberty, education, and civilization.

I have no light or knowledge not common to my countrymen. I do not prophesy. The present is all-absorbing to me, but I cannot bound my vision by the blood-stained trenches around Manila, where every red drop, whether from the veins of an American soldier or a misguided Filipino, is anguish to my heart; but by the broad range of future years, when that group of islands, under the impulse of the year just past, shall have become the gems and glories of those tropical seas; a land of plenty and of increasing possibilities; a people redeemed from savage indolence and habits, devoted to the arts of peace, in touch with the commerce and trade of all nations, enjoying the blessings of freedom, of civil and religious liberty, of education and of homes, and whose children and children's children shall for ages hence bless the American Republic because it emancipated and redeemed their fatherland and set them in the pathway of the world's best civilization.

DEBATE ON THE TARIFF
SPEECH OF THOMAS B. REED

Whether the universal sentiment in favor of protection as applied to every country is sound or not, I do not stop to discuss. Whether it is best for the United States of America alone concerns me now, and the first thing I have to say is, that after thirty years of protection, undisturbed by any menace of free trade, up to the very year now last past, this country was the greatest and most flourishing nation on the face of this earth. Moreover, with the shadow of this unjustifiable bill resting cold upon it, with mills closed, with hundreds of thousands of men unemployed, industry at a standstill, and prospects before it more gloomy than ever marked its history--except once--this country is still the greatest and the richest that the sun shines on, or ever did shine on.

According to the usual story that is told, England had been engaged with a long and vain struggle with the demon of protection, and had been year after year sinking farther into the depths until at a moment when she was in her distress and saddest plight her manufacturing system broke down, "protection, having destroyed home trade by reducing," as Mr. Atkinson says, "the entire population to beggary, destitution, and want." Mr. Cobden and his friends providentially appeared, and after a hard struggle established a principle for all time and for all the world, and straightway England enjoyed the sum of human happiness. Hence all good nations should do as England has done and be happy ever after.

Suppose England, instead of being a little island in the sea, had been the half of a great continent full of raw material, capable of an internal commerce which would rival the commerce of all the rest of the world.

Suppose every year new millions were flocking to her shores, and every one of those new millions in a few years, as soon as they tasted the delights of a broader life, would become as great a consumer as any one of her own people.

Suppose that these millions, and the 70,000,000 already gathered under the folds of her flag, were every year demanding and receiving a higher wage and therefore broadening her market as fast as her machinery could furnish production. Suppose she had produced cheap food beyond all her wants, and that her laborers spent so much money that whether wheat was sixty cents a bushel or twice that sum hardly entered the thoughts of one of them, except when some Democratic tariff bill was paralyzing his business.

Suppose that she was not only but a cannon shot from France, but that every country in Europe had been brought as near to her as Baltimore is to Washington--for that is what cheap ocean freights mean between us and European producers. Suppose all those countries had her machinery, her skilled workmen, her industrial system, and labor forty per cent cheaper. Suppose under that state of facts, with all her manufacturers proclaiming against it, frantic in their disapproval, England had been called upon by Cobden to make the plunge into free trade, would she have done it? Not if Cobden had been backed by the angelic host. History gives England credit for great sense.

SPEECH OF CHARLES F. CRISP

I assume that the cause of protection has no more able advocate than the gentleman from Maine. I assume that the argument for protection can be put in no more alluring form than that to which we have listened to- day. So assuming, I shall ask you calmly and dispassionately to examine with me that argument, to see upon what it is based, and then I shall invoke the unprejudiced judgment of this House as to whether the cause attempted to be sustained by the gentleman from Maine has been sustained, or can be before any tribunal where the voice of reason is heard or the sense of justice is felt.

The gentleman from Maine, with a facility that is unequaled, when he encounters an argument which he is unable to answer passes it by with some bright and witty saying and thereby invites and receives the applause of those who believe as he does. But the gentleman does not attempt, the gentleman has not to-day attempted, to reply to the real arguments that are made in favor of freer trade and greater liberty of commerce.

The gentleman points to the progress of the United States, he points to the rate of wages in the United States, he points to the aggregated wealth of the United States, and claims all this is due to protection. But he does not explain how we owe these blessings to protection. He says, we have protection in the United States, wages are high in the United States; therefore protection makes high wages.

When we ask the gentleman from Maine to give us a reason why a high protective tariff increases the rate of wages he points to the glory, the prosperity, and the honor of our country. We on this side unite with him in every sentiment, in every purpose, in every effort that has for its object the advancement of the general welfare of the people of the United States, but we differ from him as to the method of promoting their welfare. The gentleman belongs to that school who believe that scarcity is a blessing, and that abundance should be prohibited by law. We belong to that school who believe that scarcity is a calamity to be avoided, and that abundance should be, if possible, encouraged by law.

The gentleman belongs to that class who believe that by a system of taxation we can make the country rich. He believes that it is possible by tax laws to advance the prosperity of all the industries and all the people in the United States.

Either, Mr. Speaker, that statement is an absurdity upon its face, or it implies that in some way we have the power to make some persons not resident of the United States pay the taxes that we impose. I insist that you do not increase the taxable wealth of the United States when you tax a gentleman in Illinois and give the benefit of that tax to a gentleman in Maine. Such a course prevents the natural and honest distribution of wealth, but it does not create or augment it.

SOUTH CAROLINA AND MASSACHUSETTS
Delivered in the United States Senate, January, 1830
BY ROBERT Y. HAYNE

The gentleman has made a great flourish about his fidelity to Massachusetts. I shall make no profession of zeal for the interests and honor of South Carolina; of that my constituents shall judge. If there be one State in the Union, Mr. President (and I say it not in a boastful spirit), that may challenge comparison with any other for a uniform, zealous, ardent, and uncalculating devotion to the Union, that State is South Carolina. Sir, from the very commencement of the Revolution up to this hour there is no sacrifice, however great, she has not cheerfully made, no service she has ever hesitated to perform. She has adhered to you in your prosperity; but in your adversity she has clung to you with more than filial affection. No matter what was the condition of her domestic affairs, though deprived of her resources, divided by parties, or surrounded with difficulties, the call of the country has been to her as the voice of God. Domestic discord ceased at the sound; every man became at once reconciled to his brethren, and the sons of Carolina were all seen crowding together to the temple, bringing their gifts to the altar of their common country.

What, sir, was the conduct of the South during the Revolution? Sir, I honor New

England for her conduct in that glorious struggle. But great as is the praise which belongs to her, I think at least equal honor is due to the South. They espoused the quarrel of their brethren with a generous zeal, which did not suffer them to stop to calculate their interest in the dispute. Favorites of the mother country, possessed of neither ships nor seamen to create a commercial rivalship, they might have found in their situation a guaranty that their trade would be forever fostered and protected by Great Britain. But, trampling on all considerations either of interest or of safety, they rushed into the conflict, and, fighting for principle, periled all in the sacred cause of freedom. Never were there exhibited in the history of the world higher examples of noble daring, dreadful suffering, and heroic endurance than by the Whigs of Carolina during the Revolution. The whole State, from the mountains to the sea, was overrun by an overwhelming force of the enemy. The fruits of industry perished on the spot where they were produced, or were consumed by the foe. The "plains of Carolina" drank up the most precious blood of her citizens. Black and smoking ruins marked the places where had been the habitations of her children. Driven from their homes into the gloomy and almost impenetrable swamps, even there the spirit of liberty survived, and South Carolina (sustained by the example of her Sumters and her Marions) proved by her conduct that, though her soil might be overrun, the spirit of her people was invincible.

REPLY BY DANIEL WEBSTER

The eulogium pronounced by the honorable gentleman on the character of the State of South Carolina for her Revolutionary and other merits meets my hearty concurrence. I shall not acknowledge that the honorable member goes before me in regard for whatever of distinguished talent, or distinguished character, South Carolina has produced. I claim part of the honor, I partake in the pride, of her great names. I claim them for countrymen, one and all,--the Laurenses, the Rutledges, the Pinckneys, the Sumters, the Marions, Americans all, whose fame is no more to be hemmed in by State lines than their talents and patriotism were capable of being circumscribed within the same narrow limits. In their day and generation they served and honored the country, and the whole country; and their renown is of the treasures of the whole country. Him whose honored name the gentleman himself bears,--does he esteem me less capable of gratitude for his patriotism, or sympathy for his sufferings, than if his eyes had first opened upon the light of Massachusetts instead of South Carolina? Sir, does he suppose it in his power to exhibit a Carolina name so bright as to produce envy in my bosom? No, sir, increased gratification and delight, rather. I thank God that, if I am gifted with little of the spirit which is able to raise mortals to the skies, I have yet none, as I trust, of that other spirit which would drag angels down. When I shall be found, sir, in my place here in the Senate or elsewhere, to sneer at public merit because it happens to spring up beyond the little limits of my own State or neighborhood; when I refuse, for any such cause, or for any cause, the homage due to American talent, to elevated patriotism, to sincere devotion to liberty and the country; or, if I see an uncommon endowment of Heaven, if I see extraordinary capacity and virtue in any son of the South, and if, moved by local prejudice or gangrened by State jealousy, I get up here to abate the tithe of a hair from his just character and just fame,--may my tongue cleave to the roof of my mouth!

Sir, let me recur to pleasing recollections; let me indulge in refreshing remembrance of the past; let me remind you that, in early times, no States cherished greater harmony, both of principle and feeling, than Massachusetts and South Carolina. Would to God that harmony might again return! Shoulder to shoulder they went through the Revolution; hand in hand they stood round the administration of Washington, and felt his own great arm lean on them for support. Unkind feeling, if it exist, alienation and distrust, are the growth, unnatural to such soils, of false principles since sown. They are weeds, the seeds of which that same great arm never scattered.

Mr. President, I shall enter on no encomium upon Massachusetts; she needs none. There she is. Behold her, and judge for yourselves. There is her history; the world knows it by heart. The past, at least, is secure. There is Boston, and Concord, and Lexington, and Bunker Hill; and there they will remain forever. The bones of her sons, falling in the great struggle for independence, now lie mingled with the soil of every State from New England to Georgia; and there they will lie forever. And, sir, where American liberty raised its first voice, and where its youth was nurtured and sustained, there it still lives in the strength of its manhood and full of its original spirit. If discord and party strife shall succeed in separating it from that Union by which alone its existence is made sure,--it will stand in the end by the side of that cradle in which its infancy was rocked, and it will fall at last, if fall it must, amidst the proudest monuments of its own glory and on the very spot of its origin.

THE REPUBLICAN PARTY

BY JOHN HAY

Our platform is before the country. Perhaps it is lacking in novelty. There is certainly nothing sensational about it. Its principles have been tested by eight years of splendid success and have received the approval of the country. It is in line with all our platforms of the past, except where prophecy and promise in those days have become history in these. We stand by the ancient ways which have proved good. We come before the country in a position which cannot be successfully attacked in front, or flank, or rear. What we have done, what we are doing, and what we intend to do--on all three we confidently challenge the verdict of the American people. The record of fifty years will show whether as a party we are fit to govern; the state of our domestic and foreign affairs will show whether as a party we have fallen off; and both together will show whether we can be trusted for a while longer.

I want to say a word to the young men whose political life is beginning. Any one entering business would be glad of the chance to become one of an established firm with years of success behind it, with a wide connection, with unblemished character, with credit founded on a rock. How infinitely brighter the future when the present is so sure, the past so glorious! Everything great done by this country in the last fifty years has been done under the auspices of the Republican Party. Is not this consciousness a great asset to have in your mind and memory? As a mere item of personal comfort is it not worth having? Lincoln and Grant, Hayes and Garfield, Harrison and McKinley--names secure in the heaven of fame--they all are gone, leaving small estates in worldly goods, but what vast possessions in principles, memories, sacred associations! It is a start in life to share that wealth. Who now boasts that he opposed Lincoln? who brags of his voting against Grant? though both acts may have been from the best of motives. In our form of government there must be two parties, and tradition, circumstances, temperament, will always create a sufficient opposition. But what young man would not rather belong to the party that does things, instead of one that opposes them; to the party that looks up, rather than down; to the party of the dawn, rather than of the sunset? For fifty years the Republican Party has believed in the country and labored for it in hope and joy;

it has reverenced the flag and followed it; it has carried it under strange skies and planted it on far- receding horizons. It has seen the nation grow greater every year and more respected; by just dealing, by intelligent labor, by a genius for enterprise, it has seen the country extend its intercourse and its influence to regions unknown to our fathers. Yet it has never abated one jot or tittle of the ancient law imposed on us by our God-fearing ancestors. We have fought a good fight, but also we have kept the faith. The Constitution of our fathers has been the light to our feet; our path is, and will ever remain, that of ordered progress, of liberty under the law. The country has vastly increased, but the great-brained statesmen who preceded us provided for infinite growth. The discoveries of science have made miraculous additions to our knowledge. But we are not daunted by progress; we are not afraid of the light. The fabric our fathers builded on such sure foundations will stand all shocks of fate or fortune. There will always be a proud pleasure in looking back on the history they made; but, guided by their example, the coming generation has the right to anticipate work not less important, days equally memorable to mankind. We who are passing off the stage bid you, as the children of Israel encamping by the sea were bidden, to Go Forward; we whose hands can no longer hold the flaming torch pass it on to you that its clear light may show the truth to the ages that are to come.

NOMINATING ULYSSES S. GRANT

BY ROSCOE CONKLING

In obedience to instructions I should never dare to disregard-- expressing, also, my own firm convictions--I rise to propose a nomination with which the country and the Republican party can grandly win. The election before us is to be the Austerlitz of American politics. It will decide, for many years, whether the country shall be Republican or Cossack. The supreme need of the hour is not a candidate who can carry Michigan. All Republican candidates can do that. The need is not of a candidate who is popular in the Territories, because they have no vote. The need is of a candidate who can carry doubtful States. Not the doubtful States of the North alone, but doubtful States of the South, which we have heard, if I understand it aright, ought to take little or no part here, because the South has nothing to give, but everything to receive. No, gentlemen, the need that presses upon the conscience of this Convention is of a candidate who can carry doubtful States both North and South. And believing that he, more surely than any other man, can carry

New York against any opponent, and can carry not only the North, but several States of the South, New York is for Ulysses S. Grant. Never defeated in peace or in war, his name is the most illustrious borne by living man.

His services attest his greatness, and the country--nay, the world-- knows them by heart. His fame was earned not alone in things written and said, but by the arduous greatness of things done. And perils and emergencies will search in vain in the future, as they have searched in vain in the past, for any other on whom the nation leans with such confidence and trust. Never having had a policy to enforce against the will of the people, he never betrayed a cause or a friend, and the people will never desert nor betray him. Standing on the highest eminence of human distinction, modest, firm, simple, and self-poised, having filled all lands with his renown, he has seen not only the highborn and the titled, but the poor and the lowly, in the uttermost ends of the earth, rise and uncover before him. He has studied the needs and the defects of many systems of government, and he has returned a better American than ever.

His integrity, his common-sense, his courage, his unequaled experience, are the qualities offered to his country. The only argument, the only one that the wit of man or the stress of politics has devised is one that would have dumbfounded Solomon, because he thought there was nothing new under the sun. Having tried Grant twice and found him faithful, we are told that we must not, even after an interval of years, trust him again. My countrymen! my countrymen! what stultification does not such a fallacy involve! Is this an electioneering juggle, or is it hypocrisy's masquerade? There is no field of human activity, responsibility, or reason, in which rational beings object to an agent because he has been weighed in the balance and not found wanting. There is, I say, no department of human reason in which sane men reject an agent because he has had experience making him exceptionally competent and fit.

This Convention is master of a supreme opportunity. It can name the next President. It can make sure of his election. It can make sure not only of his election, but of his certain and peaceful inauguration.

Gentlemen, we have only to listen above the din and look beyond the dust of an hour to behold the Republican party advancing with its ensigns resplendent with illustrious achievements, marching to certain and lasting victory with its greatest

Marshal at its head.

THE CHOICE OF A PARTY

From a speech delivered in New York, 1880. Depew's "Library of Oratory," E. J. Bowen and Company, New York, publishers.

BY ROSCOE CONKLING

We are citizens of a republic. We govern ourselves. Here no pomp of eager array in chambers of royalty awaits the birth of boy or girl to wield an hereditary scepter. We know no scepter save a majority's constitutional will. To wield that scepter in equal share is the duty and the right, nay, the birthright, of every citizen. The supreme, the final, the only peaceful arbiter here, is the ballot box; and in that urn should be gathered and from it should be sacredly recorded the conscience, the judgment, the intelligence of all. The right of free self-government has been in all ages the bright dream of oppressed humanity,--the sighed-for privilege to which thrones, dynasties, and power have so long blocked the way. In the fullness of freedom the Republic of America is alone in the earth; alone in its grandeur; alone in its blessings; alone in its promises and possibilities, and therefore alone in the devotion due from its citizens.

The time has come when law, duty, and interest require the nation to determine for at least four years its policy in many things. Two parties exist; parties should always exist in a government of majorities, and to support and strengthen the party which most nearly holds his views is among the most laudable, meritorious acts of an American citizen; and this whether he be in official or in private station. Two parties contend for the management of national affairs. The question is, Which of the two is it safer and wiser to trust? It is not a question of candidates. A candidate, if he be an honest, genuine man, will not seek and accept a party nomination to the presidency, vice presidency, or Congress, and after he is elected become a law unto himself. The higher obligations among men are not set down in writing and signed or sealed; they reside in honor and good faith. The fidelity of a nominee belongs to this exalted class, and therefore the candidate of a party is but the exponent of a party. The object of political discussion and action is to settle principles, policies, and issues. It is a paltry incident of an election affecting fifty million people that it decides for an occasion the aspirations of individual men. The Democratic party is the Democratic candidate, and I am against the ticket and all its works.

A triumphant nationality--a regenerated constitution--a free Republic-- an unbroken country--untarnished credit--solvent finances--unparalleled prosperity--all these are ours despite the policy and the efforts of the Democratic party. Along with the amazing improvement in national finances, we have amazing individual thrift on every side. In every walk of life new activity is felt. Labor, agriculture, manufactures, commerce, enterprises, and investments, all are flourishing, content and hopeful. But in the midst of this harmony and encouragement comes a harsh discord crying, "Give us a change--anything for a change." This is not a bearing year for "a change." Every other crop is good, but not the crop of "change"--that crop is good only when the rest are bad. The country does not need nor wish the change proposed, and to the pressing invitation of our Democratic friends a good-natured but firm "No, I thank you," will be the response at the polls.

Upon its record and its candidates the Republican party asks the country's approval, and stands ready to avow its purposes for the future. It proposes to rebuild our commercial marine. It proposes to foster labor, industry, and enterprise. It proposes to stand for education, humanity, and progress. It proposes to administer the government honestly, to preserve amity with all the world, observing our own obligations with others and seeing that others observe theirs with us, to protect every citizen in his rights and equality before the law, to uphold the public credit and the sanctity of engagements; and by doing these things the Republican party proposes to assure to industry, humanity, and civilization in America the amplest welcome and the safest home.

NOMINATING JOHN SHERMAN

From a speech nominating a candidate for President of the United States at the Republican National Convention, 1880

BY JAMES A. GARFIELD

I have witnessed the extraordinary scenes of this Convention with deep solicitude. Nothing touches my heart more quickly than a tribute of honor to a great and noble character; but as I sat in my seat and witnessed this demonstration, this assemblage seemed to me a human ocean in tempest. I have seen the sea lashed into fury and tossed into spray, and its grandeur moves the soul of the dullest man; but I remember that it is not the billows, but the calm level of the sea, from which all heights and depths are measured. When the storm has passed and the hour of calm settles on the ocean, when the sunlight bathes its peaceful surface, then the astronomer and surveyor take the level from which they measure all terrestrial heights and depths.

Gentlemen of the Convention, your present temper may not mark the healthful pulse of our people. Not here, in this brilliant circle, where fifteen thousand men and women are gathered, is the destiny of the Republic to be decreed for the next four years. Not here, where I see the enthusiastic faces of seven hundred and fifty-six delegates, waiting to cast their lots into the urn and determine the choice of the Republic, but by four millions of Republican firesides, where the thoughtful voters, with wives and children about them, with the calm thoughts inspired by love of home and country, with the history of the past, the hopes of the future, and reverence for the great men who have adorned and blessed our nation in days gone by, burning in their hearts,--there God prepares the verdict which will determine the wisdom of our work to-night. Not in Chicago, in the heat of June, but at the ballot boxes of the Republic, in the quiet of November, after the silence of deliberate judgment, will this question be settled.

Now, gentlemen, I am about to present a name for your consideration,-- the name of one who was the comrade, associate, and friend of nearly all the noble dead, whose faces look down upon us from these walls to- night; a man who began his career of public service twenty-five years ago.

You ask for his monument. I point you to twenty-five years of national statutes. Not one great, beneficent law has been placed on our statute books without his intelligent and powerful aid. He aided in formulating the laws to raise the great armies and navies which carried us through the war. His hand was seen in the workmanship of those statutes that restored and brought back "the unity and married calm of States." His hand was in all that great legislation that created the war currency, and in all the still greater work that redeemed the promises of the government and made the currency equal to gold.

When at last he passed from the halls of legislation into a high executive office, he displayed that experience, intelligence, firmness, and poise of character, which have carried us through a stormy period of three years, with one half the public press crying "Crucify him!" and a hostile Congress seeking to prevent success. In all this he remained unmoved until victory crowned him. The great fiscal affairs of the nation, and the vast business interests of the country, he guarded and preserved while executing the law of resumption, and effected its object without a jar and against the false prophecies of one half of the press and of all the Democratic party.

He has shown himself able to meet with calmness the great emergencies of the government. For twenty-five years he has trodden the perilous heights of public duty, and against all the shafts of malice has borne his breast unharmed. He has stood in the blaze of "that fierce light that beats against the throne"; but its fiercest ray has found no flaw in his armor, no stain upon his shield. I do not present him as a better Republican or a better man than thousands of others that we honor; but I present him for your deliberate and favorable consideration. I nominate JOHN SHERMAN, OF OHIO.

THE DEMOCRATIC PARTY

From "The Speeches and Addresses of William E. Russell." Copyrighted 1893, by Little, Brown and Company, Boston, publishers.

BY WILLIAM E. RUSSELL

As I stand here to-night, a Democrat, speaking to Democrats, and to men whose conscience party could not bind,--men who carry their sovereignty each under his own hat,--there comes vividly back to me the stirring words with which the chairman opened a similar meeting on the eve of the great battle of 1884, "This is a union meeting;" and, as he spoke, the minds of his hearers went back to war days, when principle was placed above party, and patriotism above partisanship.

Our union is not for the triumph of any man, but for the triumph of ideas; for a living faith, a progressive spirit. It is of that to-night I speak.

It has often been said that there was little difference between the two parties. Perhaps that was the criticism of honest men, whose earnest desire for honest candidates led them to look no farther. To-day every intelligent man in Massachusetts knows that there is a wide difference between the parties,--all the difference that there is between standing still and moving forward. I do not believe that this difference is accidental. It is the natural evolution of the history and purpose of the parties. A political prophet of a generation ago, who knew this history, who had studied the Democratic faith, had seen the birth of the Republican party and its purpose, could have predicted the position of the parties to-day. The Democratic party is old enough to have outlived and defeated all other parties, young enough to represent the progressive spirit of to-day. It must be founded on vital principles and have a living faith. Its creed from its first to its thirty-ninth article is an abiding trust in the people, a belief that men, irrespective of the accident of birth or fortune, have a right to a voice in the government that rules them. Its principles are the equality and freedom of all men in affairs of State and before the altar of their God,--that there should be allowed the greatest possible personal liberty, that a government least felt is best, that it should lightly and never unnecessarily impose its burdens of taxation and restriction, that in its administration there should be simplicity, purity, and economy, and in its form it should be closely within the reach and control of the people.

Progress, merely as progress, is nothing; but progress that sees the changes of a generation,--a blessed, lasting peace in place of the horrors and burdens of civil war, a reunited, loyal country; progress that hears the demand of the people for pure and economic administration, for relief from restrictions and taxation; progress that feels the discontent and suffering of great masses of the people,--this progress, if willing and ready to shape into legislation the new wishes and the new wants, rises to the height of statesmanship.

THE CALL TO DEMOCRATS

From a speech opening the National Democratic Convention, at Baltimore, Maryland, June, 1912.

BY ALTON B. PARKER

It is not the wild and cruel methods of revolution and violence that are needed to correct the abuses incident to our Government as to all things human. Neither material nor moral progress lies that way. We have made our Government and our complicated institutions by appeals to reason, seeking to educate all our people that, day after day, year after year, century after century, they may see more clearly, act more justly, become more and more attached to the fundamental ideas that underlie our society. If we are to preserve undiminished the heritage bequeathed us, and add to it those accretions without which society would perish, we shall need all the powers that the school, the church, the court, the deliberative assembly, and the quiet thought of our people can bring to bear.

We are called upon to do battle against the unfaithful guardians of our Constitution and liberties and the hordes of ignorance which are pushing forward only to the ruin of our social and governmental fabric.

Too long has the country endured the offenses of the leaders of a party which once knew greatness. Too long have we been blind to the bacchanal of corruption. Too long have we listlessly watched the assembling of the forces that threaten our country and our firesides.

The time has come when the salvation of the country demands the restoration to place and power of men of high ideals who will wage unceasing war against corruption in politics, who will enforce the law against both rich and poor, and who will treat guilt as personal and punish it accordingly.

What is our duty? To think alike as to men and measures? Impossible! Even for our great party! There is not a reactionary among us. All Democrats are Progressives. But it is inevitably human that we shall not all agree that in a single highway is found the only road to progress, or each make the same man of all our worthy candidates his first choice.

It is possible, however, and it is our duty to put aside all selfishness, to consent cheerfully that the majority shall speak for each of us, and to march out of this convention shoulder to shoulder, intoning the praises of our chosen leader--and that will be his due, whichever of the honorable and able men now claiming our attention shall be chosen.

NOMINATING WOODROW WILSON
At the National Democratic Convention, Baltimore, Maryland, June, 1912.
BY JOHN W. WESCOTT

The New Jersey delegation is commissioned to represent the great cause of Democracy and to offer you as its militant and triumphant leader a scholar, not a charlatan; a statesman, not a doctrinaire; a profound lawyer, not a splitter of legal hairs; a political economist, not an egotistical theorist; a practical politician, who constructs, modifies, restrains, without disturbance and destruction; a resistless debater and consummate master of statement, not a mere sophist; a humanitarian, not a defamer of characters and lives; a man whose mind is at once cosmopolitan and composite of America; a gentleman of unpretentious habits, with the fear of God in his heart and the love of mankind exhibited in every act of his life; above all a public servant who has been tried to the uttermost and never found wanting--matchless, unconquerable, the ultimate Democrat, Woodrow Wilson.

New Jersey has reasons for her course. Let us not be deceived in our premises. Campaigns of vilification, corruption and false pretense have lost their usefulness. The evolution of national energy is towards a more intelligent morality in politics and in all other relations. The situation admits of no compromise. The temper and purpose of the American public will tolerate no other view. The indifference of the American people to politics has disappeared. Any platform and any candidate not conforming to this vast social and commercial behest will go down to ignominious defeat at the polls.

Men are known by what they say and do. They are known by those who hate and oppose them. Many years ago Woodrow Wilson said, "No man is great who thinks himself so, and no man is good who does not try to secure the happiness and comfort of others." This is the secret of his life. The deeds of this moral and intellectual giant are known to all men. They accord, not with the shams and false pretences of politics, but make national harmony with the millions of patriots determined to correct the wrongs of plutocracy and reestablish the maxims of American liberty in all their regnant beauty and practical effectiveness. New Jersey loves Woodrow Wilson not for the enemies he has made. New Jersey loves him for what he is. New Jersey argues that Woodrow Wilson is the only candidate who can not only make Democratic success a certainty, but secure the electoral vote of almost every State in the Union.

New Jersey will indorse his nomination by a majority of 100,000 of her liberated citizens. We are not building for a day, or even a generation, but for all time. New Jersey believes that there is an omniscience in national instinct. That instinct centers in Woodrow Wilson. He has been in political life less than two years. He has had no organization; only a practical ideal--the reestablishment of equal opportunity. Not his deeds alone, not his immortal words alone, not his personality alone, not his matchless powers alone, but all combined compel national faith and confidence in him. Every crisis evolves its master. Time and circumstance have evolved Woodrow Wilson. The North, the South, the East, and the West unite in him. New Jersey appeals to this convention to give the nation Woodrow Wilson, that he may open the gates of opportunity to every man, woman, and child under our flag, by reforming abuses, and thereby teaching them, in his matchless words, "to release their energies intelligently, that peace, justice and prosperity may reign." New Jersey rejoices, through her freely chosen representatives, to name for the presidency of the United States the Princeton schoolmaster, Woodrow Wilson.

DEMOCRATIC FAITH

From "The Speeches and Addresses of William E. Russell." Copyrighted, 1894, by Little, Brown and Company, Boston, Publishers

BY WILLIAM E. RUSSELL

For the honor and privilege of addressing this gathering of Young Democracy I am deeply grateful. With earnestness and enthusiasm, with devotion to the party and its principles, and with unflinching loyalty to its glorious leaders, Young Democracy meets to-day for organization and action. Gladly it volunteers in a campaign where its very faith is at stake; impatiently it awaits the coming of the battle.

We fight for measures, not men; the principles of government, not men's characters, are to be discussed; a nation's policy, not personal ambition, is to be determined.

Thank God, we enter the fight with a living faith, founded upon principles that are just, enduring, as old as the nation itself, yet ever young, vigorous, and progressive, because there is ever work for them to do. Our party was not founded for a single mission, which accomplished, left it drifting with no fixed star of principle to guide it. It was born and has lived to uphold great truths of government that need always to be enforced. The influence of the past speaks to us in the voice of the present. Jefferson and Jackson still lead us, not because they are glorious reminiscences, but because the philosophy of the one, the courage of the other, the Democracy of both, are potent factors in determining Democracy to-day.

We believe that a government which controls the lives, liberties, and property of a people in its administration should be honest, economical, and efficient; and in its form a local self-government kept near to the power that makes and obeys it. To safeguard the rights and liberty of the individual, the Democratic party demands home rule. Democracy stands beside the humblest citizen to protect him from oppressive government; it is the bulwark of the silent people to resist having the power and purpose of government warped by the clamorous demands of selfish interests. Its greatest good, its highest glory, is that it is, and is to be, the people's party. To it government is a power to protect and encourage men to make the most of themselves, and not something for men to make the most out of.

And, lastly, we believe in the success, the glory, and the splendid destiny of this great Republic. It leaped into life from the hands of Democrats. More than three quarters of a century it has been nurtured and strengthened by Democratic rule. Under Democratic administrations, in its mighty sweep, it has stretched from ocean to ocean, not as a North and South and East and West, but now as a glorious Union of sovereign States, reunited in love and loyalty, a great nation of millions of loyal subjects.

The faith we profess is distinctly an American faith; the principles we proclaim are distinctly American principles, and have been from their first utterance in the Declaration of Independence to their latest in the platform of the St. Louis Convention; the policy they demand of us as Democrats is emphatically an American policy.

Our great leader lives in the faith we profess. He speaks in the principles we assert. He leads because we follow Democracy, its faith, its principles, and its policy and hail him as the foremost Democrat of the Nation. Thus comes victory. Thus victory means something. Thus power and responsibility go together, and the only influence behind him are the wishes, the rights, and the welfare of the great American people. In such a cause, with such a leader, there is no room for failure.

"To doubt would be disloyalty,

To falter would be sin."
ENGLAND AND AMERICA
BY JOHN BRIGHT

What can be more monstrous than that we, as we call ourselves, to some extent, an educated, a moral, and a Christian nation--at a moment when an accident of this kind occurs, before we have made a representation to the American government, before we have heard a word from it in reply--should be all up in arms, every sword leaping from its scabbard, and every man looking about for his pistols and his blunderbusses? I think the conduct pursued--and I have no doubt just the same is pursued by a certain class in America--is much more the conduct of savages than of Christian and civilized men. No, let us be calm. You recollect how we were dragged into the Russian war--how we "drifted" into it. You know that I, at least, have not upon my head any of the guilt of that fearful war. You know that it cost one hundred millions of money to this country; that it cost at least the lives of forty thousand Englishmen; that it disturbed your trade; that it nearly doubled the armies of Europe; that it placed the relations of Europe on a much less peaceful footing than before; and that it did not effect a single thing of all those that it was promised to effect.

Now, then, before I sit down, let me ask you what is this people, about which so many men in England at this moment are writing, and speaking, and thinking, with harshness, I think with injustice, if not with great bitterness? Two centuries ago, multitudes of the people of this country found a refuge on the North American continent, escaping from the tyranny of the Stuarts and from the bigotry of Laud. Many noble spirits from our country made great experiments in favor of human freedom on that continent. Bancroft, the great historian of his own country, has said, in his own graphic and emphatic language, "The history of the colonization of America is the history of the crimes of Europe."

At this very moment, then, there are millions in the United States who personally, or whose immediate parents have at one time been citizens of this country. They found a home in the Far West; they subdued the wilderness; they met with plenty there, which was not afforded them in their native country; and they have become a great people. There may be persons in England who are jealous of those States. There may be men who dislike democracy, and who hate a republic; there may be those whose sympathies warm only toward an oligarchy or a monarchy. But of this I am certain, that only misrepresentation the most gross, or calumny the most wicked, can sever the tie which unites the great mass of the people of this country with their friends and brethren beyond the Atlantic.

Now, whether the Union will be restored or not, or the South achieve an unhonored independence or not, I know not, and I predict not. But this I think I know--that in a few years, a very few years, the twenty millions of freemen in the North will be thirty millions, or even fifty millions--a population equal to or exceeding that of this kingdom. When that time comes, I pray that it may not be said among them, that in the darkest hour of their country's trials, England, the land of their fathers, looked on with icy coldness and saw unmoved the perils and calamities of her children. As for me, I have but this to say: I am but one in this audience, and but one in the citizenship of this country; but if all other tongues are silent, mine shall speak for that policy which tends, and which always shall tend, to generous thoughts, and generous words, and generous deeds, between the two great nations who speak the English language, and from their origin are alike entitled to the English name.

ON HOME RULE IN IRELAND

BY WILLIAM E. GLADSTONE

There has been no great day of hope for Ireland, no day when you might hope completely and definitely to end the controversy till now--more than ninety years. The long periodic time has at last run out, and the star has again mounted into the heavens. What Ireland was doing for herself in 1795 we at length have done. The Roman Catholics have been emancipated--emancipated after a woeful disregard of solemn promises through twenty-nine years, emancipated slowly, sullenly, not from good will, but from abject terror, with all the fruits and consequences which will always follow that method of legislation. The second problem has been also solved, and the representation of Ireland has been thoroughly reformed; and I am thankful to say that the franchise was given to Ireland on the readjustment of last year with a free heart, with an open hand; and the gift of that franchise was the last act required to make the success of Ireland in her final effort absolutely sure. We have given Ireland a voice; we must all listen for a moment to what she says. We must all listen, both sides, both parties--I mean as they are divided on this question--divided, I am afraid, by an almost immeasurable gap. We do not undervalue or despise the forces opposed to us. I have described them as the forces of class and its dependents; and that as a general description--as a slight and rude outline of a description--is, I believe, perfectly true. You have power, you have wealth, you have rank, you have station, you have organization. What have we? We think that we have the people's heart; we believe and we know we have the promise of the harvest of the future. As to the people's heart, you may dispute it, and dispute it with perfect sincerity. Let that matter make its own proof. As to the harvest of the future, I doubt if you have so much confidence; and I believe that there is in the breast of many a man who means to vote against us to- night a profound misgiving, approaching even to a deep conviction, that the end will be as we foresee, and not as you do--that the ebbing tide is with you, and the flowing tide with us. Ireland stands at your bar, expectant, hopeful, almost suppliant. Her words are the words of truth and soberness. She asks a blessed oblivion of the past, and in that oblivion our interest is deeper than even hers. My right honorable friend, the member for East Edinburgh, asks us tonight to abide by the traditions of which we are the heirs. What traditions? By the Irish traditions? Go into the length and breadth of the world, ransack the literature of all countries, find, if you can, a single voice, a single book--find, I would almost say, as much as a single newspaper article, unless the product of the day,--in which the conduct of England towards Ireland is anywhere treated except with profound and bitter condemnation. Are these the traditions by which we are exhorted to stand? No; they are a sad exception to the glory of our country. They are a broad and black blot upon the pages of its history; and what we want to do is to stand by the traditions of which we are the heirs in all matters except our relations with Ireland, and to make our relations with Ireland to conform to the other traditions of our country. So we treat our traditions, so we hail the demand of Ireland for what I call a blessed oblivion of the past. She asks also a boon for the future; and that boon for the future, unless we are much mistaken, will be a boon to us in respect of honor, no less than a boon to her in respect of happiness, prosperity, and peace. Such, sir, is her prayer. Think, I beseech you, think well, think wisely, think, not for the moment, but for the years that are to come, before you reject this Bill.

THE LEGAL PLEA

THE DARTMOUTH COLLEGE CASE
BY DANIEL WEBSTER

The case before the court is not of ordinary importance, nor of everyday occurrence. It affects not this college only, but every college, and all the literary institutions of the country. They have flourished hitherto, and have become in a high degree respectable and useful to the community. They have all a common principle of existence, the inviolability of their charters. It will be a dangerous, a most dangerous experiment to hold these institutions subject to the rise and fall of popular parties, and the fluctuations of political opinions. If the franchise may be at any time taken away, or impaired, the property also may be taken away, or its use perverted. Benefactors will have no certainty of effecting the object of their bounty; and learned men will be deterred from devoting themselves to the service of such institutions, from the precarious title of their offices. Colleges and halls will be deserted by all better spirits, and become a theater for the contentions of politics. Party and faction will be cherished in the places consecrated to piety and learning.

When the court in North Carolina declared the law of the State, which repealed a grant to its university, unconstitutional and void, the legislature had the candor and the wisdom to repeal the law. This example, so honorable to the State which exhibited it, is most fit to be followed on this occasion. And there is good reason to hope that a State which has hitherto been so much distinguished for temperate counsels, cautious legislation, and regard to law, will not fail to adopt a course which will accord with her highest and best interests, and in no small degree elevate her reputation.

It was for many and obvious reasons most anxiously desired that the question of the power of the legislature over this charter should have been finally decided in the State court. An earnest hope was entertained that the judges of the court might have reviewed the case in a light favorable to the rights of the trustees. That hope has failed. It is here that those rights are now to be maintained, or they are prostrated forever.

This, sir, is my case. It is the case, not merely of that humble institution, it is the case of every college in the land. It is more. It is the case of every eleemosynary institution throughout our country--of all those great charities formed by the piety of our ancestors, to alleviate human misery, and scatter blessings along the pathway of life. It is more! It is, in some sense, the case of every man among us who has property, of which he may be stripped, for the question is simply this: Shall our State legislatures be allowed to take that which is not their own; to turn it from its original use, and to apply it to such ends or purposes as they in their discretion shall see fit?

Sir, you may destroy this little institution; it is weak; it is in your hands! I know it is one of the lesser lights in the literary horizon of our country. You may put it out. But, if you do so, you must carry through your work! You must extinguish, one after another, all those greater lights of science, which, for more than a century, have thrown their radiance over our land!

It is, sir, as I have said, a small college, and yet there are those who love it.

Sir, I know not how others may feel, but for myself, when I see my Alma Mater surrounded, like Caesar, in the senate house, by those who are reiterating stab after stab, I would not, for this right hand, have her turn to me, and say, *et tu quoque, mi fili! And thou too, my son!*

IN DEFENSE OF THE KENNISTONS
BY DANIEL WEBSTER

Gentlemen of the Jury,--It is true that the offense charged in the indictment in this case is not capital; but perhaps this can hardly be considered as favorable to the defendants. To those who are guilty, and without hope of escape, no doubt the lightness of the penalty of transgression gives consolation. But if the defendants are innocent, it is more natural for them to be thinking upon what they have lost by that alteration of the law which has left highway robbery no longer capital, than what the guilty might gain by it. They have lost those great privileges in their trial, which the law allows, in capital cases, for the protection of innocence against unfounded accusation. They have lost the right of being previously furnished with a copy of the indictment, and a list of the government witnesses. They have lost the right of peremptory challenge; and, notwithstanding the prejudices which they know have been excited against them, they must show legal cause of challenge, in each individual case, or else take the jury as they find it. They have lost the benefit of assignment of counsel by the court. They have lost the benefit of the Commonwealth's process to bring in witnesses in their behalf. When to these circumstances it is added that they are strangers, almost wholly without friends, and without the means for preparing their defense, it is evident they must take their trial under great disadvantages.

But without dwelling on these considerations, I proceed, Gentlemen of the Jury, to ask your attention to those circumstances which cannot but cast doubts on the story of the prosecutor.

The jury will naturally look to the appearances exhibited on the field after the robbery. The portmanteau was there. The witnesses say that the straps which fastened it to the saddle had been neither cut nor broken. They were carefully unbuckled. This was very considerate for robbers. It had been opened, and its contents were scattered about the field. The pocket book, too, had been opened, and many papers it contained found on the ground. Nothing valuable was lost but money. The robbers did not think it well to go off at once with the portmanteau and the pocket book. The place was so secure, so remote, so unfrequented; they were so far from the highway, at least one full rod; there were so few persons passing, probably not more than four or five then in the road, within hearing of the pistols and the cries of Goodridge; there being, too, not above five or six dwelling-houses, full of people, within the hearing of the report of a pistol; these circumstances were all so favorable to their safety, that the robbers sat down to look over the prosecutor's papers, carefully examined the contents of his pocket book and portmanteau, and took only the things which they needed! There was money belonging to other persons. The robbers did not take it. They found out it was not the prosecutor's, and left it. It may be said to be favorable to the prosecutor's story, that the money which did not belong to him, and the plunder of which would seem to be the most probable inducement he could have to feign a robbery, was not taken. But the jury will consider whether this circumstance does not bear quite as strongly the other way, and whether they can believe that robbers could have left this money, either from accident or design.

II

The witnesses on the part of the prosecution have testified that the defendants, when arrested, manifested great agitation and alarm; paleness overspread their faces, and drops of sweat stood on their temples. This satisfied the witnesses of the defendants' guilt, and they now state the circumstances as being indubitable proof. This argument manifests, in those who use it, an equal want of sense and sensibility. It is precisely fitted to the feeling and the intellect of a bum-bailiff. In a court of justice it deserves nothing but contempt. Is there nothing that can agitate the frame or excite the blood but the consciousness of guilt? If the defendants were innocent, would they not feel indignation at this unjust accusation? If they saw an attempt to produce false evidence against them, would they not be angry? And, seeing the production of such evidence, might they not feel fear and alarm? And have indignation, and anger, and terror no power to affect the human countenance or the human frame?

Miserable, miserable, indeed, is the reasoning which would infer any man's guilt from his agitation when he found himself accused of a heinous offense; when he saw evidence which he might know to be false and fraudulent brought against him; when his house was filled, from the garret to the cellar, by those whom he might esteem as false witnesses; and when he himself, instead of being at liberty to observe their conduct and watch their motions, was a prisoner in close custody in his own house, with the fists of a catchpoll clenched upon his throat.

From the time of the robbery to the arrest, five or six weeks, the defendants were engaged in their usual occupations. They are not found to have passed a dollar of money to anybody. They continued their ordinary habits of labor. No man saw money about them, nor any circumstance that might lead to a suspicion that they had money. Nothing occurred tending in any degree to excite suspicion against them. When arrested, and when all this array of evidence was brought against them, and when they could hope in nothing but their innocence, immunity was offered them again if they would confess. They were pressed, and urged, and allured, by every motive which could be set before them, to acknowledge their participation in the offense, and to bring out their accomplices. They steadily protested that they could confess nothing because they knew nothing. In defiance of all the discoveries made in their house, they have trusted to their innocence. On that, and on the candor and discernment of an enlightened jury, they still rely.

If the jury are satisfied that there is the highest improbability that these persons could have had any previous knowledge of Goodridge, or been concerned in any previous concert to rob him; if their conduct that evening and the next day was marked by no circumstance of suspicion; if from that moment until their arrest nothing appeared against them; if they neither passed money, nor are found to have had money; if the manner of the search of their house, and the circumstances attending it, excite strong suspicions of unfair and fraudulent practices; if, in the hour of their utmost peril, no promises of safety could draw from the defendants any confession affecting themselves or others, it will be for the jury to say whether they can pronounce them guilty.

IN DEFENCE OF JOHN E. COOK

Published in Depew's "Library of Oratory," E. J. Bowen and Company, New York, publishers.

BY D. W. VOORHEES

Who is John E. Cook?

He has the right himself to be heard before you; but I will answer for him. Sprung from an ancestry of loyal attachment to the American government, he inherits no blood of tainted impurity. His grandfather, an officer of the Revolution, by which your liberty, as well as mine, was achieved, and his gray-haired father, who lived to weep over him, a soldier of the war of 1812, he brings no dishonored lineage into your presence. Born of a parent stock occupying the middle walks of life, and possessed of all those tender and domestic virtues which escape the contamination of those vices that dwell on the frozen peaks, or in the dark and deep caverns of society, he would not have been here had precept and example been remembered in the prodigal wanderings of his short and checkered life.

Poor deluded boy! wayward, misled child! An evil star presided over thy natal hour and smote it with gloom.

In an evil hour--and may it be forever accursed!--John E. Cook met John Brown on the prostituted plains of Kansas. On that field of fanaticism, three years ago, this fair and gentle youth was thrown into contact with the pirate and robber of civil warfare.

Now look at John Cook, the follower. He is in evidence before you. Never did I plead for a face that I was more willing to show. If evil is there, I have not seen it. If murder is there, I am to learn to mark the lines of the murderer anew. If the assassin is in that young face, then commend me to the look of an assassin. No, gentlemen, it is a face for a mother to love, and a sister to idolize, and in which the natural goodness of his heart pleads trumpet-tongued against the deep damnation that estranged him from home and its principles.

John Brown was the despotic leader and John E. Cook was an ill-fated follower of an enterprise whose horror be now realizes and deplores. I defy the man, here or elsewhere, who has ever known John E. Cook, who has ever looked once fully into his face, and learned anything of his history, to lay his hand on his heart and say that he believes him guilty of the origin or the results of the outbreak at Harper's Ferry.

Here, then, are the two characters whom you are thinking to punish alike. Can it be that a jury of Christian men will find no discrimination should be made between them? Are the tempter and the tempted the same in your eyes? Is the beguiled youth to die the same as the old offender who has pondered his crimes for thirty years? Are there no grades in your estimations of guilt? Is each one, without respect to age or circumstances, to be beaten with the same number of stripes?

Such is not the law, human or divine. We are all to be rewarded according to our works, whether in punishment for evil, or blessings for good that we have done. You are here to do justice, and if justice requires the same fate to befall Cook that befalls Brown, I know nothing of her rules, and do not care to learn. They are as widely asunder, in all that constitutes guilt, as the poles of the earth, and should be dealt with accordingly. It is in your power to do so, and by the principles by which you yourselves are willing to be judged hereafter, I implore you to do it!

IN DEFENSE OF THE SOLDIERS

Published in "Depew's Library of Oratory," E. J. Bowen and Company, New York, publishers

BY JOSIAH QUINCY, JR.

May it please your honors, and you gentlemen of the jury,--We have at length gone through the evidence in behalf of the prisoners. The witnesses have now placed before you that state of facts from which results our defense.

I stated to you, gentlemen, your duty in opening this cause--do not forget the discharge of it. You are paying a debt you owe the community for your own protection and safety: by the same mode of trial are your own rights to receive a determination; and in your turn a time may come when you will expect and claim a similar return from some other jury of your fellow subjects.

How much need was there for my desire that you should suspend your judgment till the witnesses were all examined? How different is the complexion of the cause? Will not all this serve to show every honest man the little truth to be attained in partial hearings? In the present case, how great was the prepossession against us? And I appeal to you, gentlemen, what cause there now is to alter our sentiments? Will any sober, prudent man countenance the proceedings of the people in King Street,--can any one justify their conduct,--is there any one man or any body of men who are interested to espouse and support their conduct?

Surely, no! But our inquiry must be confined to the legality of their conduct, and here can be no difficulty. It was certainly illegal, unless many witnesses are directly perjured: witnesses, who have no apparent interest to falsify,--witnesses who have given their testimony with candor and accuracy,--witnesses whose credibility stands untouched,--whose credibility the counsel for the king do not pretend to impeach or hint a suggestion to their disadvantage.

I say, gentlemen, by the standard of the law are we to judge the actions of the people who were the assailants and those who were the assailed and then on duty. And here, gentlemen, the rule we formerly laid down takes place. To the facts, gentlemen, apply yourselves. Consider them as testified; weigh the credibility of the witnesses-- balance their testimony--compare the several parts of it--see the amount of it; and then, according to your oath, "make true deliverance according to your evidence." That is, gentlemen, having settled the facts, bring them truly to the standard of the law; the king's judges, who are acquainted with it, who are presumed best to know it, will then inspect this great standard of right and wrong, truth and justice; and they are to determine the degree of guilt to which the fact rises.

II

May it please your honors, and you gentlemen of the jury,--After having thus gone through the evidence and considered it as applicatory to all and every one of the prisoners, let us take once more a brief and cursory survey of matters supported by the evidence. And here let me ask in sober reason, what language more opprobrious, what actions more exasperating, than those used on this occasion? Words, I am sensible, are no justification of blows, but they serve as the grand clew to discover the temper and the designs of the agents; they serve also to give us light in discerning the apprehensions and thoughts of those who are the objects of abuse.

"You lobsters!"--"You bloody-back!"--"You coward!"--"You dastard!" are but some of the expressions proved. What words more galling? What more cutting and provoking to a soldier? But accouple these words with the succeeding actions,-- "You dastard!"--"You coward!" A soldier and a coward!

This was touching "the point of honor and the pride of virtue." But while these are as yet fomenting the passions and swelling the bosom, the attack is made; and probably the latter words were reiterated at the onset; at least, were yet sounding in the ear. Gentlemen of the jury, for Heaven's sake, let us put ourselves in the same situation! Would you not spurn at that spiritless institution of society which tells you to be a subject at the expense of your manhood?

But does the soldier step out of his ranks to seek his revenge? Not a witness pretends it. Did not the people repeatedly come within the points of their bayonets and strike on the muzzles of the guns? You have heard the witnesses.

Does the law allow one member of the community to behave in this manner towards his fellow citizen, and then bid the injured party be calm and moderate? The expressions from one party were--"Stand off, stand off!"--"I am upon my station."--"If they molest me upon my post, I will fire."--"Keep off!"

These words were likely to produce reflection and procure peace. But had the words on the other hand a similar tendency? Consider the temper prevalent among all parties at this time. Consider the situation of the soldiery; and come to the heat and pressure of the action. The materials are laid, the spark is raised, the fire enkindles, all prudence and true wisdom are utterly consumed. Does common sense, does the law expect impossibilities?

Here, to expect equanimity of temper, would be as irrational as to expect discretion in a madman. But was anything done on the part of the assailants similar to the conduct, warnings, and declarations of the prisoners? Answer for yourselves, gentlemen! The words reiterated all around stabbed to the heart; the actions of the assailants tended to a worse end,--to awaken every passion of which the human breast is susceptible; fear, anger, pride, resentment, revenge, alternately take possession of the whole man.

To expect, under these circumstances, that such words would assuage the tempest, that such actions would allay the flames,--you might as rationally expect the inundations of a torrent would suppress a deluge, or rather that the flames of Aetna would extinguish a conflagration!

III

Gentlemen of the Jury,--This case has taken up much of your time, and is likely to take up so much more that I must hasten to a close. Indeed, I should not have troubled you, by being thus lengthy, but from a sense of duty to the prisoners; they who in some sense may be said to have put their lives in my hands; they whose situation was so peculiar that we have necessarily taken up more time than ordinary cases require. They, under all these circumstances, placed a confidence it was my duty not to disappoint, and which I have aimed at discharging with fidelity. I trust you, gentlemen, will do the like; that you will examine and judge with a becoming temper of mind; remembering that they who are under oath to declare the whole truth think and act very differently from bystanders, who, being under no ties of this kind, take a latitude which is by no means admissible in a court of law.

I cannot close this cause better than by desiring you to consider well the genius and spirit of the law which will be laid down, and to govern yourselves by this great standard of truth. To some purposes, you may be said, gentlemen, to be ministers of justice; and "ministers," says a learned judge, "appointed for the ends of public justice, should have written on their hearts the solemn engagements of his Majesty, at his coronation, to cause law and justice in mercy to be executed in all his judgments."

"The quality of mercy is not strained;
It droppeth as the gentle rain from heaven:...
It is twice blessed;

It blesseth him that gives, and him that takes."

I leave you, gentlemen, hoping you will be directed in your inquiry and judgment to a right discharge of your duty. We shall all of us, gentlemen, have an hour of cool reflection when the feelings and agitations of the day shall have subsided; when we shall view things through a different and a much juster medium. It is then we all wish an absolving conscience. May you, gentlemen, now act such a part as will hereafter insure it; such a part as may occasion the prisoners to rejoice. May the blessing of those who were in jeopardy of life come upon you--may the blessing of Him who is "not faulty to die" descend and rest upon you and your posterity.

IN DEFENSE OF LORD GEORGE GORDON
Before the Court of King's Bench, 1781
BY LORD THOMAS ERSKINE

Gentlemen,--You have now heard, upon the solemn oaths of honest, disinterested men, a faithful history of the conduct of Lord George Gordon, from the day that he became a member of the Protestant Association to the day that he was committed a prisoner to the Tower. And I have no doubt, from the attention with which I have been honored from the beginning, that you have still kept in your minds the principles to which I entreated you would apply it, and that you have measured it by that standard. You have, therefore, only to look back to the whole of it together; to reflect on all you have heard concerning him; to trace him in your recollection through every part of the transaction; and, considering it with one manly, liberal view, to ask your own honest hearts, whether you can say that this noble and unfortunate youth is a wicked and deliberate traitor, who deserves by your verdict to suffer a shameful and ignominious death, which will stain the ancient honors of his house forever.

The crime which the Crown would have fixed upon him is, that he assembled the Protestant Association round the House of Commons, not merely to influence and persuade Parliament by the earnestness of their supplications, but actually to coerce it by hostile, rebellious force; that, finding himself disappointed in the success of that coercion, he afterward incited his followers to abolish the legal indulgences to Papists, which the object of the petition was to repeal, by the burning of their houses of worship, and the destruction of their property, which ended, at last, in a general attack on the property of all orders of men, religious and civil, on the public treasures of the nation, and on the very being of the government.

To support a charge of so atrocious and unnatural a complexion, the laws of the most arbitrary nations would require the most incontrovertible proof. And what evidence, gentlemen of the jury, does the Crown offer to you in compliance with these sound and sacred doctrines of justice? A few broken, interrupted, disjoint-ed words, without context or connection--uttered by the speaker in agitation and heat--heard, by those who relate them to you, in the midst of tumult and confu-sion--and even those words, mutilated as they are, in direct opposition to, and in-consistent with, repeated and earnest declarations delivered at the very same time and on the very same occasion, related to you by a much greater number of persons, and absolutely incompatible with the whole tenor of his conduct. Which of us all, gentlemen, would be safe, standing at the bar of God or man, if we were not to be judged by the regular current of our lives and conversations, but by detached and unguarded expressions, picked out by malice, and recorded, without context or cir-cumstances, against us? Yet such is the only evidence on which the Crown asks you to dip your hands, and to stain your consciences, in the innocent blood of the noble and unfortunate youth who stands before you.

I am sure you cannot but see, notwithstanding my great inability, increased by a perturbation of mind (arising, thank God! from no dishonest cause), that there has been not only no evidence on the part of the Crown to fix the guilt of the late com-motions upon the prisoner, but that, on the contrary, we have been able to resist the probability, I might almost say the possibility of the charge, not only by living witnesses, whom we only ceased to call because the trial would never have ended, but by the evidence of all the blood that has paid the forfeit of that guilt already; since, out of all the felons who were let loose from prisons, and who assisted in the destruction of our property, not a single wretch was to be found who could even attempt to save his own life by the plausible promise of giving evidence to-day.

What can overturn such a proof as this? Surely a good man might, without superstition, believe that such a union of events was something more than natural, and that a Divine Providence was watchful for the protection of innocence and truth.

I may now, therefore, relieve you from the pain of hearing me any longer, and be myself relieved from speaking on a subject which agitates and distresses me. Since Lord George Gordon stands clear of every hostile act or purpose against the Legislature of his country, or the properties of his fellow-subjects--since the whole tenor of conduct repels the belief of the ***traitorous intention*** charged by the indictment--my task is finished. I shall make no address to your passions. I will not remind you of the long and rigorous imprisonment he has suffered; I will not speak to you of his great youth, of his illustrious birth, and of his uniformly animated and generous zeal in Parliament for the Constitution of his country. Such topics might be useful in the balance; yet, even then, I should have trusted to the honest hearts of Englishmen to have felt them without excitation. At present, the plain and rigid rules of justice and truth are sufficient to entitle me to your verdict.

PRONOUNCING SENTENCE FOR HIGH TREASON
BY SIR ALFRED WILLS

Arthur Alfred Lynch, otherwise Arthur Lynch, the jury have found you guilty of the crime of high treason, a crime happily so rare that in the present day a trial for treason seems to be almost an anachronism-- a thing of the past. The misdeeds which have been done in this case, and which have brought you to the lamentable pass in which you stand, must surely convince the most skeptical and apathetic of the gravity and reality of the crime. What was your action in the darkest hour of your country's fortunes, when she was engaged in the deadly struggle from which she has just emerged? You joined the ranks of your country's foes. Born in Australia, a land which has nobly shown its devotion to its parent country, you have indeed taken a different course from that which was adopted by her sons. You have fought against your country, not with it. You have sought, as far as you could, to dethrone Great Britain from her place among the nations, to make her name a byword and a reproach, a synonym for weakness and irresolution. Nor can I forget that you have shed the blood, or done your best to shed the blood, of your countrymen who were fighting for their country. How many wives have been made widows, how many children orphans, by what you and those who acted under your command have done, Heaven only knows! You thought it safe at that dark hour of the Empire's fate, when Ladysmith, when Kimberley, when Mafeking, were in the very jaws of deadly peril--you thought it safe, no doubt, to lift the parricidal hand against your country. You thought she would shrink from the costly struggle wearied out by her gigantic efforts, and that, at the worst, a general peace would be made which would comprehend a general amnesty and cover up such acts as yours and save you from personal peril. You misjudged your country and failed to appreciate that, though slow to enter into a quarrel, however slow to take up arms, it has yet been her wont that in the quarrel she shall bear herself so that the opposer may beware of her, and that she is seldom so dangerous to her enemies as when the hour of national calamity has raised the dormant energies of her people--knit together every nerve and fiber of the body politic, and has made her sons determined to do all, to sacrifice all on behalf of the country that gave them birth. And against what a Sovereign and what a country did you lift your hand! A Sovereign the best beloved and most deeply honored of all the long line of English Kings and Queens, and whose lamented death was called back to my remembrance only yesterday as a fresh sorrow to many an English household. Against a country which has been the home of progress and freedom, and under whose beneficent sway, whenever you have chosen to stay within her dominions, you have enjoyed a liberty of person, a freedom of speech and action, such as you can have in no other country in Europe, and it is not too much to say in no other country in the world. The only--I will not say excuse, but palliation that I can find for conduct like yours is that it has been for some years past the fashion to treat lightly matters of this kind, so that men have been perhaps encouraged to play with sedition and to toy with treason, wrapt in a certain proud consciousness of strength begotten of the deep-seated and well-founded conviction that the loyalty of her people is supreme, and true authority in this country has slumbered or has treated with contemptuous indifference speeches and acts of sedition. It may be that you have been misled into the notion that, no matter what you did, so long as your conduct could be called a political crime, it was of no consequence. But it is one thing to talk sedition and to do small seditious acts, it is quite another thing to bear arms in the ranks of the foes of your country, and against it. Between the two the difference is immeasurable. But had you and those with whom you associated yourself succeeded, what fatal mischief might have been done to the great inheritance which has been bequeathed to us by our forefathers--that inheritance of power which it must be our work to use nobly and for good things; an inheritance of influence which will be of little effect even for good unless backed by power, and of duty which cannot be effectually performed if our power be shattered and our influence impaired. He who has attempted to do his country such irreparable wrong must be prepared to submit to the sentence which it is now my duty to pronounce upon you. The sentence of this Court--and it is pronounced in regard to each count of the indictment--is that you be taken hence to the place from which you came, and from thence to a place of execution, there to be hanged by the neck until you are dead.

THE IMPEACHMENT OF ANDREW JOHNSON
From the Official Records of the Trial in the United States Senate, 1868
BY GEORGE S. BOUTWELL

Andrew Johnson has disregarded and violated the laws and Constitution of his own country. Under his administration the government has not been strengthened, but weakened. Its reputation and influence at home and abroad have been injured and diminished. Ten States of this Union are without law, without security, without safety; public order everywhere violated, public justice nowhere respected; and all in consequence of the evil purposes and machinations of the President. Forty millions of people have been rendered anxious and uncertain as to the preservation of public peace and the perpetuity of the institutions of freedom in this country. All classes are oppressed by the private and public calamities which he has brought upon them. They appeal to you for relief. The nation waits in anxiety for the conclusion of these proceedings. Forty millions of people, whose interest in public affairs is in the wise and just administration of the laws, look to this tribunal as a sure defense against the encroachments of a criminally minded Chief Magistrate.

Will any one say that the heaviest judgment which you can render is any adequate punishment for these crimes? Your office is not punishment, but to secure the safety of the republic. But human tribunals are inadequate to punish those criminals who, as rulers or magistrates, by their example, conduct, policy, and crimes, become the scourge of communities and nations. No picture, no power of the imagination, can illustrate or conceive the suffering of the poor but loyal people of the South. A patriotic, virtuous, law-abiding chief magistrate would have healed the wounds of war, soothed private and public sorrows, protected the weak, encouraged the strong, and lifted from the Southern people the burdens which now are greater than they can bear.

Travelers and astronomers inform us that in the southern heavens, near the southern cross, there is a vast space which the uneducated call the hole in the sky, where the eye of man, with the aid of the powers of the telescope, has been unable to discover nebulae, or asteroid, or comet, or planet, or star, or sun. In that dreary, cold, dark region of space, which is only known to be less than infinite by the evidences of creation elsewhere, the Great Author of celestial mechanism has left the chaos which was in the beginning. If this earth were capable of the sentiments and emotions of justice and virtue, which in human mortal beings are the evidences and the pledge of our Divine origin and immortal destiny, it would heave and throw, with the energy of the elemental forces of nature, and project this enemy of two races of men into that vast region, there forever to exist in a solitude eternal as life, or as the absence of life, emblematical of, if not really, that "outer darkness" of which the Savior of man spoke in warning to those who are the enemies of themselves, of their race, and of their God. But it is yours to relieve, not to punish. This done and our country is again advanced in the intelligent opinion of mankind. In other governments an unfaithful ruler can be removed only by revolution, violence, or force. The proceeding here is judicial, and according to the forms of law. Your judgment will be enforced without the aid of a policeman or a soldier. What other evidence will be needed of the value of republican institutions? What other test of the strength and vigor of our government? What other assurance that the virtue of the people is equal to any emergency of national life?

BY WILLIAM M. EVARTS

Mr. Chief Justice and Senators,--If indeed we have arrived at a settled conclusion that this is a court, that it is governed by the law, that it is to confine its attention to the facts applicable to the law, and regard the sole evidence of those facts to be embraced within the testimony of witnesses or documents produced in court, we have made great progress in separating, at least, from your further consideration much that has been impressed upon your attention heretofore. It follows from this that the President is to be tried upon the charges which are produced here, and not upon common fame.

I may as conveniently at this point of the argument as at any other pay some attention to the astronomical punishment which the learned and honorable manager, Mr. Boutwell, thinks should be applied to this novel case of impeachment of the President. Cicero I think it is who says that a lawyer should know everything, for sooner or later there is no fact in history, in science, or of human knowledge that will not come into play in his arguments. Painfully sensible of my ignorance, being devoted to a profession which "sharpens and does not enlarge the mind," I yet can admire without envy the superior knowledge evinced by the honorable manager. Indeed, upon my soul, I believe he is aware of an astronomical fact which many professors of that science are wholly ignorant of. But nevertheless, while some of his honorable colleagues were paying attention to an unoccupied and unappropriated island on the surface of the seas, Mr. Manager Boutwell, more ambitious, had discovered an untenanted and unappropriated region in the skies, reserved, he would have us think, in the final councils of the Almighty, as the place of punishment for convicted and deposed American Presidents.

At first I thought that his mind had become so "enlarged" that it was not "sharp" enough to discover the Constitution had limited the punishment; but on reflection I saw that he was as legal and logical as he was ambitious and astronomical, for the Constitution has said "removal from office," and has put no limit to the distance of the removal, so that it may be, without shedding a drop of his blood, or taking a penny of his property, or confining his limbs, instant removal from office and transportation to the skies. Truly, this is a great undertaking; and if the learned manager can only get over the obstacles of the laws of nature the Constitution will not stand in his way. He can contrive no method but that of a convulsion of the earth that shall project the deposed President to this infinitely distant space; but a shock of nature of so vast an energy and for so great a result on him might unsettle even the footing of the firm members of Congress. We certainly need not resort to so perilous a method as that. How shall we accomplish it? Why, in the first place, nobody knows where that space is but the learned manager himself, and he is the necessary deputy to execute the judgment of the court.

Let it then be provided that in case of your sentence of deposition and removal from office the honorable and astronomical manager shall take into his own hands the execution of the sentence. With the President made fast to his broad and strong shoulders, and, having already essayed the flight by imagination, better prepared than anybody else to execute it in form, taking the advantage of ladders as far as ladders will go to the top of this great Capitol, and spurning then with his foot the crest of Liberty, let him set out upon his flight, while the two houses of Congress and all the people of the United States shall shout, "Sic itur ad astra."

II

But here a distressing doubt strikes me; how will the manager get back? He will have got far beyond the reach of gravitation to restore him, and so ambitious a wing as his could never stoop to a downward flight. Indeed, as he passes through the constellations, that famous question of Carlyle by which he derides the littleness of human affairs upon the scale of the measure of the heavens, "What thinks Boeotes as he drives his dogs up the zenith in their race of sidereal fire?" will force itself on his notice. What, indeed, would Boeotes think of this new constellation?

Besides, reaching this space, beyond the power of Congress even "to send for persons and papers," how shall he return, and how decide in the contest, there become personal and perpetual, the struggle of strength between him and the President? In this new revolution, thus established forever, who shall decide which is the sun and which is the moon? Who determine the only scientific test which reflects the hardest upon the other?

Mr. Chief Justice and Senators, we have come all at once to the great experiences and trials of a full-grown nation, all of which we thought we should escape--the distractions of civil strife, the exhaustions of powerful war. We could summon from the people a million of men and inexhaustible treasure to help the Constitution in its time of need. Can we summon now resources enough of civil prudence and of restraint of passion to carry us through this trial, so that whatever result may follow, in whatever form, the people may feel that the Constitution has received no wound! To this court, the last and best resort for this determination, it is to be left. And oh, if you could only carry yourselves back to the spirit and the purpose and the wisdom and the courage of the framers of the government, how safe would it be in your hands? How safe is it now in your hands, for you who have entered into their labors will see to it that the structure of your work comports in durability and excellence with theirs. Indeed, so familiar has the course of the argument made us with the names of the men of the convention and of the first Congress that I could sometimes seem to think that the presence even of the Chief Justice was replaced by the serene majesty of Washington, and that from Massachusetts we had Adams and Ames, from Connecticut, Sherman and Ellsworth, from New Jersey, Paterson and Boudinot, and from New York, Hamilton and Benson, and that they were to determine this case for us. Act, then, as if under this serene and majestic presence your deliberations were to be conducted to their close, and the Constitution was to come out from the watchful solicitude of these great guardians of it as if from their own judgment in this court of impeachment.

THE AFTER-DINNER SPEECH

AT A UNIVERSITY CLUB DINNER
Reprinted, with the author's permission, from a speech at a dinner of The Harvard Club of New York City.
BY HENRY E. HOWLAND
There should be a proper amount of modesty in one called upon to address such an intelligent audience of educated men as I see before me, and I am conscious of it in the same sense as the patient who said to his physician, "I suffer a great deal from nervous dyspepsia, and I attribute it to the fact that I attend so many public dinners." "Ah, I see," said the doctor, "you are often called upon to speak, and the nervous apprehension upsets your digestion." "Not at all; my apprehension is entirely on account of the other speakers; I never say a thing;" and it is with some hesitation that I respond to your call.

Following out that line of thought, there is a great deal that is attractive in a gathering of College men. They have such a winsome and a winning way with them.

Richest in endowments, foremost in progress, honored by the renown of a long line of distinguished sons, the university that claims you is worthy of the homage and respect which it receives from the educated men of America.

The study of the development of the human race by educational processes which change by necessity under changing conditions and environment, is one of the most interesting that we can engage in. The greatest men of this country, or any other, have not always been made by the university, however it may be with the average. You cannot always tell by a man's degree what manner of man he is likely to be. But the value of a technical or academic training is apparent as time goes on, population increases, occupations multiply and compete, and the strife of life becomes more fierce and strenuous.

Many in these days seem to prefer notoriety to fame, because it runs along the line of least resistance. A man has to climb for fame, but he can get notoriety by an easy tumble. And others forget the one essential necessary to success, of personal effort, and, assuming there is a royal road to learning, are content with the distinction of a degree from a university, without caring for what it implies, and answer as the son did to his father who asked him: "Why don't you work, my son? If you only knew how much happiness work brings, you would begin at once." "Father, I am trying to lead a life of self-denial in which happiness cuts no figure; do not tempt me."

But notwithstanding all these tendencies, the level of mankind is raised at these fountains of learning, the tone is higher, and the standards are continually advanced. The discipline and the training reaches and acts upon a willing and eager army of young recruits and works its salutary effect, like that upon a man who listened with rapt attention to a discourse from the pulpit and was congratulated upon his devotion, and asked if he was not impressed. "Yes," he replied, "for it is a mighty poor sermon that doesn't hit me somewhere."

However discouraging the action of our governing bodies through the obstruction and perverse action of an ignorant or corrupt majority or minority in them may be in the administration of great public affairs, the time at last comes when the nation arouses from its lethargy, shakes off its torpor, shows the strain of its blood, and follows its trained and intelligent leaders, like the man who, in a time of sore distress, after the ancient fashion, put ashes on his head, rent his garments, tore off his coat, his waistcoat, his shirt, and his undershirt, and at last came to himself. At such times, by the universal voice of public opinion and amid hearty applause of the whole people, we welcome to public office and the highest responsible stations such men as our universities have given to the country. It matters not to what family we belong--Harvard, Yale, Columbia, or Princeton--we are all of us one in our welcome to them, for they represent the university spirit and what it teaches--honor, high- mindedness, intelligence, truthfulness, unselfishness, courage, and patriotism.

THE EVACUATION OF NEW YORK
Reprinted with the author's permission
BY JOSEPH H. CHOATE

Mr. President and Gentlemen,--I came here to-night with some notes for a speech in my pocket, but I have been sitting next to General Butler, and in the course of the evening they have mysteriously disappeared. The consequence is, gentlemen, that you may expect a very good speech from him and a very poor one from me. When I read this toast which you have just drunk in honor of Her Gracious Majesty, the Queen of Great Britain, and heard how you received the letter of the British Minister that was read in response, and how heartily you joined in singing "God Save the Queen," when I look up and down these tables and see among you so many representatives of English capital and English trade, I have my doubts whether the evacuation of New York by the British was quite as thorough and lasting as history would fain have us believe. If George III, who certainly did all he could to despoil us of our rights and liberties and bring us to ruin--if he could rise from his grave and see how his granddaughter is honored at your hands to-night, why, I think he would return whence he came, thanking God that his efforts to enslave us, in which for eight long years he drained the resources of the British Empire, were not successful.

The truth is, the boasted triumph of New York in getting rid of the British once and forever has proved, after all, to be but a dismal failure. We drove them out in one century only to see them return in the next to devour our substance and to carry off all the honors. We have just seen the noble Chief Justice of England, the feasted favorite of all America, making a triumphal tour across the Continent and carrying all before him at the rate of fifty miles an hour. Night after night at our very great cost we have been paying the richest tribute to the reigning monarch of the British stage, and nowhere in the world are English men and women of character and culture received with a more hearty welcome, a more earnest hospitality, than in this very state of New York. The truth is, that this event that we celebrate to-day, which sealed the independence of America and seemed for a time to give a staggering blow to the prestige and the power of England, has proved to be no less a blessing to her own people than to ours. The latest and best of the English historians has said that, however important the independence of America might be in the history of England, it was of overwhelming importance in the history of the world, and that though it might have crippled for a while the supremacy of the English nation, it founded the supremacy of the English race. And in the same spirit we welcome the fact that those social, political, and material barriers that separated the two nations a century ago have now utterly vanished; that year by year we are being drawn closer and closer together, and that this day may be celebrated with equal fitness on both sides of the Atlantic and by all who speak the English tongue.

TIES OF KINSHIP

From "Modern Eloquence," Vol. I, Geo. L. Shuman and Company, Chicago, publishers.

BY SIR EDWIN ARNOLD

When I was conversing recently with Lord Tennyson, he said to me: "It is bad for us that English will always be a spoken speech, since that means that it will always be changing, and so the time will come when you and I will be as hard to read for the common people as Chaucer is to-day." You remember what opinion your brilliant humorist, Artemus Ward, let fall concerning that ancient singer. "Mr. Chaucer," he observed casually, "is an admirable poet, but as a spellist, a very decided failure."

To the treasure house of that noble tongue the United States has splendidly contributed. It would be far poorer to-day without the tender lines of Longfellow, the serene and philosophic pages of Emerson, the convincing wit and clear criticism of my illustrious departed friend, James Russell Lowell, the Catullus-like perfection of the lyrics of Edgar Allan Poe, and the glorious, large-tempered dithyrambs of Walt Whitman.

These stately and sacred laurel groves grow here in a garden forever extending, ever carrying further forward, for the sake of humanity, the irresistible flag of our Saxon supremacy, leading one to falter in an attempt to eulogize America and the idea of her potency and her promise. The most elaborate panegyric would seem but a weak impertinence, which would remind you, perhaps too vividly, of Sydney Smith, who, when he saw his grandchild pat the back of a large turtle, asked her why she did so. The little maid replied: "Grandpa, I do it to please the turtle." "My child," he answered, "you might as well stroke the dome of St. Paul's to please the Dean and chapter"

I myself once heard, in our Zoological gardens in London, another little girl ask her mamma whether it would hurt the elephant if she offered him a chocolate drop. In that guarded and respectful spirit is it that I venture to tell you here to-night how truly in England the peace and prosperity of your republic is desired, and that nothing except good will is felt by the mass of our people toward you, and nothing but the greatest satisfaction in your wealth and progress.

Between these two majestic sisters of the Saxon blood the hatchet of war is, please God, buried. No cause of quarrel, I think and hope, can ever be otherwise than truly out of proportion to the vaster causes of affection and accord. We have no longer to prove to each other, or to the world, that Englishmen and Americans are high-spirited and fearless; that Englishmen and Americans alike will do justice, and will have justice, and will put up with nothing else from each other and from the nations at large. Our proofs are made on both sides, and indelibly written on the page of history. Not that I wish to speak platitudes about war. It has been necessary to human progress; it has bred and preserved noble virtues; it has been inevitable, and may be again; but it belongs to a low civilization. Other countries have, perhaps, not yet reached that point of intimate contact and rational advance, but for us two, at least, the time seems to have come when violent decisions, and even talk of them, should be as much abolished between us as cannibalism.

I ventured, when in Washington, to propose to President Harrison that we should some day, the sooner the better, choose five men of public worth in the United States, and five in England; give them gold coats if you please, and a handsome salary, and establish them as a standing and supreme tribunal of arbitration, referring to them the little family fallings-out of America and of England, whenever something goes wrong between us about a sealskin in Behring Strait, a lobster pot, an ambassador's letter, a border tariff, or an Irish vote. He showed himself very well disposed toward my suggestion.

Mr. President, in the sacred hope that you take me to be a better poet than orator, I thank you all from the bottom of my heart for your reception to-night, and personally pray for the tranquility and prosperity of this free and magnificent republic.

CANADA, ENGLAND, AND THE UNITED STATES

From an address in Brewer's "The World's Best Orations," Vol. VII, Ferd P.

Kaiser, St. Louis, Chicago, publishers.

BY SIR WILFRED LAURIER

Mr. Toastmaster, Mr. President, and Gentlemen,--I very fully and very cordially appreciate the very kind feelings which have just now been uttered by the toastmaster in terms so eloquent, and which you gentlemen have accepted and received in so sympathetic a manner. Let me say at once, in the name of my fellow-Canadians who are here with me and also, I may say, in the name of the Canadian people, that these feelings we shall at all times reciprocate; reciprocate, not only in words evanescent, but in actual living deeds.

Because I must say that I feel that, though the relations between Canada and the United States are good, though they are brotherly, though they are satisfactory, in my judgment they are not as good, as brotherly, as satisfactory as they ought to be. We are of the same stock. We spring from the same races on one side of the line as on the other. We speak the same language. We have the same literature, and for more than a thousand years we have had a common history.

Let me recall to you the lines which, in the darkest days of the Civil War, the Puritan poet of America issued to England:--

"Oh, Englishmen! Oh, Englishmen!
In hope and creed,
In blood and tongue, are brothers,
We all are heirs of Runnymede."

Brothers we are, in the language of your own poet. May I not say that while our relations are not always as brotherly as they should have been, may I not ask, Mr. President, on the part of Canada and on the part of the United States, if we are sometimes too prone to stand by the full conceptions of our rights, and exact all our rights to the last pound of flesh? May I not ask if there have not been too often between us petty quarrels, which happily do not wound the heart of the nation?

There was a civil war in the last century. There was a civil war between England, then, and her colonies. The union which then existed between England and her colonies was severed. If it was severed, American citizens, as you know it was, through no fault of your fathers, the fault was altogether the fault of the British

Government of that day. If the British Government of that day had treated the American colonies as the British Government for the last twenty or fifty years has treated its colonies; if Great Britain had given you then the same degree of liberty which it gives to Canada, my country; if it had given you, as it has given us, legislative independence absolute,--the result would have been different; the course of victory, the course of history, would have been very different.

But what has been done cannot be undone. You cannot expect that the union which was then severed shall ever be restored; but can we not expect--can we not hope that the banners of England and the banners of the United States shall never, never again meet in conflict, except those conflicts provided by the arts of peace, such as we see to-day in the harbor of New York in the contest between the *Shamrock* and the *Columbia* for the supremacy of naval architecture and naval prowess? Can we not hope that if ever the banners of England and the banners of the United States are again to meet on the battlefield, they shall meet entwined together in the defense of some holy cause, in the defense of holy justice, for the defense of the oppressed, for the enfranchisement of the downtrodden, and for the advancement of liberty, progress, and civilization?

MONSIEUR AND MADAME

From a speech in "Modern Eloquence," Vol. I, Geo. L. Shuman and Company, Chicago, publishers.

BY PAUL BLOUET (MAX O'RELL)

Now, the attitude of men towards women is very different, according to the different nations to which they belong. You will find a good illustration of that different attitude of men toward women in France, in England, and in America, if you go to the dining-rooms of their hotels. You go to the dining-room, and you take, if you can, a seat near the entrance door, and you watch the arrival of the couples, and also watch them as they cross the room and go to the table that is assigned to them by the head waiter. Now, in Europe, you would find a very polite head waiter, who invites you to go in, and asks you where you will sit; but in America the head waiter is a most magnificent potentate who lies in wait for you at the door, and bids you to follow him sometimes in the following respectful manner, beckoning, "There." And you have got to do it, too.

I traveled six times in America, and I never saw a man so daring as not to sit there. In the tremendous hotels of the large cities, where you have got to go to Number 992 or something of the sort, I generally got a little entertainment out of the head waiter. He is so thoroughly persuaded that it would never enter my head not to follow him, he will never look round to see if I am there. Why, he knows I am there, but I'm not. I wait my time, and when he has got to the end I am sitting down waiting for a chance to be left alone. He says, "You cannot sit here." I say: "Why not? What is the matter with this seat?" He says, "You must not sit there." I say, "I don't want a constitutional walk; don't bother, I'm all right." Once, indeed, after an article in the **North American Review**--for your head waiter in America reads reviews--a head waiter told me to sit where I pleased. I said, "Now, wait a minute, give me time to realize that; do I understand that in this hotel I am going to sit where I like?" He said, "Certainly!" He was in earnest. I said, "I should like to sit over there at that table near the window." He said, "All right, come with me." When I came out, there were some newspaper people in the hotel waiting for me, and it was reported in half a column in one of the papers, with one of those charming headlines which are so characteristic of American journalism, "Max sits where he likes!" Well, I said, you go to the dining-room, you take your seat, and you watch the arrival of the couples, and you will know the position of men. In France Monsieur and Madame come in together abreast, as a rule arm in arm. They look pleasant, smile, and talk to each other. They smile at each other, even though married.

In England, in the same class of hotel, John Bull comes in first. He does not look happy. John Bull loves privacy. He does not like to be obliged to eat in the presence of lots of people who have not been introduced to him, and he thinks it very hard he should not have the whole dining-room to himself. That man, though, mind you, in his own house undoubtedly the most hospitable, the most kind, the most considerate of hosts in the world, that man in the dining-room of a hotel always comes in with a frown. He does not like it, he grumbles, and mild and demure, with her hands hanging down, modestly follows Mrs. John Bull. But in America, behold the arrival of Mrs. Jonathan! behold her triumphant entry, pulling Jonathan behind! Well, I like my own country, and I cannot help thinking that the proper and right way is the French. Ladies, you know all our shortcomings. Our hearts are exposed ever since the rib which covered them was taken off. Yet we ask you kindly to allow us to go through life with you, like the French, arm in arm, in good friendship and camaraderie.

THE TYPICAL AMERICAN

From "The New South," with the permission of Henry W. Grady, Jr.

BY HENRY W. GRADY

Pardon me one word, Mr. President, spoken for the sole purpose of getting into the volumes that go out annually freighted with the rich eloquence of your speakers--the fact that the Cavalier as well as the Puritan was on the continent in its early days, and that he was "up and able to be about." I have read your books carefully and I find no mention of that fact, which seems to me an important one for preserving a sort of historical equilibrium if for nothing else. Let me remind you that the Virginia Cavalier first challenged France on this continent-- that Cavalier, John Smith, gave New England its very name, and was so pleased with the job that he has been handing his own name around ever since--and that while Miles Standish was cutting off men's ears for courting a girl without her parents' consent, and forbade men to kiss their wives on Sunday, the Cavalier was courting everything in sight, and that the Almighty had vouchsafed great increase to the Cavalier colonies, the huts in the wilderness being full as the nests in the woods.

But having incorporated the Cavalier as a fact in your charming little books, I shall let him work out his own salvation, as he always has done with engaging gallantry, and we will hold no controversy as to his merits. Why should we? Neither Puritan nor Cavalier long survive as such. The virtues and traditions of both happily still live for the inspiration of their sons and the saving of the old fashion. But both Puritan and Cavalier were lost in the storm of the first Revolution; and the American citizen, supplanting both and stronger than either, took possession of the Republic bought by their common blood and fashioned to wisdom, and charged himself with teaching men government and establishing the voice of the people as the voice of God.

My friend Dr. Talmage has told you that the typical American has yet to come. Let me tell you that he has already come. Great types, like valuable plants, are slow to flower and fruit. But from the union of these colonist Puritans and Cavaliers, from the straightening of their purposes and the crossing of their blood, slow perfecting through a century, came he who stands as the first typical American, the first who comprehended within himself all the strength and gentleness, all the majesty and grace, of this Republic--Abraham Lincoln. He was the sum of Puritan and Cavalier, for in his ardent nature were fused the virtues of both, and in the depths of his great soul the faults of both were lost. He was greater than Puritan, greater than Cavalier, in that he was American, and in that in his homely form were first gathered the vast and thrilling forces of his ideal government--charging it with such tremendous meaning and so elevating it above human suffering that martyrdom, though infamously aimed, came as a fitting crown to a life consecrated from the cradle to human liberty. Let us, each cherishing the traditions and honoring his fathers, build with reverent hands to the type of this simple but sublime life, in which all types are honored; and in our common glory as Americans there will be plenty and to spare for your forefathers and for mine.

THE PILGRIM MOTHERS
Reprinted with the author's permission
BY JOSEPH H. CHOATE

I really don't know, at this late hour, Mr. Chairman, how you expect me to treat this difficult and tender subject.

I might take up the subject etymologically, and try and explain how woman ever acquired that remarkable name. But that has been done before me by a poet with whose stanzas you are not familiar, but whom you will recognize as deeply versed in this subject, for he says:--

"When Eve brought woe to all mankind,
Old Adam called her woe-man,
But when she woo'd with love so kind,
He then pronounced her woman.

"But now, with folly and with pride,
Their husbands' pockets trimming,
The ladies are so full of whims
That people call them w(h)imen."

Mr. Chairman, I believe you said I should say something about the Pilgrim mothers. Well, sir, it is rather late in the evening to venture upon that historic subject. But, for one, I pity them. The occupants of the galleries will bear me witness that even these modern Pilgrims-- these Pilgrims with all the modern improvements--how hard it is to put up with their weaknesses, their follies, their tyrannies, their oppressions, their desire of dominion and rule. But when you go back to the stern horrors of the Pilgrim rule, when you contemplate the rugged character of the Pilgrim fathers, why, you give credence to what a witty woman of Boston said--she had heard enough of the glories and sufferings of the Pilgrim fathers; for her part, she had a world of sympathy for the Pilgrim mothers, because they not only endured all that the Pilgrim fathers had done, but they also had to endure the Pilgrim fathers to boot. Well, sir, they were afraid of woman. They thought she was almost too refined a luxury for them to indulge in. Miles Standish spoke for them all, and I am sure that General Sherman, who so much resembles Miles Standish, not only in his military renown but in his rugged exterior and in his warm and tender heart, will echo his words when he says:--

"I can march up to a fortress, and summon the place to surrender, But march up to a woman with such a proposal, I dare not. I am not afraid of bullets, nor shot from the mouth of a cannon, But of a thundering 'No!' point-blank from the mouth of a woman, That I confess I'm afraid of, nor am I ashamed to confess it."

Mr. President, did you ever see a more self-satisfied or contented set of men than these that are gathered at these tables this evening? I never come to the Pilgrim dinner and see these men, who have achieved in the various departments of life such definite and satisfactory success, but that I look back twenty or thirty or forty years, and see the lantern-jawed boy who started out from the banks of the Connecticut, or some more remote river of New England, with five dollars in his pocket and his father's blessing on his head and his mother's Bible in his carpetbag, to seek those fortunes which now they have so gloriously made. And there is one woman whom each of these, through all his progress and to the last expiring hour of his life, bears in tender remembrance. It is the mother who sent him forth with her blessing. A mother is a mother still--the holiest thing alive; and if I could dismiss you with a benediction to-night, it would be by invoking upon the heads of you all the blessing of the mothers that we left behind us.

BRIGHT LAND TO WESTWARD

From "Modern Eloquence," Vol. III, Geo. L. Shuman and Company, Chicago, publishers.

BY E. O. WOLCOTT

Mr. President and Gentlemen,--It was with great diffidence that I accepted the invitation of your President to respond to a toast to- night. I realized my incapacity to do justice to the occasion, while at the same time I recognized the high compliment conveyed. I felt somewhat as the man did respecting the Shakespeare-Bacon controversy; he said he didn't know whether Lord Bacon wrote Shakespeare's works or not, but if he didn't, he missed the greatest opportunity of his life.

We are a plain people, and live far away. We are provincial; we have no distinctive literature and no great poets; our leading personage abroad of late seems to be the Honorable "Buffalo Bill"; and we use our adjectives so recklessly that the polite badinage indulged in toward each other by your New York editors to us seems tame and spiritless. In mental achievement we may not have fully acquired the use of the fork, and are "but in the gristle and not yet hardened into the bone of manhood." We stand toward the East somewhat as country to city cousin; about as New to Old England, only we don't feel half so badly about it, and on the whole are rather pleased with ourselves. There is not in the whole broad West a ranch so lonely or so remote that a public school is not within reach of it. With generous help from the East, Western colleges are elevating and directing Western thought, and men busy making States yet find time to live manly lives and to lend a hand. All this may not be aesthetic, but it is virile, and it leads up and not down.

There are some things more important than the highest culture. The West is the Almighty's reserve ground, and as the world is filling up, He is turning even the old arid plains and deserts into fertile acres, and is sending there the rain as well as the sunshine. A high and glorious destiny awaits us; soon the balance of population will lie the other side of the Mississippi, and the millions that are coming must find waiting for them schools and churches, good government, and a happy people:--

"Who love the land because it is their own,
And scorn to give aught other reason why;
Would shake hands with a King upon his throne,

And think it kindness to his Majesty."

In everything which pertains to progress in the West, the Yankee reenforce-
ments step rapidly to the front. Every year she needs more of them, and as the
country grows the annual demand becomes greater. Genuine New Englanders are
to be had on tap only in six small States, and remembering this we feel that we have
the right to demand that in the future, even more than in the past, the heads of the
New England households weary not in the good work.

In these days of "booms" and New Souths and Great Wests, when everybody
up North who fired a gun is made to feel that he ought to apologize for it, and good
fellowship everywhere abounds, there is a sort of tendency to fuse; only big and
conspicuous things are much considered; and New England being small in area
and most of her distinguished people being dead, she is just now somewhat under
an eclipse. But in her past she has undying fame. You of New England and her
borders live always in the atmosphere of her glories; the scenes which tell of her
achievements are ever near at hand, and familiarity and contact may rob them of
their charms, and dim to your eyes their sacredness. The sons of New England in
the West revisit her as men who make pilgrimage to some holy shrine, and her hills
and valleys are still instinct with noble traditions. In her glories and her history we
claim a common heritage, and we never wander so far away from her that, with
each recurring anniversary of this day, our hearts do not turn to her with renewed
love and devotion for our beloved New England; yet--

"Not by Eastern windows only,
When daylight comes, comes in the light;
In front the sun climbs slow, how slowly,
But Westward, look, the land is bright!"

WOMAN

From "Modern Eloquence," Vol. Ill, Geo. L. Shuman and Company, Chicago, publishers.

BY THEODORE TILTON

You must not forget, Mr. President, in eulogizing the early men of New England, who are your clients to-night, that it was only through the help of the early women of New England, who are mine, that your boasted heroes could ever have earned their title of the Pilgrim Fathers. A health, therefore, to the women in the cabin of the Mayflower! A cluster of Mayflowers themselves, transplanted from summer in the old world to winter in the new! Counting over those matrons and maidens, they numbered, all told, just eighteen. Their names are now written among the heroines of history! For as over the ashes of Cornelia stood the epitaph "The Mother of the Gracchi," so over these women of the Pilgrimage we write as proudly "The Mothers of the Republic." There was good Mistress Bradford, whose feet were not allowed of God to kiss Plymouth Rock, and who, like Moses, came only near enough to see but not to enter the Promised Land. She was washed overboard from the deck--and to this day the sea is her grave and Cape Cod her monument! There was Mistress Carver, wife of the first governor, who, when her husband fell under the stroke of sudden death, followed him first with heroic grief to the grave, and then, a fortnight after, followed him with heroic joy up into Heaven! There was Mistress White--the mother of the first child born to the New England Pilgrims on this continent. And it was a good omen, sir, that this historic babe was brought into the world on board the Mayflower between the time of the casting of her anchor and the landing of her passengers--a kind of amphibious prophecy that the newborn nation was to have a birthright inheritance over the sea and over the land. There also was Rose Standish, whose name is a perpetual June fragrance, to mellow and sweeten those December winds.

Then, after the first vessel with these women, there came other women-- loving hearts drawn from the olden land by those silken threads which afterwards harden into golden chains. For instance, Governor Bradford, a lonesome widower, went down to the seabeach, and, facing the waves, tossed a love letter over the wide ocean into the lap of Alice Southworth in old England, who caught it up, and read it, and said, "Yes, I will go." And she went! And it is said that the governor, at his second wedding, married his first love! Which, according to the New Theology, furnishes the providential reason why the first Mrs. Bradford fell overboard!

Now, gentlemen, as you sit to-night in this elegant hall, think of the houses in which the *Mayflower* men and women lived in that first winter! Think of a cabin in the wilderness--where winds whistled--where wolves howled--where Indians yelled! And yet, within that log house, burning like a lamp, was the pure flame of Christian faith, love, patience, fortitude, heroism! As the Star of the East rested over the rude manger where Christ lay, so--speaking not irreverently--there rested over the roofs of the Pilgrims a Star of the West--the Star of Empire; and to-day that empire is the proudest in the world!

And now, to close, let me give you just a bit of good advice. The cottages of our forefathers had few pictures on the walls, but many families had a print of "King Charles's Twelve Good Rules," the eleventh of which was, "Make no long meals." Now King Charles lost his head, and you will have leave to make a long meal. But when, after your long meal, you go home in the wee small hours, what do you expect to find? You will find my toast--"Woman, a beautiful rod!" Now my advice is, "Kiss the rod!"

ABRAHAM LINCOLN
Reprinted with the author's permission
BY HORACE PORTER

The story of the life of Abraham Lincoln savors more of romance than reality. It is more like a fable of the ancient days than the story of a plain American of the nineteenth century. The singular vicissitudes in the life of our martyred President surround him with an interest which attaches to few men in history. He sprang from that class which he always alluded to as the "plain people," and never attempted to disdain them. He believed that the government was made for the people, not the people for the government. He felt that true Republicanism is a torch--the more it is shaken in the hands of the people the brighter it will burn. He was transcendently fit to be the first successful standard bearer of the progressive, aggressive, invincible Republican party. He might well have said to those who chanced to sneer at his humble origin what a marshal of France raised from the ranks said to the haughty nobles of Vienna boasting of their long line of descent, when they refused to associate with him: "I am an ancestor; you are only descendants!" He was never guilty of any posing for effect, any attitudinizing in public, any mawkish sentimentality, any of that puppyism so often bred by power, that dogmatism which Johnson said was only puppyism grown to maturity. He made no claim to knowledge he did not possess. He felt with Addison that pedantry and learning are like hypocrisy in religion--the form of knowledge without the power of it. He had nothing in common with those men of mental malformation who are educated beyond their intellects.

The names of Washington and Lincoln are inseparably associated, and yet as the popular historian would have us believe one spent his entire life in chopping down acorn trees and the other splitting them up into rails. Washington could not tell a story. Lincoln always could. And Lincoln's stories always possessed the true geometrical requisites, they were never too long, and never too broad.

But his heart was not always attuned to mirth; its chords were often set to strains of sadness. Yet throughout all his trials he never lost the courage of his convictions. When he was surrounded on all sides by doubting Thomases, by unbelieving Saracens, by discontented Catilines, his faith was strongest. As the Danes destroyed the hearing of their war horses in order that they might not be affrighted by the din of battle, so Lincoln turned a deaf ear to all that might have discouraged him, and exhibited an unwavering faith in the justice of the cause and the integrity of the Union.

It is said that for three hundred years after the battle of Thermopylae every child in the public schools of Greece was required to recite from memory the names of the three hundred martyrs who fell in the defense of that pass. It would be a crowning triumph in patriotic education if every school child in America could contemplate each day the grand character and utter the inspiring name of Abraham Lincoln, who has handed down unto a grateful people the richest legacy which man can leave to man--the memory of a good name, the inheritance of a great example!

TO ATHLETIC VICTORS

From a speech at a dinner of graduates of Yale University, in New York, 1889. By the kindness of the author.

BY HENRY E. HOWLAND

On Boston Common, under the shadow of the State House, and within the atmosphere of Harvard University, there is an inscription on a column, in honor of those who, on land and sea, maintained the cause of their country during four years of civil war. The visitor approaches it with respect and reverently uncovers as he reads.

With similar high emotions we, as citizens of the world of letters, and acknowledging particular allegiance to the province thereof founded by Elihu Yale, are assembled to pour libations, to partake of a sacrificial feast, and to crown with honors and with bays those who, on land and sea, with unparalleled courage and devotion, have borne their flag to victory in desperate encounters.

Peace hath her victories no less renowned than war.

On large fields of strife, the record of success like that which we are called upon to commemorate would give the victors a high place in history and liken their country to ancient Thebes,--

"Which spread her conquest o'er a thousand states,
And poured her heroes through a hundred gates."

There are many reasons why Yale men win. One is that which was stated by Lord Beaconsfield, "The Secret of success is constancy of purpose." That alone sufficiently accounts for it.

We are here present in no vain spirit of boasting, though if our right to exalt ourselves were questioned, we might reply in the words of the American girl who was shown some cannon at Woolwich Arsenal, the sergeant in charge remarking, "You know we took them from you at Bunker Hill." "Yes," she replied, "I see you've got the cannon, but I guess we've got the hill."

We come rather in a spirit of true modesty to recognize the plaudits of an admiring world, to tell you how they were won. It was said in the days of Athenian pride and glory that it was easier to find a god in Athens than a man. We must be careful in these days of admiration of athletic effort that no such imputation is laid upon us, and that the deification of the human form divine is not carried to extremes.

It is a curious coincidence that a love of the classics and proficiency in intellectual pursuits should coexist with admiration for physical perfection and with athletic superiority during all the centuries of which the history is written. The youth who lisped in Attic numbers and was brought up on the language we now so painfully and imperfectly acquire, who was lulled to sleep by songs of AEschylus and Sophocles, who discussed philosophy in the porches of Plato, Aristotle, and Epicurus, was a more accomplished classical scholar than the most learned pundit of modern times, and was a model of manly beauty, yet he would have died to win the wreath of parsley at the Olympian games, which all esteemed an immortal prize. While, in our time, to be the winning crew on the Isis, the Cam, the English or American Thames, is equal in honor and influence to the position of senior wrangler, valedictorian, or Deforest prize man.

The man who wins the world's honors to-day must not be overtrained mentally or physically; not, as John Randolph said of the soil of Virginia,--"poor by nature and ruined by cultivation," hollow-chested, convex in back, imperfect in sight, shuffling in gait, and flabby in muscle. The work of such a man will be musty like his closet, narrow as the groove he moves in, tinctured with the peculiarities that border on insanity, and out of tune with nature.

No man can work in the world unless he knows it, struggles with it, and becomes a part of it, and the statement of the English statesman that the undergraduate of Oxford or Cambridge who had the best stomach, the hardest muscles, and the greatest ambition would be the future Lord Chancellor of England, had a solid basis of truth.

Gentlemen of the bat, the oar, the racquet, the cinder path, and the leathern sphere, never were conquerors more welcome guests, in palace or in hall, at the tables of their friends than you are here.

You come with your laurels fresh from the fields you have won, to receive the praise which is your due and which we so gladly bestow. Your self-denial, devotion, skill, and courage have brought honor to your University, and for it we honor you.

THE BABIES

At a banquet in honor of General Grant, Chicago, 1877

BY SAMUEL L. CLEMENS (Mark Twain)

MR. CHAIRMAN AND GENTLEMEN,--"The Babies." Now, that's something like. We haven't all had the good fortune to be ladies; we have not all been generals, or poets, or statesmen; but when the toast works down to the babies, we stand on common ground--for we've all been babies. It is a shame that for a thousand years the world's banquets have utterly ignored the baby, as if he didn't amount to anything! If you, gentlemen, will stop and think a minute--if you will try to go back fifty or a hundred years, to your early married life, and recontemplate your first baby--you will remember that he amounted to a good deal--and even something over.

You soldiers all know that when that little fellow arrived at family headquarters, you had to hand in your resignation. He took entire command. You had to execute his order whether it was possible or not. And there was only one form of marching in his manual of tactics, and that was the double-quick. When he called for soothing syrup, did you venture to throw out any remarks about certain services unbecoming to an officer and a gentleman? No; you got up and got it! If he ordered his pap bottle, and it wasn't warm, did you talk back? Not you; you went to work and warmed it. You even descended so far in your menial office as to take a suck at that warm, insipid stuff yourself, to see if it was right!--three parts water to one of milk, a touch of sugar to modify the colic, and a drop of peppermint to kill those immortal hiccoughs. I can taste that stuff yet.

And how many things you learned as you went along! Sentimental young folks still take stock in that beautiful old saying, that when a baby smiles in his sleep it is because the angels are whispering to him. Very pretty, but "too thin"--simply wind on the stomach, my friends. I like the idea that a baby doesn't amount to anything! Why, one baby is just a house and a front yard full by itself; one baby can furnish more business than you and your whole interior department can attend to; he is enterprising, irrepressible, brimful of lawless activities. Do what you please you can't make him stay on the reservation. Sufficient unto the day is one baby. As long as you are in your right mind don't ever pray for twins. Twins amount to a permanent riot; and there ain't any real difference between triplets and insurrections.

Among the three or four million cradles now rocking in the land there are some which this nation would preserve for ages as sacred things, if we could know which ones they are. For in one of these cradles the unconscious Farragut of the future is at this moment teething; in another the future great historian is lying, and doubtless he will continue to lie until his earthly mission is ended. And in still one more cradle, somewhere under the flag, the future illustrious commander-in-chief of the American armies is so little burdened with his approaching grandeurs and responsibilities as to be giving his whole strategic mind at this moment, to trying to find out some way to get his own big toe into his mouth, an achievement to which (meaning no disrespect) the illustrious guest of this evening also turned his attention some fifty-six years ago! And if the child is but the prophecy of the man, there are mighty few will doubt that he succeeded.

THE OCCASIONAL POEM

CHARLES DICKENS

Read by Mr. Watson in New York, at the celebration of the Dickens Centenary, 1912. Reprinted from the public press.

BY WILLIAM WATSON

When Nature first designed In her all-procreant mind The man whom here tonight we are met to honor-- When first the idea of Dickens flashed upon her-- "Where, where" she said, "upon my populous earth Shall this prodigious child be brought to birth? Where shall we have his earliest wondering look Into my magic book? Shall he be born where life runs like a brook, Pleasant and placid as of old it ran, Far from the sound and shock of mighty deeds, Among soft English meads? Or shall he first my pictured volume scan Where London lifts its hot and fevered brow For cooling night to fan?" "Nay, nay," she said, "I have a happier plan For where at Portsmouth, on the embattled tides The ships of war step out with thundering prow And shake their stormy sides-- In yonder place of arms, whose gaunt sea wall Flings to the clouds the far-heard bugle call-- He shall be born amid the drums and guns, He shall be born among my fighting sons, Perhaps the greatest warrior of them all."

II

So there, where from the forts and battle gear And all the proud sea babbles Nelson's name, Into the world this later hero came-- He, too, a man that knew all moods but fear-- He, too, a fighter. Yet not his the strife That leaves dark scars on the fair face of life. He did not fight to rend the world apart; He fought to make it one in mind and heart, Building a broad and noble bridge to span The icy chasm that sunders man from man. Wherever wrong had fixed its bastions deep, There did his fierce yet gay assault surprise Some fortress girt with lucre or with lies; There his light battery stormed some ponderous keep; There charged he up the steep, A knight on whom no palsying torpor fell, Keen to the last to break a lance with Hell. And still undimmed his conquering weapons shine; On his bright sword no spot of rust appears, And still across the years His soul goes forth to battle, and in the face Of whatso'er is false, or cruel, or base, He hurls his gage and leaps among the spears, Being armed with pity and love and scorn divine, Immortal laughter and immortal tears.

THE MARINERS OF ENGLAND

BY THOMAS CAMPBELL

Ye Mariners of England That guard our native seas! Whose flag has braved, a thousand years, The battle and the breeze! Your glorious standard launch again To match another foe: And sweep through the deep, While the stormy winds do blow; While the battle rages loud and long And the stormy winds do blow.

The spirit of your fathers Shall start from every wave, For the deck it is our field of fame, And Ocean was their grave: Where Blake and mighty Nelson fell Your manly heart shall glow, As ye sweep through the deep, While the stormy winds do blow; While the battle rages loud and long And the stormy winds do blow.

Britannia needs no bulwarks, No towers along the steep; Her march is o'er the mountain waves, Her home is on the deep. With thunders from her native oak She quells the floods below, As they roar on the shore, When the stormy winds do blow; When the battle rages loud and long And the stormy winds do blow.

The meteor-flag of England Shall yet terrific burn; Till danger's troubled night depart And the star of peace return. Then, then, ye ocean warriors! Our song and feast shall flow To the fame of your name, When the storm has ceased to blow; When the fiery fight is heard no more, And the storm has ceased to blow.

CLASS POEM

Read in Sanders Theater at the Harvard Class Day Exercises, 1903. Reprinted with permission.

BY LANGDON WARNER

Not unto every one of us shall come

The bugle call that sounds for famous deeds; Not far lands, but the pleasant paths of home,

Not broad seas to traffic, but the meads Of fruitful midland ways, where daily life

Down trellised vistas, heavy in the Fall, Seems but the decent way apart from strife;

And love, and work, and laughter there seem all.

War, and the Orient Sun uprising,

The East, the West, and Man's shrill clamorous strife, Travail, disaster, flood, and far emprising,

Man may not reach, yet take fast hold on life. Let us now praise men who are not famous,

Striving for good name rather than for great; Hear we the quiet voice calling to claim us,

Heed it no less than the trumpet-call of fate!

Profit we to-day by the men who've gone before us,

Men who dared, and lived, and died, to speed us on our way. Fair is their fame, who make that mighty chorus,

And gentle is the heritage that comes to us to-day.

They pulled with the strength that was in them,

But 'twas not for the pewter cup, And not for the fame 'twould win them When the length of the race was up. For the college stood by the river,

And they heard, with cheeks that glowed, The voice of the coxswain calling At the end of the course--"Well rowed!"

We have pulled at the sweep and run at the games, We have striven to stand to our boyhood aims, And we know the worth of our fathers' names;

Shall we have less care for our own? The praise of men they dared despise, They set the game above the prize, Must we fear to look in our fathers' eyes,

Nor reap where they have sown?

Do we lose the zest we've known before? The joy of running?--The kick of the oar

When the ash sweeps buckle and bend?

Is the goal too far?--Too hard to gain? We know that the candle is not the play, We know the reward is not to-day,

And may not come at the end.

But we hear the voice of each bygone class From the river's bank when our own crews pass,

And the backs of the men are bowed, With a steady lift and a squandering strength, For the heave that shall drive us a nation's length,

Till the coxswain calls--"Well rowed."

Now all to the tasks that may find us--

To the saddle, the home, or the sea, Still hearing the voices behind us

The voices that set us free; Free to be bound by our honor,

Free to our birthright of toil, The masters, and slaves, of the nation,

The Serfs, and the Lords, of the soil!

Proudly we lift the burdens

That humbled the ages past, And pray to the God that gave them

We may bear them on to the last;

That our sons and our younger brothers,

When our gaps in the front they fill, May know that the class has faltered not, And the line is even still.

Then out to the wind and weather!

Down the course our fathers showed, And finish well together,

As the coxswain calls--"Well rowed!"

A TROOP OF THE GUARD

Harvard Class Poem, 1907, Houghton Mifflin Company, Boston, publishers, Reprinted with permission.

BY HERMANN HAGEDORN, JR.

There's a trampling of hoofs in the busy street,

There's a clanking of sabers on floor and stair, There's a sound of restless, hurrying feet, Of voices that whisper, of lips that entreat,--

Will they live, will they die, will they strive, will they dare?-- The houses are garlanded, flags flutter gay, For a troop of the Guard rides forth to-day.

Oh, the troopers will ride and their hearts will leap,

When it's shoulder to shoulder and friend to friend-- But it's some to the pinnacle, some to the deep, And some in the glow of their strength to sleep,

And for all it's a fight to the tale's far end, And it's each to his goal, nor turn nor sway, When the troop of the Guard rides forth to-day.

The dawn is upon us, the pale light speeds

To the zenith with glamour and golden dart. On, up! Boot and saddle! Give spurs to your steeds! There's a city beleaguered that cries for men's deeds,
With the pain of the world in its cavernous heart.

Ours be the triumph! Humanity calls!
Life's not a dream in the clover!
On to the walls, on to the walls,
On to the walls, and over!

The wine is spent, the tale is spun, The revelry of youth is done. The horses prance, the bridles clink, While maidens fair in bright array With us the last sweet goblet drink, Then bid us, "Mount and away!" Into the dawn, we ride, we ride, Fellow and fellow, side by side; Galloping over the field and hill, Over the marshland, stalwart still, Into the forest's shadowy hush, Where specters walk in sunless day, And in dark pool and branch and bush The treacherous will-o'-the-wisp lights play. Out of the wood 'neath the risen sun, Weary we gallop, one and one, To a richer hope and a stronger foe And a hotter fight in the fields below-- Each man his own slave, each his lord, For the golden spurs and the victor's sword!

An anxious generation sends us forth On the far conquest of the thrones of might. From west to east, from south to north, Earth's children, weary-eyed from too much light, Cry from their dream-forsaken vales of pain, "Give us our gods, give us our gods again!" A lofty and relentless century, Gazing with Argus eyes, Has pierced the very inmost halls of faith; And left no shelter whither man may flee From the cold storms of night and lovelessness and death.

Old gods have fallen and the new must rise! Out of the dust of doubt and broken creeds, The sons of those who cast men's idols low Must build up for a hungry people's needs New gods, new hopes, new strength to toil and grow; Knowing that nought that ever lived can die,-- No act, no dream but spreads its sails, sublime, Sweeping across the visible seas of time Into the treasure-haven of eternity. The portals are open, the white road leads

Through thicket and garden, o'er stone and sod. On, up! Boot and saddle! Give spurs to your steeds! There's a city beleaguered that cries for men's deeds,
For the faith that is strength and the love that is God!

On, through the dawning! Humanity calls!
Life's not a dream in the clover!
On to the walls, on to the walls,
On to the walls, and over!
THE BOYS

At a class reunion. By permission of, and by special arrangement with, Hough-ton Mifflin Company, authorized publishers of this author's works.

BY OLIVER WENDELL HOLMES

Has there any old fellow got mixed with the boys? If there has, take him out, without making a noise. Hang the Almanac's cheat and the Catalogue's spite! Old Time is a liar! We're twenty to-night!

We're twenty! We're twenty! Who says we are more? He's tipsy, young jackanapes!--show him the door! 'Gray temples at twenty?'--Yes! *white* if we please; Where the snowflakes fall thickest there's nothing can freeze!

Was it snowing I spoke of? Excuse the mistake! Look close,--you will see not a sign of a flake! We want some new garlands for those we have shed,-- And these are white roses in place of the red.

We've a trick, we young fellows, you may have been told, Of talking (in public) as if we were old:-- That boy we call 'Doctor,' and this we call 'Judge'; It's a neat little fiction,--of course it's all fudge.

That fellow's the 'Speaker,'--the one on the right: 'Mr. Mayor,' my young one, how are you to-night? That's our 'Member of Congress,' we say when we chaff; There's the 'Reverend' What's his name?--don't make me laugh.

That boy with the grave mathematical look Made believe he had written a wonderful book, And the ROYAL SOCIETY thought it was *true*! So they chose him right in; a good joke it was, too!

There's a boy, we pretend, with a three-decker brain, That could harness a team with a logical chain; When he spoke for our manhood in syllabled fire, We called him 'The Justice,' but now he's 'The Squire.'

And there's a nice youngster of excellent pith,-- Fate tried to conceal him by naming him Smith; But he shouted a song for the brave and the free,-- Just read on his medal, 'My country,' 'of thee!'

You hear that boy laughing?--You think he's all fun; But the angels laugh, too, at the good he has done; The children laugh loud as they troop to his call, And the poor man that knows him laughs loudest of all!

Yes, we're boys,--always playing with tongue or with pen,-- And I sometimes have asked,--Shall we ever be men? Shall we always be youthful, and laughing, and gay, Till the last dear companion drops smiling away?

Then here's to our boyhood, its gold and its gray! The stars of its winter, the dews of its May! And when we have done with our life-lasting toys, Dear Father, take care of thy children, the BOYS!

THE ANECDOTE

THE MOB CONQUERED
From "The Orations and Addresses of George William Curtis," Vol. 1 Copyright 1893, by Harper and Brothers. Reprinted with permission.

BY GEORGE WILLIAM CURTIS

It is especially necessary for us to perceive the vital relation of individual courage and character to the common welfare, because ours is a government of public opinion, and public opinion is but the aggregate of individual thought. We have the awful responsibility as a community of doing what we choose; and it is of the last importance that we choose to do what is wise and right. In the early days of the antislavery agitation a meeting was called at Faneuil Hall, in Boston, which a good-natured mob of sailors was hired to suppress. They took possession of the floor and danced breakdowns and shouted choruses and refused to hear any of the orators upon the platform. The most eloquent pleaded with them in vain. They were urged by the memories of the Cradle of Liberty, for the honor of Massachusetts, for their own honor as Boston boys, to respect liberty of speech. But they still laughed and sang and danced, and were proof against every appeal. At last a man suddenly arose from among themselves, and began to speak. Struck by his tone and quaint appearance, and with the thought that he might be one of themselves, the mob became suddenly still, "Well, fellow-citizens," he said, "I wouldn't be quiet if I didn't want to." The words were greeted with a roar of delight from the mob, which supposed it had found its champion, and the applause was unceasing for five minutes, during which the strange orator tranquilly awaited his chance to continue. The wish to hear more hushed the tumult, and when the hall was still he resumed: "No, I certainly wouldn't stop if I hadn't a mind to; but then, if I were you, I *would* have a mind to!" The oddity of the remark and the earnestness of the tone, held the crowd silent, and the speaker continued, "not because this is Faneuil Hall, nor for the honor of Massachusetts, nor because you are Boston boys, but because you are men, and because honorable and generous men always love fair play." The mob was conquered. Free speech and fair play were secured. Public opinion can do what it has a mind to in this country. If it be debased and demoralized, it is the most odious of tyrants. It is Nero and Caligula multiplied by millions. Can there then be a more stringent public duty for every man--and the greater the intelligence the greater the duty--than to take care, by all the influence he can command, that the country, the majority, public opinion, shall have a mind to do only what is just and pure and humane?

AN EXAMPLE OF FAITH
From "The New South." Reprinted with permission
BY HENRY W. GRADY

Permitted, through your kindness, to catch my second wind, let me say that I appreciate the significance of being the first Southerner to speak at this board, which bears the substance, if it surpasses the semblance, of original New England hospitality--and honors the sentiment that in turn honors you, but in which my personality is lost, and the compliment to my people made plain.

I bespeak the utmost stretch of your courtesy to-night. I am not troubled about those from whom I come. You remember the man whose wife sent him to a neighbor with a pitcher of milk, and who, tripping on the top step, fell with such casual interruptions as the landings afforded into the basement, and, while picking himself up, had the pleasure of hearing his wife call out: "John, did you break the pitcher?"

"No, I didn't," said John, "but I'll be dinged if I don't."

So, while those who call me from behind may inspire me with energy, if not with courage, I ask an indulgent hearing from you. I beg that you will bring your full faith in American fairness and frankness to judgment upon what I shall say. There was an old preacher once who told some boys of the Bible lesson he was going to read in the morning. The boys, finding the place, glued together the connecting pages. The next morning he read on the bottom of one page, "When Noah was one hundred and twenty years old he took unto himself a wife, who was--" then turning the page--"140 cubits long, 40 cubits wide, built of gopher wood--and covered with pitch inside and out." He was naturally puzzled at this. He read it again, verified it, and then said, "My friends, this is the first time I ever met this in the Bible, but I accept this as an evidence of the assertion that we are fearfully and wonderfully made." If I could get you to hold such faith to-night I could proceed cheerfully to the task I otherwise approach with a sense of consecration.

THE RAIL-SPLITTER

From "The Lincoln Story Book," with the permission of G. W. Dillingham and Co., New York, publishers.

BY H. L. WILLIAMS

The Illinois Republican State Convention of 1860 met at Decatur, in a wigwam built for the purpose, a type of that noted in the Lincoln Annals as at Chicago. A special welcome was given to Abraham Lincoln as a "distinguished citizen of Illinois, and one she will ever be delighted to honor." The session was suddenly interrupted by the chairman saying: "There is an old Democrat outside who has something to present to the convention."

The present was two old fence rails, carried on the shoulder of an elderly man, recognized by Lincoln as his cousin John Hanks, and by the Sangamon folks as an old settler in the Bottoms. The rails were explained by a banner reading:

"Two rails from a lot made by Abraham Lincoln and John Hanks, in the Sangamon Bottom, in the year 1830."

Thunderous cheers for "the rail-splitter" resounded, for this slur on the statesman had recoiled on aspersers and was used as a title of honor. The call for confirmation of the assertion led Lincoln to rise, and blushing--so recorded--said:

"Gentlemen,--I suppose you want to know something about those things. Well, the truth is, John and I did make rails in the Sangamon Bottom." He eyed the wood with the knowingness of an authority on "stumpage," and added: "I don't know whether we made those rails or not; the fact is, I don't think they are a credit to the makers!" It was John Hanks' turn to blush. "But I do know this: I made rails then, and, I think, I could make better ones now!"

Whereupon, by acclamation, Abraham Lincoln was declared to be "first choice of the Republican party in Illinois for the Presidency."

Riding a man in on a rail became of different and honorable meaning from that out.

This incident was a prepared theatrical effect. Governor Oglesby arranged with Lincoln's stepbrother, John D. Johnston, to provide two rails, and with Lincoln's mother's cousin, Dennis Hanks, for the latter to bring in the rails at the telling juncture. Lincoln's guarded manner about identifying the rails, and sly slap at his ability to make better ones, show that he was in the scheme, though recognizing that the dodge was of value politically.

O'CONNELL'S WIT

From a lecture on Daniel O'Connell in "Speeches and Lectures," with the permission of Lothrop, Lee and Shepard, Boston, publishers.

BY WENDELL PHILLIPS

We used to say of Webster, "This is a great effort"; of Everett, "It is a beautiful effort"; but you never used the word "effort" in speaking of O'Connell. It provoked you that he would not make an effort. I heard him perhaps a score of times, and I do not think more than three times he ever lifted himself to the full sweep of his power.

And this wonderful power, it was not a thunderstorm: he flanked you with his wit, he surprised you out of yourself; you were conquered before you knew it.

He was once summoned to court out of the hunting field, when a young friend of his of humble birth was on trial for his life. The evidence gathered around a hat found next the body of the murdered man, which was recognized as the hat of the prisoner. The lawyers tried to break down the evidence, confuse the testimony, and get some relief from the directness of the circumstances, but in vain, until at last they called for O'Connell. He came in, flung his riding-whip and hat on the table, was told the circumstances, and, taking up the hat, said to the witness, "Whose hat is this?" "Well, Mr. O'Connell, that is Mike's hat." "How do you know it?" "I will swear to it, sir." "And did you really find it by the body of the murdered man?" "I did that, sir." "But you're not ready to swear to that?" "I am, indeed, Mr. O'Connell." "Pat, do you know what hangs on your word? A human soul. And with that dread burden, are you ready to tell this jury that the hat, to your certain knowledge, belongs to the prisoner?" "Y-yes, Mr. O'Connell; yes, I am."

O'Connell takes the hat to the nearest window, and peers into it--"J-a- m-e-s, James. Now, Pat, did you see that name in the hat?" "I did, Mr. O'Connell." "You knew it was there?" "Yes, sir; I read it after I picked it up."----"No name in the hat, your Honor."

So again in the House of Commons. When he took his seat in the House in 1830, the London *Times* visited him with its constant indignation, reported his speeches awry, turned them inside out, and made nonsense of them; treated him as the New York *Herald* use to treat us Abolitionists twenty years ago. So one morning he rose and said, "Mr. Speaker, you know I have never opened my lips in this House, and I expended twenty years of hard work in getting the right to enter it,--I have never lifted my voice in this House, but in behalf of the saddest people the sun shines on. Is it fair play, Mr. Speaker, is it what you call 'English fair play' that the press of this city will not let my voice be heard?" The next day the *Times* sent him word that, as he found fault with their manner of reporting him, they never would report him at all, they never would print his name in their parliamentary columns. So the next day when prayers were ended O'Connell rose. Those reporters of the *Times* who were in the gallery rose also, ostentatiously put away their pencils, folded their arms, and made all the show they could, to let everybody know how it was. Well, you know nobody has a right to be in the gallery during the session, and if any member notices them, the mere notice clears the gallery; only the reporters can stay after that notice. O'Connell rose. One of the members said, "Before the member from Clare opens his speech, let me call his attention to the gallery and the instance of that 'passive resistance' which he is about to preach." "Thank you," said O'Connell. "Mr. Speaker, I observe the strangers in the gallery." Of course they left; of course the next day, in the columns of the London *Times*, there were no parliamentary debates. And for the first time, except in Richard Cobden's case, the London *Times* cried for quarter, and said to O'Connell, "If you give up the quarrel, we will."

A RELIABLE TEAM

From "Hunting the Grizzly," with the permission of G. P. Putnam's Sons, New York and London, Publishers.

BY THEODORE ROOSEVELT

In the cow country there is nothing more refreshing than the light-hearted belief entertained by the average man to the effect that any animal which by main force has been saddled and ridden, or harnessed and driven a couple of times, is a "broke horse." My present foreman is firmly wedded to this idea, as well as to its complement, the belief that any animal with hoofs, before any vehicle with wheels, can be driven across any country. One summer on reaching the ranch I was entertained with the usual accounts of the adventures and misadventures which had befallen my own men and my neighbors since I had been out last. In the course of the conversation my foreman remarked: "We had a great time out here about six weeks ago. There was a professor from Ann Arbor came out with his wife to see the Bad Lands, and they asked if we could rig them up a team, and we said we guessed we could, and Foley's boy and I did; but it ran away with him and broke his leg! He was here for a month. I guess he didn't mind it, though." Of this I was less certain, forlorn little Medora being a "busted" cow town, concerning which I once heard another of my men remark, in reply to an inquisitive commercial traveler: "How many people lives here? Eleven--counting the chickens--when they're all in town!"

My foreman continued: "By George, there was something that professor said afterward that made me feel hot. I sent word up to him by Foley's boy that seein' as how it had come out, we wouldn't charge him nothin' for the rig; and that professor answered that he was glad we were showing him some sign of consideration, for he'd begun to believe he'd fallen into a den of sharks, and that we gave him a runaway team apurpose. That made me hot, calling that a runaway team. Why, there was one of them horses never *could* have run away before; it hadn't never been druv but twice! and the other horse maybe had run away a few times, but there was lots of times he *hadn't* run away. I esteemed that team full as liable not to run away as it was to run away," concluded my foreman, evidently deeming this as good a warranty of gentleness in a horse as the most exacting could possibly require.

MEG'S MARRIAGE

From a lecture entitled "Clear Grit," published in "Modern Eloquence," Vol. IV, Geo. L. Shuman and Company, Chicago.

BY ROBERT COLLYER

In what we call the good old times--say, three hundred years ago--a family lived on the border between England and Scotland, with one daughter of a marvelous homeliness. Her name was Meg. She was a capital girl, as homely girls generally are. She knew she had no beauty, so she made sure of quality and faculty. But the Scotch say that "while beauty may not make the best kail, it looks best by the side of the kail-pot." So Meg had no offer of a husband, and was likely to die in what we call "single blessedness." Everybody on the border in those days used to steal, and their best "holt," as we say, was cattle. If they wanted meat and had no money, they would go out and steal as many beef cattle as they could lay their hands on, from somebody on the other side of the border. Well, they generally had no money, and they were always wanting beef, and they could always be hung for stealing by the man they stole from if he could catch them, and so they had what an Irishman would call a fine time entirely. One day a young chief, wanting some beef as usual, went out with part of his clan, came upon a splendid herd on the lands of Meg's father, and went to work to drive them across to his own. But the old fellow was on the lookout, mustered his clan, bore down on the marauders, beat them, took the young chief prisoner, and then went home to his peel very much delighted. Meg's mother, of course, wanted to know all about it, and then she said, "Noo, laird, what are you gaun to do with the prisoner?" "I am gaun to hang him," the old man thundered, "just as soon as I have had my dinner." "But I think ye're noo wise to do that," she said. "He has got a braw place, ye ken, over the border, and he is a braw fellow. Noo I'll tell ye what I would do. I would give him his chance to be hung or marry oor Meg." It struck the old man as a good idea, and so he went presently down into the dungeon, told the young fellow to get ready to be hung in thirty minutes, but then got round to the alternative, and offered to spare his life if he would marry Meg, and give him the beef into the bargain. He had heard something about Meg's wonderful want of beauty, and so, with a fine Scotch prudence, he said, "Ye will let me see her, laird, before I mak' up my mind, because maybe I would rather be hung." "Aye, mon, that's fair," the old chief answered, and went in to bid the mother get Meg ready for the interview. The mother did her best, you may be sure, to make Meg look winsome, but when the poor fellow saw his unintentional intended he turned round to the chief and said, "Laird, if ye have nae objection, I think I would rather be hung." "And sae ye shall, me lad, and welcome," the old chief replied, in a rage. So they led him out, got the rope around his neck; and then the young man changed his mind, and shouted, "Laird, I'll tak' her." So he was marched back into the castle, married before he had time to change his mind, if that was possible, and the tradition is that there never was a happier pair in Scotland, and never a better wife in the world than Meg. But I have told the story because it touches this point, of the way they hold their own over there when there are great families of children. They tell me that the family flourishes famously still; no sign of dying out or being lost about it. Meg's main feature was a very large mouth, and now in the direct line in almost every generation the neighbors and friends are delighted, as they say, to get Meg back. "Here's Meg again," they cry when a child is born with that wonderful mouth. Sir Walter Scott was one of the descendants of the family. He had Meg's mouth, in a measure, and was very proud of it when he would tell the story.

OUTDOING MRS. PARTINGTON

From a speech published in Brewer's "The World's Best Orations," Vol. IX, Ferd. P. Kaiser, St. Louis, Chicago, publisher.

BY SIDNEY SMITH I have spoken so often on this subject, that I am sure both you and the gentlemen here present will be obliged to me for saying but little, and that favor I am as willing to confer, as you can be to receive it. I feel most deeply the event which has taken place, because, by putting the two houses of Parliament in collision with each other, it will impede the public business and diminish the public prosperity. I feel it as a churchman, because I cannot but blush to see so many dignitaries of the Church arrayed against the wishes and happiness of the people. I feel it more than all, because I believe it will sow the seeds of deadly hatred between the aristocracy and the great mass of the people. The loss of the bill I do not feel, and for the best of all possible reasons--because I have not the slightest idea that it is lost. I have no more doubt, before the expiration of the winter, that this bill will pass, than I have that the annual tax bills will pass, and greater certainty than this no man can have, for Franklin tells us there are but two things certain in this world--death and taxes. As for the possibility of the House of Lords preventing ere long a reform of Parliament, I hold it to be the most absurd notion that ever entered into human imagination. I do not mean to be disrespectful, but the attempt of the lords to stop the progress of reform reminds me very forcibly of the great storm of Sidmouth, and of the conduct of the excellent Mrs. Partington on that occasion. In the winter of 1824, there set in a great flood upon that town, the tide rose to an incredible height, the waves rushed in upon the houses, and everything was threatened with destruction. In the midst of this sublime and terrible storm, Dame Partington, who lived upon the beach, was seen at the top of her house with mop and pattens, trundling her mop, squeezing out the water, and vigorously pushing away the Atlantic Ocean.

The Atlantic was roused. Mrs. Partington's spirit was up; but I need not tell you that the contest was unequal. The Atlantic Ocean beat Mrs. Partington. She was excellent at a slop or a puddle, but she should not have meddled with a tempest. Gentlemen, be at your ease--be quiet and steady. You will beat Mrs. Partington.

CIRCUMSTANCE NOT A CAUSE

From the same speech as the foregoing

BY SIDNEY SMITH

An honorable member of the honorable house, much connected with this town, and once its representative, seems to be amazingly surprised, and equally dissatisfied, at this combination of king, ministers, nobles, and people, against his opinion,--like the gentleman who came home from serving on a jury very much disconcerted, and complaining he had met with eleven of the most obstinate people he had ever seen in his life, whom he found it absolutely impossible by the strongest arguments to bring over to his way of thinking.

They tell you, gentlemen, that you have grown rich and powerful with these rotten boroughs, and that it would be madness to part with them, or to alter a constitution which had produced such happy effects. There happens, gentlemen, to live near my parsonage a laboring man of very superior character and understanding to his fellow laborers, and who has made such good use of that superiority that he has saved what is (for his station in life) a very considerable sum of money, and if his existence is extended to the common period he will die rich. It happens, however, that he is (and long has been) troubled with violent stomachic pains, for which he has hitherto obtained no relief, and which really are the bane and torment of his life. Now, if my excellent laborer were to send for a physician and to consult him respecting this malady, would it not be very singular language if our doctor were to say to him: "My good friend, you surely will not be so rash as to attempt to get rid of these pains in your stomach. Have you not grown rich with these pains in your stomach? have you not risen under them from poverty to prosperity? has not your situation since you were first attacked been improving every year? You surely will not be so foolish and so indiscreet as to part with the pains in your stomach?" Why, what would be the answer of the rustic to this nonsensical monition? "Monster of rhubarb! (he would say) I am not rich in consequence of the pains in my stomach, but in spite of the pains in my stomach; and I should have been ten times richer, and fifty times happier, if I had never had any pains in my stomach at all." Gentlemen, these rotten boroughs are your pains in the stomach--and you would have been a much richer and greater people if you had never had them at all. Your wealth and your power have been owing not to the debased and corrupted parts of the House of Commons, but to the many independent and honorable members whom it has always contained within its walls. If there had been a few more of these very valuable members for close boroughs we should, I verily believe, have been by this time about as free as Denmark, Sweden, or the Germanized States of Italy.

This is the greatest measure which has ever been before Parliament in my time, and the most pregnant with good or evil to the country; and though I seldom meddle with political meetings, I could not reconcile it to my conscience to be absent from this.

Every year for this half century, the question of reform has been pressing upon us, till it has swelled up at last into this great and awful combination; so that almost every city and every borough in England are at this moment assembled for the same purpose, and are doing the same thing we are doing.

MORE TERRIBLE THAN THE LIONS

From "Modern Eloquence," Vol. X, Geo. L. Shuman and Company, Chicago, publishers.

BY A. A. MCCORMICK

I do not want to be in the position of a man I once heard of who was a lion tamer. He was a very brave man. There was no lion, no matter how big, or strong, or vicious, that had not succumbed to this man's fearlessness. This man had a wife, and she did not like him to stay out late at night, and big as he was, and as brave, he had never dared to disrespect his wife's wishes, until one evening, meeting some old friends, he fell to talking over old times with them, their early adventures and experiences. Finally, looking at his watch, to his amazement he discovered it was midnight. What to do he knew not. He didn't dare to go home. If he went to a hotel, his wife might discover him before he discovered her. Finally, in desperation, he sped to the menagerie, hurriedly passed through and went to the cage of lions. Entering this he closed and locked the door, and gave a sigh of relief. He quieted the dangerous brutes, and lay down with his head resting on the mane of the largest and most dangerous of them all. His wife waited. Her anger increased as the night wore on. At the first sign of dawn she went in search of her recreant lord and master. Not finding him in any of the haunts that he generally frequented, she went to the menagerie. She also passed through and went to the cage of the lions. Peering in she saw her husband, the fearless lion tamer, crouching at the back of the cage. A look of chagrin came over her face, closely followed by one of scorn and fine contempt, as she shook her finger and hissed, "You coward!"

IRVING, THE ACTOR

From "In Lighter Vein," with the permission of Paul Elder and Company, San Francisco, publishers.

BY JOHN DE MORGAN

Henry Irving, the actor, was always fond of playing practical jokes. Clement Scott tells of one played by Irving and Harry Montague upon a number of their associates. Irving and Montague, hitherto the best of friends, began to quarrel on their way to a picnic, and their friends feared some tragic consequences. After luncheon both of the men disappeared. Business Manager Smale's face turned pale. He felt that his worst fears had been realized. With one cry, "They're gone! What on earth has become of them?" he made a dash down the Dargle, over the rocks and bowlders, with the remainder of the picnickers at his heels. At the bottom of a "dreadful hollow behind the little wood," a fearful sight presented itself to the astonished friends. There, on a stone, sat Henry Irving, in his shirtsleeves, his long hair matted over his eyes, his thin hands and white face all smeared with blood, and dangling an open clasp-knife. He was muttering to himself, in a savage tone: "I've done it, I've done it! I said I would, I said I would!" Tom Smale, in an agony of fear, rushed up to Irving. "For Heaven's sake, man," he screamed, "tell us where he is!" Irving, scarcely moving a muscle, pointed to a heap of dead leaves, and, in that sepulchral tone of his, cried: "He's there! I've done for him! I've murdered him!" Smale literally bounded to the heap, almost paralyzed with fear, and began pulling the leaves away. Presently he found Montague lying face downward and nearly convulsed with laughter. Never was better acting seen on any stage.

WENDELL PHILLIPS'S TACT

From "Memories of the Lyceum," in "Modern Eloquence," Vol. VI, Geo. L. Shuman and Company, Chicago, publishers.

BY JAMES BURTON POND

Wendell Phillips was the most polished and graceful orator our country ever produced. He spoke as quietly as if he were talking in his own parlor and almost entirely without gestures, yet he had as great a power over all kinds of audiences as any American of whom we have any record. Often called before howling mobs, who had come to the lecture- room to prevent him from being heard, and who would shout and sing to drown his voice, he never failed to subdue them in a short time. One illustration of his power and tact occurred in Boston. The majority of the audience were hostile. They yelled and sang and completely drowned his voice. The reporters were seated in a row just under the platform, in the place where the orchestra plays in an ordinary theater. Phillips made no attempt to address the noisy crowd, but bent over and seemed to be speaking in a low tone to the reporters. By and by the curiosity of the audience was excited; they ceased to clamor and tried to hear what he was saying to the reporters. Phillips looked at them and said quietly:--

"Go on, gentlemen, go on. I do not need your ears. Through these pencils I speak to thirty millions of people."

Not a voice was raised again. The mob had found its master and stayed whipped until he sat down.

Eloquent as he was as a lecturer, he was far more effective as a debater. Debate was for him the flint and steel which brought out all his fire. His memory was something wonderful, He would listen to an elaborate speech for hours, and, without a single note of what had been said, in writing, reply to every part of it as fully and completely as if the speech were written out before him. Those who heard him only on the platform, and when not confronted by an opponent, have a very limited comprehension of his wonderful resources as a speaker. He never hesitated for a word or failed to employ the word best fitted to express his thought on the point under discussion.

BAKED BEANS AND CULTURE

From "Writings in Prose and Verse, by Eugene Field," with the permission of Charles Scribner's Sons, New York, publishers.

BY EUGENE FIELD

The members of the Boston Commercial Club are charming gentlemen. They are now the guests of the Chicago Commercial Club, and are being shown every attention that our market affords.

Last night five or six of these Boston merchants sat around the office of the hotel and discussed matters and things. Pretty soon they got to talking about beans; this was the subject which they dwelt on with evident pleasure.

"Waal, sir," said Ephraim Taft, a wholesale dealer in maple sugar and flavored lozenges, "you kin talk 'bout your new-fashioned dishes an' high-falutin' vittles; but when you come right down to it, there ain't no better eatin' than a dish o' baked pork 'n' beans."

"That's so, b'gosh!" chorused the others.

"The truth o' the matter is," continued Mr. Taft, "that beans is good for every-body--'t don't make no difference whether he's well or sick. Why, I've known a thousand folks--waal, mebbe not quite a thousand; but--waal, now, jest to show, take the case of Bill Holbrook,--you remember Bill, don't ye?"

"Bill Holbrook?" said Mr. Ezra Eastman. "Why, of course I do. Used to live down to Brimfield, next to Moses Howard farm."

"That's the man," resumed Mr. Taft. "Waal, Bill fell sick--kinder moped 'round, tired-like, for a week or two, an' then tuck to his bed. His folks sent for Dock Smith--ol' Dock Smith that used to carry a pair o' leather saddlebags. Gosh, they don't have no sech doctors nowadays! Waal, the dock he come; an' he looked at Bill's tongue, an' felt uv his pulse, an' said that Bill had typhus fever."

Ol' Dock Smith was a very careful, conserv'tive man, an' he never said nothin' unless he knowed he was right.

"Bill began to git wuss, an' he kep' a-gittin' wuss every day. One mornin' ol' Dock Smith sez, 'Look a-here, Bill, I guess you're a goner; as I figger it, you can't hol' out till nightfall.'

"Bill's mother insisted on a con-sul-tation bein' held; so ol' Dock Smith sent over for young Dock Brainerd. I calc'late that, next *to* ol' Dock Smith, young Dock Brainerd was the smartest doctor that ever lived.

"Waal, pretty soon along come Dock Brainerd; an' he an' Dock Smith went all over Bill, an' looked at his tongue, an' felt uv his pulse, an' told him it was a gone case, an' that he had got to die. Then they went on into the spare chamber to hold their con-sul-tation.

"Waal, Bill he lay there in the front room a-pantin' an' a-gaspin', an' a wond'rin' whether it wuz true. As he wuz thinkin', up comes the girl to git a clean tablecloth out of the clothespress, an' she left the door ajar as she come in. Bill he gave a sniff, an' his eyes grew more natural like; he gathered together all the strength he had, an' he raised himself up on one elbow an' sniffed again.

"'Sary,' says he, 'wot's that a-cookin'?'

"'Beans,' says she; 'beans for dinner.'

"'Sary,' says the dyin' man, 'I must hev a plate uv them beans!'

"'Sakes alive, Mr. Holbrook!' says she; 'if you wuz to eat any o' them beans it'd kill ye!'

"'If I've got to die,' says he, 'I'm goin' to die happy; fetch me a plate uv them beans.'

"Waal, Sary she pikes off to the doctor's.

"'Look a-here,' says she; 'Mr. Holbrook smelt the beans cookin' an' he says he's got to have some. Now, what shall I do about it?'

"'Waal, Doctor,' says Dock Smith, 'what do you think 'bout it?'

"'He's got to die anyhow,' says Dock Brainerd, 'an' I don't suppose the beans 'll make any diff'rence.'

"'That's the way I figger it,' says Dock Smith; 'in all my practice I never knew of beans hurtin' anybody.'

"So Sary went down to the kitchen an' brought up a plateful of hot baked beans. Dock Smith raised Bill up in bed, an' Dock Brainerd put a piller under the small of Bill's back. Then Sary sat down by the bed an' fed them beans into Bill until Bill couldn't hold any more.

"'How air you feelin' now?' asked Dock Smith.

"Bill didn't say nuthin; he jest smiled sort uv peaceful-like and closed his eyes.

"'The end hez come,'f said Dock Brainerd sof'ly; 'Bill is dyin'.'

"Then Bill murmured kind o' far-away like; 'I ain't dyin'; I'm dead an' in heaven.'

"Next mornin' Bill got out uv bed an' done a big day's work on the farm, an' he ain't bed a sick spell since. Them beans cured him!"

SECRETARY CHASE'S CHIN-FLY

From "Speeches and Addresses of Abraham Lincoln," Current Literature Publishing Company, New York, publishers.

BY F. B. CARPENTER

"Within a month after Mr. Lincoln's first accession to office," says the Hon. Mr. Raymond, "when the South was threatening civil war, and armies of office seekers were besieging him in the Executive Mansion, he said to a friend that he wished he could get time to attend to the Southern question; he thought he knew what was wanted, and believed he could do something towards quieting the rising discontent; but the office seekers demanded all his time. 'I am,' said he, 'like a man so busy in letting rooms in one end of his house that he can't stop to put out the fire that is burning the other.' Two or three years later when the people had made him a candidate for reflection, the same friend spoke to him of a member of his Cabinet who was a candidate also. Mr. Lincoln said that he did not concern himself much about that. It was important to the country that the department over which his rival presided should be administered with vigor and energy, and whatever would stimulate the Secretary to such action would do good. 'R----,' said he, 'you were brought up on a farm, were you not? Then you know what a *chin-fly* is. My brother and I,' he added, 'were once plowing corn on a Kentucky farm, I driving the horse, and he holding the plow. The horse was lazy; but on one occasion rushed across the field so that I, with my long legs, could scarcely keep pace with him. On reaching the end of the furrow, I found an enormous *chin-fly* fastened upon him, and knocked him off. My brother asked me what I did that for. I told him I didn't want the old horse bitten in that way. "Why," said my brother, "that's all that made him go!" Now,' said Mr. Lincoln, 'if Mr. ---- has a presidential *chin-fly* biting him, I'm not going to knock him off if it will only make his department *go*.'"

REVIEW EXERCISES

EXERCISES

There exercises should be practiced in only a moderately strong voice, at times perhaps in a very soft voice, and always with a good degree of ease and naturalness. They had better be memorized, and as the technique becomes more sure, less thought may be given to that and more to the true expression of the spirit of each passage--or let the spirit from the first, if it will, help the technique.

TONE

For rounding and expanding the voice. To be given in an even sustained tone, with rather open throat and easy low breathing. Suspend the speech where pauses are marked, for a momentary recovery of breath. Keep the breath easily firm. Don't drive the breath through the tone.

1

Roll on, | thou deep and dark blue Ocean, | roll! Ten thousand fleets | sweep over thee | in vain; Man marks the earth | with ruin--his control | Stops | with the shore.

2

O Tiber, | Father Tiber | To whom the Romans pray, A Roman's life, | a Roman's arms, Take thou in charge | this day |

3

O Rome! | my country! | city of the soul! The orphans of the heart | must turn to thee, Lone mother of dead empires! | and control In their shut breasts | their petty misery.

4

Ring joyous chords!-- | ring out again! A swifter still | and a wilder strain! And bring fresh wreaths!-- | we will banish all Save the free in heart | from our banquet hall.

5

O joy to the people | and joy to the throne, Come to us, | love us | and make us your own: For Saxon | or Dane | or Norman | we, Teuton or Celt, | or what ever we be, We are all of us Danes | in our welcome of thee, Alexandra!

6

Liberty! | Freedom! | Tyranny is dead!-- Run hence, | proclaim, | cry it about the streets. Some to the common pulpits, | and cry out, "Liberty, | freedom, | and enfranchisement!"

INFLECTION

Give these with a rather vigorous colloquial effect, with clear-cut form, with point and spirit.

1

Armed, say you?
Armed, my lord.
From top to toe?
My lord, from head to foot.
Then saw you not
His face?
Oh, yes, my lord; he wore his beaver up.
What, looked he frowningly?
A countenance more
In sorrow than in anger.
Pale or red?
Nay, very pale.
And fixed his eyes upon you?
Most constantly.

2

But, sir, the Coalition! The Coalition! Aye, "the murdered Coalition!" The gentleman asks if I were led or frighted into this debate by the specter of the Coalition. "Was it the ghost of the murdered Coalition," he exclaims, "which haunted the member from Massachusetts; and which, like the ghost of Banquo, would never down?" "The murdered Coalition."

3

Should he have asked Aguinaldo for an armistice? If so, upon what basis should he have requested it? What should he say to him? "Please stop this fighting?" "What for?" Aguinaldo would say; "do you propose to retire?" "No." "Do you propose to grant us independence?" "No, not now." "Well, why then, an armistice?"

4

Alas, poor Yorick!--I knew him, Horatio; a fellow of infinite jest, of most excellent fancy: he hath borne me on his back a thousand times; and now, how abhorred in my imagination it is! my gorge rises at it.--Where be your gibes now? your gambols? your songs? your flashes of merriment, that were wont to set the table in a roar? Not one now, to mock your own grinning? quite chop-fallen? Now get you to my lady's chamber, and tell her, let her paint an inch thick, to this favor she must come; make her laugh at that.

ENUNCIATION

Keep first of all a good form to the vowels. Make consonants definitely by sufficient action of jaw, tongue, and lips. Keep the throat easy; avoid stiffening and strain. A particularly light, soft, pure tone, with fine articulation, may generally be best for practice.

In these first passages, carry the tone well in the head, so as to give a pure, soft, clear sound to the *m*'s, *n*'s, *ng*'s, and *l*'s. If need be, these letters may be marked.

1

One cry of wonder, Shrill as the loon's call, Rang through the forest, Startling the silence, Startling the mourners Chanting the death-song.

2

One after one, by the star-dogged Moon, Too quick for groan or sigh, Each turned his face with a ghastly pang, And cursed me with his eye.

Four times fifty living men, (And I heard nor sigh nor groan,) With heavy thump, a lifeless lump, They dropped down one by one.

3

These abominable principles, and this more abominable avowal of them, demand the most decisive indignation.

4

Lay the proud usurpers low! Tyrants fall in every foe! Liberty's in every blow!

Forward! let us do or die!

5

I closed my lids, and kept them close, And the balls like pulses beat; For the sky and the sea, and the sea and the sky Lay like a load on my weary eye, And the dead were at my feet.

REVIEW EXERCISES

Give clearly the *k* and the *g* forms, making a slight percussion in the back of the mouth. Finish clearly all main words.

1

With throats unslaked, with black lips baked, We could nor laugh nor wail; Through utter drought all dumb we stood! I bit my arm, I sucked the blood, And cried, A sail! a sail!

With throats unslaked, with black lips baked, Agape they heard me call: Gramercy! they for joy did grin, And all at once their breath drew in, As they were drinking all.

2

Where dwellest thou? Under the canopy. Under the canopy! Ay! Where's that? I' the city of kites and crows. I' the city of kites and crows!-- Then thou dwellest with daws, too? No: I serve not thy master.

3

Strike | till the last armed foe | expires! Strike | for your altars and your fires! Strike | for the green graves of your sires! God | and your native land!

For flexibility of the lips, form well the *o*'s and *w*'s.

1

Blow, blow, thou winter wind, Thou art not so unkind as man's ingratitude.

2

O wonderful, wonderful, and most wonderful, wonderful! and yet again wonderful, and after that, out of all hooping!

3

Water, water, everywhere, And all the boards did shrink; Water, water, everywhere, Nor any drop to drink.

4

O Wedding-Guest! this soul hath been Alone on a wide, wide sea: So lonely 'twas, that God himself Scarce seemed there to be.

Have care for *t*'s, *d*'s, *s*'s, the *th* and the *st*'s.

1

Day after day, day after day, We stuck, nor breath nor motion; As idle as a painted ship Upon a painted ocean.

Down dropt the breeze, the sails dropt down, 'Twas sad as sad could be; And we did speak only to break The silence of the sea!

2

What loud uproar bursts from that door! The wedding-guests are there: But in the garden-bower the bride And bride-maids singing are: And hark the little vesper bell, Which biddeth me to prayer!

3

Farewell, farewell! but this I tell To thee, thou Wedding-Guest! He prayeth well, who loveth well Both man and bird and beast.

He prayeth best, who loveth best All things both great and small; For the dear God who loveth us, He made and loveth all.

Attend especially to *b*'s and in passage 2 to *p*'s. Give a very soft, slightly echoing continuation to the *ing* in "dying."

1

Blow, bugle, blow, set the wild echoes flying, Blow, bugle; answer, echoes, dying, dying, dying. Blow, let us hear the purple glens replying: Blow, bugle; answer, echoes, dying, dying, dying.

2

Hop, and Mop, and Drop so clear, Pip, and Trip, and Skip that were To Mab their sovereign dear,

Her special maids of honor; Fib, and Tib, and Pinck, and Pin, Tit, and Nit, and Wap, and Win,

The train that wait upon her.

EMPHASIS

Determine the exact sense and express it pointedly. The primary or central emphasis takes an absolute fall from a pitch above the general level; the secondary emphasis takes a circumflex inflection--a fall and a slight rise. Primary, Hebrew Letter Yod; secondary Gujarati Vowel Sign li. In the question, the main part of the inflection is usually rising instead of falling. The effect of suspense or of forward look requires the slightly upward final turn to the inflection. Note this in passages 4, 5, and 6.

1

In 1825 the gentleman told the world that the public lands "ought *not* to be treated as a *treasure*." He now tells us that "they *must* be treated as *so much treasure*." What the deliberate opinion of the gentleman on this subject may be, belongs not to me to determine.

2

Compare the two. This I offer to give you is *plain* and *simple;* the other full of perplexed and intricate *mazes*. This is mild; that *harsh*. This is found by experience *effectual for its purposes*; the other is a *new project*. This is *universal*; the other calculated for *certain colonies only*. This is *immediate in its conciliatory operation*; the other *remote, contingent*, full of *hazard*.

3

As Caesar *loved me*, I *weep* for him; as he was *fortunate*, I *rejoice* at it; as he was *valiant*, I *honor* him; but as he was *ambitious*, I *slew* him. There is *tears* for his *love*; *joy* for his *fortune*; *honor* for his *valor*; and *death* for his *ambition*.

4

One moment he stood erect, strong, confident in the years stretching peacefully out before him; the next he lay wounded, bleeding, *helpless*, doomed to weary weeks of torture, to silence and the grave.

5

For no cause, in the very frenzy of wantonness and wickedness, by the red hand of Murder he was thrust from the full tide of this world's interest, from its hopes, its aspirations, its victories, into the visible presence of death; and he *did not quail*.

6

There was no flinching as he charged. He had just turned to give a cheer when the fatal ball struck him. There was a convulsion of the upward hand--his eyes, pleading and loyal, turned their last glance to the flag--his lips parted--he fell *dead*, and at nightfall lay with his face to the stars. Home they brought him, fairer than

Adonis over whom the goddess of beauty wept.

7

But the gentleman inquires why *he* was made the object of such a reply. Why was *he* singled out? If an attack has been made on the *East, he*, he assures us, did not *begin* it; it was made by the gentleman from *Missouri*. Sir, I answered the gentleman's speech because I happened to *hear* it; and because, also, I chose to give an answer to that speech which, if *unanswered*, I thought most likely to produce *injurious impressions*.

MELODY

Give musical tone and a fitting modulation, or tune, avoiding the so- called singsong. Note the occasional closing cadence. Observe the rhythmic movement, with beat and pause.

1

You think me a fanatic to-night, for you read history not with your eyes, but with your prejudices. But fifty years hence, when Truth gets a hearing, the Muse of History will put Phocian for the Greek, and Brutus for the Roman, Hampden for England, Fayette for France, choose Washington as the bright consummate flower of our earlier civilization, and John Brown the ripe fruit of our noonday, then, dipping her pen in the sunlight, will write in the clear blue, above them all, the name of the soldier, the statesman, the martyr, Toussaint L'Ouverture.

2

Have you read in the Talmud of old, In the Legends the Rabbins have told Of the limitless realms of the air, Have you read it,--the marvelous story Of Sandalphon, the Angel of Glory, Sandalphon, the Angel of Prayer?

3

You remember King Charles' Twelve Good Rules, the eleventh of which was, "Make no long meals." Now King Charles lost his head, and you will have leave to make a long meal. But when, after your long meal, you go home in the wee small hours, what do you expect to find? You will find my toast--"Woman, a beautiful rod!" Now my advice is, "Kiss the rod!"

4

Then here's to our boyhood, its gold and its gray! The stars of its winter, the dews of its May! And when we have done with our life-lasting toys, Dear Father, take care of Thy children, the Boys!

FEELING

Have great care not to put any strain upon the throat. Breathe low. Be moderate in force.

1

O mighty Caesar! dost thou lie so low? Are all thy conquests, glories, triumphs, spoils, shrunk to this little measure? Fare thee well.

2

Yes, I attack Louis Napoleon; I attack him openly, before all the world. I attack him before God and man. I attack him boldly and recklessly for love of the people and for love of France.

3

I am asked what I have to say why sentence of death should not be pronounced on me according to law. I am charged with being an emissary of France! and for what end? No; I am no emissary.

4

I see a race without disease of flesh or brain,--shapely and fair,--the married harmony of form and function,--and as I look, life lengthens, joy deepens, love canopies the earth.

TONE COLOR

Use the imagination to see and hear. Suit the voice to the sound, form or movement of your image, or to the mood of mind indicated. Read with melody and pause. Take plenty of time.

1

There's a lurid light | in the clouds to-night, In the wind | there's a desolate moan, And the rage of the furious sea | is white, Where it breaks | on the crags of stone.

2

The Sun's rim dips; the stars rush out: At one stride | comes the dark; With far-heard whisper, | o'er the sea, Off shot | the specter-bark.

3

Is this a time to be gloomy and sad; When our mother Nature | laughs around; When even the deep blue heavens | look glad, And gladness breathes from the blossoming ground?

4

The breeze comes whispering in our ear, That dandelions | are blossoming near,

That maize | has sprouted, that streams | are flowing, That the river is bluer | than the sky, That the robin | is plastering his nest | hard by; And if the breeze kept the good news back, For other couriers | we should not lack;

We could guess it all | by yon heifer's | lowing,-- And hark! how clear | bold chanticleer, Warmed | by the new wine | of the year,

Tells all | by his lusty | crowing!

VARIETY--IN PITCH, TIME, FORCE, COLOR, AND MODULATION

1

Ring out, wild bells, to the wild sky; Ring out the false, ring in the true.

2

Good work is the most honorable and lasting thing in the world.

3

O Thou that rollest above, round as the shield of my fathers, whence are thy beams, O Sun, thy everlasting light!

4

I am thy father's spirit, Doomed for a certain term to walk the night, And for the day confined to fast in fires, Till the foul crimes done in my days of nature Are burnt and purg'd away.

5

"Well, gentlemen, I am a Whig. If you break up the Whig party, where am *I* to go?" And, says Lowell, we all held our breath, thinking where he *could* go. But, says Lowell, if he had been five feet three, we should have said, Who *cares* where you go?

GESTURE

Have the action simple and unstudied, expressing the dominant purpose rather than illustrating mere words or phrases. Avoid stiltedness and elaboration. Try to judge where and how the gesture would be made.

I

Nor do not *saw the air* too much with your *hand, thus*, but use all gently; for in the very torrent, tempest, and, as I may say, the whirlwind of passion, *you must acquire and beget a temperance* that may give it smoothness.

2

In my native town of Athens is a monument that crowns its central hills--a plain, white shaft. *Deep cut into its shining side is a name* dear to me above the names of men, that of a brave and simple man who died in brave and simple faith. Not for all the glories of New England--from Plymouth Rock all the way--would I exchange the heritage he left me in his soldier's death.

3

Sir, when I heard the gentleman lay down principles which place the murderers of Alton side by side with Otis and Hancock, with Quincy and Adams, *I thought those pictured lips* (pointing to the portraits in the Hall) would have broken into voice to rebuke the recreant American,--the slanderer of the dead.

4

Suppose I stood at the foot of Vesuvius, or AEtna, and, seeing a hamlet or a homestead planted on its slope, I said to the dwellers in that hamlet, or in that homestead, "You see that vapor which ascends from the summit of the mountain. That vapor may become a dense, black smoke, that will obscure the sky. *You see the trickling of lava from the crevices in the side of the mountain.* That trickling of lava may become a river of fire. *You hear that muttering in the bowels of the mountain.* That muttering may become a bellowing thunder, the voice of violent convulsion, that may shake half a continent."

5

And what have we to oppose them? Shall we try argument? Sir, we have been trying that for the last ten years. Have we anything new to offer upon the subject? Nothing. We have held the subject up in every light of which it is capable; but it has been all in vain. Shall we resort to entreaty and humble supplication? What terms shall we find which have not been already exhausted? Let us not, I beseech you, sir, deceive ourselves longer.

CHARACTERIZATION

1

Learn from real life. Don't go by the spelling. Don't overdo the dialect.

   'E carried me away

To where a dooli lay,
An' a bullet come an' drilled the beggar clean.
'E put me safe inside,
An' just before 'e died:
"I 'ope you liked your drink," sez Gunga Din.

2

Sergeant Buzfuz began by saying that never, in the whole course of his experience,--never, from the very first moment of his applying himself to the study and practice of the law, had he approached a case with such a heavy sense of the responsibility imposed upon him.

3

I'm a walkin' pedestrian, a travelin' philosopher. Terry O'Mulligan's me name. I'm from Dublin, where many philosophers before me was raised and bred. Oh, philosophy is a foine study! I don't know anything about it, but it's a foine study!

4

It is de ladies who do sweeten de cares of life. It is de ladies who are de guiding stars of our existence. It is de ladies who do cheer but not inebriate, and, derefore, vid all homage to de dear sex, de toast dat I have to propose is, "De Ladies! God bless dem all!"

5

What tho' on hamely fare we dine, Wear hoddin' gray, an' a' that; Gie fools their silks, and knaves their wine-- A man's a man, for a' that.

For a' that, an' a' that, Their tinsel show, an' a' that, The honest man, though e'er sae poor, Is king o' men for a' that!

6

A keerless man in his talk was Jim, And an awkward hand in a row, But he never flunked, and he never lied,-- I reckon he never knowed how. He seen his duty, a dead-sure thing,-- And he went for it thar and then; And Christ ain't agoing to be too hard On a man that died for men.

The Codes Of Hammurabi And Moses
W. W. Davies

QTY

The discovery of the Hammurabi Code is one of the greatest achievements of archaeology, and is of paramount interest, not only to the student of the Bible, but also to all those interested in ancient history...

Religion   **ISBN:** *1-59462-338-4*   **Pages:132**
MSRP $12.95

The Theory of Moral Sentiments
Adam Smith

QTY

This work from 1749. contains original theories of conscience amd moral judgment and it is the foundation for systemof morals.

Philosophy **ISBN:** *1-59462-777-0*   **Pages:536**
MSRP $19.95

Jessica's First Prayer
Hesba Stretton

QTY

In a screened and secluded corner of one of the many railway-bridges which span the streets of London there could be seen a few years ago, from five o'clock every morning until half past eight, a tidily set-out coffee-stall, consisting of a trestle and board, upon which stood two large tin cans, with a small fire of charcoal burning under each so as to keep the coffee boiling during the early hours of the morning when the work-people were thronging into the city on their way to their daily toil...

Childrens   **ISBN:** *1-59462-373-2*   **Pages:84**
MSRP $9.95

My Life and Work
Henry Ford

QTY

Henry Ford revolutionized the world with his implementation of mass production for the Model T automobile. Gain valuable business insight into his life and work with his own auto-biography... "We have only started on our development of our country we have not as yet, with all our talk of wonderful progress, done more than scratch the surface. The progress has been wonderful enough but..."

Biographies/   **ISBN:** *1-59462-198-5*   **Pages:300**
MSRP $21.95

The Art of Cross-Examination
Francis Wellman

QTY

I presume it is the experience of every author, after his first book is published upon an important subject, to be almost overwhelmed with a wealth of ideas and illustrations which could readily have been included in his book, and which to his own mind, at least, seem to make a second edition inevitable. Such certainly was the case with me; and when the first edition had reached its sixth impression in five months, I rejoiced to learn that it seemed to my publishers that the book had met with a sufficiently favorable reception to justify a second and considerably enlarged edition. ..

Reference   **ISBN: *1-59462-647-2***   **Pages:412**

MSRP *$19.95*

On the Duty of Civil Disobedience
Henry David Thoreau

QTY

Thoreau wrote his famous essay, On the Duty of Civil Disobedience, as a protest against an unjust but popular war and the immoral but popular institution of slave-owning. He did more than write—he declined to pay his taxes, and was hauled off to gaol in consequence. Who can say how much this refusal of his hastened the end of the war and of slavery ?

Law   **ISBN: *1-59462-747-9***   **Pages:48**

MSRP *$7.45*

Dream Psychology Psychoanalysis for Beginners
Sigmund Freud

QTY

Sigmund Freud, born Sigismund Schlomo Freud (May 6, 1856 - September 23, 1939), was a Jewish-Austrian neurologist and psychiatrist who co-founded the psychoanalytic school of psychology. Freud is best known for his theories of the unconscious mind, especially involving the mechanism of repression; his redefinition of sexual desire as mobile and directed towards a wide variety of objects; and his therapeutic techniques, especially his understanding of transference in the therapeutic relationship and the presumed value of dreams as sources of insight into unconscious desires.

Psychology   **ISBN: *1-59462-905-6***   **Pages:196**

MSRP *$15.45*

The Miracle of Right Thought
Orison Swett Marden

QTY

Believe with all of your heart that you will do what you were made to do. When the mind has once formed the habit of holding cheerful, happy, prosperous pictures, it will not be easy to form the opposite habit. It does not matter how improbable or how far away this realization may see, or how dark the prospects may be, if we visualize them as best we can, as vividly as possible, hold tenaciously to them and vigorously struggle to attain them, they will gradually become actualized, realized in the life. But a desire, a longing without endeavor, a yearning abandoned or held indifferently will vanish without realization.

Self Help   **ISBN: *1-59462-644-8***   **Pages:360**

MSRP *$25.45*

www.bookjungle.com *email: sales@bookjungle.com fax: 630-214-0564 mail: Book Jungle PO Box 2226 Champaign, IL 61825*

QTY

The Rosicrucian Cosmo-Conception Mystic Christianity *by Max Heindel*   ISBN: *1-59462-188-8*   **$38.95**
The Rosicrucian Cosmo-conception is not dogmatic, neither does it appeal to any other authority than the reason of the student. It is: not controversial, but is: sent forth in the, hope that it may help to clear...   New Age/Religion Pages 646

Abandonment To Divine Providence *by Jean-Pierre de Caussade*   ISBN: *1-59462-228-0*   **$25.95**
"The Rev. Jean Pierre de Caussade was one of the most remarkable spiritual writers of the Society of Jesus in France in the 18th Century. His death took place at Toulouse in 1751. His works have gone through many editions and have been republished...   Inspirational/Religion Pages 400

Mental Chemistry *by Charles Haanel*   ISBN: *1-59462-192-6*   **$23.95**
Mental Chemistry allows the change of material conditions by combining and appropriately utilizing the power of the mind. Much like applied chemistry creates something new and unique out of careful combinations of chemicals the mastery of mental chemistry...   New Age Pages 354

The Letters of Robert Browning and Elizabeth Barret Barrett 1845-1846 vol II   ISBN: *1-59462-193-4*   **$35.95**
by Robert Browning and Elizabeth Barrett   Biographies Pages 596

Gleanings In Genesis (volume I) *by Arthur W. Pink*   ISBN: *1-59462-130-6*   **$27.45**
Appropriately has Genesis been termed "the seed plot of the Bible" for in it we have, in germ form, almost all of the great doctrines which are afterwards fully developed in the books of Scripture which follow...   Religion/Inspirational Pages 420

The Master Key *by L. W. de Laurence*   ISBN: *1-59462-001-6*   **$30.95**
In no branch of human knowledge has there been a more lively increase of the spirit of research during the past few years than in the study of Psychology, Concentration and Mental Discipline. The requests for authentic lessons in Thought Control, Mental Discipline and...   New Age/Business Pages 422

The Lesser Key Of Solomon Goetia *by L. W. de Laurence*   ISBN: *1-59462-092-X*   **$9.95**
This translation of the first book of the "Lemegton" which is now for the first time made accessible to students of Talismanic Magic was done, after careful collation and edition, from numerous Ancient Manuscripts in Hebrew, Latin, and French...   New Age/Occult Pages 92

Rubaiyat Of Omar Khayyam *by Edward Fitzgerald*   ISBN:*1-59462-332-5*   **$13.95**
Edward Fitzgerald, whom the world has already learned, in spite of his own efforts to remain within the shadow of anonymity, to look upon as one of the rarest poets of the century, was born at Bredfield, in Suffolk, on the 31st of March, 1809. He was the third son of John Purcell...   Music Pages 172

Ancient Law *by Henry Maine*   ISBN: *1-59462-128-4*   **$29.95**
The chief object of the following pages is to indicate some of the earliest ideas of mankind, as they are reflected in Ancient Law, and to point out the relation of those ideas to modern thought.   Religion/History Pages 452

Far-Away Stories *by William J. Locke*   ISBN: *1-59462-129-2*   **$19.45**
"Good wine needs no bush, but a collection of mixed vintages does. And this book is just such a collection. Some of the stories I do not want to remain buried for ever in the museum files of dead magazine-numbers an author's not unpardonable vanity..."   Fiction Pages 272

Life of David Crockett *by David Crockett*   ISBN: *1-59462-250-7*   **$27.45**
"Colonel David Crockett was one of the most remarkable men of the times in which he lived. Born in humble life, but gifted with a strong will, an indomitable courage, and unremitting perseverance...   Biographies/New Age Pages 424

Lip-Reading *by Edward Nitchie*   ISBN: *1-59462-206-X*   **$25.95**
Edward B. Nitchie, founder of the New York School for the Hard of Hearing, now the Nitchie School of Lip-Reading, Inc, wrote "LIP-READING Principles and Practice". The development and perfecting of this meritorious work on lip-reading was an undertaking...   How-to Pages 400

A Handbook of Suggestive Therapeutics, Applied Hypnotism, Psychic Science   ISBN: *1-59462-214-0*   **$24.95**
by Henry Munro   Health/New Age/Health/Self-help Pages 376

A Doll's House: and Two Other Plays *by Henrik Ibsen*   ISBN: *1-59462-112-8*   **$19.95**
Henrik Ibsen created this classic when in revolutionary 1848 Rome. Introducing some striking concepts in playwriting for the realist genre, this play has been studied the world over.   Fiction/Classics/Plays 308

The Light of Asia *by sir Edwin Arnold*   ISBN: *1-59462-204-3*   **$13.95**
In this poetic masterpiece, Edwin Arnold describes the life and teachings of Buddha. The man who was to become known as Buddha to the world was born as Prince Gautama of India but he rejected the worldly riches and abandoned the reigns of power when...   Religion/History/Biographies Pages 170

The Complete Works of Guy de Maupassant *by Guy de Maupassant*   ISBN: *1-59462-157-8*   **$16.95**
"For days and days, nights and nights, I had dreamed of that first kiss which was to consecrate our engagement, and I knew not on what spot I should put my lips..."   Fiction/Classics Pages 240

The Art of Cross-Examination *by Francis L. Wellman*   ISBN: *1-59462-309-0*   **$26.95**
Written by a renowned trial lawyer, Wellman imparts his experience and uses case studies to explain how to use psychology to extract desired information through questioning.   How-to/Science/Reference Pages 408

Answered or Unanswered? *by Louisa Vaughan*   ISBN: *1-59462-248-5*   **$10.95**
Miracles of Faith in China   Religion Pages 112

The Edinburgh Lectures on Mental Science (1909) *by Thomas*   ISBN: *1-59462-008-3*   **$11.95**
This book contains the substance of a course of lectures recently given by the writer in the Queen Street Hail, Edinburgh. Its purpose is to indicate the Natural Principles governing the relation between Mental Action and Material Conditions...   New Age/Psychology Pages 148

Ayesha *by H. Rider Haggard*   ISBN: *1-59462-301-5*   **$24.95**
Verily and indeed it is the unexpected that happens! Probably if there was one person upon the earth from whom the Editor of this, and of a certain previous history, did not expect to hear again...   Classics Pages 380

Ayala's Angel *by Anthony Trollope*   ISBN: *1-59462-352-X*   **$29.95**
The two girls were both pretty, but Lucy who was twenty-one who supposed to be simple and comparatively unattractive, whereas Ayala was credited, as her Bombwhat romantic name might show, with poetic charm and a taste for romance. Ayala when her father died was nineteen...   Fiction Pages 484

The American Commonwealth *by James Bryce*   ISBN: *1-59462-286-8*   **$34.45**
An interpretation of American democratic political theory. It examines political mechanics and society from the perspective of Scotsman James Bryce   Politics Pages 572

Stories of the Pilgrims *by Margaret P. Pumphrey*   ISBN: *1-59462-116-0*   **$17.95**
This book explores pilgrims religious oppression in England as well as their escape to Holland and eventual crossing to America on the Mayflower, and their early days in New England...   History Pages 268

www.bookjungle.com *email: sales@bookjungle.com fax: 630-214-0564 mail: Book Jungle PO Box 2226 Champaign, IL 61825*

QTY

The Fasting Cure *by Sinclair Upton*　　　　　　　　ISBN: *1-59462-222-1*　**$13.95**
In the Cosmopolitan Magazine for May, 1910, and in the Contemporary Review (London) for April, 1910, I published an article dealing with my experiences in fasting. I have written a great many magazine articles, but never one which attracted so much attention... New Age/Self Help/Health Pages 164

Hebrew Astrology *by Sepharial*　　　　　　　　　ISBN: *1-59462-308-2*　**$13.45**
In these days of advanced thinking it is a matter of common observation that we have left many of the old landmarks behind and that we are now pressing forward to greater heights and to a wider horizon than that which represented the mind-content of our progenitors... Astrology Pages 144

Thought Vibration or The Law of Attraction in the Thought World　　ISBN: *1-59462-127-6*　**$12.95**

by William Walker Atkinson　　　　　　　　　　　　　　　Psychology/Religion Pages 144

Optimism *by Helen Keller*　　　　　　　　　　　ISBN: *1-59462-108-X*　**$15.95**
Helen Keller was blind, deaf, and mute since 19 months old, yet famously learned how to overcome these handicaps, communicate with the world, and spread her lectures promoting optimism. An inspiring read for everyone... Biographies/Inspirational Pages 84

Sara Crewe *by Frances Burnett*　　　　　　　　ISBN: *1-59462-360-0*　**$9.45**
In the first place, Miss Minchin lived in London. Her home was a large, dull, tall one, in a large, dull square, where all the houses were alike, and all the sparrows were alike, and where all the door-knockers made the same heavy sound... Childrens/Classic Pages 88

The Autobiography of Benjamin Franklin *by Benjamin Franklin*　　ISBN: *1-59462-135-7*　**$24.95**
The Autobiography of Benjamin Franklin has probably been more extensively read than any other American historical work, and no other book of its kind has had such ups and downs of fortune. Franklin lived for many years in England, where he was agent... Biographies/History Pages 332

Name	
Email	
Telephone	
Address	
City, State ZIP	

☐ **Credit Card**　　　　　☐ **Check / Money Order**

Credit Card Number	
Expiration Date	
Signature	

Please Mail to:　Book Jungle
PO Box 2226
Champaign, IL 61825
or Fax to:　　630-214-0564

ORDERING INFORMATION

web*: www.bookjungle.com*
email*: sales@bookjungle.com*
fax*: 630-214-0564*
mail*: Book Jungle PO Box 2226 Champaign, IL 61825*
or PayPal *to sales@bookjungle.com*

Please contact us for bulk discounts

DIRECT-ORDER TERMS

**20% Discount if You Order
Two or More Books**
Free Domestic Shipping!
Accepted: Master Card, Visa,
Discover, American Express